MATE

ALI HAZELWOOD

BERKLEY ROMANCE
NEW YORK

BERKLEY ROMANCE
Published by Berkley
An imprint of Penguin Random House LLC
1745 Broadway, New York, NY 10019
penguinrandomhouse.com

Book design by Daniel Brount
Edited by Sarah Blumenstock

Library of Congress Cataloging-in-Publication Data

Names: Hazelwood, Ali, author
Title: Mate / Ali Hazelwood.
Description: First edition. | New York: Berkley Romance, 2025.
Identifiers: LCCN 2025010272 (print) | LCCN 2025010273 (ebook) |
ISBN 9780593952580 paperback | ISBN 9780593952597 ebook
Subjects: LCGFT: Werewolf fiction | Romance fiction | Novels
Classification: LCC PS3608.A98845 M38 2025 (print) |
LCC PS3608.A98845 (ebook) | DDC 813/.6—dc23/eng/20250307
LC record available at https://lccn.loc.gov/2025010272
LC ebook record available at https://lccn.loc.gov/2025010273

Berkley hardcover edition ISBN: 9780593955017
Berkley signed hardcover edition ISBN: 9798217190652
Barnes & Noble edition ISBN: 9798217188956
BAM edition ISBN: 9798217189045
Target edition ISBN: 9798217188949
Walmart edition ISBN: 9798217188963

Printed in the United States of America
2nd Printing

The authorized representative in the EU for product safety and compliance is
Penguin Random House Ireland, Morrison Chambers, 32 Nassau Street,
Dublin D02 YH68, Ireland, https://eu-contact.penguin.ie.

To LiveJournal users tehdirtiestsock, the_miss_lv, and pianoforeplay, as well as the anonymous prompters. I hope you're thriving, wherever you are.

MATE

PROLOGUE

THE CHILD HAD BEEN TRAINED WELL—NOT BY HER FAMILY, BUT by life.

When the door broke down and she ran for her mother, it wasn't to seek comfort, but to provide it. *Come with me*, she wanted to beg, but since the words wouldn't come out, she tugged at her sleeve. *Come with me. It's better this way.*

But the mother freed herself and didn't spare a single glance for the girl, who had no choice but to retreat upstairs, alone. There was a man sleeping in the bedroom, a cruel, nasty Were who scared her nearly as much as the people breaking in. Still, she shook him awake to warn him.

"I'm tryin' to get some fucking rest for once," he roared, pushing her away. The girl ducked down before he could hit her. "If you can't keep quiet—" He stopped, realizing that something was amiss. She glanced around for a hiding spot and slipped inside the closet.

For a while, that was it. She hugged her knees and breathed

through the musty scent of old clothes. When the screams started, she began counting. The people in the house always called her stupid, but she could go up to a thousand, and the numbers in her head, stacked one after the other after the other, covered the wails of pain, the snarled insults, the sounds of snapping bones. She kept silent, even as the noises grew closer and louder.

Two hundred and five. Two hundred and six. Two hundred and—

A pool of viscous blood seeped in from under the door, and the child could no longer control herself. Her gasp ricocheted off the walls of the overstuffed closet before she could cover her mouth. She knew then that she was as good as dead.

No. No, no, *no.*

Trembling, she bit her lip and prayed to her mother's old god. In the darkness, she could not make out the color of the blood. *Stay calm*, she told herself, shrinking into a pile of ancient blankets. The pleas had stopped a whole minute earlier, but there was still movement all over the house. Maybe it was her mother. Maybe she was coming upstairs to look for her—

The closet door opened abruptly. A dark figure stared down at the girl, its tall silhouette framed by a glowing halo from the ceiling light.

He was Death. Who Death would be if it were a person.

Seized by terror, the girl opened her mouth and filled her lungs with air, ready to scream. But the man lifted his finger to his lips, and the simple command froze her.

"Not a huge fan of shrieks," he explained, coming closer. Behind him was the corpse of the Were she'd tried to warn, forest-green liquid oozing from the gash in his neck.

And she was going to be next.

"Don't beat yourself up. It's not because you made noise."

Death's voice was a low rumble cutting through the silence. He seemed distracted, glancing around the room, as if looking for something he may have misplaced. "I could smell you the second I walked inside." He crouched down to her height, carelessly stepping in blood.

The child's teeth chattered with pure fear. *Beg,* a voice ordered. *Beg him.* But her mouth wouldn't open.

"You up there?" someone yelled from the first floor, and the girl jerked. She tried to be brave, but tears began streaming down her face. The man noticed, and his expression became displeased, just like Mother's had when the girl used to complain about their new life.

Weak. Crybaby. Selfish.

He reached for her with a sigh, and she screwed her eyes shut. In the riot of her heartbeat, she wished only for the end to be quick. *Let it be quick. It can be painful as long as it's quick.*

But then a thumb gently wiped tears from her face, and her eyes sprang open.

"Hey!" Another voice traveled up the stairs, closer this time. "Anything you need?"

The man's dark eyes held hers. He sighed again. "Call the social worker."

"Shit. How many this time?"

"One." The man's jaw ticced as his finger did one last pass.

"Don't cry. Or do, if you like. But it's better this way. I sincerely hope that this will be the worst day of your life." His lips curved in a small smile. "When's the last time you ate?"

She blinked, taken aback by the change of topic. Truth was, she couldn't remember. Yesterday? Two days ago?

"C'mon. Let's get you something warm." He held out his arms, and since the child couldn't avoid the sticky green puddle on her own, she let him pick her up, not sure why she was allowing a murderer to carry her downstairs. *Maybe he helped Mother, too*, she thought, knowing that the man was strong enough for the task.

Yes, he certainly had. She was sure that they were going to her right now. So she buried her face in the stranger's neck and let his slow heartbeat lull her to calm. And since she was able to, she started to count to a thousand once more.

CHAPTER 1

She tore him apart and remade him.
It took her less than a second.

Present day

IF SUCH A THING AS AN IDEAL NIGHT TO DIE EXISTED, IT WOULD not be this one.

There's *so much* wrong with it. I could bitch about the recent rainstorm, the weak garlic-clove-sized moon, the uncharged phone sitting on my nightstand. The main issue, though, is that I'm wearing no more than two items of clothing: undies and a camisole. They were both perfectly adequate underneath my fluffy comforter. Unfortunately, I left that back at the cabin. When I woke up at one a.m. to the realization that someone was breaking in.

It's fall. In a place that a year or so ago—back when I still foolishly believed I was Human—I would have called Oregon. Now that my Were genes are taking over, stuff like cartography and state lines have become comically trivial, but the crux of the matter remains: November in the Northwest is cold, and I'm not dressed appropriately.

The goddamn timing, I mouth to myself, darting behind the gnarly trunk of a Douglas fir. Chest heaving, I stare down at my very Human-shaped hand. I visualize the change, willing my bitten-to-the-quick nails to turn into claws.

Shift into a wolf, Serena. Shift into a fucking wolf, or I swear to God that . . .

That *nothing*. My body refuses to be shamed into compliance. I glance up at the sky, but the much-publicized pull of the moon offers only the most apathetic of tugs. With a muted groan, I resume my sprint through the forest, bare feet slipping through fresh mud. A dozen little cuts crisscross my soles and shins. The longer I run, the fainter my hope that the soil will conceal the iron scent of my blood.

And I've been running for a while.

The intruder is tracking me. Gaining ground. The wind carries his ever-closer smell, and I don't like what it tells me. Vampyre. Adult in his prime. Eager. The thrill of the chase titillates him, and his arousal scrapes against the bottom of my stomach. As revolting as that is, though, it's the least of my problems. Because if I can smell him this clearly, there's a very high chance that *he*'s close enough to—

"At long fucking last." The words hiss like bullets in my ear. An instant later, my back is slammed into a trunk. I don't know what hurts most—the bark biting into my skin, the hand he curls around my throat, or his disgusting, maniacal stench.

The forest is pitch black. There's no darkness through which Weres cannot see, but I got only half of those nice wolf genes, which means that my night vision is hit or miss. Still, the Vampyre's bloodlust is unmistakable. As is the blade in his hand. "Not very fast, are you?" he growls.

No shit. I swallow an eye roll and make myself moan helplessly.

"Please," I beg. His scent explodes, like having women at his mercy is his kink of choice—how predictable—so I give him some more. "Please, don't kill me. I'll do whatever you want."

"Whatever I want?"

He's *so* interested. I let out a whimper and widen my eyes. "Anything."

His eyes travel down my body, as if to assess what I might be useful for—organ trafficking, bone broth, yard maintenance. Unlike me, he *is* fast. Preternaturally so. With dizzying speed, his knife slices through the front of my silk top, deepening the neckline.

This *fucker*.

But as he leers, his scent spikes. Which means that he's distracted enough by what he's uncovered that I get a chance to put the self-defense classes my sister forced me to attend to good use.

Knee to the groin.

Headbutt to the nose.

And, as a little extra, an elbow to the stomach. I mean, why not?

The Vampyre grunts. Mutters a few variations of "fucking whore." I'm free, though. I might not be able to outrun him, but I *can* grab a fistful of soil and throw it at his eyes, which does just enough damage to slow him down. I frantically look around and— *yes*. I spot a sharp, jagged rock. Bend down to palm it.

"You fucking *freak of nature*." The Vampyre is on me again, twisting my arm behind my back. I let out a yelp, but the rock is in my hand. Tragically, he's holding my wrist at the wrong angle for me to strike.

In theory, I know what the next step is—*move closer, lower your center of gravity, rotate your body, strike with your free hand*—and boy, do I try. Sadly, the Vampyre is a notch or two above the average fighter, and none of it works.

7

That's when my stomach starts churning for real. This is not going to end well. "Let. Me. Go," I spit out.

"Shut up." The vinegar of his scent stings my nose. He's even more worked up now. And I'm in even deeper shit. "I may not be allowed to kill you, but I can make you hurt a whole fucking lot before I—"

"Can you, though?" A male voice interrupts him. It travels in our direction from some place in the thicket of trees. A rich, slow curl, at once vicious and detached. No answer exists that could faze this voice. "Can you really, buddy?"

The Vampyre's frame stiffens. Before he can leash his instinctive reaction, I smell utter, abject, acrid fear.

I close my eyes. Force my burning lungs to inhale slowly. Let my prospect of the next ten minutes readjust, mold to a shape that is . . . still unfortunate, yes, but a touch less.

Koen.

Koen's here.

It will be all right.

The Vampyre yanks me in front of him, holding his knife to my throat. I wonder if he means to use me as a hostage, or as a meat shield that barely reaches the top of his chest. "What are you doing here?" he barks.

It's a fair question. Koen lives several hours away and hasn't been around in nearly two months, since the day he dropped me off at the cabin, at my request, with a metric ton of supplies, a lingering stare, and a mocking *Have fun chatting up the spruces, killer* that didn't quite match the intensity in his eyes.

"Did you just ask what *I'm* doing in *my* territory? What the fuck are *you* doing, shitdump?" A handful of long, unhurried strides, and Koen emerges from the thicket.

He's different. From anyone else, yes, but also since I last saw him. His black hair is tied back at the top of his head in an over-grown, unkempt version of his latest cut. He hasn't shaved in weeks, and I suspect he might be a touch behind on sleep, too. His presence, though, has the usual effect on me: it gives me ballast and bolts me to the ground when I'm on the verge of being spirited away.

Alpha.

His deep scent is unmistakable. Solid and placating. The perfect counterpoint to the panic of the Vampyre.

Who snarls, "I'll kill her if you come closer."

Koen, of course, comes closer. With the placid air of someone who has never doubted his ability to hammer the world to his will. "Uh-uh. Serena, he says he's going to kill you. You cool with that?" His tone is pure intellectual curiosity. Charcoal eyes glow steadily in the night.

"I did run out of instant noodles last week," I croak. Not my best idea, since the Vampyre nearly twists my humerus out of its socket. But the amused twitch of Koen's mouth *almost* makes up for it.

"You are Koen Alexander, aren't you? The Alpha of the North-west."

"I sure am. What's *your* name, bud?"

"That's not important. If you come any closer—"

Koen clucks his tongue. "You gotta tell me your name, or I'll have to make one up. Any ideas, Serena?"

I clear my throat. "I like Bob."

"Bob the Vampyre. Love it."

"That's *not* my na—"

"It is if the lady says so, shartstain. Wanna tell me what you're doing in my territory before I rip off your balls and shove them down your throat?"

The Vampyre doesn't reply but wrenches my arm so violently, my vision spots and I nearly lose consciousness. When I can parse out sounds again, he's pulling me into his body and snarling, "She might be too valuable to kill, but I can do a whole lot of damage."

"Go ahead, then." For the first time since he appeared, Koen's eyes catch on mine. I read absolutely nothing in them. "This girl can take a lot. Am I wrong, Serena?"

I somehow find the strength to shake my head—a blatant lie. And yet. It might be a pain-induced olfactory hallucination, but I think I smell how pleased it makes him.

"You sure?" the Vampyre asks. "She's half *Human*, after all."

"And you're half jackass. What a stunning coincidence."

"They all want her, you know. Since that interview she gave, every Vampyre on the continent has been looking for her."

"Yeah. I'm sure there are plenty of vivisection tables with her name on it."

"But do you know how much they'll pay?" The Vampyre's voice takes on a sudden persuasive bent. "As the person who brings the hybrid to them, I will be able to name my price."

"Sure. And they definitely won't get rid of you the second you hand her over."

The Vampyre snorts. "I'm smarter than that. I'm the first who found her—do you think I'm the only one after her bounty? Others are going to follow. Once they discover that you're giving her sanctuary, they'll flock here. Are you sure you want to spend the rest of your life protecting a half Human? Let me take her off your hands. Look the other way."

"As far as offers go, Bob, this one is lazy as fuck." Koen spreads his arms. "What do *I* get out of it? You're supposed to offer something in return. Split the reward, wash my car—"

"They say she's your mate."

It's like the forest hears the words. Like it *understands* them. For a brief second every critter, every leaf, every drop of water stills, as if waiting for Koen's reaction.

"Do they, now?" He advances, still relaxed. He's taking a night stroll. Wandering around a museum. Unburdened of all worries.

"Yes. And you know what else they say?"

"Bet you're going to tell me."

"That she rejected you."

"Ouch." Koen doesn't look to be in any pain. "And your unimpeachable reasoning is that I'll happily exact my revenge on her by allowing you to take her."

"Wouldn't it be better? To be done with her once and for all?"

Koen lifts a hand, making the Vampyre jolt. All he does, though, is massage his temple like an exhausted parent would. Wondering why his toddler is stuffing another crayon up a nostril. "Man. I'm going to have to kill you, and Jorma's gonna make me do a fuckton of paperwork for that." He sighs, and the trace of impatience in his voice makes my blood curdle.

Not the Vampyre's, though. Because what he says next is "And she's pretty, isn't she?"

I go very, very still. And so does Koen.

"And right now she's not in a position to *reject* anyone."

No response.

"Do you get my meaning? *Alpha?*"

Any pretense of casualness melts out of Koen's demeanor. Every atom of his body is now on high alert, orienting toward prey. Toward *me.*

"Like I said, she's very beautiful. I wouldn't mind tossing her your way, after I'm done with her," he offers. Koen's eyes contract to displeased pinpricks, and his scent gives off such unequivocal aversion, even the Vampyre knows to backtrack. "Or you could have your fun with her. Then I'd take her away, no questions asked. She'd have no one to complain to."

An owl hoots in the distance. I hold my breath, waiting for Koen to tell the Vampyre to fuck off, but the silence lingers, and his eyes grow opaque, and after a while he . . .

Koen *nods*.

My heart plummets.

No. He wouldn't. He would never.

"Koen?" I say. Half question, half plea.

"In my defense, Serena . . ." Koen lifts his shoulders. "It's always fucking something with you."

Ice prickles all over my skin. "No. Don't. Koen, *don't*—"

"I took the liberty to get started," the Vampyre says, and before I can wonder what he means, his free hand lowers the torn half of my top down my shoulder.

Koen's eyes linger on my nearly bare chest like I'm no more than a cut of flesh. An offering to be appraised. Something created for him to use. I watch his pupils do an odd dance, sense a shift in his scent before he murmurs, "See, *this* is how you make a deal. I knew you had it in you, Bob."

Once again, I beg my body to shift to its wolf form. Once again, I am ignored. With a furious grunt, I begin thrashing in the Vampyre's grip, desperately trying to break free. But he's stronger than me, and Koen's probably stronger than the two of us put together. I can knock out one of them, and I'd still be screwed.

I clutch the rock in my palm, but folded as he has me, I still cannot use it.

Terror rushes through my body. Thumps against my chest.

"She's all yours, Alpha. Do what you will with her." The Vampyre lets out a winded, obnoxious laugh. He lowers his blade and pushes me a few inches forward without letting go of my wrists. He stinks like he knows that it's all over for me—that he's *won*. "Maybe she'd even enjoy it?"

Koen considers the matter as he steps closer, near enough that I can feel his heat, and I bare my teeth at him as I squirm in the Vampyre's clutch. This can't be for real. *Alpha protects*, says a calm Were voice that lives inside my bones. *Alpha is home. Koen is not like that.*

Except, I'm not so sure.

Koen stops in front of me, staring like I'm at his disposal, and yeah. He is *exactly* like that.

"Would she?" he wonders, voice low and rich, eyes caressing my face and lingering on my bare breast. Closer still, and his presence envelops me like a warm blanket. His scent blooms in my nostrils, safe, grounding, so breathtakingly perfect that for a moment I forget about the Vampyre behind me, the pine needles jabbed into the soles of my feet.

"Please," I mouth softly, but I don't think Koen hears me. His hand comes up to my face. Wraps around my cheek, thumb pressing into my lower lip.

"Would you, Serena? Enjoy it?"

Panic bursts anew in my chest. I shake my head violently. No. *No.*

"Well, then." His eyes soften, and he lets out a half-resigned, half-amused sigh. "Better make use of that rock in your hand, killer."

It takes me a beat to understand his meaning, and to realize that the Vampyre's hold on my wrist has loosened. Twisting my arm free and stabbing the jagged edge of the rock into his stomach takes so little effort, it's almost anticlimactic.

"What the—" The Vampyre doubles over. I'm about to hit him again, but he bounces back and slams me to the ground. He lifts his knife above his head, aiming for my throat. "You fucking *bitch*—"

He stops with an abrupt gasp, as though in the grip of a sudden illuminating revelation. He stares down at me, eyes bulging, mouth wide open, and I almost expect him to . . . apologize? Then, after coughing up a small rivulet of mulberry-colored blood, he loses his balance. I observe his descent, horrified, as he collapses right by my side, face-first into a patch of moss.

He does *not* move again.

Neither do I. I don't know what it says about me, but I'm incapable of *not* staring as blood gurgles out of the deep claw-shaped parallel wounds on his back, iron blending with the earthy smell of the soil.

It's a long while before I'm able to glance down at my body—miraculously intact, if mostly naked—and then up at Koen—glibly unimpressed. Anyone else would be helping me up, but not the Alpha of the Northwest pack. Instead, he slowly shakes his head, wiping the hand he just used to kill a man across his flannel. The deep-violet strokes create an oddly pretty painting over the black-and-white canvas.

It takes him a while to remember that I exist. "Evening, Serena." The intensity of a few moments ago has dissolved, and he sounds indifferent. Maybe he knows that a single ounce of sympathy would knock me over. Maybe he truly does not, and has never, given a fuck about anything. "How's your night been?"

"Uneventful," I rasp out.

"Yeah? You look like shit."

"Do I." Gelid sweat slides down my temple and between my breasts, which I hurry to cover as best as I can. "Is this the way you talk to your beloved mate?"

A single eyebrow lifts "I said you were my mate. Not that I loved you."

I gasp out a single, outraged laugh, but at least I'm not crying. It's nice to keep what little dignity I have left as Koen gives me a cool, appraising look and crouches next to me.

"We have to go," he tells me.

"Where?"

"To the Den." He picks me up with his arms under my back and knees. The chill becomes a distant memory. "Woodland retreat's over, killer."

CHAPTER 2

"Absolutely fucking no."

"If you don't tell her, Koen, she'll find out anyway."

"How? Will she steal my diary? Is she able to read minds?"

Lowe, in his defense, has the grace to look vaguely self-conscious. "I won't hide it from Misery. And Misery won't hide it from her."

"Oh, fuck off. I liked it better when you were lonely and sad and depressed. Listen, I tell Serena, and then what? Nothing could ever come of it, even if she's interested."

"If we made it publicly known . . . If she's the mate of the Alpha of the Northwest, no Were will harm her. Hybrid or not."

A mix of anger and outrage simmers in the pit of Koen's stomach. "No Were will harm her, because I'll be there to fucking kill them."

"Will you? Misery is here, and Serena wants to be with Misery. You won't be around."

"Then I'll move into the Moreland compound. My pack runs itself."

But Lowe just looks at him like he did when he was twelve, already way too fucking serious for his age, like the pillars of Earth rest in his clenched sphincter, and Koen has never been able to stand it. Back then, all he wanted was to shield Lowe from the ugliness of being the kind of Weres they are. He still does.

"You're so fucking annoying." Koen drags a hand down his face.

"Yup." Lowe stands. "Had a great role model."

Four and a half months earlier
Southwest territory

KOEN ALEXANDER'S FIRST WORDS TO ME ARE "IT'S NOT plugged in."

Memorable stuff, really.

I'm sure it's the start of every epic love story: a girl, trying to turn on a laptop and jabbing the power button with increasing violence. A very big man in a plaid shirt, leaning cross armed against a doorjamb, staring skeptically at her. The ego-pulverizing embarrassment of making a less-than-excellent first impression on someone your friends love and respect.

Koen appeared in Lowe's driveway a couple of hours ago, Lowe's little sister in tow, triggering the family reunion that's currently going on downstairs. It involves Ana being bubbly, Misery pretending not to adore her, and Lowe pretending not to be awestruck by Misery's inability to successfully hide her adoration. It's cute, and it deserves some privacy.

Misery is at her best. I may not be at my worst, but I'm still a definite work in progress.

I spent the last two months imprisoned in Vampyre territory. I was certain that my abduction would end with my spleen being fed to the raccoons, meaning that this is a second chance at life that I don't yet know what to do with. I've been wading through time and space slowly, never fully coherent, constantly overstimulated. After months of silence, whispers are too loud. The cicadas feel single-mindedly focused on rupturing my eardrums. My skin is either boiling hot or a glacier. These days, I enjoy being on my own. So I snuck up to Lowe's office. Sat on a leather chair. Grabbed a laptop and made the radical choice to check my email.

That's where Koen found me and decided to educate me about electricity.

"Oh." I glance at the, yes, very dangling power cord. "Duh." I smile, trying to display the right ratio of self-deprecating to mortified, and look for an outlet.

"On your left," he says.

I turn.

"Your *other* left."

I want to go outside, swallow a porcupine, and wait for the internal hemorrhaging to finish me. Instead, I set the laptop aside and stand. "Koen, right? Nice to meet you." I offer my hand—which he looks at but doesn't take. *Okay*, I think, tucking it in my back pocket.

Maybe it's a Were thing. Maybe Koen's hand-shaking partners must clear a certain IQ threshold, which I clearly do not. Misery mentioned something about him being "an exceptional asshole"—a seldom-offered compliment from her—so if he doesn't like me, I'm not going to bawl. There's more pressing stuff taking up my brainpower. "Was there anything you needed?" I ask with a polite smile.

"To talk. Do you have a minute?"

"Of course. What's up?"

He doesn't tell me. Instead he looks, and looks, and looks some more. His eyes are . . . not black. Not gray, either. Somewhere in between. Reflective. They feel like tar: viscous, sticky, well-laid traps. I cannot tear mine away, but neither can I hold his gaze.

"Are you here to behold the hybrid?" I ask without hostility. The Weres I've met so far have shown me nothing but kindness, and their curiosity is a small price to pay for their welcome. Especially considering that most Humans would shoot me on sight. "Here I am." I twirl around to give him the best three-sixty view of my aberrant self. "Honestly, I think I just look Human, but . . ." I cut off, because his eyes . . . That thing they're doing, it's not normal. They glow and contract and—

Koen grunts. His head tips back, showing a strong neck and a working throat. "What the fuck have I done to deserve this?" he mutters.

"Excuse me?"

"Actually, I just remembered." He lowers his chin and sighs. His voice is deep and gravelly. "I've been a piece of shit for most of my life, that's what."

"I . . . don't follow?"

Heavy steps thud up the stairs. It's Lowe, who joins us and asks, "You told her?"

"Not yet."

Lowe nods, and I get my first hint that whatever Koen wants from me, it's probably a bit more serious than *May I ask about your hybrid diet and musculoskeletal system and whether you molt in the fall?*

"Where's Misery?" I ask, suddenly terrified. "And Ana?"

"They're fine. Both downstairs." Lowe pauses. "Do you want Misery here?"

"I . . ." Yes. Kind of. But also, I do miss being a functioning adult who can operate without her Vampyre security blanket. "Nah."

Lowe turns to Koen. "You really want to tell her now?"

"Might as well."

The two men stand, silent, staring—Lowe like I'm a wounded kitten he's trying to corner for an injection, and Koen . . . I can't get a good read on him, which might account for how alarming I find him.

Or it could be the scars. The three parallel claw marks on his face, for instance. The one in the middle is the longest: it starts up in his forehead, dissects his brow, and continues down his cheek in a thin, straight line. He also has small ones on his upper lip, at the base of his jaw, past his collarbone. But none are hungry or red or new. None suggest that he's itching for a fight.

He's big, too—as in, *big*. Just a couple of inches taller than Lowe, but approximately ninety times more intimidating. *It's because Lowe feels domesticated*, a wise, instinctual voice explains from the recesses of my skull. *Lowe can, and will, control and pace himself. Koen is a wild card. Koen is raw. Koen will do whatever the hell he—*

"You are my mate," he says. With little inflection.

So little, I must have misheard. I learned it back in college. Linguistics elective, junior year. *The rhythmic patterns of language contribute to listening comprehension.* "Excuse me?"

"You and the Vampyre are close, right?" he asks, full of that calm that borders on indifference. Is he making fun of me? "She explained what a mate is?"

Slowly, I nod.

"What Misery is to Lowe, you are to me."

Oh.

Oh?

Oh. "Is this a, um . . . terminal diagnosis?"

His lips twitch. "No cure, I'm afraid."

"I see." I clear my throat. "Well, this relationship sure escalated quickly."

His words surprised me, but the way the corners of his eyes crease in amusement shocks me tenfold. His laugh is a deep, warm chuckle that makes my heart stumble. "You have no idea, kid."

I cross my arms. "Should you be calling me 'kid,' given the situation?"

"I'm not married to it. What would you prefer?"

"Well, there's always my actual name. But if you insist on a nick-name, I'd prefer something with a bit more . . ."

"More?"

"More teeth."

His eyebrow rises. "Root canal?"

"No. Come on, you know what I mean. Something that inspires fear."

"Real estate market crash."

"Okay, maybe less fear and more . . . awe. Warrior-like."

His once-over is skeptical. "You're what? Five feet?"

"I'm two and a half inches over that. And for your information, the other day these stubby little legs butchered several Vampyres."

"Look at you go, killer."

"Guys." Lowe's voice startles me. I forgot he was there. "We should get back to the matter at hand."

Koen and I exchange a brief *Can you believe this narc?* glance.

"I think that part of the conversation is over," Koen says, push-ing nonchalantly away from the doorway. "She's been informed. She understands. We can all resume our normal activities, such as running packs, or"—he glances at my laptop—"boycotting power outlets."

I stave off a smile. "I forget *one time* and—"

"Serena." Lowe. Interrupting again. "Do you *really* understand what it means?" The urgency in his tone is a confusing contrast to Koen's indifference.

And then the full impact of it slams into me.

No, I *don't* understand. Because I haven't even stopped to *con-sider* it. "Is it . . . Does it mean that he . . ." On the mate thing, Misery was light on the specifics. And it's not as though Lowe unburdens his secret heart to me. "Does it mean that he likes me?"

"Yes," Lowe says—which perfectly covers Koen's "No."

I frown. "Wow. This is bringing me lots of clarity. Thanks, guys."

Lowe glares at Koen, who's sporting a shit-eating grin. "Look, I'm sure you're a very likable person. It's not what this is about, though."

"What *is* it about?"

Lowe massaged the bridge of his nose. "For a Were, finding a mate triggers a chain of physiological changes. Misery compared it to falling in love at first sight, and there's some truth to that, but—"

"I'm sorry." I cut in. "Could you leave the two of us alone?" I'm looking at Koen, but the question is for Lowe—whose concerned scent signals a *strong* objection.

In all fairness, a one-on-one with a possible nutjob who wants me to become his mail-order bride *does* seem like a terrible idea. But I suspect that if Koen wanted to hurt me, he could do it whether Lowe was babysitting us or not.

More importantly: I suspect that Koen has no interest in doing any of that.

"Please," I add calmly.

In response to Lowe's searching gaze, Koen nods. Once.

"Call if you need *anything*," Lowe says gruffly before turning on his heel, an invite interestingly directed at both me *and* Koen.

Then we're alone. Somehow, my stomach feels ten pounds lighter. Weird. "Will you come in, please? And, ah, sit down."

He does, no questions asked—kneeling briefly to plug my damn charger into the damn socket. I pretend not to see it, and close the door.

Koen slouches lazily on the chair next to mine, almost too relaxed, a large apex predator examining its quarry. Like we're about

MATE

to discuss the new garbage collection schedule, and not a major psychosocial milestone in the life of a Were. Maybe this mate business isn't that big of a deal?

"Lowe seems . . ." I return to my chair. Run my palms down the legs of my sweats. "Very protective. Of me *and* of you, I think."

"Isn't he fucking adorable?" Koen's tone is pure fondness. "Always been like that, since before his balls dropped. Best Were I've ever met."

I smile. "I'm glad Misery is in good hands."

"And vice versa."

I tilt my head. "It doesn't bother you that she's a Vampyre?"

"They obviously care for each other." He sounds as though nothing else would ever factor into his approval, which I find very endearing.

"So." I run my tongue against the back of my teeth. "Love at first sight, huh?"

Koen winces. "Not quite. Lowe's a bit of a romantic."

"Oh?"

"A side effect of all that decency, probably. Colors his perception of the world."

"But *your* perception is unmarred. Because you're *not* decent?"

He doesn't reply, but he smells like he agrees. "What's happening here has very little to do with loving or liking, Serena."

"What *does* it have to do with, then?"

A beat. His lips curve. "Really?"

I stare at him, stumped.

"Oh, killer. I'm happy to spell it out for you, if you need me to."

"I *do* need you to. Like I'm five, preferably."

"Not sure I can make it anything under NC-17."

ALI HAZELWOOD

"What do you—*ooh.*" My cheeks flood with heat. After gawking owl-eyed at Koen for a long stretch, I realize that I'm clutching my chest like a Victorian governess and abruptly let go.

"I . . ." I shake my head, not wanting to come across as some sex-ed-deprived orphan who thinks that childbirth occurs when nose boogers reach critical mass.

I'm not. Although I used to be, in my teens. Misery was the Vampyre Collateral, obligated to live among Humans, to be killed if the Vampyres violated the rules of the ceasefire between the two species. I was her companion—an orphan randomly selected to be her friend and make sure that she wouldn't get too lonely (something *no one* gave a shit about) or too disruptive (something *everyone* was scared shitless of). Except that the Randomly Selected Human Orphan turned out to be more like the Purposefully Chosen Human-Were Hybrid Who Needed to Be Kept Under Surveillance by the Vampyres to Prevent the World from Finding Out That Humans and Weres Are Actually Reproductively Compatible and Might Therefore Decide to Not Hate Each Other or Even Form Alliances Against the Vampyres.

Plot twist.

But at the time, no one knew that. Back then, my entire *value* was exclusively reflected in Misery. My education hinged on hers. And since no one was certified to teach reproductive anatomy to a Vampyre, I didn't get sex ed, either.

Once we got out, though, we had unlimited access to the internet and dates and boyfriends. And, of course, sex.

Except, that was a lifetime ago. A handful of years that might as well be entire geologic eras. Back then, I was *Human.* I wasn't terrified of the full moon, or of what color my blood would spill if I cut myself. Once I began to realize that there was something very,

24

very wrong with me, the entire concept of sex became laughably trivial. At the beginning of my abduction, I was briefly concerned that it might be forced upon me. When that wasn't the case, it was pleasantly forgotten.

And now here I am. Thinking about it. Sex is a giant winged dragon, stretching awake in my head.

"Can you . . ." I swallow. "These biological changes you mentioned. Can you control yourself?"

The meaning takes a minute to sink in. When it does, I half expect Koen to resent my question, but there's no trace of defensiveness in his firm "Always."

It makes it easier to believe him. "So, basically, you just want to . . . ?"

"Correct." He nods casually. *Yes, I would love a cup of Earl Grey. Yes, I'll respond to a brief survey in exchange for a ten percent discount on my purchase. Yes, I do want to f—*

"I hope I don't sound conceited, but . . . how is it different from the reaction of most Human men I've met?" I cringe the instant the words are out. "God. I *do* sound conceited. I'm sorry. I promise I don't walk around thinking that my face launches a thousand erections—"

"You're the most beautiful woman that I've ever seen," he says simply.

Like it's not a big deal.

Like he's complimenting my taste in socks.

Like I could resemble the reflection of a wart on a doorknob, and it would change nothing for him.

Which might be just what I need. My looks have always been a sore point for me. Something ugly, to be ashamed of. *Sexualized too young*, a friend with a psychology degree once said. Misery and I turned twelve, and our paths diverged. She became longer, graceful, ethereal. I, softer. Rounder. Suddenly my body *burst*. I bloomed into something with hips and breasts, and people—mostly adult men—would look at me in ways that hopscotched between uncomfortable and dangerous.

Maybe it's a good thing, Misery said skeptically, noticing the way Mr. Elrod would track my movements. *Maybe it means that you're beautiful?*

I doubt men twice my age looking at me is a proxy for anything other than them wanting to take advantage. And that was the crux of it. Misery was the Collateral. Misery needed to be kept alive, or an interspecies war would ravage the south of the North American continent. Above all, Misery was *special*, and therefore off-limits.

I, on the other hand, was a Human orphan. Replaceable. A dime a dozen—less than. My value was null, and the staff was fully aware. I saw it in their stares. Heard it in the comments they never bothered to whisper. Felt it in how intensely I had to request, press, beg, advocate, to receive my first bra, or clothes that I wouldn't outgrow in a few months. I was there at their discretion, and without protection. If I wasn't careful, who knew what might happen?

I knew. And when I was twelve, I began wedging a chair under the door of my room every night.

"I don't doubt you're approached by many men. But I'm not Human, so I'm not sure how it differs." He shrugs, once again bored by the conversation. "It might be just quantitative. In the end, it's hormones. Sex. The rest—liking, or loving, doesn't come with it."

"I see." I drum my fingers over my armrest and lean back, observing. Not just Koen, but also the way Koen makes *me* feel. In my previous life, I wouldn't have spared him a single glance. Were Serena, though, studies the lock of black hair falling over his forehead; the clean-shaven aggressively handsome face. He is too intense, too brash. Too rough around the edges, and at least a decade older than me.

I have—had?—a type: cute, polite, solicitous. Boyish. My age. Gentle guys who underlined their favorite prose passages in books we buddy read, and who were secure enough in their masculinity to borrow my moisturizer when they spent the night. I never enjoyed being overwhelmed.

Koen is the Alpha of a pack that takes up a quarter of the country. Koen confuses me just by breathing the same air. Koen is so diametrically opposed to the kind of men I prefer, a protractor must be involved. "The gist of this," I summarize, as though taking minutes for a meeting, "is that you find me attractive."

"That might be the dictionary definition of 'understatement,' but yes."

I'm a little heated. "But you won't, um, die of a broken heart over me?"

He sighs. "Humans are so fucking dramatic."

"And Weres are such dicks," I reply sweetly.

"Lucky for you, you're a mix of both."

I bite the inside of my cheek, desperate to hide how entertained I am. Going by the swirl of amusement in his eyes, he's perfectly aware.

"Well, this attraction you have for me is clearly beyond your control, so I won't tell you that I'm flattered. And you seem like a great guy. You're, um, gainfully employed, and look like you spend lots of time shirtless chopping firewood—"

"I don't."

"No?"

"I'm Were. I produce my own warmth."

Makes sense. "What I meant is, you're clearly a catch. But I know very little about you. I have no clue about your age, your last name, your favorite color . . ." I study him. "It's probably black. It's black, isn't it?"

"I'm actually partial to red."

"Like Human blood?"

He does *not* deny it.

"Okay. Well. As I said, thank you for your consideration. Unfortunately, I'm not in the position to start a relationship, so I must decline your offer, and—"

"What offer?"

"The one that you . . ." I frown. Because he did *not* make an offer.

"This conversation is *not* an invitation, killer."

That is . . . true, even though I'm not sure why I'm realizing it just now. Koen is not hitting on me. He's not trying to cha-cha real smooth into my life. He did *not* decide that pairing up with me would perfectly round out Lowe and Misery's nuclear family and allow us to host holiday meals at alternating intervals.

There is no expectation of anything.

But . . . "Why did you want me to know, then?"

"It's the truth. You should be aware." He says it matter-of-factly, like *real* and *shared* are overlapping constructs.

"And you and the truth are particularly tight?"

He assesses me for a beat. "I'm not going to *lie* to you, Serena."

"Well, I'm probably going to lie to you *a lot*."

"Yeah?" His smile is almost charmed. "What kind of lies do you tell?"

"All sorts." I swallow. Glance at my own knees. "But only if it's for the greater good."

"You sure?"

Yes. "What about you? Are *you* sure?"

"Sure of . . . ?"

"How do you know that I'm really your mate?"

"I just do. Trust me on it."

I do, surprisingly. In fact, I'm less concerned with what he feels, and more with . . . "How can I tell if someone is my mate? I want to know if I feel the same about you."

He waves the question away. "You don't."

"How do you know?"

"If you did, you'd be aware."

"That's not true. Maybe the signs are there, but I'm missing them because I'm only half Were."

"You couldn't miss them."

My throat is dry. My stomach, heavy with disappointment. Did I . . . ? No. Come on. I don't *want* a mate, whatever that means. My sex drive's cobwebs have grown their own cobwebs. I've always needed bucketloads of time alone. Plus, I'm still figuring out *what* I am. This isn't the start of anything.

Except.

"I do feel . . . very safe. Here, with you," I confess, retreating inward for a moment, groping at my unintelligible body and my tricky mind for clarity. Koen's presence is cumbersome, and I feel like I'm stuffed too tight by him, but I am experiencing a stunningly quiet moment. No anxiety. No choking dread of what's to come. "I'm usually . . . Well, it's been a bit draining, finding out that I'm a hybrid. But right now, I'm not afraid at all."

"That's because I'm Alpha. We bring calm and order."

"But I don't feel the same with Lowe."

He quickly discounts it. "Don't read too much into that. It's not a sign of anything."

"But . . ." Why am I even pushing back? He just gave me an out. "Okay. Well, then, since this is clearly one of those unrequited lust situations we, um, all have to deal with sometimes . . ."

"Yes?" He seems amused. Like he knows something I don't. Shouldn't he feel despondent and rejected?

"You're my closest friend's husb—mate's closest friend. And I'd love to get along with you. So maybe we could be, you know, friends."

"What about polite acquaintances?" he counters.

I cannot tell whether he's serious, so I nod. "Deal. And you may quietly pine after me, if you must."

He exhales a rough, quiet laugh. It mostly sits around the edges of his eyes, but it envelops me all the same. "Thank you." He doesn't seem too devastated. Or maybe he's just the type to find humor in every situation. It's what Misery and I used to do whenever things went to shit, which was always: laugh about them. Watch them go to shit even harder. Become hysterical, but in a diverting way.

That's still who I am. Misery may be settled, overflowing with belonging, but I'm a fucking disaster. "You wouldn't want me anyway, if it weren't for the whole biology thing. I'm a mess," I say, subdued, barely audible.

He hears me, though. "Oh, yeah. You are."

"Hey." My chin juts out. "*I* can say it. *You* shouldn't."

"Serena, you're a half-Human Were who admits to being a serial liar, doesn't know how electricity works, and is undoubtedly swimming in complex PTSD. Believe me, a *toddler* can say it."

I really want to be indignant, but a laugh snorts out of me all on its own. And then Koen is standing, heading for the door, and there's once again a weight in my stomach, one that seems to get heavier just because he's leaving, and heavier still because I'd like him to stay for a second longer.

And then the understanding rolls into me, as inexorable as a little earthquake, that—this is it. The rest of my life. And maybe I could slowly, cautiously, start living it.

"You know," I say when he opens the door and I'm brusquely reminded that a world exists outside the walls of this room. "I actually think that maybe I could . . ."

He looks at me over his shoulder.

"Just." My belly feels warm. "You seem . . . Misery and Ana love you, which means that you're a nice guy. We could maybe, um, try to hang out sometime? Coffee, maybe. Or . . . I'm not sure what you guys do when you go out, but . . . The thing is, I know you very little, but so far, I kind of like you."

No *Hey, I'd love to go on a date with you* was ever uttered more clumsily, but it's okay. Because Koen's eyes soften with amusement, and indulgence, and maybe some affection, too.

That's what makes his words feel like a razor-sharp knife sliding between my ribs.

"I meant what I said, killer. This mate thing is about fucking. The part of me that matters isn't interested in you. Like me, or don't," he says kindly. "I really couldn't care less."

CHAPTER 3

She expects little and is not easily offended. It makes pushing her away frustratingly hard.

Present day

KOEN ALEXANDER, THE FERAL ALPHA OF THE MOST DANGER-ous pack on the continent, undisputed ruler in a wild territory known for its exceptional bloodthirst, listens to Human classical music while driving.

I did *not* see that coming.

And yet here he is. Post Vampyre slaughtering, blissfully unaffected as he chauffeurs me back to the Southwest pack. Lightly tapping his long fingers against the steering wheel to keep rhythm like a connoisseur. Would it be insulting to openly manifest my shock? Do I care about offending Koen?

Yes. And *yes*, since I'll be alone with him in this car for the next few hours. At the mercy he may not have.

"Is this Bach?" I ask, with no real clue what Bach sounds like. In my previous life, back when I was a Human financial reporter whose idea of a mightily stressful time included judging the ripeness of watermelons or having to sneeze while driving, I gravitated toward pop.

"Why didn't you shift?" Koen asks instead of answering. His eyes never leave the road ahead.

"Sorry?"

"Why didn't you shift to wolf form to run from Bob?"

"Right. Who *is* Bob anyway?"

The look he gives me lasts a quarter of a second but perfectly relays what Koen thinks about people who answer his questions with more questions. How lovely to learn that his patience and willingness to filter himself have not increased in the weeks since he shuttled me to the cabin. I fidget with the sleeves of the extra-large hoodie he lent me, and for the tenth time since I got in the car, I tell myself to forget the way he stared at my naked chest in the woods.

It was a ruse. To distract the Vampyre. To save my life. He was never going to harm me, and I have zero reasons to be afraid of him.

Well, I have *one*: he's objectively terrifying.

"I can't shift when the moon is this small," I tell him.

It's the way it works with Weres: when the moon is fat and round in the sky, we can barely resist its call and need all our self-control to avoid shifting to wolf form. The feeling of something awakening inside me, clawing to be let out once a month, always during the same lunar phase—that's what first clued me in that maybe I wasn't all that Human, after all.

Conversely, when the moon is weak, only highly powerful and dominant Weres can shift. I'm neither, and my ineptitude should be plenty believable to Koen.

If only.

"And yet," he muses in his deep voice, "back when I first met you, you could shift at will."

"Not when the moon was like this."

"When it was smaller, if I recall correctly. And I do."

I force myself not to tense. Weres pick up on physiological changes like sentient lie detectors, and I nurse too many secrets to have someone as perceptive as Koen on my back. "Maybe you have me mixed up with someone else."

He shoots me another dissecting, eviscerating look. "Does your sudden inability to shift have anything to do with the reason you decided to disappear on a two-month holiday in the middle of the forest?"

Yes, it does, and no, it's none of his business. "The reason I decided to *disappear*, if that's even a word you can use for someone whose whereabouts were never *not* accounted for, is that the things I had to deal with in the past year include, in chronological but not traumatogenic order"—I lift my hand and begin counting with my fingers—"the slow realization that I'm not fully Human; the even slower realization that I'm much wolfier than I ever believed; my abduction and subsequent imprisonment at the hands of the Vampyres; baby's first mass murder—in which I partook as the *murderer*; and, at long last, coming out to the rest of the planet as the first Human-Were hybrid." I thrust my splayed hand in Koen's face like it's the world's most fucked-up bingo card and bat my eyes at him. "I think my need for rest and relaxation was justified."

"Not to kill your buzz, but I doubt you get to claim a Mass Murderer commemorative coin if it was in self-defense."

He's probably right. And I don't feel bad about the (two? Three? Seven? It's all a blur.) Vampyres I killed to protect Misery. "Still. Rearranging my self-image from law-abiding citizen to opportunistic slaughterer did require some inward work. Ego-concept adjustments. Self-reflection. Bawling. That kind of stuff." I gather my knees to my chest, pull the hoodie over my scratched-up shins, and ask, "How did you know, by the way?"

"Know what?"

"That someone was going to come for me at the cabin."

"Lowe called me earlier today. Two Vampyres, Bob and some other jizzmuffin, tried to hack the Southwest and triggered some intrusion detection systems. Alex, their IT guy, realized that they were looking for your location." A beat. "And Ana's."

I cover my mouth with my hand. Ana and I have one thing in common: we're Human-Were hybrids. But while I went public with my real nature, hers is on a strict need-to-know basis.

Because Ana is *seven years old*.

"Is she—"

"Okay, yes. Bob was able to track you through your sat phone and followed you up north. There was no information on Ana. But Alex planted some to lure the other jizzmuffin deeper into Southwest territory."

"And?"

"Lowe killed him, of course. But prior to his . . . untimely demise, Lowe's mate did that"—he makes a vague circular motion—"hypnosis thing on him."

"What hypnosis— Oh. The thrall?"

"Yeah. That." Koen's expression clearly states, *Not a fan*. It's a common Were feeling.

"So Misery thralled Jizzmuffin? What did he say?"

"A member of the Vampyre council is offering several life-changing amounts of money for a hybrid."

"Which member?"

"The fact-finding didn't get that far. Either Jizzmuffin didn't know, or Lowe got impatient and graduated early to the massacre part of the night."

That's unfortunate, but I'm inordinately proud. "Good on Misery. And to think that she used to say I was the only person she could competently thrall." Koen's glare is bemused, so I hurry to explain, "Consensually. She practiced on me when we were kids."

"She *practiced* on you."

"Of course. How else was she supposed to learn? She needed a brain to train on, and mine was right there."

"Maybe there was permanent damage. That would explain it."

"Explain what?"

"The many things that are wrong with you."

I frown. "Like what?"

"Your self-imposed isolation. How much weaker you've gotten since I last saw you. The fact that you smell exhausted. Your affinity for lies. Your refusal to shift even when your life depends on it—"

"You know," I challenge him mildly, "if you're accusing me of something, you can just come out and say it."

"Nah. It's more fun to corner you into admitting it." He clearly has feelings about what happened tonight. They include frustration, worry, anger, and even a hint of distrust. I'm not sure how I know, since his stony profile hasn't moved a millimeter. Maybe I'm getting better at guessing others' emotions by scent, like a *real* Were.

Look at me, the little hybrid that could.

"There is nothing to admit," I say blandly. "Do you think Bob told anyone about our locations?"

"No. He's an idiot who entered Northwest territory on his own."

"Was."

"Was," Koen concedes, disturbingly pleased. Were justice is swift and brutal, and the Northwest's most of all. The pack is known for spending more time in wolf form than others, for being vicious beyond what is necessary to maintain their borders, and for holding grudges. The Northwest has fewer members than the Southwest, but its territory is wider and more remote. Which is why, when I decided that I needed to be alone, it seemed like the best option.

But now that I have Koen breathing down my neck, I'm rethinking things.

"You're tired, and we have a long drive," he says, abruptly changing the topic. "Go to sleep."

I *am* tired. But: "What are we going to do about Ana?"

He frowns in surprise. "I told you, Ana is fine."

"Ana is *seven*. We need to have a plan in place to protect her."

"We?"

"We," I repeat. When *I* was seven, I was an orphan. When *I* was seven, nothing but horrible things happened around me. Too much of this hits too close to home, and I don't want her to ever feel like I used to.

"Ana has Lowe, and the Vampyre—"

"Her name is Misery."

"—and an entire pack that is ready to die and, more productively, to *kill* for her."

"I should help, too. I can—"

"Serena." There is an edge to his voice. His grip on the steering wheel tightens. "Did you hit your head earlier?"

"What?" I instinctively massage the back of my skull. "I don't think so. Why?"

"Just trying to figure out what caused the memory loss."

"I don't have—"

"Clearly you forgot that you were assaulted about forty-five minutes ago."

"I didn't."

"Really? That's fucking great." There is a deep V between his dark, reflective eyes, one that makes his scars pop. "Then I won't have to remind you that you're twenty times more at risk than Ana is."

"That's not true."

"*Ana* is the sister of an Alpha, and her existence is a well-kept secret. *You* have no family, no pack, no influence, no resources— you don't even have a home. You are virtually alone in the world, and you've been under surveillance your entire life, which makes predicting your next move very easy for a specific contingent of people. And don't forget that for the last few months, your face has been plastered on every single news segment all over the world. Now, for a thought experiment: If someone decides that they want to play mad scientist with a hybrid, who do you think they'll go for, killer?"

Koen is angry—whether at my stupidity or at being saddled with me, I'm not sure. Still, the depth of my lack of . . . of *everything* is not something I want to contemplate at the moment. "You are correct," I say calmly, feeling a burning pressure behind my eyes. "And I'm not going to say that I can fend off whoever comes for me. However, if I know about a threat, I *can* prepare and take care of myself—"

"*I* will take care of you," he says roughly.

Oh. "Oh."

He sighs and runs a hand through his thick, unkempt hair.

"Koen, you don't have to—"

"Serena." I hear it in his voice, how little patience he has to spare. For the first time, it occurs to me to wonder what his night was like before he appeared to take care of Bob—and of *me*. The warning phone call from Lowe. The furious drive to reach me. The fear of being too late.

The part of me that matters isn't interested in you, he'd said, and I do not doubt it. But even if the mate thing means nothing to Koen, even if he doesn't care about me as a person, I'm still a hybrid who could bridge the gap between Weres and Humans. I'm under his protection, and hearing that I was in danger cannot have been easy. "Thank you," I say with sincere appreciation. "For coming to get me. For being there right on time."

"Don't thank me."

"Why?"

"I fucking hate it."

"You hate to be . . . thanked?"

"Yup."

"I . . . Why?"

"If I'm doing something, you can be sure that I chose to of my own free will." He falls silent for a moment. Then his nostrils flare and he turns to scan my face, his expression increasingly horrified.

"What?" I ask. "Is a moth crawling up my nostril, or—" I pat my cheek with my palm, and it comes back wet.

That's what's upsetting him.

"Oh." Koen just killed someone without batting an eye but cannot take me shedding a single teardrop. "I'm fine," I reassure him. His alarm doesn't abate. It's like I've just been shot in front of his eyes. "I'm okay, I promise. I'm just tired."

"Then go the fuck to sleep." he orders, panicky. *Big Bad Murderous Wolf in Charge of Thousands Cannot Handle Girl Crying*. What a headline. "What are you waiting for? Do you need a bedtime story?"

I chew back a smile. Settle against the headrest. "Why? Do you have any?"

"Me?"

"No—Weres. *Us*, I guess."

"Sure, but they're bleak. Humans and Vampyres coming for us if we nip our teachers too hard. The gods of nature toying with their beastly children. Cosmic horror—that kind of shit."

"Wow. Do children like them?"

"I didn't. Had nightmares about them for years."

I nod slowly. "That explains it."

"What?"

"The many things that are wrong with *you*."

Even under the beard, I can see it. A small smile. A soft snort.

"Go to sleep, Serena." This time, his tone is a gentle push that has me instantly yawning. *It's an Alpha thing*, Misery said. *They're great at making their suggestions sound like the best option for everyone involved.*

So I close my eyes and let the time and the road flow by. Until I remember something. "Koen?" I'm almost fully asleep, my lids too heavy to open.

"Yeah?"

"I think you owe me an apology."

"For what?"

"The way you stared at my tits."

Silence. Then, instead of the *I'm sorry* or *Go to fucking sleep* I expect, he says, "I think *you* owe me an apology."

"For what?"

"How spectacular your tits are."

God, he really is an epic asshole. "You might be the worst person I've ever met."

"Wouldn't be surprised," he mutters.

I fall asleep with a small smile on my face. And for a few hours, I don't think about how little time I have left to live.

CHAPTER 4

He's toweling himself off after a shower, and the call is on speaker. It gives him hope that he may have misunderstood.

"Are you serious?" He doesn't wait for Lowe's reply. As a rule, Lowe doesn't joke. "Who the fuck gave her the idea?"

"Maddie Garcia asked."

"For fuck's sake, the Human governor's the one who leaked her existence to the press to begin with. She can suck shit out of a straw."

"We cannot be sure." A pause. "But yes. Her team likely did. And when the knowledge of the existence of a hybrid wasn't enough to sway public opinion, she asked Serena to publicly come forward. Serena said yes."

"And you let her."

"I have no say in the matter."

"Do you realize the danger she'll be in afterward? Being known as my mate won't protect her in Vampyre or Human territory."

"Serena believes that the benefits outweigh the costs. And, Koen . . ." A sigh. "However much you hate this, Misery loathes it more."

He doubts it.

"But," Lowe continues, "if Serena's sister is willing to acknowledge that a lot of good can come from this, then you, too, should—"

"I fucking won't."

"That bad?" Lowe asks after a long silence.

No. It's worse than that.

Two and a half months earlier
Human territory

THE THING I HATE THE MOST—AND THERE'S *PLENTY* TO HATE here—is the sticky heat of the camera lights. It sends little beads of perspiration down my spine and makes the skin of my back plaster to my ("Light pink!" per Ana's request) blouse.

"We cranked the AC all the way up," one of the producers tells me, apologetic, "but Governor Garcia sent over twenty Secret Service agents to protect you. We're working on a skeleton crew, but the studio's not built for a crowd this size."

I smile, grateful. Nod, appreciative. Wonder if he knows that on top of the Human agents, there are approximately fifteen Weres milling around incognito. Half Koen's, half Lowe's.

Maddie said that she'd provide security, I pointed out to them two days ago, when they briefed me on their plan. *Don't you trust her?*

Lowe's diplomatic *Yes, but* completely overlapped with Koen's curt *No.* His favorite word, coupled with his favorite tone.

I cocked my head at him, fascinated. *Do you trust anyone at all?*

With your precious life, killer? How could I?

This is Koen in a nutshell. Mocking and unreadable and maybe even a little cruel. He does, however, get shit done.

"We're on in five," the producer reminds me. "Anything else you need?"

"I'm good, thank you."

A few feet away, the star journalist who'll conduct the interview is recording a teaser. ". . . the answer that every Human has been seeking for the past month: When was the first known Were-Human hybrid born? How did she manage to stay undetected until her early twenties? What was her life like? Who is she, and above all, why is she coming forward right now? Stick around to learn more . . ."

I zone out. Dissociate. Try not to think about what's at stake. In a shocking revelation, the business of going on TV to speak on how alien one is can be a bit alienating. Solitary. Misery and Lowe insisted on being here, but the less obvious my link to the Southwest, the better for Ana. Maddie's presence would only fuel the (correct) rumors that I'm her carefully chosen political pawn. And it's not as though I could've asked Danny, the last guy I dated before realizing I was a Were, to be my plus-one as I out myself as the Hybrid Whose Existence Has Been Leaked to the Press.

Hence, Koen.

The stage lighting fuzzes the crowd behind the cameras, but the tallest outline, the cross-armed, stern one, can only be him. I smile in his direction, fully aware that even if I could see it, there would be no response.

He's so opposed to what I'm about to do, it's almost funny. His disapproval vibrates through time and space and anchors me to this moment. Nothing else here feels *real*.

"You ready?" the interviewer asks, taking a seat across from me. She's older. Elegant. Her scent betrays how disquieting she finds me, but her poker face is titanium solid. Honestly, I'm impressed. "That's what the viewers at home are seeing now." She points at the monitors. "An interview with the geneticist that I recorded yesterday."

The road to this hothouse of a studio was paved with buccal swabs, blood draws, and lab testing. *Six* independent groups of scientists have confirmed that I am "an interspecific cross" (Latin for *freak*, I believe) and not, as some pundits and social media trolls have decreed, "a grifter making shit up for clout."

"*. . . was not believed possible. We don't have reports of hybrids, even* *from territories such as Europe. in which Weres and Humans live more amalgamated lives. What changed?"*

"The most likely hypothesis is that random genetic mutations have oc-curred within North American packs."

"Genetic mutations like what?"

"It's impossible to say without more data. My hunch would be muta-tions in the genes that encode for gamete recognition, or regulatory genes. The bottom line is that these mutations made Weres reproductively com-patible with Humans."

"And these mutations, they affect all Weres, all over the world?"

"Unlikely. Were packs tend to be self-sufficient and isolated. For in-stance, packs such as the Northwest and the Southwest are known allies, which may come with genetic exchanges between them. But according to most Human observers, those two packs rarely interact with the New En-gland packs. And the same is true for other North American and Euro-pean packs: very few connections."

"So what are the chances that Humans and Weres will become one single species?"

The geneticist laughs. *"I wouldn't worry about it. Keep in mind, most hybrids are not fertile."*

"What about this one?"

"She's highly unlikely to be able to have children, with Humans or with Weres. The difference in chromosome structure will make it hard for her to produce functional gametes . . ."

An out-of-body experience, that's what this is. My soul is up on the ceiling, dangling monkey-bar-style from a truss, staring down at my unresponsive body as it learns that it might not be able to have children.

For the first time.

In front of dozens of people.

From someone who laughs it off as a best-case scenario.

It's okay, I remind my body as the inside of its stomach is being raked bloody. *It changes nothing. It's the least of your problems. You knew that this would be supremely shitty when you agreed to it. Stay on task. Focus on—*

". . . made you decide to come forward and speak to us?" the interviewer is asking.

We're on air. I switch on. Plunge back into the moment. "Frankly, realizing that it was either that or letting others take control of the narrative." I smile the same confident, self-assured smile I used to pitch stories to my editor or to charm the pizza place guy into giving me the slice with the most pepperoni. "Since my existence was made public three weeks ago, a lot of inaccuracies have been reported. I'd like to set the record straight."

"I see. And to remind our viewers, *The Herald*, Ms. Paris's former place of employment, received information about the alleged existence of hybrids from an undisclosed Human source. Its veracity was widely debated. Then, a few days ago, you made a statement to the press revealing your name."

"Thank you for giving me the opportunity to share my story."

"Could you explain why you believed you were Human until last year?"

People *adore* being served a good conspiracy theory. However, one must choose its platter and garnishments very carefully. Take my situation: I *could* tell the truth—that I was under surveillance my entire life because a few despotic members of Human, Were, and Vampyre societies were so power hungry and pathologically unwilling to coexist, they engaged in a complex web of sloppy but decades-enduring deceit. Problem is, it sounds . . . sketchy. Farfetched. The responsibility is too diffused.

More importantly, it would only reinforce Humans' hostility toward the other two species, and there are buckets of that going around already.

That's why, after agreeing to this interview, Maddie, Lowe, and I put our heads down and workshopped a few talking points. The title of our story is *An Evil Human Ex-Governor Locked Poor Little Hybrid Me in a Basement Because He Hated Peace*. It's palatable. Easy to understand. Might even allow the average Human to feel morally superior.

They would never imprison an orphan and lie to them.

They could even be inclined to open their hearts to a victim of injustice.

They might decide to see Weres as people, instead of glowy-eyed butchering machines.

And in the end, this is what we hope to accomplish: buy goodwill for Maddie Garcia, the new Human governor, and enough public support to make reforms possible.

"My real nature was kept from me. The former governor was afraid that as a hybrid, I had the potential to become a symbol of unity between Weres and Humans—an unwelcome one, since his political career was based on divisiveness and fearmongering."

"You're talking about former Human Governor Davenport, who unexpectedly died in prison two days ago?"

"Yes."

It wasn't us, Lowe was quick to say when the news broke of the governor's death. A little too quick, considering I hadn't even asked.

You sure about that?

Tragically, yes. Koen sounded disappointed. *Though his Vampyre and Human accomplices may have had something to do with it. His death is very fortuitous for them.*

My demure nod and murmured "Yes. May he rest in peace" should earn me several acting award statuettes. "He knew that I was half Were."

"How?"

"That, we're still researching. Unfortunately, I don't have many memories of the first few years of my life, or of my parents. All we know is that by the time I was seven, I was living in a Human orphanage in The City. I suspect that through some routine checkup, one of the doctors realized that I was part Were and alerted Governor Davenport." None of what I just said is a lie, which is highly unusual on my part.

"And what did Governor Davenport do?"

"At the time, he knew I was genetically half Were, but I presented as Human. Still, he thought it best to keep an eye on me."

"And that's why you grew up in the Vampyre Collateral's mansion, as Misery Lark's companion. She was the second-to-last Collateral before the program was discontinued."

"Correct."

"And when did you start exhibiting Were traits?"

"About two years ago."

"By then, you were living freely in Human society, correct? Was Governor Davenport still watching you?"

I nod. "He had me abducted and imprisoned for several weeks."

"Why?"

"I believe he felt threatened by the Human public's possible reaction to my existence. At the time, Maddie Garcia's gubernatorial campaign was picking up steam, and she was later elected. It was clear that many voters wanted to see some change in the Were-Human relationships, and Governor Davenport thought my presence might galvanize them even more."

"Did he act alone?"

"As far as I know." Blatant erasure of the Vampyres and Weres he was in cahoots with. I'm sure I'll hear all about it when we meet again, in hell.

"How did you get free?"

Oh, boy. "I shifted to wolf form and escaped."

"So you *are* able to shift?"

"I am." Is it a lie? I'm not even sure anymore. "But it's a new skill for me."

"In what ways are you Human?"

"Well, my blood is red. My strength and senses acuity are somewhere in the middle between a Were and a Human's."

"I see. Serena, this must all be very painful to relive—thank you for sharing it with us. What about the rumors that there are others?"

"Others?"

"Other hybrids. *The Herald*'s article suggested that you might be one of two."

And this, *this*, is the real reason I'm here. Everything else—Maddie, peace, reforms, public opinion . . . well, it all matters. But not as much as shoving the spotlight away from Ana.

That's why I spent the last week leaning across the porcelain sink of Lowe's bathroom, rehearsing my frown until it was flawless. When I see it furrow my brow on multiple screens, I decide that all that practice was worth it. "If there are other hybrids, I've never heard of them. But I'd love to meet them."

The interviewer leans forward a little, ready to dig. I recognize the ambitious gleam in her eyes, the thrill of the chase. I was like her. I used to ask the hard questions. I wanted the truth.

Now all I want is to get this over with.

"The article that outed you," she says, "alleged the existence of a younger female hybrid, one who lives with the Weres."

"Oh, right. Yes." I force a kick of understanding to spill onto my expression. "I wonder if the source was mistaken. What was said about the other Were used to be true of me when I was younger . . . Maybe that's where the confusion originated?" I shrug cluelessly.

"The article itself did state that the source could not provide evidence on the existence of this second hybrid," the interviewer agrees. My posture doesn't change, but I *feel* my muscles melt into the chair.

I had a single fucking job, and I did it. I'm *so* ready to go home and throw up in the bathtub, but this lady is still asking questions. ". . . you've been staying with the Southwest pack. Do you miss living among the Humans?"

"Yes, of course," I say, instead of a more truthful *Not at all.*

The thing is, Humans have been less than outstanding to me of late. My former colleagues at *The Herald* wrote an op-ed about feeling betrayed and traumatized by the way I "deliberately misrepresented" myself "in a professional setting, no less." A waiter from a restaurant I never even set foot inside went on record about the time I ordered a steak and promised a 40 percent tip to make it extra rare. Pete, an engineer I went on *three* dates with, sold his story to a tabloid. *I always suspected there was something wrong about her. She didn't seem to enjoy what most women do.* His dick, he meant. I can't believe I'm getting internationally dragged for refusing to screw a guy who told me that I looked just like his mother.

So, yeah. Humans are on my shit list, and I don't miss them. What I do miss is the period of my life in which the word *problem* could apply to the printer not working.

"However," I add, "I'm very grateful for the opportunity to spend time with Weres and learn their customs."

"And what do you say to those who believe that hybrids such as you are a threat to society and should be eliminated?"

I smile pleasantly, like she didn't just ask me, *What's it like when people want to watch you croak with their beady little eyes?* Gotta love journalism. "They are free to believe what they like. But centuries of conflict have benefited no one except those in power. I think that the genetic bridge between the two species could be the harbinger of a better future."

There are a few more softballs, and I spout a few more platitudes, which should get me a seven-figure aphorism book deal any day now. Once the interview ends, Koen waits for me on the side of the stage, looking as pleased as ever.

Which is not at all.

"Are you her, um, Alpha?" the interviewer asks, taking him in. She smells terrified. And aroused.

"Sure," Koen drawls, right as I snort, "He's more like my baby-sitter."

"And she's more like a pain in my—"

"Let's go," I nearly scream, tugging at the sleeve of his plaid shirt. He's the only person in the building not wearing business attire. I'd say he didn't get the memo, but knowing Koen, he sent it back with *I do whatever the fuck I want* scribbled all over it. In blood, most likely.

In the elevator it's me, him, and a gaggle of Human agents standing behind us.

"Did you know?" he asks under his breath, staring ahead at the doors.

My heart plummets. He's talking about what the geneticist revealed about hybrids having children. I have no clue how, but I'm certain of it. "No."

His jaw shifts from side to side.

In the network's lobby, a valet timidly approaches him. "Sir, your car is waiting outside."

Koen's eyebrow, the one dissected by scars, arches at an angle that clearly states *I've never been called Sir before, and it better not happen again*. I turn my head to hide a smile, and that's when I hear it.

"—the gall of coming here and forcing Secret Service agents to guard her. Like we won't be first in line to get rid of her." The man in black behind us is mumbling in his buddy's direction. Low enough not to be overheard—if Koen and I were Humans.

But we aren't. And the agent is apparently *that* stupid, because he continues, "Can't believe her fucking kind."

I spin, ready to politely request that he repeat it to my face, but Koen wraps an arm around my waist and pulls me into the hard heat of his body. From the outside, it probably looks like a playful, affectionate gesture. I take it for what it is: a firm command *not to kill*.

"Not with an audience this big, at least," he murmurs lightly against the shell of my ear. Without letting go of me, he uncoils to his full height. "Listen, bud," he tells the men, at once easygoing and assertive.

This is Koen, being in charge, herding people, straightening spines. I wonder if the agents know he's an Alpha. For me, it's impossible to miss. Those eyes. His overpowering scent. How difficult it is to tell him anything approaching *no*. "I don't like her kind, either. Do I think she should have come here? Fuck no."

The agent blinks. I can almost hear his skin break into goose bumps.

"Women? They belong in the kitchen. *I* don't, though." I can't see Koen's face, but the smile in his voice is *bloodcurdling.* "I get around. Would you like to apologize to the lady, or would you like to learn what that means?"

The man's scent is pure terror, mixed with a drop of shame. He started shit but doesn't want to lose face in front of his colleagues. "Is this a threat?"

"If you have to ask, I must be doing something wrong." Koen shifts me and hooks me at his side. The agent's friend—older and clearly wiser—takes about five steps back and reaches for his weapon.

So does every other person in the lobby.

Koen ignores them all. "You have two options, shitmuncher. You can apologize to the lady this very instant, or you can wait till later to be fucked up. Your choice. And don't worry, I won't be disappointed either way."

"I'm not afraid of your animals. Send them after me, and see what—"

"Whoa. *Highly* offensive. Whatever have I done to make you think that I wouldn't kill you myself?"

Something in Koen's tone must alert the man that this is no joke. His throat bobs. His cheek tics. After a few seconds of angry deliberation, he hisses at me, "I'm sorry."

My shoulders slump in relief.

"Not that hard, was it?" Koen beams. He holds out his hand, grasping the other man's in a friendly, peacekeeping shake that lasts less than a second. "Careful, buddy. Looks like you hurt yourself."

The man lifts his arm, puzzled to find thick red blood streaming down his pale flesh, past his wrists and into the sleeve of his suit. He seems to be unable to grasp what just happened, and I don't blame him, because neither can I—at least, until I notice the two vertical cuts slicing his wrist. They are claw shaped. Deep. And they run parallel to the long vein in his inner arm.

In fact, they barely missed it.

"If you make any more comments about this girl over here and I find out," Koen says, too low for anyone but the three of us to hear, "it'll be your throat."

I shiver. The man breathes hard, clutching his wrist to his chest.

"Show me you understood."

He nods quickly.

"Very good. C'mon, Serena." Koen's arm wraps around my shoulder. "I need you to make me a sandwich."

I let him lead me to the door, feeling as though I'm moving through water. "Koen?"

"Hmm?"

"What just happened?"

"You gave an interview that stuck a bull's-eye on your back, despite my repeatedly stated and very valid objections."

"No, I meant—" Stepping outside is like walking into a wall made of screams. Unsurprisingly, my presence here has attracted a crowd big enough that the network busted out the VIP barriers.

"—abomination—"

"—never forget what the Weres did to my people—"

"—liar, you're a liar—"

"—blessed with the power of blood and the blood of power, the flesh will be reborn and take new shapes—"

The last one is my personal favorite. Koen's, too, judging from how his pupils turn into slits.

But there are half a dozen *We love you, Serena, you're so brave, you're still one of us* signs, and I smile at their owners as Koen pushes me forward and opens the passenger door of the car for me.

He grabs the edge of the roof to protect my head. When I slip onto the seat, he leans against the door and says into my ear, "You did good in there, killer."

The shrieks, the interview, the man bleeding in the lobby—it all becomes background noise.

I look up at him. Don't bother hiding my smile. "High praise."

"Didn't say you did *great*," he mutters, closing the door after me.

We do have sandwiches for dinner, but Koen's the one who ends up making them, with a little help from Ana.

CHAPTER 5

His seconds like her, they have from the very start.
Traitors.

Present day

I WAKE UP FLOATING SEVERAL FEET ABOVE THE GROUND—AND promptly decide to go back to sleep.

This is nice. I am, for once, not cold. My bed smells pleasant and woodsy, not at all like rancid nightmare sweat. The pillow is the perfect consistency. Everything about the situation is cozy and restful, and I see no reason to interrupt it—until a worried voice pierces through my cocoon of joy.

"Please, tell me that she's sleeping and not unconscious."

My eyes flutter open, and two realizations hit me: the person speaking is Amanda, Koen's closest second.

And I'm very much *not* in bed.

Koen is carrying me inside a cabin that doesn't look too different from the one in which I'd spent the last weeks, one arm hooked under my bent knees, the other cradling me to his chest. My head nestles in the side of his throat, where the scratch of his beard tickles my cheek. The events of last night wash over me in rolling waves.

Look at me, living to see another day.

"What time is it?" I ask.

"Almost dawn."

We must be a few hours away from my cabin, then. "Are we in the Southwest?" That's where he's going to take me, right? Back to Misery and Lowe.

"Still Northwest. We stopped at one of our safe houses."

Lazily, I paw at Koen's shoulder and stretch in his arms. "I can walk."

"Me too. Wanna start a club?"

"Can I be president?"

"Treasurer at most."

"No deal." I yawn into the spot at the base of his neck, which causes his grip to falter first and then tighten. "Seriously, you can let go of me."

He does, but only because we've reached our destination. He deposits me on a worn-out but clean sectional and then proceeds to look down at me with a frown.

"You okay?" he asks, gruff. "Anything feel . . . loose inside?"

"Loose? Like what?"

"I don't fucking know. An artery?"

I decide to ignore the question, and ask, "Do you know what a man bun is?"

"A what?"

"Hmm. Must not have made it to the Weres. I was just wondering whether the lumbersexual vibes were on purpose?"

He scowls. Leans down. Cups my nape with one hand, while

the fingers of the other slide through my hair, now matted with sweat, mud, and Bob's blood. His grip is gentle. Soothing.

"What are you doing?"

"Feeling for a bump."

"Why?"

"Might explain the sudden onset of aphasia."

I snort out a laugh. "Come on, Koen. Tell me you at least yell 'timber' every once in a while."

The only thing he's ready to tell me is that he'll have me institutionalized. It's for the best, then, that Amanda sinks down next to me and wraps me in a hug.

"Look at you. Not even a little bit dead." She grins. By the time she pulls away, Koen is gone. "Despite your high-stakes, violent existence."

I snort again, looking at her round face, flawless dark skin, full lips. She's around Koen's age, even though she could pass for a high schooler. That's where the similarities end: she's kind and humorous, and I don't believe I've ever heard her call someone a "rotten cockwomble."

"I missed you," she tells me. She and I met only recently, but we got close very quickly. Koen wouldn't allow me to move into the cabin without periodic supervision and tasked her with coming to check on me once a week or so. I don't really consider myself in the market for new friendships, not at this stage of my . . . *life*, let's call it, but there are only so many games of I Spy one can play (seventeen, to be precise) before starting to miss meaningful conversation. By the second visit, we were dumping on each other like coal trimmers on the *Titanic*. Pretty cathartic—if mostly abridged and highly redacted on my part. "You don't look too well."

I smile. "Yeah. So I hear."

"Sorry some asshole Vampyre interfered with your search for, uh, inner peace."

I am profoundly embarrassed that my cover story for needing to stay at the cabin required me to utter words like *harmony* and *serenity* with a straight face. Sometimes, you just do what you have to. "It's okay. It's been very . . restorative," I lie bald-facedly. Weres can usually pick up fibs, but they struggle to make sense of me. Being a hybrid has its pros. Well . . . pro. Singular.

"Thank God Koen was in your area to meet with huddle leaders." Amanda takes my hand. "I was shitting myself when Lowe told us about the Vampyre tracking you."

"I was not," Jorma says, stepping inside the room. He's another of Koen's seconds—a stern, statuesque man with white-blond curls and icy-blue eyes. Jorma loves rules, unnecessary clerical work, waiting in line, and—hazarding a guess, here—bland foods covered in protein powder. His childhood dream was probably to become a hall monitor. I've seen him smile only once, and it was a terrifying process, like he'd learned how to move his facial muscles from a book. I hope it never happens again. "Serena has bested several Vampyres in a fight before." He nods at me in approval. "No reason to worry about her."

I should be grateful for what's obviously as close to a compliment as Jorma gets, but his misplaced faith just makes me want to shrink into the couch. "Yeah. Thanks," I croak.

The last second in the cabin is Saul—who, unlike Jorma, has never filled out a form in his life, communicates mostly through grins and winks, and is the biggest, loudest flirt I've ever met. "Honey," he says instead of *Hello*. He takes me in with a pained expression. "The hoodie-chic, blood-spattered, final-girl outfit suits you. The hair, not so much."

I pout. "But my stylist said it was so *me*."

"You deserve a refund." He bends to kiss my cheek. "You look rough. Need a hug? Chamomile tea? A coloring book with some pencils? All of the above?"

Every time Saul comes up in conversation, someone feels the need to mention how incredibly handsome he is, but I don't see it. Maybe it's because I know that he's Amanda's ex. Maybe he just doesn't do it for me. I guess I'm more into . . .

"She's fine," Koen orders, returning to the room with something in his hand. "Stop fussing."

It's an odd thing to say, considering that it's followed by him kneeling in front of me and taking the heel of one of my feet in his palm. He runs a damp washcloth all over the little abrasions the forest floor left on my skin, the ones that are already starting to heal. The warmth feels so indecently good, I swallow a moan.

"You're fine. Aren't you, killer?" he asks, holding my eyes.

I nod, a little breathless.

"You need a bed and some rest," Saul continues, undeterred.

"And a hot meal," Amanda adds. "Should I—"

"She's an adult Were who doesn't require coddling," Koen interrupts. Once again, a bit jarring to hear, especially as he rolls thick, soft socks up my shins. They reach just below my knees. I might just go to my deathbed wearing them.

"Doesn't mean we can't worry about her," Amanda points out.

"Last week Colin came back from a sweep with his arm nearly hanging off, and you all laughed in his face."

"As is appropriate when one loses a fight against a bear," Jorma says, straight-faced.

Saul seems to agree. "I'd forgotten that you'd declared it against the law to be excellent to each other, Koen."

"Make sure you write it down, then."

"Once again, if we had an HR department, they would be so busy dealing with . . ." Saul's phone pings. He trails off to read a message, and when he looks up, he's all business. "Alpha, Lowe is ready to talk."

Koen nods. I expect him to walk out to take the call, but Amanda fiddles with a cable, and a moment later a flat screen I hadn't noticed slowly whirs to life.

Several people appear, all of them known to me from my time in the Southwest. There's Lowe, of course. The redheaded second whose name has clearly rotted out of my mind. Alex, the IT guy who taught me how to play *Grand Theft Auto*. And . . .

"Look who ran out of toilet paper and decided to rejoin civilization," Misery says with a wide smile. Her pale elfin face is as close as I'll ever get to having a home. I guess it's fitting, then, how foreign she looks of late.

She stopped bothering with contacts or filing her canines, which fills me with joy. For the first time in her life, she's happy, protected, and invested in the world around her. *Are you jealous of her relationship with Lowe?* Amanda once asked me, and I get why she'd think that. Growing up, it used to be Misery and me—just the two of us, hand in hand against the world. Now it's Misery and Lowe and the cute child she's somehow step-mommying despite having no business being left alone with someone whose fontanelles have barely closed. And yes, me too. Somewhere out yonder. In the periphery.

But I told Amanda that I wasn't, and it's the truth. I don't think I'm capable of jealousy. It's a feeling that requires the assumption that something is due, and I never developed that. Years in an orphanage, then more years as the Collateral's baby doll, will beat the possessiveness out of anyone.

Still, change requires adjustment—and secrets require distance. When I realized that I needed to step away, I mixed truth and lies, said I was overstimulated, and asked for an isolated place to acclimatize to my Were senses. Misery and Lowe didn't love the idea of me leaving the Southwest, but they believed the tale I spun.

Want to know who *didn't* believe it? Koen. Why some guy I'd met two months earlier was better than my lifelong friend at reading through my bullshit is something I have no intention of pondering.

"Just kidding about the toilet paper," Misery adds. "I know you people just shift into wolves and lick your own butts."

Next to her, Lowe winces but pulls her closer. If things go to shit tomorrow, today, in five minutes, at least I can be reassured that the person I care about the most is in excellent hands. I'm genuinely happy for her.

Though maybe a little less when she tells me, "Serena, you look like shit."

"Seriously?" I scowl. "Is no one interested in sparing my feelings?"

Misery's and Koen's "nope" are perfectly in unison. He takes a seat next to me, close enough for our thighs to touch, legs stretched out on the coffee table and calves crossed. The picture of relaxed boredom. "So," he starts, "what the fuck just happened, and who do I kill?"

I refrain from pointing out the obvious: *Bob the Vampyre* and *You already have.*

Lowe sighs. "We are producing a list."

"Nice." Koen sounds ready to roll up his sleeves. "I'll take the first ten names."

"What happened up at the cabin?" Lowe asks.

"Yeah, Serena," Misery adds. "How hard did you maul the guy who tried to come for you?"

I freeze, loath to admit how much of a wimp I am.

"He won't be bothering her anymore," Koen says flatly. "She made sure of it." Definitely not the whole truth, but Misery equivocates and gives me a proud, fangy smile.

"Actually," I start guiltily, "if Koen hadn't been there—"

I stop, because suddenly the screen is fully taken up by a pair of piercing light green eyes. They blink at me as a small, sleepy voice asks, "Serena, did they tell you I lost two tooths?" The angle shifts, and a small tongue wiggles in and out of a wide front gap. For *way* longer than is needed for a demonstration.

Ana. My heart nearly bursts with love for her. For some reason, my hands start trembling. "Nope." I try to firm up my voice. "They rudely kept it from me."

"I thought so." She pulls back, just enough for me to see her give the adults behind her a disappointed look. "Someone will bring me money. A fairy. A creepy fairy made of tooths."

"We've been over this, pest. The fairy *takes* the teeth, but she's not made of . . ." Misery waves her hand. "You know what? Sure. The damn fairy is made of enamel and pulp."

"Ana, it's too early for you to be up," Lowe says, failing to sound stern. "Remember that you promised that after saying hi to Serena, you'd go back to bed?"

"Okay. Bye, Serena," she says cheerfully, stopping to kiss her brother on the cheek and to blow a raspberry on a resigned Misery's arm.

I watch her disappear, trying not to think about the fact that there are people out there who would be willing and capable of hurting her, until Koen says, "I thought the Vampyre council had agreed to stop fucking with Weres."

"It's a complicated situation," Lowe acknowledges. "As you know, Owen, Misery's brother, has been trying to consolidate control over the Vampyre council and convince them to agree to a trilateral peace treaty with the Weres and the Humans."

"With mixed results, given the frequent mentions of his suddenly receding hairline," Misery informs us. It's unclear whom the recap is for. Probably me, the one voted most likely to forsake an internet connection and melt into the underbrush.

"After Serena's interview," Lowe continues, "Human public opinion has become highly favorable toward Weres. Disclosing the genetic compatibility was a gamble, and it paid off. The alliance Maddie and I have formed is stronger than ever. Peaceful coexistence, demilitarized areas, softer borders—none of this would have been possible even six months ago."

"And the Vampyres are feeling left out?" Saul asks.

"The Vampyres have been invited to the playdate," Misery says. "But for interspecies alliances the council needs a supermajority, and some members think it's all a trick to weaken their position in the Southwest area."

Koen snorts. "These crusty Vampyres really believe other species think about them that much, huh?"

"That's exactly what *I* said," Misery points out. They share a look, brief but full of contempt. Shocking, how well they get along. "Basically," Misery continues, "someone on the council wants to blow up the alliance between the Weres and the Humans, and they put a bounty on Serena's head, and now any Vampyre in want of a fortune is after her."

"How did they track her down?" Koen asks. "Only Amanda and I knew her location."

"That is my . . . well, I don't know that one would say *fault*, per se, *but* . . ." Alex timidly clears his throat, wringing his hands. I suspect he finds regular Koen terrifying—and *angry* Koen bloodcurdling. "When I gave Serena the satellite phone, I, um, recorded it with her initials to keep, uh, track of it," he finishes in a hush.

"How thorough of you. Why not add a couple recent pictures, just to give the kidnappers a visual aid?"

"Actually." Alex swallows. "There may have been one."

Never mind Alex, *I* am scared of Koen. I slide my hand on his leg, feeling the warm flesh of his thigh through his jeans. His muscles clench tight, then abruptly relax.

"Do we know which councilmembers set the bounty?" I ask.

Misery shakes her head. "Owen has a network of informants and thinks that Councilwoman Selamio or Councilman Ross might be behind this. Others might be involved, too. In a way, it's not a bad thing. If they are caught participating in something that might start an interspecies war, they'll be instantly killed, and their seats will pass to their heirs. Selamio Jr. and Baby Ross are assholes, but they're not stupid. They know that entering the trilateral alliance would be for the best."

"So . . . why are their parents still alive?" Koen asks. His leadership philosophy seems to be *if inconvenient, why not dead?*

"They've been covering their tracks," Lowe admits reluctantly. "Without proof, Owen can't make accusations."

Koen grunts, unhappy with the concept of due process. "What do they even want with Serena?"

"To prove she's an imposter. To use her DNA to dilute the

symbolic power of a Were-Human hybrid by creating Were-Vampyre or Vampyre-Human hybrids. Who knows?" Misery massages her forehead, like the sheer idiocy is giving her a headache. "But they're willing to part with a lot of money to have Serena delivered to them, *alive*, and . . ." She presses her lips together. Stares at me with those unblinking lilac eyes. "Serena, did you just shrug?"

"What? No."

"She did," the redhead mutters.

"I saw her too," Jorma says.

"Yup." Saul.

"Could it have been a shiver?" Amanda asks.

"I . . . Maybe I shrugged." I glare around the room, defensive. "Is it, like, against pack rules?"

"It's just, you know." Misery gestures vaguely. "A weird reaction to have when someone tells you that there are hordes of financially strapped assassins after you."

"For one, they're not assassins. They want me alive so they can scrape DNA off the inside of my cheek and use it to grow baby werebananas. And honestly . . ." I shrug again. *Consciously*, this time. "I knew my name was in a bunch of little black books. Now it's in more, bigger black books, but I've maxed out my levels of distress." Perspective is a hell of a drug. "It's fine, really," I tell several increasingly understanding pairs of eyes, proud of the way I seem to have convinced everyone—and then I meet Koen's gaze.

Who, clearly, has never encountered a lie of mine he couldn't shuck like sweet corn.

"I *am* concerned for Ana, though," I hasten to add, tearing my eyes away. "She's already a bunch of stressors stacked in a trench coat. There are only that many kidnapping and murder attempts a child can endure before developing serious issues and self-destructive behaviors. We wouldn't want her to grow up and, say, go to grad school."

"Don't worry," Misery reassures me, "every day I drill into her that we'll be disappointed in anything but a DJing career."

"You're such a good role model."

"I know. Right, Lowe?"

Lowe just looks exhausted, like he did every day of the weeks I spent at his house. In his defense, we *are* a lot.

"How did the Vampyres even learn about Ana?" I ask. "I thought her hybrid status was strictly on a need-to-know basis?"

"It is. So far, only high-ranking Northwest and Southwest members and her physician know. And the Vampyres, they're not *sure*," Misery says. "But they're hoping. Put yourself in their shoes: someone's offering a shit ton of money in exchange for a hybrid. You're a sure bet but hard to track and known for having disposed of multiple Vampyres. Ana's a child. Much easier to take."

"Serena," Lowe interjects, "the most important thing right now is to make sure that you and Ana are safe and off the radar. We're going to get you back to the Southwest by tomorrow, and—"

"But that's a terrible idea."

Once again, everyone turns to me. Except for Koen, who keeps looking ahead as though . . . I can't shake the impression that he knows what I'm about to say.

"Excuse me?" Lowe says.

"They're going to come back for me."

"They're not going anywhere near you," Koen mutters, arrogant and a little too certain. No one else can hear it, but my cheeks feel hot anyway.

"With a financial incentive that high, they're not going to give up."

"That's the point." Misery looks at me like she suspects that my brain fell off into a septic tank. "They're not going to stop, and so we need to hide you away—"

"No. You need to hide *Ana* away."

She frowns. "Ana, yes. *And* you—"

"And *I'm* going to be hidden so poorly, it'll take them no effort to find me. I'm going to be in plain sight. I'm going to be such an easy target, it won't ever occur to them to expend resources to locate another hybrid." I smile. "And when they come for me, we'll use them to figure out who's behind the bounty."

CHAPTER 6

*He's going to take her lies and peel them off one by one.
Then he'll force her to show him what's underneath.*

MY PERFECTLY REASONABLE PLAN, AIMED AT PREVENTING the slaughter of a very cute child who once pointed at a drawing of an antelope and asked me if it was a "duocorn," is received less than marvelously.

The protests are so vehement, I cannot help wondering whether they misheard me. Maybe they think I'm planning to hijack an SUV and run over the mother of newborn kittens? It would explain the full-throttle stream of objections, which includes words like "unacceptable" (Lowe), "death sentence" (Saul), "terrible idea" (Alex), "must be the Human half speaking, 'cause this sounds crazy" (Amanda), and "this feels wrong on so many levels, some of which must be *legal*" (Jorma), as well as an additional assortment of grunts and protests.

Misery, who's taking to being an Alpha's mate a little too well, commands me to "come to bed in the Southwest right now. *Without dinner.*"

"Wrong meal, Misery. Also, I don't take orders from the chick who once gave me toenail fungus."

"Shut up. Acknowledge me as your Alpha!"

"Love, we've been over this," Lowe murmurs, patting her knee. "It's not how it works."

"And bring me gifts of gold, frankincense, and peanut butter!"

"Misery, I've seen you flick boogers at passersby."

"I was a *child*."

"You were *seventeen*."

But she won't stop protesting, and snarls that I'm "too valuable, too important, too loved" to be used as bait. God. What an inconvenient time for her to finally get in touch with her emotions.

"I'm not suicidal," I tell everyone, "nor am I suggesting I walk unarmed into Vampyre headquarters. We can safely arrange to—" I stop to hide a yawn in my palm, and that's when Koen declares the meeting over and stands.

"I'm taking her to bed." It speaks to his authority that not a single eyebrow lifts.

My abused feet make contact with the floor, and I grit my teeth. Koen instantly picks me up, one strong arm snaked around my rib cage as he presses me to his side, toes dangling a few inches from the ground.

It's undignified. And pathetically befits my status in life.

"Once again, I *am* capable of walking," I murmur against his shoulder. His beard bristles against the tender skin of my temple, ticklish but pleasant. He runs much warmer than me. The wonders of genetics not split between species with wildly different baseline temperatures.

"I heard rumors but dared not believe them." He walks through the first door on the right. There is a bit of shuffling me in his arms, then he pulls back the covers and deposits me on a soft mattress, between sheets that smell like lavender. "Show me tomorrow, after your soles have healed."

"It'll be the performance of a lifetime." I shiver at the sudden chill and pull the hem of his hoodie down my bare thighs.

I feel, once again, that *something* about Koen. How imposing he is. The kind of menacing that colors the air around him for miles. It comes not from height and muscles, but from something else, something undefinable with Human words—the only ones I have.

Vocabulary. That's what stands between me and understanding Koen.

Maybe with time, I tell myself.

And then reply, *What time, Serena?*

"You get it, right? Why I want to take the attention off Ana?"

Downstairs, he didn't say much—just sat next to me, a quiet, dark center of intense energy. It's not that I want his approval, especially after he made it clear that he couldn't care less about mine. But the others' opposition to my plan is not rational. It comes from some soft place, deep within their bellies. Misery loves me, and so does Lowe, if only for some spousal transitive property. Being in charge, though, means constructing complex trade-offs. And Koen is nothing if not *in charge*.

"Yes. This is for you." He deposits a satellite phone I've never seen before on the nightstand and holds my eyes disapprovingly as he plugs the charger into the outlet.

Shit. Did he try to call to warn me about Bob earlier today? I'll never know, 'cause my phone was dead and I left it back at the cabin. Should I reiterate that I am, in fact, able to take care of battery-operated devices? "Thank you. For this."

"You already thanked me, and I told you—not big into gratitude.

Either return the favor by coming to my house and dusting the light fixtures, or shut up."

"No, this is not about saving my life." I sit up on my heels. "Thank you for taking my side. About Ana."

"Is that your takeaway?" He scoffs. "I'm *not* taking your side, Serena."

"Downstairs, you didn't object."

"I didn't object because I don't *need* to. It's upstanding of Lowe and the Vampyre to try to convince you not to do something idiotic." His eyes bore into mine and he leans forward, palms against the mattress, caging my thighs. He's a wall of heat, all forest scent. This close, I could easily trace all the little scars on his face. "I'm simply going to lock you up, killer. If I have to chain you to my fucking bed to keep you alive, I will not hesitate."

I refuse to cower backward. "You really are a dick."

Well, duh, his gaze clearly states. "If you're into self-immolation and dying, I can easily arrange it for you. No need to involve other species."

"This is not self-immolation. It's a strategy—putting oneself in danger in order to gain something. Taking one for the team. Like Misery did when she married Lowe."

Koen's eyebrows rise. "Those two are sickeningly in love. Whatever she's taking, it's *not* for the team."

I wince. "Thank you for this *highly* disturbing mental image of my *sister*—"

"You're welcome."

"—and yes, it worked out great, but she could have gotten mangled and eaten. She could be hanging out with Lowe's gut bacteria. We all make sacrifices. Look at Lowe—he's my age and has to take care of a whole-ass pack. You're like, thirty-five, had much longer to grow accustomed to your role."

His expression clouds. "I'm not thirty-five, Serena."

I flush and scan his sculpted, complicated face. He doesn't look old, just like he's been through shit. "It's the whole"—I lift my hand to his face, gently stroking his beard—"um, facial hair and stuff. Ages you. I could trim your hair, it'd take me ten minutes, tops. I used to do it for Misery—"

"I'm thirty-*six*. Even more decrepit than you thought."

"Oh."

"I know. Highly disturbing that Weres are allowed to advance to such a ramshackle state."

"That's not what I—"

"But rest assured, killer, that I am not so enfeebled that I won't tie you up in my basement if you endanger yourself."

The thing about Koen: He *is* an asshole, but a reasonable one. Which means that the more unhinged his threats become, the less believable they sound. And the stronger my impulse to just laugh in his face. "But what about the martyr character arc I've always wanted?"

"Not on my watch. Not in my territory. Not under my protection."

I shift higher on my knees to gain a few inches. It brings our noses in touching range. "Koen, you know it's a good idea."

"If by good idea you mean bullshit. The problem with your plan, and I'm using that word generously, is that *you* do not have the resources to pull it off."

"Then *help me*." I try to wrap my hand around his wrist, but my fingers don't meet. "You care about Ana just as much as I do. What if—what if I stay in the Northwest? Where's your Den? Olympia? Take me there. Parade me around. We'll make it so easy for the Vampyres to find me, they won't even investigate Ana's where-abouts. They'll come for me, your patrols will capture them, and Owen will gain control of the council. *Please.* At least consider it."

He straightens abruptly, freeing himself from my grip with no effort. A small shudder licks up my spine, and the way he looked at me earlier, the weight of his eyes on my bared body, it all flashes through me like a bolt. For a moment I am—I don't know. Eager. Uneasy. Heated. Full. Empty. Heavy. Good, but bad. I don't know.

I don't *know* what I am or how I feel, because my stupid body isn't mine anymore, and there seems to be no one like me in the whole damn world.

"You need food," he says, heading for the door. "I'll have Saul bring you something."

My stomach rolls in vehement, impolite denial. "I'm not hungry."

Koen folds his arms. Inspects me like he has a medical degree and I'm at my yearly checkup. "You're not thirsty, either. Unusual, for a Were."

"I'm only half Were."

"You are." It's disquieting, frankly. The way he sees through the layers of bullcrap I painstakingly apply to my skin every day. "Maybe we could hunt together. Find some game. Fill that belly of yours." His eyes lower to my stomach, and I'm suddenly hot.

"I told you. I can't shift right now."

"Ah, yes. I forgot that you're . . . not very powerful." He says it—*not very powerful*—in a deep, rumbly voice, making it clear that he thinks I'm a load of dung posing as a person. "Moon too small?"

I nod.

"Can't wait for the full moon, then. I'd love to see your wolf form." He says it suggestively, but not in the try-hard way of a third date dropping hints that they've been *wondering* about the view from my apartment. This is a purely intellectual pursuit on his part: *I'd love to read that article on micro-dosing. I'd love to snorkel in the coral reef, if the opportunity were to arise. I'd love to catch you in a lie.* Still, something twisted in my brain registers it as inappropriate and dirty and disturbing and glorious and . . .

I have seen Koen's wolf form. The glossy black fur that reminds me of his hair. The large paws. That white tuft right on his chest, above the spot where his heart beats. The size of him. He is very much *Koen* at a level I cannot put in words. He could be standing next to a dozen identical animals, and I'd still be able to single him out.

God, am I about to use the word *aura*?

"In the meantime, I'll have Saul bring you food. Since you look so gaunt."

"I do *not*."

"Right. Picture of health."

I grin. "No need to mince your words. Just say that I'm fugly, call it a day, and—"

"Serena," he growls. His stare, the dull black of his eyes, is abrasive. Sands me down to the skeleton. "Sleep. When you wake up, I'm taking you back to the Southwest."

"What?" No. *No.* That's where Ana is. "Please, don't. Just think about it—"

"If you keep lying to me, I can't properly protect you. And if I can't protect you, I won't keep you around."

"I'm not— Which lie?"

He snorts softly. "You tell *that* many?"

"I . . ." I fidget with the sleeve of my hoodie. "I lie a lot."

"You shouldn't. Telling the truth can be therapeutic."

I narrow my eyes. "You know what else can be therapeutic?"

"Punching me in the nuts?"

That's *exactly* what I was going to say. "How did you know I—"

"You're pretty fucking predictable." He's leaving again, and I hate him. *So* much. Especially when I have no choice but to yell after him, "Fine."

He doesn't stop.

"I'll tell the truth."

Keeps walking.

I squeeze my eyes shut and force myself to admit it.

"I haven't been able to shift in months."

CHAPTER 7

It's not the only secret she's been keeping. It's not even the worst one. For now, though, he'll play. The alternative is unacceptable.

KOEN TAKES HIS SWEET, SWEET TIME TO TURN TO ME. HIS SURprise at my confession couldn't fill a puddle. "Was that so hard?"

I clench my fist. "Since you obviously already knew, why did you make me say it?"

"Hearing you verbally acknowledge your limitations brings flavor and spice to my life. Why were you keeping it a secret?"

"I don't know. I . . . Maybe I just didn't want you looking down on me."

"I will never *not* look down on you, chiefly because of our height difference. When did it start?"

"A while ago."

"Was it before or after I allowed you to be alone at the cabin—"

"You *allowed me?*"

"—under repeated reassurances that you could take care of yourself, *killer?*"

"I . . . Before. I already couldn't shift."

His jaw tics. "Here's the deal: you're not an idiot."

"Wow. What a compliment."

"Sure. Keep that in mind when I ask you why the fuck you are acting like one. How. Long?"

"It's genuinely hard to tell. A few days after I moved to the Southwest?"

"How many?"

I try to recall. "Maybe a week or so? The first time I tried and wasn't able to was the day after . . . after Ana returned." The day after Koen and I met. "I also started feeling poorly, and—"

"Feeling poorly?"

Tell him, I order myself. *Tell him. Tell him everything. It'll make things so much easier.*

But it wouldn't. It would be incredibly selfish. Things would be easier for me and significantly more complicated for everyone else. "Nothing bad. You're right, my appetite has been low. Nausea. Issues sleeping. One of the Southwest physicians, Dr. Henshaw, said it's stress from . . ." I shrug and smile. Artfully, if I say so myself. When it comes to my recent past, the ratio of what went wrong to what could have gone wrong is so high, it's objectively funny. "Take your pick. Basically, I just need to wait it out and chill. Hence the cabin."

"Are you in pain?"

I shake my head, instinctively. His expression looks so dubious, I wince. "It's more like discomfort."

Koen doesn't *want* to believe it, but it's obvious that he's not sure where the lie's at. "For someone juggling this many secrets, you're pretty terrible at keeping them."

"I'll try to do better, Alpha." I bat my eyes at him, which makes his scowl deepen by a factor of ten. "Could you please not tell Misery and Lowe?"

"Oh, you're hiding shit from them, too?"

"I'm an equal opportunity liar. And really, it would just give them one more thing to worry about, when Ana should be their—"

"Priority, yeah. You've mentioned her." My craning neck weeps in gratitude when Koen takes a seat on the edge of the mattress. His posture is lazy, but his eyes stay sharp. "Under Were custom, I cannot keep this from Lowe. He's your Alpha."

"Is he, though? I didn't, like, go to the DMV to sign paperwork—"

"To the what, now?"

"—and I didn't take a blood oath. You said it yourself, that I have no pack—"

"You are not an official member of any pack. You are, however, affiliated with the Southwest. The alternative is for Were society to deal with you as a rogue Were, and you do *not* want that."

"I don't understand, why does it matter—"

"Correct. You *don't* understand. Were packs are not chummy extended families, killer. To safely set foot in a pack's territory, you'll need to be affiliated with that pack or with their allies."

"And if I'm not?"

He gives me a flat look that— Okay. Got that loud and clear. "Can I change? If I were affiliated with the Northwest, then it would be okay for Lowe not to know, right?"

"That would make *me* your Alpha."

"Would you mind that?"

He stares like I'm trying to sell him a pouch of magic beans. "To be clear, I know that I'm being played. I'm just allowing it because I love the idea of telling you what to do *that* much."

I cannot help my smile. "Very well. Deal. Now that I'm officially a Northwesterner—"

"Not a name we go by."

"—in the name of Alpha-member confidentiality—"

"Which doesn't exist."

"—I ask you to please not tell Misery that I'm . . . I don't know, regressing to my Human self? She already has plenty to be nervous about." I chew on my lower lip for a moment. "Will you take me in, then? It'll ease the pressure off the Southwest. And . . . I feel safer when I'm with you."

His tongue prods at the inside of his cheek. "You do?"

I nod, wondering why it's the truth. I'm sure Lowe and his seconds are just as capable. They may even have more of an incentive to protect me, since . . . well. Lowe has never felt the need to remind me that the part of him that matters could never be interested in me. "Yeah. I do."

"Well, that's too bad. Because I don't want you to feel safe."

"You . . . don't?"

Glaring, he leans toward me, full of something vicious that I cannot name. "I want you to be scared shitless, Serena. I want you so fucking terrified of me, you won't even dream of not doing what I say. I want you to feel like your soft little throat is in my hands, and I want you to be so afraid that I'll tear into it that when I tell you to do something for your own fucking safety, you won't consider saying anything but 'Yes, Alpha.'"

The last words are hissed just inches from my face, the puff of his breath hot against my cheek, and the thing is—he *is* terrifying. He *could* carve me open like an overripe pomegranate. And he's definitely capable of forcing me to do whatever he wants. I've seen the way even his seconds look at him, love and trust and respect mixed with circumspection. I've heard Lowe and Misery whisper their worries. I am aware that there is an edge of unpredictability to Koen.

And yet the only response I can muster to his threats is a small, apologetic smile.

He didn't ask for me to be his mate. I didn't ask to be a hybrid. And yet here we both are.

I cannot help myself. I lift my hand, and with the backs of my fingers I stroke the skin of his cheek. It's the lightest touch, barely anything. But it sends currents trembling down my arm, clamoring for more.

Koen's muscles tense, and he flinches from my touch. With a roll of his eyes, he unfolds away from me, and cold seeps back into my bones.

"You're such a fucking nuisance," he murmurs, almost softly.

"I know." I press my lips together. "Thank you again for—"

"Serena."

"I know, but I have to say it, and—"

"Just mulch Saul's rose beds, and we can be even." He spins on his heel. Is he leaving?

"Are you going to bed?" I ask after him.

"After I'm done." He doesn't specify with what.

"Where will you be sleeping?"

"There are half a dozen beds in this cabin."

What a nonanswer. And on top of *thank you*, he must also not be big into *good night*, because he opens the door and—

"Koen?"

He stops. Turns to me with an expression that's equally patient, insulting, and dismissive. The quintessential *Alpha has shit to do* look.

"Just . . ." I swallow. "The mate thing."

His face doesn't move a millimeter. His biological predestination

ALI HAZELWOOD

to want sex with me seems to interest him less than the favorite yogurt flavor of the fifteen-to-twenty-one demographic.

"The rest of your pack, do they know?"

He shrugs, one shouldered. Truly, he does not give a shit about the stuff I spend my nights overthinking. "Everyone does."

"You didn't . . . It's not a secret?"

"We made sure every Were knew, Serena."

"Oh. Why?"

"No sane Were will touch you if they think you're important to me."

If they *think*.

I scratch the back of my head. "Do they think we . . . ?"

"No. We made that clear, too."

"So they know that I'm your mate but we're not together?"

"Correct."

"And doesn't it bother you?"

"Why would it?"

"I don't know. Just . . . big bad Alpha. Everyone's boss. I thought you might want to . . ."

"Spare myself the humiliation of having been rejected?" He huffs a laugh. "Serena, there are much worse things than that."

Are there? I'm not so sure. The good and the bad of my life correlate strongly with feelings of being wanted—or not. But Koen is not a Human orphan, let alone one whose claim to fame is being useless in therapy because of an overgrown case of infantile amnesia.

Like me, or don't. I really couldn't care less.

God, how many times do I have to make him tell me before I turn it into a long-term memory? "I'm sorry. I don't know why I asked. I'm just tired."

"Right. If only you had a bed to sleep in."

82

His sarcasm is a jolt of electricity. "I hate you," I say mildly.

"You need me to check the closet for monsters?"

"Nope." I already know where those are.

"Glass of water? Brush your hair one hundred strokes? The fucking chamber pot?"

I let out a small laugh and shake my head, and before I can force my "Good night" upon him, Koen is gone.

My heart feels cavern hollow. I ignore it, spend five minutes punching my pillows into shape, and fall into a deep sleep.

———※———

IT STARTS LIKE IT ALWAYS DOES. THAT IS TO SAY, NICELY ENOUGH.

I wonder how universal a truth it is that the closer to the end we get, the more mundane our oneiric activities become. Mine used to be ridiculous, equally fun and horrifying, but lately they're about only one thing: sex.

It just seems so . . . unambitious. I could be dreaming of castles, or deer with Jell-O antlers, or pizza pies in the sky. Instead, it's all work-rough palms wrapped around my kneecap, and bare, sweat-slick skin. Outdoor scents. Sticky, dripping, hazy warmth. Bites into unyielding muscles. Rolling murmurs, whispers of something dark and good I can never make out, and laughter pressing into my throat. Red cheeks, a hot olive flush, heavy, lingering touches, aches that don't hurt. Twitches of pleasure, a white-knuckled grip, the pulse of something hungry and needy. A hitch of breath. A sharp inhale. Low bass, vibrating through me. A quiet exhale. Hard and soft, muted swallows, a sloppy, lazy rhythm.

It's not even *sex*. At least, not as far as I can tell. Just the components of it, the pieces and not the whole, cluttering my mind, taking up every corner. Like I said, it's nice enough—until I wake up.

An agonized moan slips out of my throat, and I press my palm to my mouth.

I don't waste time. I know by now that hoping for the rippling pain to subside is no use. My temperature would spike even higher, and the heat would probably kill me. Fisting the edge of the mattress, I manage to roll out of bed and crawl to the bathroom. Once I'm a heap of perspiration and tears and shivers on the soft shower mat, that's when the fun starts.

Some nights, I only deal with the fever. Others—more and more frequent—my stomach demands its due. Luckily, when the first bout pours out of me, I'm standing right by the toilet bowl. It smells like acid and sickness and rot, and I gag even more, but once that's done, the pain recedes long enough for me to catch my breath.

So I focus on the *real* issue: I'm about to burst into flames.

It could be an exaggeration—or not. Will my organs melt out of my orifices if I skip the next step? It sure feels like it. So I elbow myself into the bathtub and flick on the cold water.

The first cool splash against my sizzling skin always has me sighing in relief, but it's ludicrously short-lived. It'll get better, though. Once I'm neck deep, I'll stop feeling like a small, violent mammal has crawled inside my abdomen and is gnawing at my flesh while breathing fire. For now, though, my heart hammers against my rib cage, my body arches and contracts, and I swallow the pain of a hundred bones crumbling.

And since it's all I can do, I sit, bury my face in my knees, and wait.

CHAPTER 8

She calls him out of the blue. He hasn't saved her number, but it's etched into the hidden layers of his skin. "I need a favor."

"A favor. And am I——" He stops and briefly covers the phone's mic with his palm to tell Jorma that yes, he did sign whatever the hell was on his desk this morning. "Am I your favor guy, now?"

"Um. Do you want to be?"

"No. I don't like doing nice things for people."

Her low laugh makes his body do things. "The thing is . . . when Ana was being targeted, Lowe said you hid her."

"I did."

She wets her lips. He can hear it. "He said that the Northwest is the best place to disappear."

A pause. "Is anyone after you?"

"No, no. Nothing like that. It's more like . . . I really need a break."

Two months earlier
Southwest territory

KINDA DISAPPOINTING, HOW LITTLE DIFFERENCE THERE IS BEtween Human and Were physicians' offices.

I probably should have known. When I asked Lowe if the Southwest had *a, um, holistic healer I could see, or something*, he looked at me with his resting *I must have drop-kicked a lot of puppies in my past life to deserve this* face, and said, *We do. We call them doctors. They have degrees and such.*

Clearly, *I'm* the problem here. The first time Misery brought me into Vampyre territory, I expected capes with standing collars, scarlet velvet, a menagerie of aloof Mexican free-tailed bats. Instead, I found commercial buildings and suit-wearing finance bros who crowded the elevators and screamed into their phones as though their lives depended on cryptocurrency. Even Owen, Misery's twin, was less like a demonic scion of darkness and more of a lost, indolent fuckboy with daddy issues.

Then again, my impression of him might be influenced by the fact that he hit on me relentlessly, from the moment I entered the Nest till the second I stepped out. I never told Misery, and I'll bring this to my shallow grave.

Very soon, apparently.

Dr. Henshaw's office, tragically, is a new addition in a long line of unmet expectations. The plaque on the door followed by a whole-ass MD? The lack of evolution vector concept art in which an *Australopithecus* transitions to Human and then to wolf? Zero terrifying forceps? Disinfectant wipes that smell *exactly* like the ones I used for my apartment?

As I said: disappointing. The setting *and* the news.

"Serena," he calls. He is a kindly older man, good at his job. My issues stump him and challenge his self-perception, which accounts for half of the urgency in his tone. The other half . . . It cannot be easy, delivering the kind of information he just did.

"Don't worry about it. It's not your fault," I say, hopping off the exam table with a smile.

I stuff my top back into my jeans. The weirdest part about this is that, as far as my days go, I was having a *great* one. Today I haven't puked. Haven't passed out. Haven't felt like all my mucous tissues were drenched in muriatic acid. *Is it my fucking birthday, or what?* I wondered on my way here.

Spoiler alert: it's not. "Please don't feel bad about this," I reassure him. "It's totally okay."

"Serena, I'm not . . ." He pauses to stroke his thick gray beard. "Like I said, cortisol surge disorder is a very common illness for Weres, and a leading cause of death."

"But it's very unusual for a Were as young as me to have CSD, I'm not responding to treatment, and my condition is deteriorating faster than you've ever seen before." I smile to show him that yes, I've been listening.

When I first came to Dr. Henshaw, my biggest fear was that he would tell me that my odd hybrid biology was too much of a medical head-scratcher to give me a diagnosis. It never occurred to me that my disease might be easy to identify but untreatable.

To his credit, Dr. Henshaw did everything he could. He consulted several of his colleagues. He shared my anonymized labs with specialists. He compared notes, asked for advice, and ordered additional tests on their behalf.

And today . . . Well. Today.

"Even if I am not able to do much for you, there are still accommodations to be made. You'll need palliative care to treat your symptoms. We can and should involve your family and your closest friends, like Lowe and the Vampyre, and give them as much time with you as possible."

"It's okay," I say. I feel—no, I *am* calm. Not that I've ever been one for dramatics, despite Misery's accusations that I'm "severely unstable" for crying over videos of dogs reuniting with their owners. The ease with which I'm digesting the news that I'm about to become maggot feed is almost more disquieting than the knowledge itself. "I'd rather not tell anyone."

His eyes widen. "Lowe is my Alpha. I feel uncomfortable, withholding information that—"

"I'm sorry about your discomfort," I interrupt. Gentle *and* firm. "But before I walked into this room for the first time, I made sure that you were not mandated to report your findings to Lowe, and you said—"

"Only if they threatened the safety of the pack." The eleven between his brows deepens, like he's looking for a loophole. "Serena, nearly all people with CSD display aggressive episodes as their disease progresses. You've already experienced blackouts and sleepwalking. The other day, you said you clawed into the headboard of your bed overnight—"

"I promise, I don't need the recap." I attempt an amused smile to soften my words. We were both here for the last two months, trying pills, injectables, even minor surgery. But I steadily got worse, and Dr. Henshaw's even-keeled *We just haven't found the right treatment yet* became a frustrated *You're not responding as well as I'd hoped*, then unspooled into frowns that I interpreted as *What the fuck is wrong with your body?*

Then, today, he said somberly, *My colleagues and I are in agreement that your body cannot sustain this level of adrenal imbalance for much longer. It's simply not compatible with life, both from a Were and a Human physiology standpoint. And the rate of your decline . . .*

It's okay. We tried. Didn't work out. But that's life: you win some, and you lose some—in which case, it becomes death.

"How long?" I ask him.

He doesn't waffle. "Three to six months."

Okay. That's fine. That's . . . I can work with that.

"I cannot thank you enough," I say sincerely. Maybe, after I slog my way to greener pastures, this could be my legacy. Gratitude. Wouldn't it be nice to be remembered as the hybrid who didn't ask to see the manager when things didn't go her way? "You've done so much for me. I would write you a positive online review, but I'm not sure whether *Attempted to fix a hybrid* would get you killed, so."

"Serena. I strongly advise sharing what is happening with Lowe. If nothing else, because you could easily hurt someone during an episode. You live with Ana, too, who—"

"I would *never*—" I stop and force myself not to act defensively, because he's not wrong. If I shredded a piece of wood in my sleep without realizing it, what would stop me from shredding . . . "You're correct." I go on my tiptoes to grab my jacket. "The pack *is* at risk with me around. But there are ways to deal with it."

"Such as?"

"I could ask for some isolation. Misery knows that I've been overwhelmed."

"The Vampyre won't like it."

"She's used to stuff not going her way. She's a bitter pill swallower of great skill and experience."

"Did she not agree to wed Lowe to find *you*?" Dr. Henshaw tilts his head. "And you plan to leave her with a lie?"

"If I think it'd be best for her? Yes." I've expended a lot of effort in the past few weeks to hide my condition from the people I live with. I have no intention to stop now. "Nice guilt trip, though."

"It was worth a try."

I grin at him, wondering when it will sink in that I'm about to die. The atoms that make me will be eaten by worms and turn into fungi and undergo redistribution within the universe. Why do I feel so little? "My medical records through the years, the ones I gave you. You still have them?"

He nods.

"After I . . . Feel free to make copies and share them with whoever you want—they'll come in handy as Ana grows up and—" My voice cracks. For the past decade, I've refused to let my circumstances define me. Fuck being an orphan, or poor, or the Collateral's lady-in-waiting. Fuck being a victim. Fuck navel-gazing and wallowing in my wretchedness.

And then I met Ana. Who's an orphan and a hybrid. She's everything that I used to be. And the compassion I've never been able to extend to myself *overflows* whenever I think about her.

Whoever intends to hurt her will have to crawl over my cold, rotting corpse. Literally, perhaps.

"Mine is a Were illness and likely has nothing to do with me being hybrid," I tell the doctor. "But my medical history might help, if Ana ever runs into issues, and—I did tell you that I'm happy to donate my body, right? Make sure you, um, dissect me, and all. To learn."

"Serena." Dr. Henshaw's light eyes search mine. "You should not forgo palliative care."

"If the pain gets too bad, I'll come back to you. But you know I've been surveilled my entire life, all because of my biology. Something that happened before I was even born has dictated the last two decades of my life, and . . . I think, if you try to wrap your head around it, you might be able to understand that I'd rather not spend the last months of my life being poked and prodded. I just want to *be*, for once."

"Don't you want to spend time with your sister?"

"Not if this illness turns me into a different person. Misery and

I were alone for so long. A year or so ago, when I realized that something was wrong with me, I was terrified that if I disappeared, it would destroy her. And the thing is . . . it will, when it happens. But she has people that'll help her pick up the pieces now." I smile. It's heartfelt. "That's the biggest gift I could ask for."

I wrap my hand around the door handle, ready to leave, when Dr. Henshaw asks, "What about the Northwest Alpha?"

A beat. "What about him?"

"Are you not his mate?"

I look at him over my shoulder. "He won't care. It's just—it's only hormones. Sex."

The doctor cocks his head. "I highly doubt that's true."

"Koen's a grown man. I—" I blink, feeling a burst of anger. I cannot worry about Koen. I need to make sure that Misery and Ana are safe and taken care of, and . . . Does Dr. Henshaw not get it? "He can handle wanting to fuck someone and being told no," I say, voice acid with worry and something that feels too much like regret. "If he can't, that's his problem."

I walk out, pretending not to hear Dr. Henshaw tell me that if that's the impression I'm under, either I was lied to, or I'm lying to myself.

CHAPTER 9

Jerzy's only question is, "Are you sure?"
He shakes his head, because no, of course he isn't.
"I hope I'm wrong about her."
"And if you aren't?" Karolina asks.
It changes nothing.

Present day

IN THE AFTERNOON, I HOBBLE DOWNSTAIRS WEARING A THICK sweater and rolled-up sweats that belong to someone much more vertically gifted than me. My headache pounds through the roof of my mouth. I feel thoroughly banged up. Whether it's from playing hide-and-seek with Bob the Vamp, from sleeping in a bed of ceramic, or from the simple curse of living in my unpredictable sack of meat, I have no clue.

Look at me. Spoiled for choice.

"What is your preferred morning upper?" Amanda asks with a wide smile when I find the kitchen after some wandering. "Coffee? Tea? Methamphetamine?"

I lift my eyebrows. "Is that a common breakfast option in Were B and Bs?"

"I could synthesize some real quick."

She's joking, I think. Not sure. Faced with proof of the existence of stuff like biologically mandated mates, and hybrids, and the legality of child beauty pageants, it's hard to discount . . . anything. I'm a single internet rabbit hole away from becoming a Hollow Earther. "I'm good, thanks. Trying to avoid stimulants. Where did Koen go?" I woke up *deeply* aware that he wasn't around—not in the house, not roaming the woods outside, not anywhere nearby. I'd say GPS tracking is a Were superpower, but mine doesn't extend to anyone but him.

"Off having a chat with a few of the huddle leaders."

"Aren't *you* a huddle leader?"

"Me? Oh, because I'm a second? Nope. But that's how it works in Lowe's pack, right?"

"I think so, yeah." I take a seat and hug my legs to my chest. The temperature is chilly, though one wouldn't be able to guess from Amanda's shorts and tank top. Clearly one of us is a real Were. World's easiest *find the intruder*. "How do you guys do things?" I ask, then rush to add, "If you're allowed to tell me."

"Of course I am. You're one of us." She reaches across the table, briefly covering my hand with hers. Her flesh against mine feels so intensely *wrong*, it's all I can do not to free myself in repulsion—a totally appropriate reaction to a kind gesture. I've never been particularly physical, but this hormonal stuff is making me as avoidant as Misery. "Our pack is divided into geography-based huddles, just like the Southwest. But being a huddle leader doesn't translate to becoming one of Koen's seconds."

"Then, are the seconds elected separately?"

"Elected. Ha." She slaps the table. "We're seconds because Koen wants us to be, period. We do things a bit differently here. Less democracy, and more . . . despotism?" Her grin is unapologetic. "The Northwest is made up of five peripheral huddles and a core. The five huddle leaders make up the Assembly, which is a council of sorts. They bring their territories' needs to the Alpha, advise him. Keep him in check. That kind of stuff."

"If you have the assembly, why do you still put up with an Alpha?"

She chuckles. "We're not Human, Serena. We are biologically hardwired to coalesce around a worthy figure." She tilts her head at me. "You're a Were. Not a full one, maybe, but you feel it, too, don't you? The importance Koen has as a symbol. Unity. Strength. Safety. I guess it's like faith, in a way, but also not at all, and . . ." She lets out a small laugh. "I don't know how to explain it, but you understand, right?" I don't know if I do. Not the way she'd like me to, at least. I nod anyway, and she seems pleased. "Koen will be back soon. He just needed to discuss a . . . situation."

I bury my hands inside my sleeves. "Am *I* the situation?"

"Nope."

"Oh." Heat creeps up my cheeks. "I promise I don't go about my life believing that I'm the center of the universe."

"You kinda are, at the moment. Honestly, if I were kidnapped and man-hunted at the rate you are, I'd assume, too. But this is something else—hopefully nothing to worry about."

Like the vast majority of Humans, I grew up suspecting that if I ever met a Were, I'd be skewered into a kebab before I could politely inquire about their customs and traditions. Most information publicly available on them was speculation, often contradictory, always incomplete. I get it, Weres not wanting other species to know their business—sworn enemies and all that. Still, it was *very* inconvenient for me. When I realized that I was one of them, their secrecy made it impossible to predict what their reaction to a hybrid would be, and that's what prevented me from reaching out and asking for help. But even in my hardest days, when my body clawed at me with needs that I couldn't decipher and I contemplated walking into a pack's territory, waving a white flag, and letting the chips fall where they may, I never, not *once*, considered approaching the Northwest.

Out of all the packs on the North American continent, they are the least conflict prone, mostly because their territory doesn't abut the Vampyres'. They are, however, surrounded by various Human settlements, and while they don't exactly cohost monthly block parties, I could find no indication that their borders have historically been as contentious as the ones between the Southwest and the Humans. The Northwest pack has perfected the art of, as Koen would put it, minding their goddamn business.

And yet any mention of them induces brick-shitting. In Humans, and in their own kind.

It's the zero strike policy, Alex told me while I was staying at Misery's. She and Lowe would frequently disappear to do newlywed things that, in my humble experience, should have taken no longer than fifteen minutes. Alex noticed me listlessly wandering around the garden and graciously took me under his wing for a couple of remedial history lessons. *They don't tolerate any invasion.*

Isn't that true of every pack?

Most packs will kill the intruders and call it a day. They won't line their perimeters with vertically impaled corpses.

A long pause. *Impaled on . . . ?*

Oh, you know. Just your regular, um, stakes?

Why would they do that?

To remind their neighbors of the exact location of their borders. He looked as nauseous as I felt. *You have to admit, Koen's logic is solid.*

I don't think I have to, actually.

Anyway, they're equal opportunity haters. They've done this with Humans, but also with the Canada and Midwest packs. So no one messes with them anymore.

So nice, to discover that the dude who'd told me I was his mate was impalement happy. *Koen and Lowe are allies, though*, I said. To soothe myself.

Yup. The North- and Southwest were never enemies, but they became close allies because Koen's aunt was the mate of Roscoe, our former Alpha. When Lowe turned twelve and started feeling a bit too Alpha for Roscoe, Roscoe sent him to the Northwest. An exile-in-everything-but-name type of deal.

And Koen took him in?

Yeah. Basically raised him. Rumor has it that Koen didn't want to play nanny, but it was obvious that Lowe would one day be Alpha, and he couldn't let him become too fucked up. Alex laughed, but I wasn't so certain that Koen had been joking.

They're different, though, I mused. *Lowe is much more about diplomacy, and less about . . . impalement.*

They are. But I was in the Northwest for several months a couple of summers ago, doing some IT work. I get why Koen's considered a great Alpha.

By whom? I asked skeptically. *Himself?* It was important to me that Koen Alexander was a mediocre . . . man, Were, Alpha. My pride and self-respect were at stake.

Everyone, really. He reunited the Northwest after the pack had splintered into different factions. All of a sudden, I could see the faint green undertones of Alex's skin. He smelled warm and nervous and . . . scared? *By the way, I heard about the mate thing.*

Ah. Yeah. What an unfortunate direction for this chat.

And . . . you know how the first week you were here, I kind of asked you out?

I do. In my dreams, I violently slammed my skull against the wall.

You said no. And it's totally fine. But would it be possible for you to . . . A deep breath. *Never, ever, ever mention it to Koen?*

Oh. *Alex, Koen and I are not . . .*

And if you do mention it to him, could you maybe give me a heads-up? So then I can, you know, burn my fingerprints with my sister's curling iron and go underground and maybe buy some fake documents—

I could have an orgy on Koen's yard, and he wouldn't give a shit. And . . . I liked Alex. He was, most days, the smartest person in the room. He reminded me of the kind of guys I used to date—friendly, kind, cute. And the idea of touching him made my stomach roll and my insides putrefy. *I'm sorry I said no, but you do not want to hook up with someone who doesn't even know what species box to tick on the census form.*

"Is there any strife?" I ask Amanda now. "Between Koen and the huddle leaders?"

"No. Or, no more so than usual. Koen does thrive on pissing people off—it's his main pastime."

"Is it okay to say that about your Alpha?"

"If it's true. Which it totally is." She grins and rotates her shoulders, arching up in a stretch. I can't quite swallow a gasp when my eyes stumble on her nails, elongated into sharp, lethal weapons. When she yawns, her canines are no longer blunt. "Oh, shit." She laughs and immediately backtracks her shift. "It's been months since I last was in human form for over a day. Not used to it, I guess."

Ana told me something similar. *When I was in the north, Uncle Koen spent four days in wolf form and* never *changed back,* she said, sounding the same mix of titillated and scandalized as when I'd explained to her that no, Sparkles was not going to have kittens, because his testicles resided somewhere at the bottom of a vet's composting bin. RIP, Sparkles Jr. and Sparklette. *And it was a new moon! Sooo cool!*

Here, wolf is the default. Human form is somewhere between an unavoidable hassle and an embarrassing constraint that affects only the least dominant Weres. "Feel free to shift," I tell Amanda with a smile.

"Why don't we go on a run together?"

My stomach drops. "I . . ."

"Wait, you have that call, right?"

"What call?"

"The Southwest geneticist. Juno? She has something to share, but Koen wanted me to remind you that you don't have to talk to her if you prefer not to. Shall we just go frolic in mud?" Amanda asks hopefully, and as little as I want to discuss genetics . . .

I take a big-girl breath. "Actually, I'm *dying* to catch up with Juno."

A MEETING WITH JUNO THE GENETICIST—LOVELY ALLITERATION— can mean only one thing: she inserted my DNA sample into a Big Science Machine, and the Big Science Machine spat out information about my blood relatives.

For my entire life, I've felt ambivalent about learning anything regarding my parents. Not your average orphan's attitude—though maybe it is? I'm sure some of us seek to uncover our past to better define our future, and all that therapy stuff, while others are as blasé as I am. Children raised like me develop a unique brand of pragmatism, born of the knowledge that nothing will stand as a shield between us and reality. On my second-grade career day, when I told a teacher that I wanted to become a journalist, and he laughed, saying that I was more likely to be found dead in a ditch by eighteen, no helicopter mother waltzed in to have a stern talking-to with the principal. When the cafeteria served us spoiled chicken and the dormitory looked like a splash pad of projectile vomiting, no loving father made sure we stayed hydrated. When the creepy orderly with the easily discoverable felony convictions insisted on watching us change after PE, no probation officer came to arrest him.

We had to take care of ourselves, so we did. Some pining for our lost families was involved, sure, but holding on to an idea, just like holding a grudge, takes up a significant amount of energy, one that could be used to . . . well, bully other orphans, in my less-than-uncommon experience. If Ruth from the group home had been more in touch with her emotions, maybe she wouldn't have forced me to drink toilet water for refusing to give up my sandwich.

So I haven't spent my life searching for my parents, because there's little room for this to work out in a satisfying way. Either they wanted to get rid of me (tragic, tear-jerking, the stuff where trauma thrives) or they were forced to (tragic, tear-jerking, the stuff where trauma thrives). Neither option comes with a happy ending. Sure, there's room for variation in the levels of rejection, self-loathing, and generic *mal de vivre* I'll experience as my backstory unfolds. But unless Juno's report comes with a time-travel machine and a redo in which Mommy, Daddy, Fido the goldendoodle, and I picket-fence it in the suburbs—and maybe in which I get to spit in Ruth's coffee just once—I doubt any good will come of it.

Ignorance, bliss, that kind of stuff.

And *yet*, about two months ago, after hearing my prognosis from Dr. Henshaw, I decided to not return home to Misery right away. Instead, I stopped by Juno's place. And told her that, at last, I was ready for her to compare my DNA with the available databases, to see if she could find any relative of mine.

Maybe being reminded of my own mortality made me curious. Maybe I'm afraid to be insubstantial, and that no part of me will be left once I'm gone. Maybe I'm just filling time, sitting at the desk in the bedroom where I slept last night, wrapped in a thick blanket. I'd love for Misery to be present for this, but it's the middle of day, when Vampyres are at their sleepiest. I don't want to bother her. So when I accept the call and see her next to Juno, mouth wide open in a huge, fanged yawn, my heart squeezes.

"She does *not* need to be here," Juno tells me, pointing at her.

"Eh," Misery says. "I kinda do."

Juno ignores her. "I explained the concept of confidentiality to her multiple times."

"Serena wants me here. Right?"

"She can stay, I guess," I say with an exaggerated, disaffected tone that has her blowing me a kiss.

Juno is almost pathologically humorless. Nice, though, and the flowchart I use to decide whether to consider someone a friend is made up of a single question: Have they tried to kill me or Misery? No? Fantastic. Let's have a spa day. Go zip-lining. Overshare about recurring UTIs.

"First, I'd like to say how sorry I am about your experience with the Human genetic counselor. He was being interviewed as an expert and had no right to disclose information about *your* reproductive health to the public."

"Oh." I swallow. "It's fine. I'm sure they didn't mean—"

"It's unacceptable, and your and Koen's anger is perfectly justified. He's been suspended, pending investigation." When did Juno talk with *Koen* about my anger? "Secondly, I'm sorry it took me this long to contact you. I'm sure you've been anxious about the results—"

"She absolutely has not," Misery informs her cheerfully. "Her avoidance is the stuff psychiatrists' dreams are made of."

Juno blinks. "Well, Serena, either way, the reason this took months is that I had to run your father's DNA through several Were databases, and—"

"My father? You mean . . my *father* was a Were?"

"Yes." She seems taken aback. "I thought you knew. It was widely shared in the Human news. Maddie felt that the public would want to know, and— I'm sorry."

"It's okay. It's not your fault if I spent the last few months hiding inside a walnut, and . . ." I shake my head and wait for my perception of myself to adjust. I never fully articulated it, but somewhere, in a corner of my mind made up of no words and many, *many* vibes, I assumed that the Were was my mother. Probably because that's the case with . . .

"I'm not like her," I say. The relief is a physical, tangible thing.

"Not like who?"

"Ana."

Juno nods. "Indeed."

"Does it mean that . . . Does it mean that we'll have different outcomes, too?"

"Outcomes? Of what?"

"Just . . . different challenges. Or issues." *She won't have a terminal diagnosis at twenty-five, will she?*

"Presumably. We're working on a sample of two, but you already manifest in different ways. You are closer to Human—redder blood, lower basal temperature, less acute senses. Ana may not shift, but she couldn't pass for a Human the way you did at her age. So, yes. We can assume that different genotypes will lead to different phenotypes."

Misery tilts her head. "You seem happy about it."

"Oh, no, I'm not." I notice my grin on the screen. I look on the verge of swing dancing on top of the keyboard. Probably because I am. "Just tired. Go ahead, please." Juno buys it. Misery is somewhat trickier, but I've been hiding shit from her for years now. *For her own good*, I remind myself, careful not to look at her as I change the topic. "How can you tell that my father was the Were?"

"We took a look at your mitochondrial DNA."

"Right. And mitochondrial DNA is mostly passed down from mother to child." Noticing Misery's thunderstruck expression, I ask, "What?"

"Nothing. Just, look at you. Being all sciency."

"I had a mandatory biology class in college."

"And you retained knowledge from that low C?"

"Stay out of my transcripts."

"But they're such a riveting bedtime read."

"*And* it was a C-plus."

"You woman in STEM."

She deserves being flipped off, and Juno's throat clearing signals her agreement. "I used DNA comparison to find your genetic relatives, but in the Southwest, there are no individuals with DNA segments identical to yours."

"Does that mean . . . no relatives?"

"We can be reasonably sure that your father was not Southwest."

"Bummer." Misery looks disappointed, like she wanted for the two of us to have this in common. For *her* home to be *my* home.

"So I expanded my search to other packs," Juno continues. "Which complicated things."

Misery snorts. "The other Alphas giving you access to their precious little data was not on my bingo card."

"That's good, because they didn't. However, once Lowe reached out, most of them did agree. The ones who didn't . . . they came around later, after Koen had a chat with them." It's obvious from her blank face that *chat* is not the right word for what happened. "This is where things get messy. I wasn't given direct access to the databases—their geneticists ran Serena's DNA. We have no choice but to trust that they did their job well and that their databases are accurately maintained."

"And you do?"

She hesitates. "I think so, yes. Serena is . . . a hot commodity, for many reasons. If a pack had any ground to claim her, they absolutely would. And they did not."

Misery scratches her head. "Dude, did you spring up from a cabbage patch?"

"Maybe? Could I be from another continent?"

"That's one explanation. Lowe has contacts in Europe, so we're exploring that. More likely . . ." Juno pauses. Her eyes meet mine. "There's one American pack whose structure has gone through several transformations. Most of its records were lost."

"Okay. And will you tell us which pack that is, or—"

"No need." I interrupt Misery, because I already know. "It's the Northwest, isn't it?"

CHAPTER 10

*She is braiding her hair. Bends her head forward, sectioning
the strands and paying no mind to the world around her.
Doesn't notice him lingering at the door. Her bare nape is
there for him to stare at, pink and vulnerable and accessible.
It's so flagrantly* indecent, *he must excuse himself.*

I T'S MISERY WHO ASKS THE ONLY SENSIBLE QUESTION: "HOW DO
you *lose* a genetic database? I mean, Koen's temperamental and
all that, but even he wouldn't just misplace—"

"'Destroyed' is a better word for it. I believe it was an accident."

"What kind of accident?"

Juno hesitates just a fraction of a second. "A fire, I think. Twenty
years ago."

I remember what Alex told me. "Does this have anything to do
with the fact that the Northwest was divided into different factions?"

"I'm sorry." Another infinitesimal pause. "I don't know much
about the circumstances."

I exchange a wordless glance with Misery, who picked up on
the same offbeat vibes. "What about my . . . mother?" The word
sounds disturbingly odd in my mouth. "Do the Humans have databases?"

"Nothing as thorough as ours. Their registries are mostly opt-ins, biotech companies that offer personalized screening. That covers a small percentage of the Human population on this continent, but I'll try."

I scratch the side of my neck, weighing my options. Taking the temperature. I'm disappointed, more than I thought I'd be. But it's fine. I don't *need* to know—

"Serena, I realize that this is a sensitive question, but . . . Misery mentioned that you do not remember much from your childhood. Is that true?"

I nod.

"Is there anything about your earliest memories that might help us refine our search?"

"Not really, no. I barely . . ."

What's your name, honey? Do you know how we can get in touch with your parents?

She'll be in the car for several hours. Let's make sure she's not conscious for that.

Are you stupid? I hate the dumb ones. Can she have a different bed, away from mine?

It's no big deal. Just the desert. Have you not seen a prickly pear before?

I shake my head. "I started linearly encoding my childhood memories when I was seven or eight, but I have some spotty recollection from before. The earliest is being in Paris, a small Human town north of The City. It was April, and I was . . . They estimated my age at about six. I was told that I wandered into the Child Services office with no idea how I got there." My tone is always detached when I talk about this, because I never feel as though *I'm* the one who went through it. "No one local knew me, not even when they expanded the radius of their search. I couldn't remember my own name, and the nurses got tired of calling me 'the girl.' One of them named me Serena, after her mother, and . . . Well, it stuck. Two decades, and still going strong."

"Sadly, not all of us can be named after the literal state of being in agony," Misery says. Her grin pulls me back into the present.

I return her smile. "A missed opportunity. It pains me to admit how inflated my ego has become, but given the years of cloak-and-dagger surveillance, I assume Humans have thorough files on me."

"There are none, Serena," Juno says.

"Well, that's certainly humbling."

"We believe they were destroyed by Governor Davenport's team." She purses her lips. "That's okay. For now, at least. If you recall anything else, give Lowe or me a call."

"Or *me*." Misery scowls. "Now that I think about it, Serena, send me your new phone number. So I can keep you updated on Sparkles's bowel movements, as you requested."

"I requested cute pictures. Please, stop sending cat turds."

"Nah." Her gaze flicks somewhere past my head. "I know it must be symptomatic of either overwork or severe depression, but I'm loving the *shipwreck survivor with no access to blades* look, Koen."

I turn around so fast, I nearly pull a muscle. Koen is behind me, standing at the door.

"Be good, Vampyre," he tells Misery, in that affectionate tone that he uses only with her and Ana. It should be at odds with his usual orneriness but somehow fits him like a glove. And sends odd pangs to my chest. I bet he *does* care, whether *they* like him or not.

"I'm *never* good," Misery replies, and a beat later I hear the video call being shut down.

"How long have you been here?" I ask him.

He lifts a shoulder. Widens his arms. "What is time?"

"How much did you hear?"

"I don't know. Everything?"

I frown. "Pretty sure being Alpha of this pack doesn't give you a pass to eavesdrop on people."

"Pretty sure being Alpha of this pack gives me a pass to run people through the paper shredder and make dinosaur-shaped nuggies out of what's left."

He may have just threatened to macerate me, but at least he's funny about it. "You heard the plot twist, then?"

"Which one?"

"I might be part of your pack." He stares, unreadable, until I continue. "We could be related. I could be your cousin."

He scoffs, unimpressed. "You're not."

"How do you know?"

"I *have* a cousin. Looking at her does *not* feel like looking at you."

I glance down, hot all of a sudden. Hang on. Am I flattered? None of what he just said could be construed as *nice*.

"Come on." He directs me with his head. "We're leaving."

"For where? You're not taking me back to the Southwest, right?" I ask as I rise.

"We'll see."

"Koen." I hurry down the stairs after him. "You said that if I told you the truth, you'd go along with my plan."

"Did I?"

"Yes." I fist my hand in his flannel. It looks like yesterday's, but green, and without Vampyre blood. "Please," I say when he graces me with his gaze. He's standing in my space. Or maybe I'm in his. "Let me come to the Den with you. For all we know, it's where I was born."

"You wanna be my cousin *that* bad, huh?"

I roll my eyes. "You know, being all secretive and mastermind-y is not really as charming as you—"

"Relax. I'm not taking you back to the Southwest." He must know that I'm *this* close to hugging him, because he leans closer and orders, "Dial it down."

"What?"

"That look—like I'm about to take you to the shelter to pick out a new kitten. It's not going to be fun. I won't put you up in another isolated cabin in the middle of nowhere."

"Where are we going, then?"

"You said you want to be bait." His smile is anything but pleased. "Time to put you on a hook, killer."

———— ❧ ————

"YOU NEED TO EAT," HE SAYS ONCE THE CAR IS OUT OF THE driveway.

I stare up at the hemlock-spruces that line the road, nose pressed against the cool glass, and murmur, "I'm good."

The thing about this place is: the farther north we push, the more beautiful it gets. Dramatic. A little mysterious. Lush and rich. I spot a million shades of green. Everything towers. Endless jutting trees, spongy moss, water flowing always, everywhere, vibrant and otherworldly and so *alive*, it makes *me* feel alive, too.

"You're lots of things, and *good* is not one of them."

I glance at Koen, who's not unlike the landscape: outdoorsy and remote and moody. Wild and overcast. "Must be nice," I muse.

"What?"

"Being you. Knowing *everything*."

"It is, yeah," he agrees.

"Any other unfulfilled strata in my pyramid of need that I should know about?"

"You're sleep deprived. A little dehydrated. But the hunger is what concerns me the most."

"I told you. My appetite has been—"

"Low. That's fine. We'll find something you can keep down."

Behaviors like this used to be an instant date-ender—*Yeah, you do want another drink; I promise you'll love this movie; You need someone who really gets you, babe, let me take care of you*. But with Koen, they don't really faze me. Maybe it's because with my exes it felt like posturing, little kids playing dress-up. Koen, though, takes care of thousands of people. His job, his vocation, the mission statement of his entire life is to figure out what the Weres in his territory need. It's not so far-fetched that he could take on one more person. Even if I might just be the most burdensome yet.

"Are we ever going back to the cabin where I was staying?"

"No. It's hours away." He scowls. "Why? Want to bring flowers to Bob's grave?"

"First of all, you left Bob's corpse in the very place where it dropped. He's probably been eaten by the beavers."

"Eh. Beavers are discerning."

"Secondly, *no*. It's just, all my stuff is there."

"Your what?"

"My clothes."

"I'm sure we can buy you a new burlap sack."

"Okay, well . . . Thank you. But I have other stuff there that I can't replace."

"Like what?"

I quickly cast around for a good answer. The infamous sat

phone? My sports drinks? Neither is worth driving hours for. Maybe the strong painkillers that Dr. Henshaw gave me *for when things get really bad, Serena. And they will.* But I cannot tell Koen about them, just like I cannot tell him what I really want to go back for.

So I lie. "My plushie."

"Your plushie."

"Yeah. Ana gave it to me."

"Did she, now?"

"She bought it for me with her monthly allowance." Which is nearly as high as my salary used to be. Misery is *not* strict with that child. "I sleep with it every night."

He looks at me like he's considering laying down a tarp and butchering me on it.

"It's important to me," I continue weakly. "What? You don't believe that a family can be a girl and her pink stuffed penguin?"

"I emphatically do not."

"You're so bigoted."

"Glad you finally noticed."

There's no point in arguing with him. I perform a huge, dramatic yawn and let my head fall sideways against the window, pretending to take a nap. His snort spells out how little I'm fooling him, but I don't care. As much as I'd love to stab him, his scent is safe and warm, as shrouding and all-consuming as the Douglas fir.

I try to forget the cabin—above all, I try not to think about the letters I stuffed at the bottom of the dresser. And after a while, I sink into the first restful sleep I've had in a long time.

CHAPTER 11

Unknown number: You are now officially in charge of my sister, so be aware that if she gets so much as a skinned knee, I will fuck up your life. I will steal your identity and ruin your credit score. I will plant evidence of white-collar crimes on your computer. I will take control of your webcam and film you while you're picking your nose. I will hack your pack directory and impersonate you and send everyone emails about how much you'd love for them to come over and snuggle with you. I will sell your information to the dark web and clone your credit cards and make donations to pro-cancer charities in your name and if you ever buy a smart car

Unknown number: sssli999f

Unknown number: lgi64ssss99f

Unknown number:

Unknown number: 00kk9—

Unknown number: Sorry. Ana stole my phone. Where was I?

THE COARSE CARESS OF A PALM AGAINST MY CHEEK WAKES ME up, a strand of hair tucked behind my ear. My eyes flutter open and search for the dashboard clock. I napped for over three hours.

"Holy shit."

"Told you. Sleep deprived." Koen's hand is gripping my headrest, so far from my face, I must have dreamed of his touch. Which is on-brand for my recent maelstrom of psychosexual neuroses. The fact that my stomach is not twisting and turning, even though I've been abhorring all forms of physical contact, is proof of it.

"Where are we?" I ask, sliding out of the car. A few hundred feet from us, past the evergreen shrubbery peppering the shoreline and a sandy beach that looks untouched by man, there's a lake. Or . . .

I inhale once, deeply. Again. Salt. Sea. "Is that a river? The coast?"

"An estuary. If you follow the shore all the way north to the end of the inlet, that's where the ocean starts. Follow me."

He walks uphill, opposite to the water. I linger for a moment, listening to the seagulls soaring overhead and squinting at the splashes of the dolphins—no, *seals*—in the distance. Then I hurry after him. "Are we in the Den?"

"Yes. Olympia, Humans call it."

I glance around, taking advantage of the slight elevation of the terrain. We're on top of a rolling hill, and below us is what looks like—no, it *is* a city. It sprawls for miles, gently following the curves of the river, spilling farther inland. There are clusters of buildings, roads, electric poles, bridges. It could house thousands and thousands of people. But it's also disarmingly . . .

"Horizontal," I murmur.

Koen's expression is quizzical.

"So different from Human cities. There isn't a single high-rise. And it's also . . ." The marine breeze flows through my hair. Strands stick to my lips. "A little ghostly? There are so many houses but few cars and so few people walking around . . . *Oh.*" I flush. It's not that there aren't many people. "Are they . . ." I bite my tongue, because of course the wolves milling around at the edge of the forest are Weres. Simple animals are never that large, nor do they have such all-seeing expressions. Above all, they wouldn't join a chorus of howls after spotting Koen.

Which, judging by his reaction, is a typical welcome home. He lifts his hand in greeting, a small smile on his lips, and leads me to a cabin right at the outskirts of the woods.

"Third quarter's not even over yet." He must notice my confusion, and continues, "The pull of the moon is still strong enough that over half of the Northwest can easily maintain wolf form. Give it a week and you'll see plenty of 'people walking around.'"

I climb the steps that lead up to the wraparound porch, a little embarrassed by the mockery in his voice, and admire the log exterior and tall windows. It's pretty. Rustic. The door is unlocked, and Koen opens it without knocking or announcing himself. Must belong to someone he's close to—a friend or a second or a girlfriend.

Does he? Have a girlfriend? Is that why he was so dismissive, when—

"Why do you smell so worried all of a sudden?" he asks, ushering me inside.

"Nothing." I take a few hesitant steps, wondering if I'll be mistaken for a home-wrecking intruder and deboned. What a way to go that would be. But I doubt it'll be mine, because with my first deep breath, I *know* who the cabin belongs to.

"You live here," I tell Koen. Accusingly. His scent is everywhere. It coats every object in a blanket of good and calm and safe and— did I mention *good*? I feel it stick to my nostrils and the roof of my mouth. It's like he took off his shirt and gave me permission to lick his skin, and—

What the hell? *No.*

"This is your house," I repeat—less reproachful, more sullen.

"Yup."

"The door was unlocked. And you were out of town."

"I'm the Alpha of the pack, Serena."

Fair enough. The likelihood of his space being invaded without an invitation is probably lower than someone gifting him a pet hippopotamus. Plus, there wouldn't be much to steal. This place is not like Lowe's house—large, crowded, and cluttered, an obvious labor of love. Koen's decor style of choice seems to be *I was going to hang a picture or two but got distracted, my bad*.

The door opens into a single large room—kitchen on the left, living area on the right. He's clearly not much for knickknacks and ornaments, but judging from the shelves full of books, he likes to read. On the coffee table, I spot a laptop. Some additional furniture, sparse but beautifully handcrafted. A couch. A hallway that'll likely lead to the bedrooms, and . . . that's about it. No TV. No stereo system. The appliances in the kitchen are the kind that would fetch less than the shipping cost on eBay. The fridge is an older model, not much taller than me. "Did you make this?" I ask, tracing the woodgrain of the beautiful cherry table.

"A while ago."

"Really?"

"Yeah. Shop's in the back."

"So you *do* chop firewood."

"I *work* wood. Not the same thing."

Lumberjack, I mouth to myself. "You don't spend much time here, do you?"

"Not lately, no. Just write me a list and I'll get you what you need."

Which is when my heart stops. Because I understand why he brought me here.

I need the mother of all escape plans. "I can't stay at your house," I say, calm. Reasonable. I'm an adult. I'm *not* panicking.

"Why?"

"Because." I attempt a playful smile. "I'm a kleptomaniac. I'd steal your razors and shaving gel—and *clearly*, you're in dire need of them."

"Serena."

"Not to mention, I snoop around. You'd have to hide all your porn magazines."

"I have Wi-Fi, killer."

"Well, turning on incognito browsing is a pain."

He folds his arms. "It's good that you're funny. Next time someone tries to saw you open to study your half-Human gut microbiome, you can shoo them away with a jab at their masturbation habits." He strides down the hall, and I run after him.

"Koen, seriously." We pass a bedroom that smells so ruinously *mouthwatering*, it has to be his. Enter another. "I don't think this place is a good fit for me."

He opens the cabinet in the en suite to inspect its contents. "Because . . . ?"

"Well, this is not really an isolated area, and I haven't learned how to tune out sounds yet."

"Poor baby Were." He turns to me. Suddenly, I see compassion in his eyes. "In that case, we'll find a place where you can be alone in the middle of nowhere."

My heart soars. "Really?"

"No," he says mildly. "Fuck that. You'll stay where I put you."

I slump.

Koen is not a defenseless child, or a Vampyre who passes out in the brightest hours of the day. I'm sure that if I have a violent sleep-walking episode, I'll get *exactly* what I deserve. But what if *he's* the one asleep? Not to mention, he can be highly perceptive—and that meshes poorly with my secrets.

I need to be isolated to properly rot in my dysfunctions. "Thing is," I try again, "I really like living alone."

"Maybe you had shitty roommates," he says casually, opening a closet. He grabs a set of fresh sheets and lifts them to his nose. They must pass muster, because he drops them on the mattress. "I, on the other hand, am a fucking delight."

I watch him unearth several pillows. "Does it not bother your back, Koen?"

"You mean, the supermassive weight of my ego? No, it does not."

"Oh, come *on*. How did you know—"

"You're gonna have to come up with more creative insults than that, Serena." On the way to the bed, he taps my nose with two fingers and starts unfolding one of the pillowcases.

I take a deep, bolstering breath. "I *really* wouldn't want to impose."

"Pretty fucking late to worry about that," he says distractedly, continuing to make the bed.

"Well." I scowl. "I'm sorry. I didn't ask to be a hybrid hunted by every single species."

"You didn't. You didn't ask to be my mate, either." He stops mid fitting a bottom sheet to look me square in the eye. "However, you did ask me to take you in and use you to lure Vampyres away from Ana. *That* was your mistake." His mouth curls in a small, sardonic smile. "I won't be sleeping in the cabin with you, if that's what worries you."

I flush. "No, that's not what— Wait. Where *will* you be sleeping?"

"Outside," he says, like I deserve to take remedial Were classes just for asking.

"You sleep outside."

"Yes."

"In the great outdoors."

"Yup."

"Every night."

A brief pause. "Not every night."

"Oh. Good."

"Just every night in which I have time to sleep."

"You mean that you don't sleep every— You know, don't answer that." And I used to think that my job was stressful. "Did you just never outgrow your backyard camping phase— Oh. You sleep in *wolf* form."

"Like God intended," he says, with the tone of someone whose opinion of God's will is that it's secondary to his own. Rationally, I know that Koen wasn't born with a pack to boss around. There must have been a time in his life in which people surrounding him would *not* have thrown themselves under a banana car just because he snapped his fingers at them.

And yet I can't picture it. "I can't stay with you, Koen. I need to be on my own."

"Do you need to, or do you want to?"

"Does it matter?"

"No. You'll do what I say anyway."

I close my eyes. "Maybe I should just go back to Lowe and Misery—"

"Who, notoriously, have nothing and no one more important than you to worry about," he drawls.

I press my lips together.

"Word of advice, killer?" he murmurs. "Stubborn and stupid is just a couple letters' difference."

"You're not the best speller, are you?"

A smile pulls at the edge of his mouth—and then mine. We share a long look, equally frustrated and amused by each other. A weird string strains between us, tugging at me, reminding me that I like him, I liked him from the start, I don't *want* to fight with him.

Maybe I could tell him. He would understand, I think. He's gruff and abrasive, a little mean, but also aware of cumbersome stuff like duty, responsibility, love. He wouldn't judge me for doing what I needed to do. Maybe he'd help me through my last few months. Maybe I wouldn't be so alone.

That just sounds . . . good. So good, I nearly say, *Koen, I need you to know something.*

But he would never keep a secret that big. And then Misery and Lowe and Ana would know, and I want better for them.

So I ask, in my most hard-ass tone, "What do I have to do to get you to let me stay on my own?"

He pauses, staring at me in that serious, uncompromising way I should be afraid of. "You want to be on your own?"

I nod, eager.

"Okay." He drops the pillow. Flicks his fingers for me to follow. "I'll allow it. *If* you prove to me that you can handle it."

———— ⟶⟍⎪⟋ ————

DURING THE TEN-MINUTE DRIVE, I EXPERIENCE MOUNTAINS OF RE-
lief, picturing Koen dropping me off at a quaint little cottage after
proof that, at long last, I have acquired the ability to plug a charger
into a socket.

I should have expected something more like me on a gym mat.
Wearing borrowed shorts and a white tee. Standing in front of a
tall blond woman who looks like an underwear model tough
enough to survive an extinction-level event. She's inscrutable in a
pants-pissing way.

"This is Brenna," Koen says, much closer to her than he is to
me. I don't know why I notice, or why it makes my belly heavy.
"One of my seconds. She manages this gym and trains most younger members of the pack in hand-to-hand combat." They exchange
a small smile. Clearly, they go way back. "Serena here said that if
she's expecting an attack, she can fend for herself."

"Would you like me to prove her wrong?" Brenna sounds
bored. I doubt she thinks much of me. Then again, do *I* think much
of me?

"I need to make sure she won't die on my watch. Lowe's mate
likes her," he adds.

"You do have a soft spot for Lowe," Brenna agrees, like it's his
fatal flaw.

"This is unnecessary," I say. "For one, regular Weres are much
stronger than Vampyres. And in a scenario in which I live alone, I
would have weapons."

"I don't mind if she uses a weapon," Brenna offers, challenge
shimmering in her eyes.

"Well, she can't. And highly trained Vampyres defeat Weres in combat all the time." He gestures toward me with a small flourish. "Show me that you can be the last one standing in hand-to-hand, and I'll let you live wherever the hell you want. Okay?"

I can tell he expects more protests. So I smile sweetly. "Okay." And add, under my breath, "*Alpha*." His jaw twitches like he did *not* like that, but I must be in the mood to taunt him. "You didn't have to take me all the way here. You could have sparred with me yourself." I tilt my head. "Unless you're afraid of me?"

His expression flattens. "Sure. I'm afraid. It's not that I have better shit to do than to wrestle spoiled little girls who love wasting my time."

My stomach drops. It's unnecessarily mean, the way Koen holds my eyes for a beat, as if to savor the hurt in them. Then he fondly clasps Brenna's shoulder, whispers something in her ear that has her smirking, and settles on the bench farthest away.

I hate him.

"Ready to start whenever you are," Brenna says once he's out of earshot.

I hate her, too. By extension. Which is unfair, but it does fuel me.

Misery and I have taken *a lot* of self-defense, and I have some moves tucked away. Not sure how they'll play out after months of poor sleep hygiene, a diet mostly made of stomach acids, and my current *condom full of chicken stock* level of fitness, but I don't care.

Brenna expects nothing from me, and I can use it to my advantage.

"I didn't think Weres went to the gym," I tell her with a small smile.

"Weres do everything Humans do. But better."

So maybe I don't hate her. Maybe I sort of like her. It's Misery's fault if I have a thing for tall blondes who use *fuck off* humor to shield their true selves. I'll write my sister a strongly worded email of condemnation.

But there's something I need to know, and I decide not to hem and haw over it. "You and Koen . . . ?"

"Yup." Light on her feet, she moves closer. We start circling each other.

"Cool." She throws a jab at my torso. I hop back and dodge it. For some reason, my chest hurts anyway. "How, um, long have you been together?"

"We no longer are."

Oh.

I evade a few more punches and try a low attack, but she gets me with a leg kick. I fall on my ass but manage to roll back up before she can . . . I don't know. When does this stop? Pinfall? Knockout? First blood? She's not going to kill me, right? "You didn't break up because of the mate thing, right?" I ask, already panting a little.

"As if. You're not the hub of reality." She snorts. "It was a million years ago, and there was no *breaking up*. The fucking ground was falling from under our feet." She aims a cross at my head, which I barely slip. I counter with a jab to her ribs, quickly followed by a light kick.

I land both. And they must hurt—if not her flesh, her pride. Brenna glares, and that's when she begins to fight in earnest. I half expect the way she grabs my shoulders, and even her knee to my stomach. I block the latter, but she takes me down with a body lock that . . .

Fucking *ouch*.

"Listen." She pins me to the mat. Holds me down as she whispers right against my face. "I'm not some jealous woman quivering at the sight of a pretty trophy girlfriend. But you know *nothing*. Things could get real tough here in the Northwest. Koen could use an adult, instead of a cute little ball and chain combo that only slows him down."

Hard not to take what she's saying personally when, if the mood were to strike, she could easily choke me. "I may be ignorant of Were and Northwest customs, but in my defense, people haven't been forthcoming with information—"

"What do you wanna know? Ask away, 'cause I'm not going to baby you. Your weird hybrid shit and that rosy-cheeked, wide-eyed look, they're not *adorable* to me. I was thrown in the deep end when I was a decade younger than you are now, and no one tossed me a rope, not even a damn stick, and I'm stronger for it. You'd benefit from fewer gloves and rougher—"

I jerk my hips and push against her neck, creating enough space to flip us around. I twist her hand, pull it under my armpit, and lock her in an armbar. "Why was the Northwest divided?" I ask. Since she's so eager to talk, I'd rather it be about something that isn't me.

"That's a much smarter question than I expected from you," she chokes out, failing to free herself.

"Yeah, well. I used to think of myself as a smart person."

"Used to?"

"Not realizing what species I was for the better part of two decades had me reassessing," I huff.

"That must fuck you up real good, huh? I don't envy you."

"Why? It's been so *fun*." I think she might be chuckling. I strengthen my grip and ask, "When did the pack split?"

"Forty years ago. Little less."

"Why?"

"A disagreement between the former Alpha and the Assembly. The huddles separated and became self-governing. The Alpha remained in control of the core. The five huddles made for about half of the population, so it was an even split."

"Were the huddles and the core at war with each other?"

"What? No." More breathless laughter. "We interacted constantly. I was born in the Moon Craters huddle, but my mom was working in the Den when I was five or so. Koen and I learned to read at the same school."

"So what happened that made the core and the huddles reunite?"

"Outsiders tried to destroy us. The Northwest's strength comes from its unity."

I must have gotten too engrossed in the conversation, because Brenna frees herself. We both shoot to our feet, and then it's a flurry of hooks and push kicks. She tries to corner me, but I move laterally. I strike her with my elbow and aim at her knee, but she's no longer underestimating me, and that's a shame.

"Was it Humans?" I ask. "The threat, I mean."

"Isn't it always?" She tries an inside trip. I attempt a clinch. We both fail. "There's so fucking many of you, it's no surprise you're involved in *everything*."

I step back. Gain space. Reset the fight. I can feel the beginnings of bruises blooming under my skin. "How did Koen reunite the pack?"

"He cleaned up. Made promises. Took on and won countless challenges." She moves forward. Throws a body shot that I slow down with hits to her chest. "I lost my parents and my infant sister in the span of hours. Do you think I gave a shit about a breakup?" Her strikes become more forceful, and I can no longer parry them.

She dives in, shoulders against my abdomen, and forces me to the floor again.

"Fuck." I try to squirm away, but she's heavy on top of me.

"The worst part is . . ." We're both breathing heavily. Her blue eyes bore into mine as she tries to set up an armbar, this time on me. "I wouldn't have wished this on him."

"This?" I choke out.

"You."

My heart drops, even though there's no cattiness in the word. She's just sorry, I think. Sorry for Koen, for the way he's saddled with me, and I'm almost curious enough to ask her why. *Brenna, what specifically about me is not full-package material? Because we're positively besieged by choices here. Is it the fact that I'm a hybrid? That I don't know how to be a proper Were? That there's a bounty over my head? That I grew up with a Vampyre? That I'm unemployed?* A snort of a laugh hiccups out of me. Honestly, it's genuinely amusing, how poor a fit I am for the Alpha of this pack.

Brenna is less than entertained. "I don't want to be unfair. Your life has been hard. But I hope you will leave soon, Serena. I appreciate that you're trying to protect Lowe's sister, but I hope you'll know better than to stick around once this is over."

It would be so easy to snap back, if she was being deliberately rude. But she's obviously in pain. *And* too distracted to notice her slackening grip and the opening she's giving me. I rip my arm free, shift our positions, and swing my legs over her body. Putting pressure on the joint of her elbow, I watch her thrash for a few seconds.

It's there in her eyes, the moment she realizes that there's no way out.

"I'm not going to stick around," I puff out, winded. "I'll be out of your hair before you can swat me away. And you don't have to worry about Koen and me. We're not together. The mate thing has no bearing on our relationship. We're not secretly in love with each other. We're not even fucking."

"Oh, I know." Her smile is strained. "Believe me, we *all* know."

"Good. He explained the situation to you." I glance up and find him staring at us. At *me*. If he's angry that I won, he hides it well. There is a shadow of a smile around his eyes, at the edge of him, that resembles . . . pride.

I hope what he reads in my wide, smug grin is *Guess I'll be living on my own.*

And maybe he does. Because he nods, once, as if conceding that I'm right. I open my mouth to say something obnoxiously victorious—and that's when I realize that my celebration was premature.

With an explosive burst, Brenna lifts me off her. She breaks free and takes full advantage of my absolute shock to wrap an arm around my neck from the rear, and . . .

"He didn't need to explain any situation to anyone," she whispers in my ear. "There are *three* things I believe with utmost certainty. Death will come for all of us. No matter what, the sun will rise every morning. And Koen is never, *ever* going to touch you. Not even if you *beg* him for it on your knees."

She lets go of me so abruptly, I fall back against the mat, disoriented, dizzy, breathing in big gulps of air. When I open my eyes, Koen is staring down at me, mouth upturned in an unsurprised smile.

"For your sake, killer, you better not leave dirty dishes in the sink."

CHAPTER 12

Cute, how she thinks he'd ever let her out of his sight.

I LOST FAIR AND SQUARE, SO I FOLLOW KOEN OUT AND KEEP MY mouth shut, gingerly moving my bruised, achy body. Any half-decent guy would solicitously ask whether I'm okay, but that's clearly not him. He walks ahead, ignoring me, and when he comes to a sudden halt, I nearly bump into his back.

On the hood of his car there is a small parcel, carefully wrapped in brown paper. Someone wrote with a black Sharpie: *For the former Human.*

Instinctively, I round Koen to pick it up. A second later, I'm airborne: his arm is wrapped tight around my waist; my feet no longer touch the ground. His hand presses into my belly and pulls me closer to his chest. "Out of curiosity, do you have a death wish, or are you just being sewer-brained?"

I tug at his arm, with little success. I'm still suspended. "Oh, yes, the ultimate suicidal activity. Opening my own mail."

"Serena, that is not normal."

"Packages?"

"Packages for half-Human hybrids who are under my protection, and whose existence is under threat by multiple parties." He shifts forward, aiming his words at the shell of my ear. A shiver travels through my spine. "Since you appear to need reminding, if some sketchy-looking cumduck pulls up in a white van and asks you to help him rescue his puppy—"

"Okay, I get it." He inhales deeply against my back. It's like we share a single body. "Can you tell who dropped it off?"

He shakes his head. "They covered their scent."

"Hmm. Does Brenna have security cameras?"

"Yes. But I doubt they picked up anything, or she'd already know."

"Which means?"

"Just that the person who delivered the package knew where the blind zone was."

"Is that a short list?"

"No. The point of the cameras is to monitor outsiders, not pack members." Koen lets go of me and a new dance ensues, in which the package is reasonably ascertained not to contain explosives or biological hazards, then brought inside the car.

"Makes total sense," I say.

"Hmm?"

"That the Alpha with responsibility over thousands of pack members would take on this super-risky endeavor, while the random unemployed hybrid watches at a safe distance. My life is *totally* worth more than yours," I say sweetly.

He pretends to ponder the matter. "You're right. I should just off you myself and get it over with."

I bite back a smile and watch him slowly tear into the paper. There is a card inside, which has Koen's features tensing with worry.

The note, unsigned, simply says, *From your mother.*

Underneath there is a silver necklace: a moon scratched by four claw marks.

—✧—

"WASHER AND DRYER ARE DOWN THE HALL," KOEN TELLS ME BACK at his house. It's like we never left at all. "There's a bathroom in your bedroom."

There is. Unfortunately, it doesn't have a tub, which is a crucial part of my nighttime routine. Fortunately, I think I spot one in Koen's en suite as he hands me a stack of towels that feel softer than a seal's pelt. I bury my face in them and inhale deeply. Traces of soap and his skin fill my lungs, and I flush a little when his eyebrow lifts. "Um. Thank you."

The plot twist I did *not* expect, given the scantiness of the furnishings, is the piano. I stare, intrigued. It's mahogany. At once smooth and softened by time. Little scars. Faded spots. "Do you play?"

"No."

"Then why—"

"Family heirloom."

I guess that explains the way it's pushed against the wall in the far corner, almost hidden. I want to investigate, but Koen's tone doesn't encourage follow-up questions.

Back in the kitchen, he opens the fridge. It contains a single item: a purple box of something called "unicorn waffles."

My eyebrow arches.

"From when Ana was here," he mumbles, and I'm pleased to detect some sheepishness. No waft of cold air, though, because the fridge isn't even plugged into the power outlet.

"Guess I'm not the only one who doesn't know how electricity works," I murmur under my breath. Koen slams the door closed, hooks his finger under the base of my jaw, and forces me to look at him.

"Wanna say that again to my face?"

"Not particularly." I bat my eyes at him and don't bother to free myself. I'm resigned to staying here, and I must admit it: he smells nice. His touch feels nice. Being here is nice. Nice, nice, *nice*. My mind's spinning a little. "Are most Northwest members too badass to consume food? Do you only eat in wolf form?" That must be it. He can't very well bust out his grandma's silverware and fine dine with truffle risotto and densuke watermelon if 80 percent of the time he's got paws and carnassial teeth. "Poor squirrels, getting chased up the gutter."

"Squirrels have it coming. Smug little shits," he grumbles. He cocks his head and surveys me closely, as though something just occurred to him. He inches forward and forces me to take a step back until my spine meets the counter. "Close your eyes."

"What?"

He grasps my chin. "For once, do what I say and close your damn eyes."

I acquiesce, since he's now my Alpha *and* my landlord. Try not to shiver at his proximity. "What are you doing?"

"Same thing I do with unruly toddlers. Keep your eyes closed."

"I— Excuse me?"

"Take a deep breath. Another. Good. *Another*." His voice lowers to a rumble, not deeper than usual, but more resonant. Soothing and authoritative. It projects right inside my head, and listening to its bidding is like an itch that . . . I *could* help scratching, but why would I, when obeying feels so good? "Relax. I want you to think about the last time you were in wolf form."

Of course. If that's what Alpha wants.

"Don't imagine yourself as a wolf. Focus on the way it felt, being surrounded by the noises of the forest. The other creatures. The scent of the soil and the trees." His words are calm but feel as intense as a spear running through my abdomen. "Remember the last time?"

I'd gone on only four or five runs before my problems started, but they were . . . beautiful. Magic. Nature has its own, loving way of making sense to a wolf. Everything is *body*, immersive, physical. Easy. Sun drenched, rain soaked. A stride toward something meaningful. Reaching. Forward. Reaching, reaching, *reaching* even as everything slides out of—

"Stop," Koen orders. His hand slips to my cheek. A gentle, soothing stroke. "It's okay, Serena. You're okay."

Reluctantly, I open my eyes, somehow shocked to be standing in Koen's kitchen. "What happened?"

My cheeks feel sunburnt. My shirt and my hair are soaked in sweat—so much so, the white fabric plasters to my breasts and my pebbled nipples. It's wet T-shirt contest material. Spring break. Filthy.

Koen is staring, too.

I clear my throat. Cross my arms over my chest. "What just happened?"

"Not much." His voice is rough edged. He swallows. It takes him a bit of time and a lot of effort to lift his eyes to mine. "Sometimes, when the block is mental, it can help. Being guided."

"You mean, being commanded by an Alpha? It didn't work, though. What does that say?"

"That there are other reasons at play." He wets his lips. Takes a step back and then inhales deeply. Like the air around me is toxic, and he needs a break. "It was worth a try."

"Why do I look like I just spent twelve hours in labor?"

"Because your body was trying to shift. Which is a strenuous and energy-intensive activity."

"I didn't, though."

"Your cells still worked for it."

I push back my damp, lanky hair. "Maybe I won't be able to do it again. Shifting, I mean." Even if Dr. Henshaw said that people with CSD usually can shift almost till the end. How fun, to be the exception to the rule.

"Then you won't." He shrugs. The ropes of muscles in his shoulders seem to say, *I couldn't care less.* "As long as I know what I'm working with, I can keep you alive."

I nod. My head is starting to pound. "I just want you to know, I really am grateful about the fact that—"

"Serena," he grunts. "What did we agree on?"

My mind is blank for a moment. "Oh, right. No gratitude. My bad. Wait—can I say 'my bad'?" I produce my most angelic smile. "Are apologies okay?"

He sighs. "Just go to bed, killer. You're going to have a long and unpleasant day tomorrow."

"Am I?"

"Yup. It's hybrid parade time."

"Please, tell me it's not what it sounds like."

He folds his arms. "It's *exactly* it. You want to lure the Vampyres to you, we'll have to make sure they see you with me. Which means that I'll have to show you off a little."

"How, though? There are no Vampyres walking around the Den."

"They gather information in other ways. Vampyres and Humans fly drones over our territory all the time."

"And you let them?"

"Yup. It's how we manipulate them into thinking that they know more than they do. It's highly offensive, how inept they think we are, but since it's to our advantage, I'll give it a pass." His smile doesn't reach his eyes. "They probably already suspect you're with me. We just want to give them proof."

"Why would they suspect it?"

His stare is level. "Because *with me* is where I would keep my mate."

I lower my eyes. He's right. So right, I change the topic. "About the necklace . . ."

"I told you." His voice hardens. "It's probably just some ten-year-old trying to impress his friends with some dumb prank."

"Still—"

"Still, I'll investigate the package and the note and then return it to you."

"Are you . . . Do you think there's any way that my mother could really . . . ?"

A knock at the door stops me. Jorma peeks inside. He nods politely at me, then says, "I have been calling you, Alpha."

"Must have missed it."

"Actually, you hung up on me. Twice. As soon as I mentioned the paperwork for the killed Vampyre."

A deep, irritated growl rises. From Koen's chest, I believe.

"I can help," I offer. "I kinda like paperwork."

"Go to bed, Serena."

"But—"

"Now."

He glares at me like there's little he wants more than having me out of his sight—a less than auspicious start to our cohabitation. I sigh, wave goodbye to Jorma, and stalk off like I really am an unruly toddler.

———◦ ❖ ◦———

MY NIGHT IS DELIGHTFULLY DULL, IN THAT IT INVOLVES LOTS OF sleeping and no puking. True to his word, Koen skulks outside the cabin in wolf form. My eyes catch his through the window when I sneak into his room to steal more pillows.

And his duvet.

They keep me warm. Smell good. Are soft. With a few additions, my bed feels like sinking into a hug, and I have no regrets.

When I get up in the morning, he's already awake. I spot him sitting on the porch, bare chested, like he just shifted back to human form and only pulled up a pair of sweats to spare my delicate sensibilities. Since I'm not allowed to verbally express gratitude, I decide to repay his hospitality by scrounging around his cupboards to make coffee. When I bring him a mug, I realize that he's not alone.

"Oh." I blink at the wolf curled on the porch, right at Koen's feet. "Hi." His scent tells me that he's male, fully grown. Healthy. I wonder if I should introduce myself and . . . I don't know, hold out my hand to shake his paw. Then, upon a closer look, I notice his size, the shaggy gray fur, the bushy, hanging tail, and it dawns on me. "Hang on. You're not a Were. You're just a . . . wolf."

Koen huffs a gravelly morning laugh. "Not even."

"What do you mean?"

"He's half dog."

"Wait, really? Can I . . ." But yes. I can. The wolf dog eyes me, eager to make my acquaintance. I set the mug aside and let him sniff my hand first, then butt against it. My fingers comb through his thick fur, and the loll of his tongue as I scratch around his ears feels like pure joy.

"You are *so* handsome." I laugh when his tongue slobbers against my cheek. Let him do it again. "Yes. I'm a hybrid, too. Let's be best friends. Who are you?"

"He hangs out around these parts," Koen says, amused. "From time to time."

"What's his name?"

"He's a wild animal."

"I know. But what's his name."

Koen's brow furrows. "He doesn't have one."

"What? Why?"

"What does he need a name for?"

"I don't know. For when you talk about him?"

"With whom?"

"The vet? The store clerk, when you buy his kibble?" Koen looks like I just suggested that we take the river otters and put them up at a five-star hotel. "Okay, clearly you don't do that. But—" Abruptly, the wolf dog tenses and gallops away. "Don't leave. Did we offend you?" I pout—until I spot the squirrel he's chasing.

"Those fuckers," Koen mutters, clearly empathizing. He turns to me. Scans my face, then my body under the flannel I stole from his closet to sleep in. "You look better," he declares. "Less like you're going to collapse and start fertilizing the meadow."

Hard to believe, after I caught sight of my reflection in the mirror this morning—something I've been studiously avoiding. "You're just saying that to be kind."

"If I've given you the impression that I'm *kind*, something is very wrong, either with me or with you. Ready to make your debut in Northwest society?"

"Almost."

"Almost?" He's amused. "What important business do you have on your plate, killer?"

I pretend to think about it. Then, still cross-legged next to his chair, I lift my two closed fists and ask, "Which one?"

He sits back. "There's nothing in your hands, Serena."

"Doesn't matter. It's all in my head. Choose."

"What the hell is this, now?" He sounds fed up. A little pained.

"It's a game Misery and I used to play growing up. We couldn't exactly go out shopping and buy presents most of the time, so when we wanted to do something nice for each other . . ." I show him my fists. "Choose one."

He points at my right. Which is for the best. "You get coffee," I tell him, holding out the mug.

"Hang on. What would I have gotten if I'd chosen the other?"

"A hug."

His eyes widen. Then squint. "What if I want to change my answer?"

"First of all, we both know you don't." I nudge the mug up at him until he has no choice but to accept it. "Secondly, you can't. This is like when Misery decided that she wanted me to clean her room instead of giving her a kiss on the cheek."

Koen frowns. "I want a kiss on the cheek."

"You can't change your mind after you pick—that's the whole point of the game. And the kiss wasn't even an option for you."

"Bullshit. I want *both* options."

"No way." I snort. "That's not how the world works—you can't have your cake and eat it, too. When you make a choice, you miss out on what you didn't pick. There's always a price to pay. In real life, and in the game."

"It's a dumb fucking game, then." He looks at his coffee like it's made of decaying organs. "How do I know that you didn't switch the prizes?"

I gasp. "How *dare* you accuse me?"

"You are an infamous and self-admitted liar."

"But I would *never* violate the sacrosanctity of the game." I rise to my feet as haughtily as I can. "Enjoy your coffee while I get dressed."

It's not until I'm in my room that I remember: I do not own a single stitch of clothing.

CHAPTER 13

Look at her. Just—look at her.

ONCE AGAIN, I SHOW A SHAMEFUL LACK OF RESTRAINT AT THE way the coast unfolds before my eyes. I take in the rugged shorelines, gasp dramatically, and say "Oh my God" about fifteen times, pressing my forehead to the cool glass of the passenger window to get a better view. Everywhere my eyes land is blue and green, dense and jagged, beachy, woodsy. When Koen catches me craning my neck backward to study a sea stack, the car slows down for me to admire the view.

Or maybe there's a speed limit, who knows?

This place is so peaceful. So mysterious and nostalgic. The vegetation is not unlike the forest around my old cabin, but that was inland. The ocean makes it even more breathtaking. In my previous life I longed to travel, but that required money, and I tended to use what little I had on other luxuries. Eating, for instance. Not sleeping on park benches. Paying taxes that financed my very own surveillance. How very full circle of me.

"This is the most beautiful place I've ever seen," I declare, and

Koen's self-congratulatory smile has me shaking my head with laughter. "You know you have no reason to look so smug, right? It's not *your* coast."

"It is my territory."

"Sure, but it's not like you built that offshore rock formation over there."

"As far as you know. And you might want to stop contradicting me in the heart of my region, where my every word is law."

"All I'm saying is, you *can't* take credit for it."

He gives me a flat look. "I *can* tie you to an anvil and throw you from that cliff, though. And no one will ever know."

I chuckle, wondering how many of these threats he follows through with. "It's not the huge compliment you're making it out to be." I lean into the back seat to pilfer Koen's zip-up hoodie. He doesn't need it, because he has furnace genes. I'll repossess it. Use it as a blanket. "I've only ever been in the Southwest. We're working out of a pool of two."

"At least you like mine better than Lowe's."

"We're still talking about the landscapes, right?"

"Yeah. Sure."

I laugh again, and we roll into a place that looks like the quaint seaside towns I sometimes see in movies, the ones where fiscally conservative people go for weekends of antiquing, dinner parties, and discreet cheating on their spouses. "Where are we?"

"A bit outside the Den. A friend of mine owns a store here."

"Look at you guys. Having stores."

He pulls the hand brake. "And indoor plumbing. And statistics."

"And sarcasm?"

"You catch up quickly. Come on."

There's a decent amount of foot traffic: shoppers, children playing on swings, and, of course, several Weres in wolf form. They lounge under trees, perch on branches, lie next to the statue of a book in front of a local library. They acknowledge their Alpha and then study me with a sleepy, lazy sort of curiosity.

"Hi." I wave my hand in the direction of a group huddling in a nearby pocket park. They blink in response. I instinctively recognize it as a friendly greeting.

I guess standing next to their Alpha goes a long way.

"Should I go introduce myself?" I whisper at Koen. "Is that part of the hybrid parade?"

He snorts. His palm finds the middle of my back and pushes me toward a sidewalk.

"Wouldn't it be the polite thing to do?" I truly don't know. When I was with the Southwest, I didn't exactly socialize. I holed myself up in Misery's house, let Ana braid and unbraid my hair upwards of forty times a day, and retreated into my room whenever someone new would visit.

"Killer, you're proof of concept that Humans and Weres can fuck—*fruitfully* so. Not only are you the most recognizable face on the continent, but there'll be a photo of you in every time capsule shot into space for the coming century. You're good without introductions for the next couple of years." He opens a door and signals for me to go ahead. "Come on. Let's get you some clothes."

I do need them, considering the rate at which I'm stealing his. But. "Do you know how I can access my bank?"

His hand slides up, between my shoulder blades, and guides me inside. He doesn't reply.

"I do have some money," I insist.

"You do? No need to flex, Serena."

"I mean, I just need to—"

"This conversation is very tedious." He sounds distracted as he glances around.

"Well, prepare to be tedioused even more. You're not going to pay for my stuff. It's infantilizing."

His dark eyes travel down my body. *Slowly.* "As if I could ever do *that*," he drawls.

My cheeks burst into flames. The rest of me, too. His gaze doesn't let go of me. I'm about to blurt out something supremely stupid, when: "Koen, you're early! A first."

Our heads whip around as the most elegant man to ever walk this wretched globe emerges from the back. I admire his wing tips, the perfect tan of his skin, the bounce of his gravity-defying tawny forelock. I used to be handy with a can of hair spray, back when I had a job that required personal hygiene, but boy, do I have a lot to learn from this dude.

The two men exchange one of those almost-hug handshakes. "Serena, this is Carter. Carter, Serena, who we won't bother pretending requires introductions, needs something to wear that fits her."

"Does she?" He gives me the once-over. Purses his chiseled mouth. "She seems to like your flannel."

Koen's grunt is unintelligible. I attempt a smile, but it comes out tense—which he notices. "You're not afraid, are you."

It's not really a question, and I decide to be truthful. "Just intimidated by how sophisticated Carter looks." It doesn't help that my pants are Koen's sweats rolled up about five times, giving me an exquisite *toddler wearing life buoy at the pool* je ne sais quoi.

"You can handle it," Koen says. His hand slides under the collar of my flannel, between the layers of fabric that rest on my neck. All heat, no skin-to-skin contact. He squeezes me with something that could be reassurance, or a threat of strangulation. "Since you've had so much exposure to my good looks."

Carter and I burst out laughing, then stop when we notice Koen's narrow-eyed stare.

"Absolutely," Carter says, recovering faster. "It's a valid narrative choice. The scruff, I mean." He scans Koen like he's a vision board. "The story I'm picking up is that you are resourceful enough to survive forty days and forty nights in the desert by sucking the moisture out of a prickly pear. If it isn't what you're going for—*only* if it isn't, may I recommend a haircut and a shave?"

"Don't criticize my looks. It hurts my feelings."

"Your what?" I ask.

Koen gives me a deadpan look.

"We just want what's best for you," I explain.

Carter nods. "And what's best for *us*. The Alpha is the face of the pack. And right now, we're looking pretty . . ."

"Disheveled," I finish.

"We are wolves," Koen retorts. "We eat our prey alive. We shove our noses up each other's junk. We roll in shit to mask our scents."

"Point taken," Carter concedes. "Although some would argue that no wolf has ever stooped so low as to walk around with an unkempt and obviously unpremeditated topknot—"

"Carter," Koen growls. "Get Serena something to put on right now, or I'll topknot your intestines."

"On it, Alpha." Carter bends his head, once, deep, and escorts me to the back of the store. "Koen said you need a bit of everything?"

It's not quite true, since I have no plans to venture away from the cabin or to interact with anyone who'd judge me for spending my life in a bathrobe. "I don't foresee many cocktail parties in my near future, and I don't know that this is the best time for me to take up scuba diving. Just the basics?"

"Perfect."

So, jeans. Sweats. Thermal shirts, sweaters, a heavy jacket. Carter's store is great, and I don't want to impose any more than I already am, so I agree to whatever he has me trying on, even though my skin has been very sensitive for weeks, and the denim and wool scrape against it like emery boards. The texture of fleece makes me wish there were enough traffic for me to walk into. *A normal evolution of your condition,* said Dr. Henshaw. *Make sure you dress to minimize your sensory issues.*

I used to be fastidious about my appearance. I spent a huge chunk of my first few paychecks on building a wardrobe, and I miss it—the professional grays and beiges, blue hues, strategic little splashes of color. My power blouses, Misery called them. Power slacks, power blazers, power turtlenecks. That's exactly what they were: me, asserting the little power I had scrounged for myself. After years of hand-me-downs and uniforms that never fit my ever-changing teenage body, I used to take a lot of pride in looking the way *I* chose. Learning how to dress, how to style my hair, how to do makeup felt like a radical act of agency. Joyful and *fun*. Liberating. Finding myself.

But the sallow, emaciated girl blinking at me in the changing room mirror is no one at all. Her dark hair hangs limply from a middle part, far too long. Her collarbones are sharper than knives. Her identity has been peeled off layer by layer.

"Everything okay?" Carter asks from beyond the curtain. "Does the jacket look nice?"

It looks like shit, because *I* look like shit. I guess I saw myself as the kind of person who'd hold on to her dignity in the face of great hardship. Apparently, I'm just a damn slob—and the thought has me snorting out laughter. "Great. Love it!"

The process takes about twenty minutes. Koen stays out of the way, leaning back against the glass door like the world's most obstructing bouncer, never taking his eyes off us. He answers his phone a couple of times, has a few low-pitched conversations that could probably be marketed as "highly soothing white noise" and sold for eye-watering profit. I smile at him whenever our eyes meet.

He doesn't respond.

"Koen," Carter calls, tossing a plastic package at him. "Will you grab some more of this for her?" It's underwear. Koen Alexander is choosing *and* paying for my panties. The situation is so ludicrous, I can't quite bite back a hysterical chuckle.

Before we walk out with half a dozen bags, Carter whispers in my ear to please "do something about the facial hair situation," and Koen flips him off without bothering to turn around. In the car, though, I realize that we didn't stop at the register. "Hang on. Are you guys some kind of currency-less postcapitalist utopia?"

Koen blinks. "What?"

"You didn't pay. Is it some kind of Alpha feudal right?"

His eyebrow lifts. "You think they don't know where to send their bills?"

The next stop is the department store, where Weres obtain their food when they're not in the mood for marmot kebabs. "Must be where the Northwest purchases unicorn waffles," I muse, which earns me an ear flick.

This place is much more crowded. Most of the Weres in the parking area are in human form, getting out of cars with their families or loading groceries into their trunks. A couple walks by the edge of the lot, holding hands, fully naked despite the chilly breeze, and disappears past the trees.

"We'll get you food. And other shit you need."

"Such as?"

"If you think I'm going to giggle while saying feminine hygiene products, you don't know about the number of young Were couples I've caught in compromising positions and subjected to the sex talk."

I laugh. "No offense, but . . . there has to be someone better suited to that."

"Fuck off," he says mildly. "I'm great at explaining the dangers of parasitic STIs and the importance of mutual consent."

Why can I picture that so well? "Shouldn't you guys hire a professional?"

"There is one. Now. Back then, we didn't have lots of people with degrees."

"Yeah?" I look up at him. From this angle, I can't see his eyes very well. "What changed? Did you get scholarship programs or something?"

He huffs, amused. "We just grew up, Serena."

It's a bit of an odd thing to say, and I want to dig deeper, but more Weres turn toward us. They wave at Koen. Smile at me. A small group introduce themselves, the warmth of their welcome undeniable. "I thought they'd hate me," I say as we walk through the sliding doors.

"Why?"

"I don't know. Because I'm a freak? Because I'm putting the entire territory in danger? Because I'm taking up their Alpha's time? Pick your poison."

"Most people really do see you as a symbol of unity." He fetches a cart. "And the ones who don't know better than to say anything about it." I remember the necklace. Koen's near certainty that it was just a prank. Maybe it's the only way for pack members to protest my presence?

"The Southwest has been pretty shitty to Misery. Still is."

"Vampyres are more controversial than Humans, and the Southwest is a hotbed for conflict—three species practically living on top of each other? Fuck, no. Plus, Lowe's only been in charge for a couple of years and inherited a pack from a neurotic nutjob whose decades-long power structure was built on fearmongering and misleading information. It'll take him a lot of work to undo that."

"What about you? Was your previous Alpha a nutjob?"

His jaw shifts, as though he's biting the inside of his cheeks. He eyes some fruit, pensive. "Our former Alpha made mistakes, but none came from a place of malice, like Roscoe's. We've had issues with some of the neighboring Human settlements, but we also owe them. That part of our history speaks too loudly to be ignored."

"Well, that's certainly very convenient for us half Humans."

He picks up a bag of oranges. Takes a step toward me. "We live to serve." For a moment I think he'll— Is he going to *hug* me? But no. He's just dropping the fruit in the cart. "Why's your heart beating like that, killer?"

My stomach flips. I'm about to blurt out an excuse, but a young woman interrupts us. "Alpha? Do you have a moment?" She's holding the hand of a boy of eight or so, who stares at me open-mouthed. When I wave at him, he hesitantly waves back, somewhere between starstruck and petrified. Maybe I should offer him an autograph. Capitalize on this new fame while I still can. Sell jerseys. Run for office. Sign partnership deals.

It's nightmare fuel.

The rest of the shopping trip is marvelous. It's my first time walking around in public since before my abduction, and I can almost make-believe that my life hasn't changed in every way. I could be Serena Paris, journalist for *The Herald*. This could be the store closest to my apartment. The brands are different, the junk food selection is *appallingly* limited, and I cannot help giggling at the size of the fur-care section. But overall, there is something delicious about discovering that Weres like goldfish crackers, too—except theirs are shaped after the phases of the moon.

The box says *Lunar Bites*, and I text Misery a picture. *But are they peanut butter?* is her response.

I buy ingredients for a few of the dishes I enjoy cooking, more out of habit than hunger. A couple of people introduce themselves and shake my hand—nice, if unpleasant. I read the back of a bone-health supplement jar. Study the herbal teas. Feel the texture of every single blanket they have for sale. Pick up a candle. Smell it—lavender, vetiver, a hint of vanilla. Decide that I love the scent and inhale it again. Put it back on the shelf. Investigate pillows I don't need, find the softest, and rub my face against it.

It's so mundane and wonderful and cozy, the banality of the supply chain. The quiet thrill of BOGO sales. The rack of sparkly unicorn ears that Ana would totally squeal at. Koen follows a few steps behind. I think he wants to be discreet, give me space, but I don't need much in terms of feminine hygiene products, because I've never had a period. I'm okay with using his shampoo—he smells really, *really* good—and he already gave me a spare toothbrush. Moisturizer feels like a hassle. I used to be a sunscreen evangelist, and truly believe everybody should use it, but people like me (i.e., those who won't live long enough to develop melanoma) are exempt.

"It was nice," I tell Koen in the car.

"Grocery shopping?"

I nod, unsure how to explain that I haven't felt this normal and grounded in forever.

"If this is a beloved pastime of yours, you may continue doing my grocery shopping. At no cost to you."

"Cool. I'll be in charge of buying your—"

"Unicorn waffles. Look at you, holding on to jokes like your life depends on it."

It's what I've got, I think. I lean back against the headrest, roll my chin up to look at him. "Thank you for—" I immediately start laughing when he begins to protest.

"I told you to—"

"Come on."

"—just dust the goddamn fixtures—"

"Listen, just . . ." I rub my eyes. He immediately falls quiet. "Do you think the Vampyres know I'm here by now?"

"I'm certain."

I tilt my head. "Are you ever not?"

"Not what?"

"Certain. Are you ever insecure?"

"Not really, no."

"Is it an Alpha thing?"

He shrugs. *No.* I think it means *It's a me thing. You're welcome.* The conversation pulls a little laugh out of my mouth, even though it never even happened. What a florid internal life I have.

"Well," I say, "here's hoping that it'll rub off."

He shakes his head and reaches out to me. His rough, warm fingers push a few strands of hair behind my ears, and heat glows in my belly. Up my spine. Zaps at my brain, like a lightbulb turning on.

It's an odd thing for Koen to do. It surprises him as much as it does me, I think, but he doesn't pull back. It's like the rest of the world has taken a break from existing. It's just us.

"Actually," I whisper. "I had an idea. To show the gratitude I cannot verbalize."

"We already discussed it." His voice is a low murmur, too. "Dusting."

"The problem is, you do not own a duster. You barely own fixtures."

"I'll buy more useless shit. To keep you busy."

"No, I was thinking, what about . . ." It's my turn to reach out, and he's obviously not used to this—to people, to *me*, initiating physical contact. Guess that's what happens when you're the predator at the apex. Not a lot of spontaneity and liberties taken.

But he doesn't jerk back when I tug at a wisp of hair brushing against his neck. "What if I fix this mess? Give you a makeover."

"A what, now?"

"You know. The *issue* we discussed with Carter. The one where you look like a medieval peasant who's about to die of the whooping cough. I'm a pro." I might be coming undone. Or maybe some very dumb spirit has possessed me, because I let my wrist drag against the skin at the base of his throat, as if to . . . as if to rub off on him? *More*, my instinct screams at me. *More. Make him smell like you.* But Koen's breathing speeds up, and he twists his head away after shuddering in something that could very well be revulsion. I force my arm to retreat. Clear my throat. "At the very least, I'm a *very* experienced amateur. Misery had a mullet phase."

"Uh-huh." He sounds raspy. "Was that before or after she scrambled your brain?"

"During, probably." When did he start the car? It's hard to think in here. My brain feels fuzzy. "Anyway, I can do you, too."

He winces. Runs a hand down his face. "Do you even fucking hear yourself?"

"And I can shave you! I mean, I used to shave my legs, back when I made an effort to look presentable. *All the time.* Well, not *all* the time, just before dates, but I've never nicked an artery. That I know of."

"Reassuring," he grumbles, putting down the window. Fresh air blows inside the car, and we both take deep breaths. I feel instantly more clearheaded.

"Please. Let me make you pretty."

"I'm already pretty. I'm fucking *stupendous*."

I sigh. "Oh, if only you could use suppositories to—"

"To cure my malignant narcissism?"

How does he *always* know? "Listen—I just want to make you presentable. You said that you don't have time to go get a haircut, but I'm already in your house, and you're my live-in nanny. Think of the *ease*."

"Has anyone told you that you're kind of a nuisance, killer?"

"A guy. Once or ten times." I grin. "But I could be so much worse."

"I'll take it as a threat." The car stops. Somehow, we're back at his cabin. *Excellent awareness of your surroundings, Serena.* "I have to go meet someone," he tells me, taking the bags inside. The only thing left for me to carry is Ana's unicorn headband, which is already shedding glitter around Koen's trichromatic home.

"Who?"

"A friend. It's about your necklace."

"Ah. Have you discovered who dropped it off?"

"I have not, which is a problem in and of itself."

"So it's not . . . The mother thing . . . ?"

He sighs. "I don't know yet. I'll be back in a few hours. If anything weird happens, *anything*, call my phone. And yell. Amanda is watching the northeast, and Colin the southwest."

"What about attacks from above?" I tease. There are no chairs in the kitchen, so I try to lift myself onto the counter, but it's too tall. "No werestork second on air patrol?"

"If a bald eagle dove in from the sky to abduct you, my life would be so much easier." His hands close around my waist. Lift me up like I'm a feather. "And fine—I'll get more goddamn furniture." He lingers for a fraction of a second, his nose hovering by my temple, and I hear a deep inhale. A slower exhale. A gust of warmth against my heated skin. My forehead wants, demands, clamors to lean forward and kiss Koen's collarbone. I manage to hold it back long enough for him to step away, and for the possibility to be removed.

Safer this way.

Remember? How he said that he didn't care about you? When he called you a spoiled little girl? It was less than twenty-four hours ago. He's not nice.

"I'll get everything ready, then," I yell after him as he saunters off. "For our little spa session." He flips me off without glancing back. And it's not until later, when I'm unpacking the bags and going through what we bought, that I find three important things.

The first makes me blush and roll my eyes and wish that I had a shovel to bury myself in Koen's garden: every single pair of underwear he selected for me is red. Bright red. Dull red. Wine red. Blood red.

All.

Kinds.

Of.

Red.

I'm not equipped to process it, so I focus on the *second*, which makes me smile. At first, I think he may have replaced the plushie I mentioned. Then I realize that the little pink penguin in the bag is hard, made of plastic. A few seconds of fiddling with it tells me that it's a pocketknife with a foldable blade.

It's cute—and thoughtful, especially considering that I no longer have claws at my disposal. It has a different, deeper kind of heat spreading through me, and I don't want to overthink it, so I shift my attention to the *third* thing.

And I stop breathing.

Because every single thing I glanced at, grazed, examined, eyed, or even *considered* when we were at the grocery store, every single thing I decided to walk past, every single thing I told myself I didn't need—every single thing has somehow made it here, inside Koen's house.

CHAPTER 14

He overhears her talking with Pavel.
"Hey, is it true that Humans put gnomes in their gardens?"
"Oh, yeah. It's totally a thing."
"Spine-chilling."
Her laughter adjusts the spin of his atoms.

THEY START ARRIVING IN THE LATE AFTERNOON.
I spend several hours cross-legged on the couch, trying to reconstruct my lost letters, until the door bursts open. Two men walk inside like they were just handed the deed to the place. They're both tall, both well muscled, and both completely naked.

"Oh, Serena. What's up?" the first says.

The second just grins, waves at me, and bends over to stretch his hamstrings, giving me a thorough view of his butthole. "I slept wrong last night," he moans. "Everything hurts."

"Is that why you were so slow?"

"Fuck off. At least *I* have an excuse."

I blink, wondering if this is a new symptom of CSD: vivid dreams of naked men bickering in Koen's living room. That's when an ash-colored wolf with thick fur and green eyes trots inside, comes to stand between me and the two men, and growls in their direction. In a quick symphony of bones cracking, keratin shrinking, and muscles unfolding, it transforms into a familiar shape.

Amanda.

Naked, of course. And pissed. "You guys are way early, and Koen doesn't want anyone he hasn't preapproved alone with Serena."

"Oh. We did not . . ." The men exchange looks of sheer terror. "Sorry about this. We're going to . . ." One points at the door.

"No, please. Stay." I quickly hide my writing in the pages of a book and rise to my feet. "You are . . . ?"

Amanda sighs and points at the one with freckles and a spiky red mullet. "Colin." She switches to the barrel-chested guy who clearly skips leg day. "Pavel."

"Nice to meet you," I say, relieved by the lack of handshakes. "No, really. I'm glad you came over. I'm even getting used to your junk just . . . dangling there."

Colin cocks his head. "Is it not supposed to?"

"Maybe Human genitals are usually retracted?" Pavel suggests.

"Ah, yes. In those cloacal openings." Colin nods knowingly. "Like koalas and alligators."

"Precisely. Now that I think about it, I remember reading somewhere that Humans shit and piss from the same ho—"

"Guys," Amanda snaps. "Do you want Koen to come back and find you here?"

They pale. Colin clears his throat. "Actually, we're pretty hungry. We'll go hunt some dinner and be back later—"

"I can fix you something," I offer. A vein starts pulsating on Amanda's forehead, so I hasten to add, "I wasn't doing anything, anyway. And, Amanda, you're here and you're preapproved. Koen won't mind."

In fact, Koen's behavior is less predictable than a stock market crash. But a little over an hour later, when he returns to find Amanda and five more of his now-clothed seconds eating meatballs, salad, and freshly baked bread, no one ends up impaled on his claws. They all scramble to their feet to salute as he comes in, like he's the strictest teacher at the boarding school, but return to their meal and conversation quickly enough.

"Do you always have guests sitting on the floor?" I ask him when he walks up to me, handing him a bowl of scraps. "And could you take this out? For Twinkles."

"For who, now?"

"The wolf dog I met this morning. I sent Ana a picture and she picked a name for him."

Koen crosses his arms, refusing the bowl. "What about a feral mutt covered in mud screamed Twinkles to her?"

"I believe she decided that he's Sparkles's long-lost brother, and she's committed to the theme. Elle, since Koen won't, will you put this on the porch?" I smile at the girl, who looks like a very badass kindergarten teacher. "Thank you so much."

"Did you *cook* for my seconds?" Koen sounds less than enthused.

"Yeah. Isn't that why you brought me here? To keep your home?" His face has me snorting out a laugh.

"I tried to stop her," Amanda says, joining us. "But I couldn't."

Koen glares at her. "You were unable to physically prevent a hybrid half your size from producing a vat of homemade marinara sauce."

"Well, the thing is . . . she's kind of a good cook."

"Aw, thank you. Want another helping?"

"Yes, please."

"It's on the stove."

"Nice. By the way, boss, what did the Humans say? Anything useful?"

Koen shakes his head as Amanda disappears past him with a soft "Bummer." He and I are left alone in the middle of the crowded room, and I go back to chopping veggies for my stir-fry.

"Serena."

"Hmm?"

"What the fuck are you doing?"

"It's this chicken dish that—"

"Why?"

"You're the one who invited over some of your seconds so I could meet them—without warning me beforehand, by the way. Thank God for Amanda."

"I invited them because I wanted you to know who these twat-waffles are in case you need something from them—not to play house and *entertain* them."

"But they were hungry. And I love to cook. And I never get to do it for anyone." It's always been a bit of a pipe dream of mine. Showing off my culinary chops. Feeding others. I enjoyed food a lot, *before*, and became good at preparing it, but never got to do much with those skills.

In my ideal, remarkably unremarkable future that will never be, I'd go to a job I love, come home, make dinner for someone whose face was in my head and heart all day long, and spend the rest of the night watching boring TV shows with them. Of course it'll never happen, and it sounds so basic, I'm almost sure that if I had a chance to play in that particular sandbox, I'd grow bored of it in two weeks.

But maybe I wouldn't? Mundane things can feel *so exotic* when your entire life has been one plot twist after another.

"Really, I don't mind. Would you like a plate of—"

"No," he barks. But more people are trickling in, and he's too busy telling them that "Serena doesn't want to see your sad, wrinkly scrotum, and neither do I, so stop being a turd and put on some goddamn clothes" to spend time in the kitchen.

"It's a Human thing," Colin explains to every newcomer. "They have cloacas."

I smile and work on my fruit salad.

"Koen has *a lot* of seconds," I tell Jorma half an hour later, on the porch. There are over twenty people milling around, and someone explained to me several live too far away to show up.

"Not everyone here is a second. Some brought their relatives. That girl over there? Elle's partner. And that's Brenna's brother. The woman and the twin toddlers? Pavel's family."

"Disappointing."

"Why?"

"Was hoping the babies would be involved in pack leadership."

Jorma looks at me like the concept of humor slashed his tires and shat in his rose bed, but it's pleasant, being with a group with this level of camaraderie. There's obvious affection going around, the kind that reminds me of my relationship with Misery: people who grew up together and went through shit. It's etched in their omnipresent scars, the lines on their foreheads, the crinkles at the sides of their eyes when they smile.

There's always someone around Koen. He trusts me enough to not be my shadow, but every few minutes I feel his inquisitive, lingering looks. *Everything okay?* I reassure him with a nod, but I still struggle with streams of information too intense to filter quickly, and slip to the back of the house for a breather.

". . . is he doing?" I overhear someone asking, and immediately stop in my tracks. The sun has set, and a gentle sea breeze rustles through the trees.

"Same old." It's Saul's voice.

"Highly doubt it."

"Oh, yeah, he is so fucking . . ." Laughter. "Gone. She killed him, and now she's haunting him. But he's not going to admit it. Or make it her problem."

"Does she know?"

"Never will. So . . . same old."

"That's rough. And the Favored shit?"

"We've been looking into it. It's not too unlikely."

"I thought we kept track of . . ."

"Well, yeah. But we were busy."

"Right. I remember."

"You were *eight*." Laughter. "There are missing pieces. But he won't tell her unless he's sure. Maybe not even then."

A ring clinks against a beer bottle. "If it was me, I'd rather not know."

"Yeah. No one deserves that. What about you? How's stuff up north?"

"Not bad. Did I tell you about the mountain goats incident?"

The wind picks up, and I take advantage of the sudden rise in noise to sneak back inside.

My thoughts bubble. Is it unhinged and self-centered to assume that Saul was talking about me and Koen? I'm debating the matter, but a gaggle intercepts me, and I end up having a really nice conversation about cross-species exchange-traded funds with Carl, a lovely hipsterish guy who clearly regrets making my acquaintance the second I step away for a glass of water.

"Are you insane?" I overhear Elle asking him. "Hitting on Koen's mate?"

ALI HAZELWOOD

"Dude, no. We were just talking."

"Just remember to tell Koen that while he's hanging you with your own large intestine," someone else suggests.

"Shut the hell up. He would never."

"No—he *has* never. Because no one has ever hit on his mate before."

I shake my head and rinse a few glasses, once again combing through what Saul said. When I turn around, I find . . . Boden, I think, is his name. Brenna's brother, though they don't look much alike.

"Clean cups are on that rack," I say with a smile.

"You have no right to be here."

I blink. "Okay. Clean cups are still on that rack." I lean back against the edge of the sink, studying the boy. He's tall. My age or younger. Not movie star handsome, but could snatch a TV role. He's also highly . . . *dominant*, I believe is the word, and the awareness sits in the marrow of my bones. Not as much as Koen or Amanda, though, not yet. Whatever juice they use to baste future Alphas, he's going to need a few more passes.

Still, it's clear that he feels like he has something of value to say. I fold my arms and wait for it, and he doesn't disappoint.

"You're a half Human who grew up with a Vampyre."

"Misery Lark." I nod. "She's my sister."

"She's a leech."

"True. And therefore, not the slam dunk insult you believe it to be. But if you have more biographical facts about Misery you want to get off your chest, by all means."

"I think that people with your allegiances have no place in the Northwest," he says slowly.

His demeanor is calm, but I can tell that he's furious. And in pain. And very unwilling to really listen to me. There is no point in engaging in this conversation, and I wish I could be more like Misery—take provocations as pathetic attempts at riling me up, shrug them all off, never be upset. The problem is, I've maxed out the amount of shit I'm willing to take. "Well, *I* think that people who grew up with the privilege of moral grandstanding could give some of us a little more credit."

"It's basic decency. Not moral grandstanding."

"Yes. It is." I push away from the counter and step toward him. "Good and evil are wide brushes that can't always paint the fine details of real life. Lots of Vampyres and Humans *and Weres* have done terrible things, but Misery is not one of them. And, as I'm sure you know, my presence here has been approved by your Alpha, so if you have a note for the complaint box, you may take it to him. I did not ask to be born a hybrid, and I'm not some little princess on vacation from her blessed life of leisure, so you can take your snark—"

I cut myself off. Boden's eyes have doubled in size, and while I'd love to assume that it's my little speech's doing, they're trained on a spot behind my shoulders.

When I look over, Koen's a couple of feet away. Looking bored. "Mouthy, isn't she, Boden?" He sighs. "Never thought I'd be into that, and yet. Bane of my fucking existence." His eyes flit to mine. "Don't stop on my account," he says with a lopsided smile. "I love watching asses being ridden. It's my favorite kind of porn."

Boden tenses—with anger, embarrassment, or a mix of both. "If I were Alpha of this pack, she wouldn't be allowed here."

I cringe a little, because he feels so *young*. One day his frontal lobes will develop, he'll think back to this interaction, and his friends will have to remove all sharp objects from his household.

Koen, too, seems mostly embarrassed for him. "Boden, given the number of new sphincters this girl just tore you, I don't need to tell you . . ." He stops and makes a pensive face. "Then again, I do love indulging in gratuitous displays of authority. So here you have it: Serena is my guest. Bother her again, and I'll make you regret it."

"She's not your guest." A sneer twists Boden's mouth. "Half of the members of this pack want her dead."

"Is that so."

"Yes. And we all know that you despise her just as much as everyone else does."

"Do I."

"You're just stuck with her because she's . . ."

"Because she's what?" Boden seems to have found his limit. The one thing he isn't willing to bring up. "Come on," Koen urges calmly. "Say it. What is she?"

"Your mate."

"Ah, yes. I'd forgotten about that." Koen slaps his own temple with the heel of his palm. He continues, monotone, "Since you're so sure that everyone here despises her, including me, let this be known: fuck with my mate, and I'm going to kill you so slowly, draw it out so long, tectonic plates will move and create whole new mountain ranges. And when the rest of your family comes to avenge you, I'll do the same to them. And if your friends come, I'm not going to fucking stop. Not even if all that's left of the pack is me and her. I will paint this entire territory green before I let anyone in the pack spill a single drop of red. Okay?"

My belly swoops with liquid warmth. Boden's fist clutches so tight, I brace for an attack.

But next to me, Koen never tenses. Like he knew from the very start of this conversation that Boden would eventually hang his head and say, "Yes, Alpha."

"Good." He clasps the boy's shoulder with a grin. "Now get out of my kitchen and go put product in your hair, or whatever the fuck it is that you do in your spare time."

Koen wraps his entire arm around my shoulder, the heel of his open hand bouncing loosely on my chest, and pulls me into him. It's less a gesture of affection and more of a statement, so I don't take it personally. But neither do I break away the second Boden disappears. Koen's heat is like . . . like thermal water. Like one of those pillow chairs Misery loves, the ones that are terrible for your posture. Something to *sink* into.

"That sounded mean," I say softly.

"Yeah. Unfortunately, I *am* mean." He says it like he couldn't care less but feels like he should. Kind of endearing. "And no one's touching you on my watch."

"Noted." I clear my throat. Because my heart is beating in it. Koen is just . . . very, *very* close. And his touch, unlike everyone else's, doesn't make me want to fling myself down a scarp. "That was some intense stuff. I'm . . . flattered."

"Don't be. The threats were highly embellished, and less about you than about keeping pack assholes in line."

"Right, yeah." It's not disappointment, the bitter taste in the back of my throat. Or, not precisely. "I figured."

He pulls away, and my body wants to follow him. Since I can't, I once again try to hoist myself onto the counter. Once again, his hands find my hips and settle me on the surface.

This time, they linger.

A ravenous, whiny little thing starts beating deep inside of me. "Is Boden going to be the next Alpha?" I ask to distract myself.

"I doubt it. There are a handful of young pack members that are as dominant as he is and don't even behave like skid marks on the thong of the universe."

Koen's still . . . not too close, but not far, either. Warmth flares into something liquid as I stare up at him. The beard, the long hair, they don't just hide his good looks—they are a mask of sorts. It's impossible to tell how he truly feels about anything.

A lock has escaped the infamous topknot, so I reach up and push it from his forehead. "Does it worry you? That you could be challenged at any time?" Misery has given me a very graphic rundown of how Weres become Alphas, which involves physical duels that often end in death. It's possible that she was just being dramatic, but she heavily implied the presence of cartoon fight clouds, torrents of blood, and confetti made out of skin flying about. "That one day a new Alpha will come along and try to take all of this away from you?"

He laughs softly. "Killer, none of this is *mine* to be taken. An Alpha doesn't own a pack, and whoever tells you otherwise has no business overseeing a gas station toilet, let alone thousands of Weres. It's the opposite: the pack owns the Alpha like it would a tool, and if a newer, better tool shows up, I'll gladly step down." There is no resentment in his tone.

"You don't hate it, do you?"

"What?"

"Being Alpha."

He cocks his head. "Why do you sound surprised?"

"I don't know. I guess Lowe seems to feel much more conflicted about his Alpha status."

"Lowe had a whole other life planned. He is a trained architect. I only know how to be an Alpha. As demonstrated by the fact that when he brought me to a museum, I sat on a sculpture that cost more than the gross domestic product of most packs."

"Why?"

"Because it looked like a fucking chair." I laugh, and it makes his mouth twitch upward in a curve that is so . . . so charming, I *need* to trace it. But then he continues, "Alpha is all I've ever been, and all I'll ever be."

"What about after?"

"There might not be an after. But if there is . . . I guess I'll find a hobby."

"What hobby?"

"No clue. I'll have to figure it out."

A sudden, stupid idea pops into my head. I hold out my fists and say, "Pick one."

"Not this fucking game again."

"Pick one," I insist, more forcefully. He sighs like I'm forcing him to muck a stable and points to my right hand—thank God. I don't know what his reaction to me gifting him an online architecture class would have been. "I'll teach you how to play the piano."

His brow furrows. "You can play?"

"Of course. The Collateral and her companion are well-rounded young ladies. Honestly, Misery was so terrible at it, I felt bad for our tutor." I pretend to shudder. "I'll give you lessons, and you'll have a hobby that's not, you know, just standing there and being tall and imposing and *Alpha*."

"Can't you just play something for me?"

"But that won't make you a well-rounded young lady." His laughter is a groan. "Plus, I need to earn my keep, and it's not like I can defrost your freezer. Come on, I can teach you a chord every day." I hop down from the counter, wrap my hand around two of

Koen's fingers, and pull him toward his bedroom. We get a couple of curious looks on our way, but I ignore them, and so does he. It's not like I'm planning to ravish him in the closet, anyway. I just want to . . .

"Sit," I order once we're in front of the piano, and despite his usual overburdened sigh, he obeys. The door remains wide open. Chatter and laughter seep in from all around us.

Back at the Collateral mansion, the piano came with a little bench that could house two. Koen's just has a round stool that is not wide enough for the both of us. "Hang on." I glance around. This is going to be a problem, considering his strained relationship with sittable furniture. "Let me drag another chair—"

Before I can go in search of one, he tugs at my wrist and pulls me between his knees. My ass hits the hard muscles of his quads none too gently, and his left arm loops around my hips, the back of his hand resting on the upper part of my left thigh. He angles me so that my legs occupy the slice of space between his.

"Let's just get this over with," he grumbles, low against my ear. My heart skips around for a minute, and there is no way he misses it, but . . .

Okay. Sure. Fine. Just one chord. He picked it. He won it, fair and square. "Any objection to C major?"

"Nope."

"Cool." I swallow. Take his right hand in both of mine and gently splay his fingers—thumb, index, ring. "Here," I whisper, and they seem to fall on the white keys instinctively, almost too easily. Maybe someone else tried to teach him how to play in the past? Maybe there is some knowledge of the basics, deep in the recesses of his brain? "Now, you just press—like this. Yeah." The simple chord rises up, enveloping us. "You did it. Look at you."

I grin wide, lift my eyes to meet his, and find that he's already staring at me, black eyed and voracious.

"Look at *you*," he says. At least, I *think* so. I could have imagined it, because it's little more than a whispered growl, quickly followed by a much lighter question. "Now what?" he asks.

I take a deep breath. "Now you just, um . . . I don't know. Repeat the chord over and over, and play the most boring song in history?"

His eyebrow lifts. "I think I'll do that. It's what my roommate deserves."

I snort and watch him hit the C chord ten more times in quick succession, his *this is what you get* look boring into me and making me laugh even harder. I'm so busy being amused, it takes me a second to realize that his left hand, the one on my thigh, is moving, too.

It's not unpleasant. His fingers press lightly into my flesh, the warmth of his skin branding through the cotton of my pants, a rapid beat that makes my heart speed up. It's almost as though he's walking through the chord, stepping up and down and up again in a sustained rhythm, skimming closer to the crease where my thigh and my abdomen join, and . . .

With a sharp exhale, I snap my legs shut. It's an automatic gesture, one that traps his fingers there, right between the soft fat that wraps around the inside of my thighs. I look up at him, confused. All at once, I'm hot all over. Liquid.

Koen's face, on the other hand, is etched in stone. "Serena," he murmurs, scent spiking, voice otherworldly, and it feels like . . . I don't know. A question, maybe. An invitation. A turn in the road, and the beginning of something.

We could kiss. If we wanted to, it would be the perfect position, the perfect situation.

ALI HAZELWOOD

We can't, I scream inside my head. *Are you insane?*

But that's not true at all. *I* can't, because I have no time left. Koen's Alpha. Koen can do whatever the hell he wants. Koen gets to decide if—

"I told you," he says calmly. All of a sudden, he's ice cold. "I'm not interested."

My stomach hollows. The words reverberate through me, harsher than a slap.

"Alpha?"

I turn to the door. A man with gray-streaked temples and a kind, weathered smile is studying us curiously. I make to leap away from Koen, but his fingers free themselves to tighten around my hip, stopping me.

"Sorry I'm so late. John asked for more and more stories, and . . ." The man's gaze catches on me. The way I'm perched in his Alpha's lap. "That's my six-year-old."

I try to stand again, and at last Koen lets go of me. I rise to my feet and take a step away, not hasty but determined.

What the hell was I doing?

"Bedtime is still your favorite part of the day, huh?" Koen asks breezily, and the man lets out a low, pain-filled groan. It's like nothing just happened. *Because nothing happened*, I remind myself. *He just said that he's not interested. And it wasn't the first time.* "Mai, this is Serena. Serena, Mai is in charge of our northeast borders. You've been keeping him busy."

"Me?"

Mai nods. "We stopped eleven Vampyres from entering our borders in the last two days."

I gasp. "*Eleven?* Is that a real number?"

"Would you like to see their bodies?" Koen asks.

"No."

"Good." His smile doesn't reach his eyes. "They're not in great shape."

I swallow. "Did you figure out which councilmember sent them?"

"Nope. They were all independent agents interested in the bounty and didn't know much. But I bet whoever's behind the reward is getting impatient. They'll make a stupid move soon enough."

"Good. Well, not *good*, but . . ." I wince. My heartbeat seems to have stabilized. "Thank you, Mai, for . . . keeping me safe. And I'm sorry that you got stuck with the Vampyre-killing job."

"Are you kidding? I *love* it."

"Do you?"

"Mai is my eldest second," Koen explains. "He gets his pick of assignments."

We chat for a while. Mai pulls out his phone to show us a few pictures of John, who looks adorable, and a menace, and wants to be Koen when he grows up—like most children in the pack, apparently. But something needling and confusing sticks to the walls of my head, a thought that won't let go, not even hours later, when I'm alone in bed under the covers, surrounded by home-decor-store quantities of pillows.

Mai is my eldest second. Koen said. The problem is, Mai looks half a decade older than Koen, tops. Which would put him around only forty. Not eldest material.

Unable to sleep despite my exhaustion, I retrace the last few days. Every step I've taken since entering Northwest territory. Every person I met. And when the realization hits me, I want to take my lack of observational skills and drown it in the nearby river. I can't believe it took me so long to notice how *young* everyone is.

This is *not* the typical age distribution for a pack. I've now met most of Lowe's seconds, and a third of them looked old enough to be his parents. Not to mention that Lowe's house was somewhat of a revolving door of Weres of all ages seeking audience for all sorts of problems.

So it's something else. I turn inward, gears spinning. When it comes to the Northwest, I have a lot of pieces, but I'm not sure how they fit together. *Yet.*

On impulse, I reach for my phone on the nightstand and type a text.

U up?

Misery: I'm a Vampyre and it's the middle of the night.
I roll my eyes. Can you ask Lowe how long Koen has been Alpha?
The reply comes in seconds. I won't.
Serena: Why?
Misery: Because I already know the answer.
I roll my eyes harder. Misery, how long has Koen been Alpha?
Misery: So nice of you to ask! Twenty-one years. Why?
I set the phone aside.

Koen was fifteen when he became Alpha. *Fifteen.* And around the same time, something big happened—something that killed Brenna's family, destroyed pack records, and gave the Northwest a reason to reunite.

I'm not sure what the age of majority is among Weres, but I've seen the way young Were members are treated in packs, and I can't imagine anyone would be happy with a fifteen-year-old becoming Alpha, least of all the fifteen-year-old in question.

Unless . . .

Unless there were no alternatives. Unless there were no dominant older members to take over. Because everyone who was past
their late teens left, or was . . . eliminated. Some kind of accident?
An attack? But how does that happen? What slices a pack with such
surgical precision? *Who* does?

I grab my phone again. **Ask Lowe how a boy of fifteen managed
to unify an entire pack.**

I fall asleep several minutes later, still waiting for the answer.

CHAPTER 15

The cabin smells like . . .
Impossible. He must be losing his mind.

THE NIGHT BRINGS SPANKING NEW LEVELS OF PAIN AND MOR-
tification.

The recollections do not abound, but as far as I can tell: I wake up a few hours after going to bed, gasping like a rhino with sleep apnea, and make my way to the bathroom as my body works through spasms, cramps, and the fire taking over every layer of my epidermis. I sit in the shower as cold water flows over my head and beg my soon-to-be corpse to pipe the fuck down. I picture Koen walking in to find what's left of me, a beached manta ray lifeless on the bathroom floor, deflated after puking up her internal organs.

That's when it all gets fuzzy. I don't recall getting up or leaving the bathroom. I *definitely* don't recall crawling into Koen's bed. And yet it's where I wake up. Could be a Were evolutionary trait: in the face of probable death, seek refuge close to Alpha. I might be onto something. I should ask Koen, if I'm ever able to face him after what I've done to his room.

It's . . . a lot.

In the harsh morning light, I stare down at the drenched mess of his bed. I wobble on my feet, strip the cotton sheets off the mattress, and realize that it soaked through. It's sweat. A lot of sweat. *Just spent one hour on the treadmill* sweat. My scent is thick, pungent, vaguely reminiscent of things I'd rather *not* acknowledge.

And it saturates every inch of his bed.

This is an invasion of Koen's private space.

It's *desecrating.*

Small mercy is, Koen spent the night outside. I beg the god of physiologically dysregulated bitches with sleep disorders to keep him away for ten more minutes. I stuff his bedding, then mine, in the laundry machine. Setting: bulky items. Then I clean his room, trying to force it to smell . . . like *not* me, but also like a deranged person didn't just pour disinfectant all over—a fine, impossible-to-strike balance.

I speed through my shower, rehearsing what I'll tell Koen if he calls me out on this new sanitizing facet of my personality. *Why did I wash your sheets? Because I'm a wonderful houseguest. Would you like a complimentary glass of limoncello?* I get dressed in my new clothes, but something feels . . . wrong. On my way out, I have an idea—one that no sane person would entertain, but that's no longer my side of the Venn diagram. I slip back inside Koen's room, steal one of his T-shirts, hastily put it on under my sweater.

And exhale in relief.

It's as though my fur was being brushed against the grain, but this five-dollar shirt smoothed it back down where it belongs. No, I won't be pondering the matter at this moment.

I walk to the back porch and find Amanda wearing a long parka and nothing else. "Oh my God." She lights up when I hand her a mug of coffee. *"Thank you."*

"Thank *you*."

"For what?"

"Patrolling around me."

"Are you kidding? I get to chill in wolf form. Pay attention to forest noises. Growl at the squirrels. It's everyone's favorite kind of duty. Well, except for Jorma. But that's because he's thirsty for spreadsheets."

I take a seat and follow her gaze to the group of wolves a couple hundred feet ahead of us. They sit on their hind legs, observing the spectacle—which happens to be a fight.

Which happens to involve Koen.

I stare at his wolf form. The double-layered coat. His muscular frame. His *terrifying* maw. I guess I have one, too, but I haven't seen it in a while. Nor am I currently wrapping it around the bare throat of a fellow Were, like it's an oven-roasted turkey leg.

The smaller reddish-brown wolf lets out a whimpering, submissive sound. When Koen releases her, she briefly rolls on her back to show her soft belly. Then, after an affectionate nip from her Alpha, she trots toward the rest of the group, and a new fighter takes her place. I spot Twinkles among them. He looks very excited to be in the thick of the action, if comically smaller than the Weres surrounding him. Still, Ana will be pleased to hear that he's keeping busy.

"Is that . . . normal?" I ask.

"Mm?"

"That's not the challenge, right? The one that determines the new Alpha?"

She spits out a mouthful of coffee. "Serena, they are *play-fighting*."

"Okay. Just making sure."

"It's to blow off steam." Amanda brushes liquid off her coat. "You see how the bites are softer? The ears are relaxed. Tail's neutral. It'll become easier to recognize as you spend more time in wolf form."

It won't, but I smile and nod anyway.

"Play-fight is an honored Were pastime."

"I guess not everyone has the knees for pickleball."

She laughs. "I'll teach you. And Koen, he's fun to spar with. He's strong, but his self-control is ironclad—"

She cuts off as a ruckus rises. We turn just in time to see Koen ramming his head into the flank of a newcomer. He gets in a few bruising hits, then pins the dark gray wolf to the ground with enough pressure to suffocate and stops only when he whines in pain.

Amanda clears her throat. "Maybe Koen's not the best option just now. Things are . . . a lot."

"Is something happening? Is it that meeting with the huddle leaders you mentioned?"

"No. Well, yes. But that is . . . It might be nothing. We're still hoping . . ." She scrunches her nose. "Actually, this one might have to do with you."

"With me?"

"Well, he's living under the same roof as his mate. He's around you a lot, and I think he . . . he *feels* it. If you know what I mean."

I don't, really—until I do. And no longer want to intake air.

"He . . . ?" I can't bring myself to continue.

"He's horny as fuck," Amanda says, taking pity on me. "At the mercy of his own lustful concupiscence. Probably jerks off every three hours. I assume you were about to say that?"

I was not. In fact, I was thinking about last night, about his hands on me, and wondering, If Koen wants to . . . If Koen *wants* to, with me, then why not?

The question builds a hazy, thick heat in my head, a delicious drip that coalesces into a new idea. It hammers an achy place at the bottom of my stomach. If not getting laid affects Koen to this degree, if he's shifting into wolf form and sauntering off to strangle grizzly bears . . . shouldn't *I* do something about it?

I certainly could. I've had sex with men I liked and respected less than Koen, after all. Almost exclusively. And I . . . It's not that I . . . I wouldn't mind. My flustered state of mind proves it. My heart, beating so loud against my rib cage that Amanda must be wondering whether I have angina—that proves it, too.

So why not?

Because you're about to give up the ghost. And because he has told you multiple times how little he wants you. That's why not. When it comes to Koen's desires, are you really going to believe Amanda over Koen himself?

No. I won't. The issue is simple enough: Koen may want me, but he doesn't *want* to want me.

Still, there's no reason for him to blue ball it.

"He doesn't need to be," I tell Amanda, ignoring the acid taste of the words on my tongue. Maybe she'll let him know. Maybe she'll sign him up for a dating app named Howlr, which someone should totally invent. He probably has a bunch of fuck buddies lined up already.

"What do you mean?"

"Just that since Koen and I are not . . . It doesn't mean that he has to be all . . . pent up. Not that he would need my permission. But since I'm staying at his house, it might be difficult for him to . . . I guess what I'm trying to say is, I can make myself scarce. And I wouldn't complain or anything if he were to bring someone over

to . . ." I force out a smile, feeling nauseous. "Slake his lustful concupiscence."

She studies me for such a long stretch, I wonder whether my
babbling has hypnotized her.

"Amanda? Is everything okay?"

"Has Koen not told you? Or Lowe? Or anyone else?"

"I'm not sure what you're talking about."

She takes a deep breath. Runs the back of her hand over her
mouth. And then resigns herself to be the one to give me the news.
"Serena, the Alpha of Northwest pack is traditionally asked to
honor a celibacy covenant. He's forbidden by law to engage in any
kind of intimate relationships—emotional *or* physical."

CHAPTER 16

He told her that he would never touch her because he didn't want her enough; in truth, he will never touch her because he wants her too much. The make-believe, he thinks, was kinder to both of them.

I'M STILL WORKING ON GRASPING THE IMPLICATIONS OF WHAT Amanda revealed, but she's already doling out more. ". . . not much has changed for him. Your presence, that's throwing him off. At least, I think so—Koen's not really the type to walk around griping about the discontented state of his nuts. And he never seemed affected by the covenant. He's been dealing with it for twenty years, but I doubt it was a burden to him. I've never even seen him *look* at a woman, so—"

"Why?"

"Excuse me?"

"Lowe is with Misery. I know that the Alpha of one of the New England packs has a mate. Was this rule made for Koen?"

Amanda massages her eyes. "It's complicated."

"How so?"

"The celibacy covenant used to be common practice in packs. The idea is that if a pack gives an Alpha absolute power over them, the Alpha should be able to guarantee that the well-being of the

pack will be the most important thing for them. But if every decision needs to be made for the good of the pack—"

"Other priorities are a threat," I finish, starting to understand.
"Like a partner. Or children."

"Precisely," she mumbles, frowning as she takes a sip of coffee.

"But you don't agree?"

"I . . . In theory, it makes sense. But falling in love and establish-
ing relationships are not necessarily things one can control. And
that's *before* throwing in the issue of biological mates. Only a tiny
percentage of us find one, but when we do . . ." Her eyes lift to the
clearing above us. Koen and a pewter-gray wolf almost as large as
he snarl at each other. "It was a difficult rule. Not to mention, some
Alphas would take the covenant but disregard it."

"Secret vitamin D deficient family in the basement?"

"In the crawl space, in the attic. Depending on the soil type and
the frost line, but yes, pretty much." She snorts. "The rule became
obsolete. Some packs began ignoring it, others phased it out. But
there were some hiccups." Another sip, slower this time. "Although,
if you want my opinion . . . Well, you didn't ask, so—"

"I'd love to know it, though," I hurry to say.

"In that case, prepare for a world-class harangue." She turns.
Her knee bumps into mine. "Alphas are people. And people make
mistakes. That's why packs have systems of checks and balances.
We have an Assembly that can dispute the Alpha's decisions if need
be. And rules are well and good, but all they can affect is *behavior*.
They cannot police something as personal and disorderly as a *feeling*, so—" She stops, maybe realizing that she is, in fact, harangu-
ing. When she resumes, her tone is softer. "Seventy or so years ago,
the rule was slowly being rolled back all over North America. The
Midwest pack was at the forefront of that. And after a decade or so,

the first reports of leaders taking advantage of their newfound free-
dom started bleeding through. An Alpha fucking his way through
his own pack. Granting privileges in exchange for sex. Quid pro
quo stuff."

My stomach turns. "Did they stop him?"

"He was challenged and is currently fertilizing the world's most
rancid corncob. But it felt like a cautionary tale. The Northwest
decided to keep the celibacy covenant, and for the following decades, our Alphas seemed okay with it. Not everyone wants to be
sexually active or in a relationship, you know? It was a problem for
later." Amanda chews at her lower lip. "And then later came."

"Was that four decades ago? The Alpha before Koen?"

"A little less than that. But yeah." She sets the mug down, as if
she'll need all her limbs for this. "She was a fantastic Alpha. Also,
she was in love and unapologetic about it. She asked the Assembly
to rescind the covenant. According to my mother, at the time the
Assembly was a crock of geezers whose main hobby was to shake
their fists at the clouds. Or maybe they were just cautious. They
studied every known case of Alpha misconduct, came up with a
hundred scenarios in which revoking the covenant would lead to
an asteroid shower extinguishing all aerobic life, and denied her."

"Is that why the huddles seceded?"

"Yup. I was born within the core, that year. And the huddles . . .
Even after the partitioning, most members' instinct was still to
unite under one Alpha. The Assembly continued to exist as an en-
tity, to ensure good relations among the huddles, which all formed
a loose alliance. And over the years, as new huddle leaders were
elected, its composition changed to more progressive Weres,
and . . . the tide was shifting. It seemed certain that the pack would

reunite soon enough." Her fingers tighten around the balustrade. "And then we were attacked."

"Amanda, I—"

"You're sorry, I know." She reaches out to me with a small smile. Clasps my upper arm through the fabric of my sweater. "I appreciate it, Serena."

"I know it was the Humans, and I—"

"What?" Her eyes round in surprise. "Who told you that?"

"Brenna."

She rolls her eyes. "That's *not* true, and such a bullshit read of what . . . Humans were involved, yes, but the true responsibility is with the Weres."

"Wow, that's *both* my species. What a coincidence."

Amanda laughs. Squeezes me one last time before letting go. "You're no more to blame for this than I am. Or Koen. He was fifteen, but he took over, neutralized the threat, convinced the huddles that we'd be stronger together. And when the Assembly's condition was to reintroduce the celibacy covenant . . ."

"He agreed." I nod, ignoring the rocks in my stomach. Koen doesn't need me feeling sorry for him.

"It's kinda funny. I mean, Koen truly does whatever the fuck he wants. He hasn't met a rule he didn't love to break, but the covenant . . . he's a stickler for that one." A small shrug. "I'm just not sure that he cares to be, at the moment."

I don't get it, the weight settling on my chest. Koen is a powerful man with near-unlimited resources and the adoration of the masses. *Some* masses. He even has his own private fight club—the dream of every thirty-six-year-old teenaged man.

Except, being barred from relationships cannot be an easy

decision to make, especially at fifteen. And . . . why did he not tell me? The first time we met, he informed me that I was his mate, but he never mentioned the covenant.

This conversation is not *an invitation.*

Even when I clumsily asked him out . . .

Like me, or don't. I really couldn't care less.

And last night . . .

I told you. I'm not interested.

He made it sound like he didn't *want* to be with me. Never mentioned that he wasn't *allowed* to.

"We were wondering . . ." A male voice interrupts my thoughts. When I glance up, Saul and Jorma are standing in front of the cabin, naked. I deliberately keep my eyes above their necks and try not to choke on my own breath. "Hey, guys."

Saul grins. Winks at me, like one does. "Hey, honey. Jorma and I were in the area, to . . ."

"Take Koen's beatings?" Amanda offers.

"Yeah, that. And we remembered that last night you mentioned how much you love to cook. So we figured you probably made something for breakfast today, and since it's so hard to eyeball portions, you might have leftovers. Wouldn't want it to go to waste, you know?"

I bite back a smile. "What would you guys like?"

"Oh, we don't want to put you out. Just, if you have something you're gonna toss anyway . . ."

I turn to Jorma, who's high on directness and low on bullshit. "What would he like?"

"French toast, please," Jorma says. "With a side of sausages."

"You absolutely do *not* have to cook for these losers," Amanda tells me. Then adds, "But if you do, please remember that I, too, did not have breakfast."

I grin. "Come on in, then."

Less than an hour later, my culinary ego has grown to the size of a quasar. From the window, I watch Jorma, Saul, and Amanda jump off Koen's porch and shift into majestic wolves in midair. I follow their supple forms until they disappear. That's when my phone rings with an unknown number.

In the past, I'd have eaten glass with gonorrhea smeared on it before picking up. However, because of my current high-reward social lifestyle, I have only two contacts: Misery—saved from memory—and Koen—preprogrammed. Which means that I'm not in a position to reject any unknown callers.

"It's Juno," the voice on the other end says, and I slump in relief. I don't have the emotional strength to fend off financial fraud. "The Humans have gotten back to me about your DNA."

I straighten. "Any news?"

"Yes and no."

"Hit me."

"As you know, the more distant the relation, the fewer the DNA segments shared, which decreases the likelihood of detecting—"

"Juno," I interrupt, amused.

"Yes?"

"It's okay if you just tell me the findings."

A pause. "I wouldn't want you to think that I don't trust you to understand the science behind—"

"Feel free to condescend to me anytime."

"In that case." She takes a deep breath. "Your mother's family seems to be from west of the Sawtooth Range."

ALI HAZELWOOD

Sawtooth Range. Where have I heard of it? "Isn't that part of the Rocky Mountains?"

"Correct."

I visualize a map. Meaningless state lines that Humans drew up, splicing territories they haven't visited in centuries. "Lakes area, right?"

"Correct," she repeats.

"Borders with the . . . Midwest pack?"

Half a beat. "Actually, it's closer to the eastern border of the Northwest territory."

That would support Juno's suspicion that my father was from here, too. "Is there a Human family member we could talk to?"

"The closest relatives we found were distant cousins. Not to mention . . ."

"We're Weres, and they might welcome us with a machine gun?"

"It doesn't sound too far-fetched."

"Agreed. Hmm."

From your mother, the note said. Koen thought it might be a prank, but my mother was from the area, so . . . what if she's still here? She's Human, and unlikely to make it into Northwest territory undetected. But maybe she has a Were friend who delivered it for her. Could it be my father? Could he still be in the pack? Unlikely, given how few members would be old enough. But still.

I blow my hair out of my eyes. Through the glass, I see Koen ambling back, breeze snaking through his dark fur. "I'm sorry, Juno, I need to go. Thank you for this."

"Serena, may I tell Misery? I already know she'll ask. She is very . . ."

"Nosy?"

"Yes. When it comes to you."

"You can tell her anything but if this information came to you through a computer, she's likely to know already."

"Ideal, as it would spare me an ethics-breaching conversation."

I laugh, freshening up the coffee, and send a text:

I can't help noticing that either you did not ask Lowe how a boy of fifteen managed to _nify an entire pack, or you're keeping the answer to yourself.

Misery: Lowe is in the south on pack business. I am but a lonely, neglected bride.

Serena: Don't walk into the lake without first feeding Sparkles. How is my boy, by the way?

Misery: Last I checked his intestines were happy and productive. He may look like an overgrown hamster, but he sure shits like a lion.

Serena: Fantastic. Since your intellectual curiosity is clearly at its peak, can you find out something else for me?

Misery: Probably.

Serena: I need to know what specifically happened twenty-one years ago here in the Northwest. Weres died, especially older Weres. Humans were involved.

Misery: On it.

Misery: Although, and this might be too galaxy-brain an idea to have occurred to you despite your career as a journalist: you could ask questions? For instance, to the guy you live with? Who happens to have been an active participant in the events you just mentioned?

Serena: Everyone is being very cagey. This is obviously the Northwest's big, formative trauma event, and they're not over it. It's like that thing you Vampyres always yap on about, with the blood and the wedding.

Misery: The Aster?

Serena: Yup. Except this happened years, not centuries ago, and I'm pretty sure that everyone's genealogy tree died in it. It seems more tactful to seek alternative sources.

Misery: You soft hearted bitch. I could never.

Serena: Uh-huh. Where's Ana, by the way? Snuggling on top of you? Yawning in your face? Drooling all over your pillow?

Misery: Absolutely NONE of the above.

Misery: But if she were, she'd tell me to say hi to Aunt Serena and to ask her when she's coming back for more zip-lining.

Serena: Is she asking for your phone to play Tetris?

Misery: No comment. Goodbye.

I pour some coffee in a mug and set it aside for Koen. I'm gathering the seconds' used but surprisingly clean plates when, out of the corner of my eye, I catch something in the hallway.

It's a yellow flannel. The flannel I stole from Koen and slept in last night. The one I sweated through. The one I thought I'd put in the washing machine with the sheets.

"Shit," I mutter, hurrying to pick it up. Unfortunately, at the exact same moment, the door opens.

Koen enters the cabin in human form, finishing pulling up a pair of jeans, the worn denim soft around his hips. He doesn't bother buttoning them up all the way, and . . . I don't know. I guess I could rapidly avert my eyes and maybe even flush. But in a place where no one seems to care about nudity, I'm the one making it weird.

Plus, I'm busy hiding the flannel behind my back. Which seems to accomplish very little, given the way Koen's nostrils flare. I'm suddenly seized by terror: Can he smell the remnants of my sweatfest?

Clearly, yes. Because he goes rigid as a statue and asks, "What is it?" The words sound a bit like a growl, as though they're coming from deep within his body.

"Nothing." I swallow. Smile to soften the lie. "Just, my pj's. I need to wash them."

His eyes darken. Panic prickles up my spine.

"I'll be right back. Give me a sec," I plead, turning around and starting down the hallway as fast as I can.

"Serena." His voice is so harsh, my entire body clenches.

I freeze in place. After a long moment, turn around. "W-what?"

"Don't run."

I swallow thickly. "I . . . Why?"

"Walk *slowly* to the washing machine and get rid of the clothes." His voice pins me to the ground. Something builds in my belly. "Do not make me chase after you."

I have no idea why he's asking that from me, but I do as he commands: calmly make my way down the hallway until I'm in the mudroom, watching the flannel sink into a pool of soapy water. I take a deep breath before heading back, but when I return, Koen is right where I left him, clearly unwilling or unable to move.

Neither of us mentions the exchange that just occurred—a silent, shared agreement to pretend that nothing happened. Instead, I grab the coffee from the counter and hand it to him until he accepts it with a muted grunt. His eyes don't leave mine until he tips his head back to drink.

I can't help staring at the bob of his Adam's apple through his unshaven neck. The breadth of his body, muscles working under scarred, imperfect skin. The thick outline of him. His shoulders and back strain when he sees me watching; they don't relax even as I smile.

It's focus stealing, the way he looks. But most Weres are built this way, and the reason I can't tear my eyes away from this one has more to do with the fact that . . .

He's *Koen*.

He manages entire conversations in low growls. He can tell that I'm about to make fun of him before I've even formulated the joke in my head. He disturbs the space that surrounds him, and mine with it. And his eyes are always searching mine, shaping me, trying to make sure I'm okay, and *never* asking anything of me.

I remember the disjointed, vague images I keep seeing in my dreams. Feel the same liquid, low-pooling heat. Wonder how many fucking civil, criminal, moral, *maritime* laws I would break if I were to go and wrap my arms around him. Maybe say, *Your tits are pretty spectacular, too.*

"What?" he asks when I snort out a laugh, and I shake my head.

"How many packmates have you slaughtered on this fine morning?"

He mutters something about "whiny little shits," and I try not to laugh.

"I made French toast. Want some?"

"I'm good."

He didn't eat any of the food I made last night, either. It stings, and I don't know why.

"Where did Amanda go?" he asks.

"Just left. Sorry you missed her."

"I'm not. I'm packmated out for the day."

"It's eight thirty in the morning, Koen."

Your point? his look clearly asks. "Go get dressed," he orders. "We're going somewhere."

I take a deep breath. Think about all the cruel little things he told me to push me away. About the big thing he neglected to tell me, the one that best explains the distance he's been keeping. "Actually, we're not. We're staying in for a bit. And." I glance at his shoulders. His biceps. The V of his stomach. "For what I have in mind, it's better if *you* don't get dressed."

CHAPTER 17

The covenant was never a big part of his life. He would forget about it for months, even years. It never felt like a sacrifice, just a simple trade-off, an integral feature of who he was: the Alpha of the Northwest.

Then she arrived, assumed total control of him, and left no room for anything but her.

D ON'T BE NERVOUS."

"I'm not."

"Koen. I know it's been a while for you."

"Just fucking get it over with."

"What? No, that's not how you do it. This is an *experience*."

"Then make it a *quick* experience."

"Why are you being like this? I'll be gentle. Am I not gentle?"

"You mispronounced 'annoying.'"

"Oh, come on. I'm having fun."

"I wish I could say the feeling is mutual."

"Should we put down a sheet or something? You're making way more of a mess than I thought you would. Though I guess it's normal, since it's been so long."

"If anyone's making a mess, it's you."

"Hush. I'm doing this for you. The entire pack thinks you're hopeless, but I'll help you show them that—"

The door bursts open, and Koen and I fall silent mid-haircut.

It's *very* poor timing. I'm almost done with what will surely be known, postmortem, as *Serena Paris's most challenging and powerful artistic endeavor*, but two women and a man are rudely letting themselves inside and interrupting my creative process.

"Does anyone ever knock?" I whisper.

"No, clearly. And I'm not sure what it is about me that says 'make yourself at home.'" Koen glances down at the uncompromising bend of his own arms, folded on his bare chest. Then asks, louder, "Did someone install a fucking red carpet over my porch steps?"

"I must have missed it," the man says. He is bald, with a long blond beard, thick-rimmed glasses, and a *someone just dented my paint job* frown.

"I'm not sure I feel comfortable knowing that my Alpha let some girl with scissors play around his throat," the taller of the two women says, sounding just as irritated.

Koen shrugs. "Feel free to mull it over and never let me know, Anneke."

"I think he looks good," the other woman says, which I take as a much-needed compliment.

"Why, thank you." I press one hand against my chest. "I do believe my muse is speaking to me."

The woman's laughter is low and musical. She's much smaller than Anneke, and she looks a couple of years older than Koen. Unlike the other two newcomers, her stance is laid-back. *She* did not come here for a fight. "It was time for a change. Not that the depressed Viking cosplay wasn't hot," she tells Koen, who winces and massages his forehead.

"Is there a single fucking person in this godforsaken pack who does *not* have an opinion about my grooming habits?"

"No," the three reply in unison, which gives me the boost I needed to continue shaving Koen's beard.

"The reason we are here, Alpha," the man starts, "is that—"

"The pack newsletter let you know that I have a woman—my mate, no less—staying in my cabin as we wait for this new tide of murderous psychos to ebb, and you're afraid I'm fucking her. Sound about right?"

Anneke and the man exchange surprised looks, but the older woman just smiles. I run my hand through Koen's hair and tilt back his head until his neck is exposed. He follows my directions, pliant in my hands. "He's not," I say distractedly.

"He's not . . . ?" Anneke asks.

"Breaking the covenant. I remain tragically unfucked."

There's sudden tension in his bare back, the trip of a heartbeat that I can detect only because I'm in his space, touching him. A tic of his jaw.

Ah. So you were *hoping I wouldn't find out.* "Tip your chin up, Koen—perfect." I swipe the razor down the column of his throat and run my fingers over his skin, pleased with the smooth slip. Koen didn't have any shaving cream, so I'm using a blend of soap and conditioner. I take a short moment to admire my handiwork, and then smile at Anneke. "He's not madly in love with me, either. Honestly, he barely even talks to me."

"And yet he lets you brandish a weapon around his neck."

"It's more like community service, Anneke," the older woman murmurs, and we exchange an amused look. I wonder what her name is—

"Karolina," she tells me, lips curling. "And this is Xabier. We are three-fifths of the Assembly."

"Serena. I'd shake your hand, but . . ."

"Understood."

"Now that we've exchanged friendship bracelets," Koen says, "can we move on with our day?" He makes to stand, but I push him back down with a firm hand on his shoulder.

"Not until I'm done, buddy." I step around to work on the other half of his face but stop when I notice the way they're all regarding me.

Well, not *all*. Koen is just his habitual, long-suffering self. The others, though, watch us open-mouthed. I smell a surge of panic. Sudden alert. Sphincters clenched tight enough to make diamonds.

"Are we . . . are we being attacked by the Vampyres?" I switch my hold on the razor to use it as a weapon, ready for an invasion. *So* ready. They don't need to know that earlier I pulled a muscle while combing my hair.

"It's hardly evidence that you two are not in a relationship," Xabier points out, "the way she takes liberties. Gives you orders."

"Is it?" Koen sounds bored. "You three just showed up to my house to tell me what to do. and last I checked, I'm not fucking any of you."

"Stop moving," I murmur, going back to shaving him. "Or I'm going to nick you, and they're going to think I'm pregnant with your triplets."

Koen stills, but the corners of his lips twitch. "She's not *taking* liberties, she is *given* them. If anyone here is questioning my authority, it's you."

"We are not," Anneke says. "But we *are* concerned. Must we remind you—"

"No. I don't need to be reminded of shit. But if you want to anyway, go ahead. I know it's a cherished hobby of yours."

"Koen knows why the rules are there," Karolina says, diplomatic. "Better than anyone. He has never given us reason to doubt him."

"He hasn't," Xabier agrees. "But he did not have a mate before."

Koen grunts. "When the pack reunited, I promised that if I found her, I'd immediately inform you, and I did. The day I met her. *I* am the reason you can be on me like stink on shit. Unfortunately, she's also a hybrid in need of protection, which I won't withhold just to convince the Assembly that nothing is happening."

"Plus," I ask, "wouldn't you be able to smell it?"

Karolina quirks her head. "What do you mean, Serena?"

"Well, two of the seconds are together, and last night I could easily tell that they regularly exchange bodily fluids." I finish running a warm cloth against Koen's cheeks and step back, searching for missing spots. I'll be sad, if he ever holds me again, without the scratch of his beard against my skin. I was . . . yeah. Into it.

This was a fun activity, though. My favorite in a while. There's something nice about being close to my Alpha. Taking care of him, as he does of me. Breathing in his soothing scent, preparing for what's to come, comfort for—

Whoa.

Whoa, whoa, *whoa.*

Where did my brain go just now? How long was I silent?

"I guess my point is"—I clear my throat—"that your nose would tell you if something was happening between us."

"Maybe they have a cold," Koen drawls. "Maybe that cold made their brains leak out of their ears."

"Koen, given your history—"

"My *history*?" He stands, suddenly towering over all of us. The little strands of chopped hair still clinging to his shoulders silently slip to the floor. Xabier, who spoke last, takes a step back. "Do tell me more about *my* history. What have I done to warrant these doubts?"

"Your—"

"Think *very carefully* before you finish that sentence."

"Hey." My hand meets the hard heat of Koen's stomach, and I quietly slip in front of him, ignoring the additional helping of be-fuddled looks it earns me. "Listen, you may not know me, but Koen has been your Alpha for years. There's no need to treat him like a fuckboy."

Three pairs of eyes blink at me. From behind me, Koen asks, "A what?"

"A fuckboy. Just, you know. A boy. Who fucks." God, Misery's right. Some things simply do not translate to the Weres. "What I'm trying to say is, he told me that nothing would happen between us on the day we first met. And I'm not about to try to disintegrate his free will with my magic cunt. Okay?" I hold Xabier's eyes until he nods his agreement, and while he doesn't look happy as he storms out, he's at least gone. Anneke makes to leave afterward, marginally more reassured.

"I trust you, Koen," she says. "I didn't mean to imply that I don't. But I want to remind you that no other Were is strong enough to hold the Northwest together, and if your worries about Constantine turn out to be true . . . We are in your hands, Alpha. Keep that in mind." She slips outside with considerably less stomping, leaving us to stand in a long silence, and *me* to wonder, who the hell is—

"Who told you about the covenant?" Koen asks me.

Hands on my hips, I turn around. "I find it interesting that *you* didn't tell me yourself, since you're so big on the truth."

"Didn't come up." I see forced indifference in the tension of every single muscle in his body. "Who told you?"

"I have my sources." I give him my best cryptic, superspy smile, refusing to throw Amanda under the bus.

"Isn't she lovely to have around," he tells Karolina, wrapping a hand around my shoulder. His touch hits me like a small supernova, lighting up a million nerve endings. Heat licks down my arm, up my spine, pools in my belly. "She's high maintenance. Talks too much. Can't mind her business. The very opposite of how I like my pack members—seen but not heard."

I snort. "He doesn't like to see them, either."

"Yeah. True enough."

"Fascinating." Karolina's gaze alternates between us. "You said it's not mutual? You're not her mate even though she's yours?"

Koen's nod is detached, like he's confirming something inconsequential. *Yes, leeks are indeed my favorite seasonal vegetable.*

"And yet she doesn't feel the pull to obey you."

"Should I?" I ask brightly.

"Not quite. The rumor that an Alpha can brainwash other Weres into doing his bidding is vastly exaggerated—there is no magic compulsion. But our instinct is to avoid defying them. I definitely cannot remember the last time I saw a Were give Koen orders, even one as simple as 'sit down.'"

"She's not fully Were," Koen reminds her.

"And I'm not the only one. You three came over just to yell at him."

"We are the Assembly. It's our job to hold the Alpha accountable—we are trained to go against our nature." She rolls her eyes. "Though this was an unnecessary execution of our duties."

"Let me guess," Koen drawls, "Xabier and the giant pole that lives up his rectum had a bad dream and convinced Anneke that I was a step away from eloping with Serena and becoming a deadbeat Alpha, so you followed them here to make sure I didn't dissolve them in battery acid."

Karolina tries not to smile, but her relationship with Koen seems to run deep. "I can neither confirm nor deny."

"Is the rest of the Assembly going to be balls deep up my ass?"

"Not Conan—you know how little he likes the covenant. Jerzy, maybe. He's busy dealing with the Canada pack, though."

"He knows my offer for help stands, right?"

"Of course." Karolina turns to me. "Serena, let me introduce myself properly. I am the leader of the Moon Craters huddle. Saul, whom I believe you know, is my younger brother."

"Nice to meet you," I say.

"After all of this is over," she asks, "where do you plan to go?"

Rotting down a dark hole, preferably inside a mushroom death suit is not an acceptable answer, is it? "My sister lives in the Southwest."

"Ah, yes. The Vampyre? Well, should you change your mind, you are welcome in our huddle. You were a financial reporter, right?"

"Before. Yes."

"We've been doing more and more business with the Humans. We could use someone with your background."

"Oh. That's really cool. I . . . I'll give it a think," I say, somewhat sad that it's a lie. I try to camouflage it with a smile. "I'm sure I'd thrive there. I mean, I get along with you *and* Saul. It's gotta be a sign."

"It's not a sign," Koen declares flatly. "It's fucking poaching."

Karolina laughs, reaches forward to exchange a long hug with

Koen, and then leaves as I yell after her, "Please, do share with the pack newsletter about my excellent work as Koen's personal groomer." I turn around to receive what *should* be Koen's undying gratitude but will likely be a giant load of crabbiness, and—

Suddenly, I cannot breathe.

Because I didn't expect him to be standing so close to me. But also, clean shaven and without his hair hiding his features, he seems younger. Less moody. His face feels so . . . open. Direct. *Available.* Like maybe, if I applied myself, I could tell what he's thinking half of the time. There could be room for me, in the life of a man with that face.

"Hey," I say.

His nostrils work. "Hey, killer."

I clear my throat. "You look so much more dignified, now that I've de-shed you. Cuter, too. Just like that hot guy. From that movie."

"What movie?"

"All of them." I wet my lips. Look down at my toes.

"Serena." There is something in his tone, something that I refuse to contemplate, something I need to cover up quickly.

"By the way." It comes out shrill. I don't care. "I know you have a job and everything. You don't have to stick around with me all day, if there's something else you need to be doing."

"The bowling league will wait. We're going out."

"Where?"

"I had an idea." He dusts hairs off his pecs. I really wouldn't mind it if he put on some clothes. "Well, Brenna had an idea, but if it works, I'll pass it off as mine."

"An idea for . . . ?"

"Figuring you out."

"I love it when you talk about me like I'm the ultimate escape room. Tell me more."

"You'll see when we get there. Give me five to shower." He heads for his room. Stops. "And, killer?"

"What?"

"Tuck that T-shirt in your pants. It'll look less like it's mine."

CHAPTER 18

He wants to show her every corner of his territory. The deep blue lakes and the snow-capped peaks. Moss-draped trees and rock spires. He wants to be with her for each marveled intake of breath.

THE DRIVE LASTS ABOUT HALF AN HOUR, ONCE AGAIN ALONG the jagged coast. Koen spends most of it on the phone with a dozen different people, discussing pack matters that seem to range from crop rotation to solar power to children's swimming lessons.

I listen to him talking a group of teachers out of taking a shit on their principal's desk and wonder if all Alphas are this intimately involved with the goings-on of their packs. Why am I surprised that Koen is this good at this job?

We park in front of a red-roofed farmhouse that looks like something I once saw on a postcard. "No way." I once again paste my face to the window. "This place is *unreal*."

"Of course it is. It's my territory."

"I still don't think you can take credit for that." I laugh. "Look—they have cows!"

"If I'd known what a fan of livestock manure you are, I'd have—"

I ignore him and exit the car right as a young man comes toward us. His mop of dark curls is swept around by the wind, and his frame is slight, especially for a Were. "Dr. Sem Caine," Koen explains after they exchange a hug.

My stomach drops. Did Koen find out? Does he know that I'm about to—

"Don't worry," Sem says. "You're not here as a patient. In fact, you're not even here to see *me*."

The reason we came, I discover after we step inside, is Sem's grandfather—"Dr. Silas Caine," Koen explains. "Dr. Silas is one of the elders of the pack, and he used to specialize in pediatrics. Any boy or girl who was born in the Northwest in the last sixty years was examined by him at some point."

I immediately understand where this is going. "Would he remember me, though?"

"Not your face," Sem explains. "Which is just as well, since his eyesight has been deteriorating. He's in his nineties now. But he might remember your scent. Come, he's this way."

In the living room, Dr. Silas sits between two women: the first looks so much like Sem, she has to be his sister. The second has short strawberry-blond hair and a shy smile. Her fingers slide around Sem's as he introduces her as his partner.

"Layla is one of the pack's midwives," he explains. Before adding, a little sheepishly, "We're all doctors in this room."

"You are making me look bad," Dr. Silas says from his chair. He's a robust man, with a full head of milk-white hair and a husky voice. "My entire family became doctors, and people assume that it's because I've been butting my nose into their lives and pressuring them. And now we have Sem's daughter, who cannot read yet and is already saying she'll be a surgeon."

"Don't worry, Grandpa. We'll tell everyone that you pushed us to become trapeze artists and coal miners, and that we severely disappointed you."

"Is it too much to ask for a poet? Or a musician? I so love music . . ." He sighs and turns in our direction. When he smiles, his face splinters into a million fine, leathery lines. "Koen, child. It's always a pleasure to see you. And how kind of you, to bring me the halfling."

I glance at Koen, puzzled. "The what?"

"We have stories in the north. Legends, ballads. Ancient stuff about children born of Weres and Humans. Weres and Vampyres, too. We call them halflings."

"Halflings." I taste the word, then smile. "I like it. More than 'hybrid.' Makes me sound less like a car."

"Do come closer," Silas beckons. "You will forgive me if I don't stand, won't you? Serena, right?"

I nod, taking a step toward him. Then I remember what Sem told me about Dr. Silas's eyesight and add, "It was given to me at the Human orphanage. If we met before, you might have known me under another name."

"I see, I see. Will you sit, please?"

I drop to his feet, cross-legged. "These halfling legends . . . Do you think they might hold some truth?"

"Most stories do. Although the truths we seek are often not the ones we find. But if you're asking whether you're the first of your kind . . . I do not believe so, no."

Juno said the same: hundreds of thousands of years ago, Weres and Humans and Vampyres used to be one. There are lots of theories about how speciation occurred, and I'm sure that at this very moment at least two anthropologists are fisticuffing over them at a sparsely attended academic panel. The bottom line, though, is that some groups split off and went their merry way. By the time they attempted to rejoin, they were no longer the same.

But reproductive compatibility is fluid, Juno said. *Our DNA is similar enough that all it takes is a few mutations at the individual level to allow procreation. There will be people referring to you as the harbinger of the decline of civilization, but what you are is not new, per se. It's just . . .*

A comeback?

If you will.

What you're saying is, I'm vintage.

It's not really what I—

And Renaissance Girl should be my new nickname?

I didn't—

Deal.

"How old are you?" Dr. Silas asks, leaning forward in his seat.

"Twenty-five, as far as we know." I fall quiet and fail in my quest to *not* glance back at Koen. I must have lost my object permanence skills, because I need constant reassurance that he *exists,* he's *here with me.* He gives me a small nod, and I feel marginally less like used kitty litter.

I shouldn't be nervous. I've lived my entire life not knowing who my parents were, and I've been just *fine.* I never allowed my origins to define me, because if I had, I would have been destined to remain undefined. I may be Serena Nobody, but I'm still Serena. The past doesn't have to shape the future.

Hell, I don't even *have* a future.

And yet, as Dr. Silas inhales deeply, I'm on tenterhooks. If he doesn't recognize me, what would that mean? What if he *does*? What if my parents are alive and well? What if I am forced to meet them, listen to their excuses, and maybe even forgive them? Because that's what I should do, right? Be gracious and compassionate and somehow *over it* and—

Dr. Silas slowly shakes his head, and the relief folds my insides like origami. And Koen, whose eyes never, ever, *ever* leave me, can obviously tell.

A brief silence. Dr. Silas is saying that it could mean nothing— maybe he forgot, maybe my scent changed, they know so little about halfling developmental biology. Sem is agreeing, listing possibilities. Koen's face is worried, like he's about to ask me if I'm all right.

The only thing giving me strength right now is knowing that, asshole that he is, if I vomit gastric acid on his shoes, he'll never let me live it down. "Hey, is it okay if I . . . I'd love some fresh air."

"Of course." Layla smiles. "Back door is through the kitchen, on the left. You're welcome to go for a run, too. If you like the shoreline, it's just us for about ten miles."

"Great," I say, instead of *Lovely of you, to mistake me for a high-functioning Were.* I catch Koen's eyes as I step away, watch the way his muscles begin to contract to follow me, and shake my head minutely, hoping he'll understand what I'm trying to communicate: *I'm an emotional mess and I'd love to be alone for a second, just in case I burst out crying or puke up the French toast I didn't even eat.*

He doesn't like it, but he stays put.

The Caines' yard is a grass-covered cliff above the shore, something right out of an impressionistic painting. The ocean is less than a couple hundred feet away, and when I close my eyes and tilt my chin up, the sea breeze flows over me like water. How amazing it must have been to grow up here, surrounded by the Pacific, watching the blue reach as far as the eye can see, no limits, no—

I tense.

My skin bursts into a thousand little goose bumps, because I'm no longer alone.

Someone's here. Someone who wasn't inside the house.

My hand closes around the penguin knife in my pocket, and I unbraid the notes of the intruder's scent.

Were. Man. Young. Human form. Not wearing shoes. Approaching from behind. Either he's sloppy or he underestimated me, because he doesn't know that I felt his presence.

He means to assault me, and all I have to my advantage is the element of surprise. I force my heartbeat to slow down, and bide my time. Wait for the Were to come within reach of my blade. But a handful of feet from me, he halts.

I hear something thudding to the ground.

Smell the grass, crushed.

A deep intake of breath. Then a voice, hushed, barely audible through the wind. "Eva."

I whirl around, whipping out the knife, holding the blade at abdomen height. But its tip is nowhere near the man's skin, because he is . . .

Kneeling?

I adjust my aim, ready to strike, but the naked man doesn't make a single move. He stays on his knees, face bent upward, throat bare and vulnerable. Feverishly, he whispers, "As the prophet said. As the prophet wills."

"Who are you?"

He gives me a tremulous smile and, like a supplicant, presses his forehead to the ground.

CHAPTER 19

Just this once, he could have done without being right.

"DO YOU LIVE HERE?" I ASK. IN THE AFTERNOON SUN, I HAVE TO squint to properly make him out. I guess he *could* be Sem's brother—several years younger, similar hair color. Slim build and soft, boyish jawline. He doesn't seem hostile. But he also doesn't feel like he belongs to this place that smells like moss and brine.

I don't lower my knife. "Who are you?"

He slowly looks up at me, a smudge of soil on his forehead, another on his cheekbone. "Oh, your eyes. They are so familiar to me."

I take a step back. Quickly glance around, wondering if I should call for Koen. Except, would Koen kill this boy? Yes, probably. "I need you to tell me who you are," I demand.

"What a joy. To speak with you. To *be* with you."

What. The. Fuck. "I mean, sure. You *should* feel lucky, but . . . do I know you?"

He straightens further, whispering something that ends up swallowed by the breeze and the waves. Slowly, he stands, holding out his hand. When I change my defensive grip to something that could do some real damage, he remains undeterred. "Come with me," he says.

His voice is warm, coupled with a smile that is . . . unhinged, I should say. But this boy doesn't seem like a crazed nutjob. He's coherent. Kind. Looks at me like we used to play hopscotch together *and* like someone told him that my boogers are made of emeralds. So unabashedly adoring, I clutch my weapon tighter.

"Don't be afraid. We knew he would take you here."

"Who's we?"

"You must have felt so alone."

"If you come any closer, I *will* stab you." I pointedly lower my eyes to his dick, which swings between his legs like the world's wrinkliest Christmas ornament. "Wherever it's most convenient."

His smile softens. "I understand your reservations, but I am not afraid, and neither should you be. The moment has come. You were made, and so it has begun. His domain will flourish, and—"

"Stop with the Bible camp talk." I clench my teeth. "Did you call me Eva? Earlier?"

"It's the name by which I have always known you," he says simply.

"'Always'? Did you know me as a child?"

"Always. I learned the blood and the word, and therefore you."

My heart stops. He looks younger than me. Too young. "Did we grow up together?"

"Not as such, no."

"Then why do you know me?"

With a flick of his wrist, he once again offers his hand. "Come with me, and I'll tell you. *She* will tell you. You should know the wonder that you are."

"Nice try, but I'm not going to a second location with you. I'm not even convinced I want to stay in this one." I'm getting tired of the cryptic speeches, that ethereal smile painted on his face. Fear is slowly melting into frustration. "Are you a member of the Northwest pack?"

"There is no Northwest. There are no packs, no species, no borders."

"Right. Okay . . . if you don't tell me who you are, I'm going to scream, and someone who's much less nice and patient than me will come out of the house—"

"I can be fucking nice," Koen says, coming to stand behind me. Most of my tension dissolves.

"Not patient, though," he adds. "She got *that* right."

His heat presses against my back. "Is he Northwest?" I ask under my breath.

"No." Koen's hand wraps around my hip, completely engulfing it. It's a deceptively relaxed gesture, protective and lover-like. He pulls me into him, and the back of my head brushes against his chest. Worry and fear stink like acid, but I pick up neither from him. "Which means that I can kill him for being in my territory. Want me to?" He's joking. I think.

"He came alone," I murmur. "I don't think he's a danger."

"You're right." He continues louder, this time for the other Were to hear, "But why would he breach our borders? I must assume that he means to hurt you."

The boy shakes his head forcefully, mussing up already tousled hair. "I would rather die than hurt one of us, Eva."

I smell the truth of it. So does Koen, but his hold on me tightens. "What did you call her?" I can hear the frown in his question—and the way it deepens when no answer comes.

The boy stares for a long moment at Koen's fingers on my stomach, and his smile falters for the first time. "You shouldn't touch her," he warns.

It is, demonstrably, the wrong thing to say to the Alpha of a territory he just breached. So wrong, it bothers even me. "Excuse me?" Koen asks mildly.

And that poor boy—he's finally displaying some common sense, because he's about to shit himself. But to his credit, even as he shakes like a leaf, he doesn't back down. "You want her, but you are not worthy of her."

"Man, you don't know me. I think I bring a lot to the table."

"Like several moldy unicorn waffles," I mutter. In response, Koen playfully drums his fingertips over my stomach.

"He cannot keep you here, Eva," the boy tells me. "I told them that there was no need to take you. No need for blood. I promised them that if you knew we were waiting for you, you would come."

"Bro, she's not going anywhere."

"She is your superior in every way. You cannot speak for her, Koen Alexander."

"He's right, though," I say. "I'm not coming with you."

"Not all is lost, though," Koen says, suddenly pushing me half behind his body. His posture switches—protective to predatory. "Serena is off-limits, but you may still have a playdate with me."

"Eva," the boy pleads, eyes never leaving mine. "Do you not remember us? Have you not been told the stories? You were hurt greatly, if so." His smile folds into something else. Something sad. "Will you not join me?"

"I have no idea who you are. And since you're calling me by the wrong name, I think that's mutual."

His shoulders slump. It's like I cut the string that held him up.

"If you won't come with me, then I was wrong. And if I was wrong, before I leave, I will have to pay the price."

"Good for you that you won't be going anywhere, then," Koen says.

"It was lovely to stand this close to you, Eva. To feel the same breeze and the same grass. The flesh will be reborn." The boy bows his head. His attention shifts fully to Koen. "Koen Alexander. In another universe, one not as perfect as this one, I would have called you Alpha."

"What a daunting threat," Koen says, moving forward. When the boy begins to retreat, he sighs.

"We are many. And we have learned from past mistakes."

"Sure."

"What about you, Koen Alexander? Are you your parents' son?"

Koen freezes. His shoulders go rigid. "Boy, I'm faster than you, and a hell of a lot stronger. If you run, I will catch you within one hundred feet, and I'll probably end up hurting you."

"You will pay for what you did. And Constantine will see you shortly."

To me, it all sounds like nonsense. But I can smell Koen's rage. It runs so deep, I have to make the conscious choice not to step away from him. "Constantine is dead," he spits out.

"That he is," the boy agrees with his widest smile yet, a grin of undiluted joy, and I realize that my initial assessment of his sanity may have been incorrect. Then it all happens so quickly, my glitchy, shocked brain can barely register the order of it.

Koen was right: he *is* much faster, and he *could* catch the boy in one hundred feet. Except, he doesn't have one hundred feet. Because the Were doesn't run away toward the forest. Instead he chooses the opposite direction, and I don't understand—

Koen's "Fuck" is muffled by the waves lapping onto the shore
—where does the Were think he's going—
as Koen sprints to catch him
—that's not where he came from—
or maybe to kill him
—not the right path—
and why is he not slowing down, he's almost at the edge of the
cliff, he can't
—below the cliff, wasn't there a—
The Were jumps.

He dives off the cliff without a single moment of hesitation, a
perfectly symmetrical shape, a graceful silhouette against the sun.
Even the wind ebbs, as if holding its breath, trying to keep still.

All Koen can do is skid to a stop. Let one hand tug at his hair.
Watch as the boy's body travels through the air. Listen to a long,
long silence, broken only by the sound of bones crashing against
stone.

CHAPTER 20

He wants to abscond with her. Fuck the rest of the world—it's incapable of giving her the safety she so clearly deserves. He'll fix that. He'll make up for everything she has been put through.

I T'S NOT YOUR FAULT, SERENA.

He was clearly unwell. Very unwell. On some crazed mission. Not *your fault.*

People—people who are *not* Koen—have been repeating variations on this for a while, and for a while I've been nodding and telling them, *Yes, I know. Thank you, I'm good. No need to stick around, if there's somewhere you need to be.*

The sun is about to set. There are a dozen cars parked by Koen's cabin, and more of his seconds than I even met last night milling around. I struggle to keep their names straight, but it doesn't matter. They're not here for me, except for the ones on babysitting duty. Because it's obvious that Koen tasked them with making sure that I'm not left alone. Still, I act like I don't notice the way they sit next to me, on the second-highest porch step. In ten-minute shifts.

I try to pretend that Koen isn't the only person with whom I'm interested in having any kind of conversation, but my belly is made of lead. *He* was there with me. *He* would know if it was my fault.

"Would you like something warm to drink?" I ask Saul when he comes over.

"Thanks, honey, but we're leaving soon."

"Anything else I can help with?"

"You're doing it."

I glance down at myself, and the stolen hoodie that might be my only tether to sanity. If I'm doing something, Saul and I must have a different definition of *doing*. But he's shaking his head.

"Just the fact that you're keeping your cool, helps K—*all* of us."

"Oh, great. I just figured I'd scream my little heart out later, into my pillow."

Saul laughs. "That's some grade A compartmentalization."

"Thanks." I toss my hair back. "It's the childhood trauma."

Saul chokes on his spit, and Koen arrives just in time to thump him firmly between the shoulder blades. "Give me a second with Serena," he orders. "Alone."

Unlike everyone else, he doesn't sit. Instead he squats in front of me, eye to eye.

"So," I say. What would happen if I were to demand the hug I so desperately want? Since I really can't, maybe I'll just ask him if he thinks that I—

"No," he says simply.

I blink. "What?"

"No. There is nothing you could have done to prevent him from killing himself. No, it's not your fault. No, you shouldn't have agreed to go with him."

God. I needed to hear it. From *him*. "He's the second person to die in front of me in three days, Koen."

"I know. I'm starting to think that you might be bad news, killer."

I laugh. And laugh. And then force myself to stop, because there is a sense of fullness behind my eyes, inside my throat, and it threatens to overflow. "Bob was bad enough," I whisper. "But this guy . . . he wasn't trying to hurt me. He was so young, and it feels like such a waste, and . . ." I take a deep breath. "It's just been a lot. In very little time. I think I'm ready for the musical episode, you know?"

"I have no idea what the fuck you're talking about."

I laugh again. This time he smiles, too.

Until I add, "He seemed so lucid. And then, all of a sudden, he was saying all this weird shit, and it wasn't . . . He didn't sound normal."

Koen reaches up, long fingers combing through my hair. Pressing against my scalp. The warmth of his touch has my eyelids fluttering closed. "It wasn't normal. But I won't insult your intelligence and tell you that he was talking gibberish. This is bad, Serena."

Of course it is. "Because of Constantine?"

"Among the rest." A sigh. His fingertips massage the skin at the back of my head. "Yeah."

"Can you tell me who he is?"

"He was a Were. About two decades ago, he was directly responsible for the deaths of thousands of Weres and Humans in the Northwest."

I clench my fists so hard, my nails leave imprints in my palms. "And now he's back."

"He's *dead*."

"Could reports of his passing have been greatly exaggerated?"

"I ripped his heart out of his chest, chewed it for half a minute, and then spit it into the ocean."

I nod slowly. "A simple 'no' would have sufficed."

Koen's mouth twitches. "Constantine's dead, no doubt about it. But he was the leader of a very destructive group."

"Another Alpha?"

"Nothing like that. But some considered him a prophet."

I chew on my lower lip, mulling it over. "I didn't know Weres have cults."

"Everybody has cults. They're the weeds of sentient civilization. And Constantine's was the worst of them, because . . ." He shakes his head and turns back to where his seconds are idling, waiting for him. He's borrowing precious time, just to explain shit to me. "Constantine's dead. But his right hands . . . Our understanding of their power structure may have been incomplete."

"The boy who killed himself . . . ?"

"He was in his late teens. Too young to have been part of the original cult. I doubt he ever met Constantine."

"Could he be a relative of mine?"

Koen sighs like he's been wondering the same. "We have the boy's body," he says evenly. "Lots of DNA to compare with yours, and we are already on it."

"And Constantine?"

"I . . ." He shakes his head, at a loss for words, and in this moment—when he looks as confused as I feel, when he chooses to share his lack of understanding with me, I think I love him. Just a little bit.

"Okay." I swallow. Glance into the distance, at the ocean waves crashing into the shore. The glow of the last few sunrays.

"Clearly, they think you are connected to them. Most likely, you are somehow related to one of their former members. You're very high profile, and if they're rebuilding, they'll want you back."

Right. "I might be the Eva person he was talking about." The prospect is disorienting. Makes me sick to my stomach.

Koen's hand shifts to my cheek. "Look at me."

I do. His eyes are dark and steady. Make me forget what led us here, and what's to come.

"Your name doesn't fucking matter. You are my killer. Okay?"

A laugh hiccups out of me, a little wet. "Okay."

"Good. I need to meet with the Assembly." His thumb swipes against my cheekbone. "Do you want to come with me?"

Yes, with every single cell of my body. "Why would I come with you?"

"Because the idea of having you out of my sight makes me want to flip those cars one by one."

I stifle my chuckle. "The Assembly is very concerned that you're breaking your covenant. I doubt me coming with you would help your case."

"Good point." He seems to consider it. "On the other hand, fuck my case."

I snort. Watch him rise to his feet. Feel my heart grow heavier as he walks away.

Then, just a few feet from me, he turns around. "Killer?"

"Yeah?"

There is a false start. Like the words are too foreign to flow out with ease. But then he says, "Before I leave, I think I need to hold you for a minute."

I'm in his arms before I know how I got there. He bends down to scoop me up, and my forehead fits so perfectly into the valley of his already-prickly throat, this cannot be anything but *fated.* He lifts me higher, my feet no longer touching the ground, and hides his face in my neck.

A long, deep inhale. My pulse begins to dance.

He's— I did *not* plan on this. I have no business caring so much about him, but I can't remember the last time I felt this close to someone. Koen is warm, as solid as any rocky cliffside. So what if people think we're fucking?

So what if his heart ends up broken when I die in a few weeks?

So what if the Alpha's authority becomes questionable right at a moment in which the pack is suffering from violent threats and political turmoil—

No. *No.*

"I'll be fine," I force myself to say, slowly ungluing myself from his body, pushing him to let me down and let go of me. I cover the stench of the lie with some truths. "I'm tired. I should probably sleep. Just . . . say hi to Karolina from me."

He looks the kind of unhappy that comes from knowing that I'm hiding something. I feel, in the lingering of his hand on my shoulder, that he wants to press me back into him. But his muscles relax, and that's the end of it. "I'll be back tomorrow morning. If anything happens to me, what do you do?"

"Buy a black veil, pretend I'm a widow, cash in on your life insurance."

"You call Lowe. Ask him to come get you."

"What about your seconds?"

Koen's jaw shifts. He seems to come to a bitter realization. "I trust them with my life, but apparently not with yours. Lowe can protect you better than anyone." His hand lifts to my cheek. Falls back to his side without touching me. "Well. Anyone but me. You'll be safe tonight. I have people patrolling around the cabin—"

"The two cardinal points, yes."

"I have twelve guards."

"That is . . ." I close my mouth. I'm assuming he can spare the manpower. Clearly, the headline here is *Big Man Needs Peace of Mind.* "Excessive, probably. Anyone watching out for bald eagles?"

"There'll be someone on the roof." He nods like he's about to leave again.

I can't let him go without saying, "I'm sorry."

He frowns. "None of this is your fault."

"I know. But this is difficult for you, too. And he dragged your parents into it, which I can't even imagine . . ." I swallow. "I'm sorry that you have to deal with this."

His teeth clench. There's a flicker of something unreadable in his face. "If I come back and something has happened to you, Serena, I'm going to be so fucking pissed."

I bite the inside of my lips. "That sounds like a *you* problem."

"Yeah. That it is."

I turn and walk inside the cabin. I do not watch Koen leave, nor do I listen to the engine softening in the distance. Instead I go to my room, dig into the mountain of blankets and pillows the bed has somehow accumulated, sit cross-legged with my phone in my hands, and do the only thing that makes sense.

Serena: Would you love me less if my name was Eva?

Misery: Yes.

Misery: But not like, by a lot.

I bury my face in the pillow to laugh and cry at the same time.

———— ⤝⤞ ————

I WAKE UP A FEW HOURS LATER, ON FIRE.

Pouring sweat.

Shivering.

In pain so visceral, I am willing to do anything, absolutely fuck-ing *anything* to *not* feel it. Even something as drastic as dying.

I roll out of bed and drag myself to the shower. Loud whimpers spill out of me, and I slap a hand against my mouth, until I remem-ber that Koen won't be home until morning. If I use his bathtub, he won't know. Or care.

I stumble across the hallway, taking three pit stops on the way—two to dry heave, and one to just collapse for a little while. *As one does*, I tell myself. *Totally normal. Nothing to see here.*

My head spins as I pull myself up. It helps that my claws are somehow out, something to stick through the wooden walls to lug myself to a semi-upright position.

You're doing amazing, Serena. Eva. Killer. Whoever you are.

My heart has never beaten this fast, not even after a sprint, not even after killing someone. I remember when Dr. Henshaw listed the many ways in which the fevers could lead to my death. Septic shock and widespread inflammation. Brain damage and neuronal death. Dehydration.

Cardiac stress.

I was kinda partial to metabolic imbalance, but maybe this is how I go?

Either way, I inform my body, *things end in cold water. That's non-negotiable.*

I lurch into Koen's bathroom. The underwear and flannel I'm wearing are so sweat-soaked, it hurts to peel them off my skin. I turn on the faucet, make sure that the water is gelid, and when I feel my stomach twist to expel something, I trip back toward the sink.

That's where I see my eyes

I freeze, because this is new. Or maybe, in all the fever attacks so far, I never looked at my face in a mirror. My pupils have shrunk to pinpricks. It's like my irises are eggs, and someone punctured them open with a needle. The dark brown spills out, filling the white like a puddle of something viscous that could almost be *blood*—

"Serena."

I turn around. My heart sinks.

Koen is wearing yesterday's clothes and must have *just* returned. He inhales deeply, staring at my nearly naked body, focusing on the fat drops of sweat rolling between my breasts. The hot flush that blankets my skin. My eyes, still leaking into themselves.

"I'm sorry." I'm hoarse. Weak. I force myself to take a deep breath, because I need to—cold water. Can't deal with him now. I hug myself tight, forgetting about my own sharp claws, ignoring the way they pierce the skin of my ribs. "It's b-better if you leave."

His eyes are shadowed. He takes a step forward, bringing inside a tidal wave of his scent that's *safe* and *clean* and *healthy* and—

Oh my God. *Sex.* It's so delicious, so indecent, so fundamentally erotic, I want it even more than the cold water. Which I need to *survive.*

"Please, Koen. I need you to leave."

"Where does it hurt?" He comes closer, clearly unaware that I'm scary and unpredictable. His heat *should* bother me, but by some miracle of biology it doesn't add to the fever. "And how bad?"

"It's fine. I just need to—" I can't bear his gaze on me. I turn away and spot my eyes in the mirror once again. They're even worse than before, swallowed by a rising tide of dark green, and . . . "Oh my God," I whisper, reaching up to touch them, but Koen traps both my wrists against the small of my back. He slides his other arm around my chest, plastering me to him.

"Your claws are out, and you're *already* bleeding. You need to stay still."

"My eyes—"

"It's okay."

"But they—"

"Serena." That Alpha voice. "Calm down."

I do. For about a second. Then panic rises, higher, stronger. "That's not normal."

"Stop looking at them. Deep breaths."

"I can't. What is happening?"

"Don't look at them."

Tears slide down my face. I'm about to explode. "But why are they—"

Koen's fist darts out to punch the mirror, shattering my reflection into a thousand small shards. "Here. Now they're not doing that anymore." His palm rests against my forehead. "You're burning up. This is not the first time, is it?"

Yes. No. I don't know.

"Answer me."

"N-no."

"Good girl. Is it a fever?"

I nod, and the simple gesture makes me dizzy. I sink into Koen's body even more. There is no way to describe the fabric of his clothes other than *offensive*. I need them *off*.

"Cold baths work to bring it down?"

"Yes."

He glances at the almost-full tub. A second later I'm submerged in water. Distantly, I register some surprise. Because Koen gets in with me, clothes and all, and pulls me between his spread legs.

The sudden icy cold feels like unicorns and kittens building a pillow fort on a pink cloud, then snacking on a tub of frosting. "Better?" Koen asks.

I nod. The soft weight of his lips presses against my temple.

"Anything else you do?"

I shake my head. Open my mouth to tell Koen that in a second the shock will knock me out, and I'll wake up shivering in a couple of hours. That he should let go of me. That people in my condition can harm those around them. But one of his hands splays wide on my abdomen, and the other curves around my inner thigh, and even though this might be the most shameful moment of my entire life, I'm too tired and comfortable to do anything but fall asleep.

CHAPTER 21

No.

I WAKE UP TO THE MOST BEAUTIFUL PIANO MUSIC I'VE EVER heard.

Not that it means much, given my pathological inability to listen to anything without a techno beat, but this . . . it's *spectacular*. Vaguely familiar. Probably classical. Elegant but intimate. Being awakened by any sort of loud noise is down there with eating paint chips in my list of favorite things, but this is so gentle and understated, I want to make it my forever alarm.

My eyes flutter open of their own volition, and I realize that I'm in Koen's bedroom, again. Stealing his bed, again. Unable to recall how I ended up here, *again*. My last memories are blurred. Working on a letter. Yawning till my eyes were a constant stream of tears. Sliding under the covers. I must have slept in, judging from the early afternoon light filtering inside.

Which explains the wake-up call.

Koen sits on the piano stool, his back a bare expanse interrupted only by the waistband of his jeans. He is, at once, relaxed and in movement, muscles shifting occasionally, always in time with the music. What would it be like, to feel them vibrate against my cheek, or the flesh of my palm?

Sitting up is difficult, because my limbs are pulled pork. "Is this . . . ?"

"Still not Bach, killer." His long fingers don't miss a single key.

I really need to broaden my operatic horizons. "How did your meeting with the huddle leaders go?"

Koen feels distant, which surprises me after our hug yesterday, on the porch. He's not the type for mood swings—his mood tends to be consistently shitty. Am I missing something? "They all acknowledge the threat, and we're all on the same page. Which is more than I can say about the first time this happened." One last, oddly strident note, and he turns to face me directly. He leans forward, elbows on his spread thighs. His eyes *bore*, debone me, until I can't help fidgeting.

"Is anything . . ." I run a hand through my hair. "Are you—"

Why is my hair wet?

What is this T-shirt that I'm wearing?

And the claw marks on my forearms—

Last night's events hit me like a sledgehammer. Fuck.

Fuck.

I pull back the covers, intending to run for the bathroom mirror, but my quads are incapable of supporting me, and I fall back into the mattress. "My eyes—"

"Are as usual," he replies calmly.

I rub my face. Shit. That was bad. That was *so* bad—

"How long have you been feeling poorly?" Koen asks, rudely interrupting my panic tailspin.

I can tell with a millisecond-long glance that he's willing to slow roast the truth out of me. But what kind of veteran liar would I even be if I didn't attempt a weak "I'm not. It was just—"

"Serena." He looks at me like I'm not just insulting his intelligence, but also lowering the IQ of the entire pack.

Okay. Fine. No games. "I don't know."

"You don't *know*."

"Four months. Twelve years."

His eyes harden. "What a helpfully narrow interval."

"I really don't know. None of this is normal, Koen. None of this is *not* terrible, and—" I stop. Take a deep breath, letting the soothing scents of Koen and tea spread through my lungs. There is a steaming mug on the nightstand, and after a few sips I no longer feel like blurting my entire miserable story out to him. Progress. "The fevers began four or five months ago. But Dr. Henshaw says that this is a degenerative condition that starts before symptoms manifest." Koen stares at me like I'm wasting his time by not telling him everything that happened in the last decade of my life, so I continue. "It's a Were disorder that has no equivalent among Humans. Relatively common among Weres in their ninth or tenth decade, but not unheard of in younger patients. It's called CSD, which stands for—"

"Cortisol surge disorder."

"You're familiar. Good." His look tells me that nothing about this is in any realm adjacent to *good*. I avert my gaze. "The fevers are caused by . . . Basically, chronic stress fucked up my inflammatory and anti-inflammatory signals. Again, not uncommon."

"CSD can be treated."

"Yeah. In Weres, it can. Sometimes. But my hybrid biology hasn't been responding to meds. My hormonal levels are getting worse, and Dr. Henshaw said . . ." I suck my teeth. "Not compatible with life. That's how he put it."

Koen's eyelids are the only moving parts of his body. They flutter closed, then open again as he asks calmly, "How long?"

"Six months at the most. But that was . . . two months ago."

"I see." He seems bizarrely unperturbed. An Alpha trait, maybe: set aside emotions, absorb information. I'm sure it's useful in a crisis, but his cold grilling is somewhat disturbing. "What treatments did he attempt?"

"All of them. He involved his colleagues, and . . . believe me when I say, no stone was left unturned. But the side effects were bad, and my deterioration was steady. Linear, originally, then exponential."

"Is it still? Getting worse?"

After a beat, I nod. "The fevers are almost nightly. And the eye thing, the claws . . . those are new. I don't know what that was."

"Arms and eyes are where the shift to wolf form starts," he explains. "Their motor proteins activate first."

"Really? Is that the reason . . . ?"

"Maybe your fever triggers the shift, but your body cannot see it through. Or vice versa. I don't know. I barely ever took a science class."

"Really?" I tilt my head. "Why?"

"Because I was too busy protecting my pack from a coup to finish high school. Does the Vampyre know?"

"Misery? No. When I started seeing Dr. Henshaw, I told her some bullshit about having headaches, and—"

Koen snorts.

"What?"

"Just shocked the Vampyre still trusts your lies, is all."

I frown. "Every lie I've told Misery was to protect her from—"

"I'm sure your pretty little head made up a million good reasons and topped them with those gross formaldehyde cherries. Still can't believe she lets you out of her sight."

"No one 'lets' me *do* stuff or *go* places," I point out tiredly. "That's not how it works, Koen."

"If you were mine, it would. And clearly, you fucking should be." I can't tell if it's a threat or a promise. All of a sudden, Koen's eyes are so full of anger, I shiver and turn aside.

"Is that why you were in the fucking woods alone for two months? Why you're here now? Some fucked-up notion of sparing your sister from finding out that the person she cares the most about in the whole world is ill?"

Guilt stuffs my throat full. This is the part I'm most embarrassed to speak out loud, but I force myself to do it anyway. "One night I woke up in Ana's room. With no idea how I'd gotten there."

Koen inhales sharply. Like he already knows where this is going. "You didn't hurt her, Serena."

"No, but I could have. I was boiling hot and disoriented, and CSD patients can often experience aggressive episodes, and . . ." I shake my head. "It's for the best. If I told Misery, she'd want to be with me. But Ana needs her more than I do, so—"

Something lands on the comforter with a soft thud.

I gasp. "These are my . . ."

"Letters. To Ana and the Vampyre."

"Where did you find them? You had no right to—"

"On your bed. Unfolded."

"That doesn't excuse—"

"Serena." It's little more than a whisper, but everything about Koen, from his voice to the taut flex in his biceps, tells me how deeply unwilling he is to let me express righteous indignation over the violation of my privacy. He continues, composed, soft spoken, just as calm: "Last night, I didn't know if you'd ever wake up again."

It's heart snapping, as far as realizations go. I worked my way up to really bad attacks, but he had no context for what he experienced a few hours ago. It hadn't occurred to me how scary it would be for him to witness it.

Because that's what he is. Scared. Terrified in a way he may have never experienced before. It makes my stomach twist and my eyes burn.

"I'm sorry." I wipe my cheek with the back of my hand. "I'd written those back at the cabin, but . . . well, I had to redo them. They're for Misery, for the most part. And Ana—from someone who's like her. And I wrote one for Lowe, too, but it's mostly about how to take care of Misery once I'm not . . . I mean, he's doing a great job already. But there are some quirks you only find out by living with someone for a decade, like Misery's penchant for hate-reading, her terrible taste in clothes if left to her own devices, the fact that sometimes she uses fancy words without really knowing their meaning. She could fall back into her mismatched socks phase, and . . ."

"Why are you crying?" Koen asks gently.

I sniffle. "I'm not sure. Could you please forget that you know? I'd rather not talk about—"

"That's no longer an option." His tone is kind but steel boned. "I'm your Alpha. And I need you to be honest with me."

I take a deep, shuddering breath. Gather myself. "Dr. Henshaw has my labs. All my data. He has a lot of information at his disposal, and he was able to reconstruct the progression of my condition. I don't know how much of this is due to me being a hybrid, but if it is, and if something similar were to happen to Ana . . . Dr. Henshaw is under instructions to inform Lowe, after . . . *afterward.* I hope it'll help, and—"

"After what, Serena?"

"—I'm not precious about that stuff. It's more that I don't want them to freak out or feel like they have to—"

"After. What," he repeats. He's not on the stool anymore. Instead, his palms brace both sides of my bare thighs, and he leans into me. Close enough that his scent becomes my entire universe. Close enough for me to see little freckles on his skin, to count the scars that crisscross all over his torso. He looks down, inexorable, eyes blacker than black. "Say it. After what?"

I have to. Out loud. For the very first time. I have no choice but to make this real. "After I die."

The second the words are out, hanging heavy in the air between us, Koen . . . smiles.

He bends further, and there isn't a single trace of doubt on his face. He's an immovable object *and* an unstoppable force. And he says, slowly, "If you think I'm going to let you die, Serena, you know fuck all."

<hr />

DR. SEM CAINE'S OFFICE IS AT THE OUTSKIRTS OF THE DEN. HE checks my vitals and listens to a detailed recap of last night's episode, but what he spends most of his time on is the records Dr. Henshaw sent over.

Koen waits by the door, cross-armed and dark-clouded. He dispassionately informs Sem of my prognosis, commands him to refute it, kill it with fire, salt it, and then simply gazes stoically into the distance as I put my clothes back on.

It was a shared but unspoken decision, him staying for my exam. Maybe he's afraid I'll bolt, even though I'm here neither reluctantly nor under duress. Maybe he cannot physically stay away. All I know is that my heart is squeezed into the tightest of fists. It's obvious what he wants to be told.

Sem glances away from his tablet to give me a warm healthcare-professional smile. "Alpha, I think it would be best if you and I could talk privately."

"About me?" I sit back in the chair and cock my head. "That has to be a HIPAA violation."

Sem's brow furrows. "A what?"

"Just . . ." I shake my head. "Whatever you have to say, you can do so in front of me. I won't make a scene."

Sem clears his throat. "May I speak freely?"

"Yes," I say—just as Koen does. The question, of course, was for him. And not for the rightful owner of the soon-to-be-rotting body.

"Okay. Well." Sem draws in a steady breath. "Quite frankly, looking at the labs, I am surprised that you're alive, Serena. Dr. Henshaw's diagnosis and prognosis seem accurate."

I knew it, of course, but hearing it still feels like a blade slicing me open. I can't see Koen's face from where I sit, but I *feel* his displeasure beating through me. It's so intense, I almost consider going to him and . . . and what? Patting his back? Giving him a hug? I'm being ridiculous.

"What if this is just the way hybrids are?" Koen asks. "We have no basis for comparison."

"Theoretically, that could be true. But her body is in obvious distress. Weight loss, nutrient deficiencies. Metabolic and cardiac stress. I wonder how she functions."

"Not compatible with life,' I say under my breath. Sem's frown deepens, but it's a fascinating turn of phrase—I found it so from the very start. And I earned it. I have a right to use it, don't I?

"What about drugs?" Koen asks, impatient.

"Dr. Henshaw was very thorough in his attempts to ease Serena's discomfort," Sem says softly.

In English. Although one wouldn't be able to tell from Koen's uncomprehending face. He steps closer and wraps a hand around my shoulders. "She's in pain. Not eating enough. Not getting enough sleep. The fucking fevers are happening every night."

"I can give her IVs and recommend easily digestible foods, but the cold baths are the safest way to—"

"She's in *pain*," Koen snarls, leaning forward over Sem's desk.

I expect the doctor to retreat or show his throat to appease his Alpha's anger. Instead, his eyes turn hooded with sadness. "I know, Koen. I'm sorry."

"Don't be sorry—that's not your job. Your fucking job is to cure ill people. Why do you have no idea how to do that?"

"Koen," I chide, feeling my chest constrict. I wrap a hand around his forearm. The long veins running through it are coursing with blood. "That's not kind."

"As we established, I'm not fucking kind." He straightens. "Find a way to get *this*"—he gestures toward me—"fixed. Okay?"

Sem nods, full of sorrow.

As we exit the building, Koen halts briefly. His throat works as he looks into the distance, tight-lipped, running his tongue over his teeth. Composing himself.

I bite into the inside of my cheek, feeling powerless. *I'm sorry*, I want to say. *I know you care. I know it's hard.* But he's unreachable—a large, silent presence at my side as we walk to the car, his legs so much longer than mine, I have to break into a light jog to keep up with him. "Will you slow down?"

"No." He nods at a group of pack members who wave at him. Speeds up even more.

"Hear me out for a second."

"I am."

"You are not—"

"I can walk and listen at the same time." He stares straight ahead. "Must be one of those elusive Alpha traits."

"Please, can you just—" I round him and block his path. When he tries to walk past me, I close my hand around the hem of his flannel. "I know how you are feeling."

At last, his eyes meet mine. They do *not* look pleased. "You mean, angry as fuck?"

"No." I stop another attempted sidestep. "Well, yes. But that's not the real issue, and—I know it takes some adjustment, learning that someone you lo—care about is going to die." I swallow. My smile is tremulous. "I've been there."

Koen's jaw shifts. Clenches and releases. I'm afraid he'll try to leave again, and maybe, just for good measure, run me over as he pulls out of the parking lot. Instead, he says, "This is why you didn't want to stay at my cabin."

I hesitate. "I . . . It's safer, I think. I can't control myself. What if I harmed someone in the pack? What if I harmed *you*?" His look is full of pity, like I'm an ant trying to stuff a full-size anvil in her cute pink backpack. "Oh, fuck off. It's very sexist of you to assume that I couldn't beat you up."

"There's a long list of women capable of kicking my ass. In your current state, you are nowhere on it."

"What if I accidentally attacked a weaker pack member?"

"Guess I'd have to spank you." He seems unbothered by the prospect. "I'm more concerned about you sleepwalking off a cliff. But don't worry, I'll be making sure that doesn't happen." His smile feels like a threat. I'm proud of myself for not flinching.

He tries to move past me again, and this time I take his hand. "I know you want to be mad at fate—"

"I'm mad at *you*, killer."

"—but I'm at peace with it. I wish I had more time. With . . . with the people I love. With the universe. With"—I gesticulate around me—"with the ocean and the trees and . . . I love this territory so much. But it's such a *privilege*, to know that even if I won't live much longer, Misery is taken care of, and so is Ana." It's the first time I've verbalized this out loud. And it makes my chest feel at once light as a feather and deep as a crater. "When I die—"

"Not on my fucking watch, Serena."

"Okay. But when I die—"

Koen's fingers abruptly slide into the hair at the side of my head. Bend my neck back, none too gently. "Serena." He stares down at me, eyes a few inches from mine. His fury is a physical, formidable thing. It doesn't scare me. "If you say anything like that ever again, I'm going to kill you myself. Understood?"

It likely speaks of how much my sanity has devolved that I exhale a laugh. "Got it."

He grunts, a fraction mellower. I wonder if he really thinks that he can will my illness into nonexistence. Maybe someone who's been Alpha for two decades is too accustomed to power to entertain the idea of something not going his way? But slowly, eventually, he lets go of me, and I take a step back, nearly walking into the parked car. I let the sleeves of his hoodie swallow my hands, and God, that shopping trip was *so* unnecessary.

"The thing is," I try to explain, "it might be for the best."

The way he looks at me is so indignant, it makes me chuckle again. Which is not appropriate for the conversation.

"I mean, it's not like you and I could . . . You have the covenant. And I'm not exactly available for a long-term relationship." My smile feels a little forced. I hope it'll work on him anyway. "The reasons why it couldn't work between us are not just yours, or just mine. None of that one-way unrequited crap. Isn't that better?"

I half expect a dismissive scoff. A curt command to get into the car. Instead, Koen studies me at length, his eyes opaque. "If I weren't Alpha," he asks, eventually. "And you weren't sick. What then, Serena?"

"What if Earth was modeled after a giant parsley leaf? What if Humans pissed moondust? What if—"

His fingers trap my chin. Tilt my head back, hitching my breath. Once again, I have no choice but to meet his eyes. "What then, Serena?"

I can't bring myself to say, *I think we both know*, but he hears it anyway, because his nod is there, barely perceptible. This time, when the pressure swells behind my eyes, I let the tears flow. I feel them splash down on my collarbones. Dampen the tips of my hair.

"Anything that's going to happen to you," he promises, voice honest and pitched low in the swish of the breeze, "is going to be over my dead body."

I laugh softly, because . . . what else can I do? I follow him with my eyes as he opens the passenger door for me. Since this is an opportunity, one of few I have left, instead of sliding inside I wrap my arms around his torso, fisting the flannel at his hip. My face presses into his side. I inhale the scent of him, wondering if anything else this good has ever existed, and ask, "Can I say something really, really selfish?"

I feel his assent. I think he might want to know everything that's in my head. I think he could shake every thought I've ever had out of my skull, rummage through them for years, and still not be bored.

I think that in a parsley-shaped world, he and I would have had some fun.

"If today was my last day, I'd be happy to have spent it with you."

Koen cups the back of my head. I lean into the soft press of his lips against my brow. He says nothing, barely breathes, but his hands don't let go of me for a long, long time.

CHAPTER 22

He easily resigned himself to a lifetime without her, but . . .
Simply put, he is unwilling to contemplate a universe in
which she no longer exists.

THAT NIGHT KOEN HAS A PACK MEETING AT THE CABIN.
I get out of the shower, quickly put on leggings and one of
his shirts (which I sniff for over a minute, with inappropriate enthusiasm). I'm about to move to the living room and *not* mind my
own business, when my phone lights up with a call. From someone
who usually prefers a string of twelve multi-paragraph texts over a
one-minute chat.

"What's up, Bleetch?" I ask, terrified that Koen might have
gone behind my back and told Misery about my situation.

I will stab him, I vow. *I will chop him into pieces and sell him at a wet
market. For pennies.*

"Not much." A beat. "First question: Are you alone?"

"You mean, existentially, or . . ."

"Is there someone around you?"

"No. Why?"

"Second question: Are you in the right headspace to receive information that could possibly hurt you?"

My heart drops. "Misery, if—"

"No, I'm serious. I talked to Lowe about the Northwest, and it's *bad.*"

"How bad?"

"*Bad* bad. Like ... *Our lives*, bad."

"Whoa."

"Yeah. I feel way less special, knowing that there's all this trauma waffling about."

I sit on the edge of the mattress. "Is this about the cult I might be related to?"

"Koen told you about it?" She sounds surprised. "Lowe said he probably wouldn't."

"Some of it. Yesterday something weird happened." Understatement of the week. Prepare the wall plaque. "A guy came at me and started yelling thesaurus prophecies."

"Hang on, I thought they killed the cult twenty years ago?"

"They thought so, too. Surprise."

A *long* pause. "Cool."

"Yeah." I sink back into the pillows. "Very."

"Serena, are we bad people?"

"Um ... Morally? Spiritually? Fiscally? Because I did your taxes every year and exploited every single loophole in the medieval castle that is our financial system, but—"

"I'm just saying that we must, to some degree, have done something to deserve the shit coming our way."

"Well." I rub my palm against my belly, wondering if the cramps I'm experiencing are a fun new addition to my symptoms dance card. "We did pretend you were overtaken by bloodlust that time Mr. Barca got a paper cut."

"And made him piss himself. You know what? Maybe it was worth it."

"Still, I don't know that our lives necessarily needed a cult plotline."

"Agreed. Wanna hang up and spend the rest of the day buddy watching that Human show about the MILFs?"

"Yeah, actually."

"Tough shit. I'm giving you the cult deets whether you want them or not. What do you know already?"

I take a deep breath. "That Constantine was like, the Were equivalent of Rasputin."

"I have no idea what that is."

History was never her strong suit. "Do you know what his ideas were?" I ask. "What he promised his followers?"

"How do you know he promised something?"

"Isn't that the whole point of a cult? I'm your leader. You do what I tell you, and I'll give you eternal life, unlimited wealth, re-birth in a world where everything tastes like pineapples—"

"What about, 'And I'll turn you into a Were'?"

I sit up in a quick, fluid movement I did *not* think my abs were capable of. "Are you for real?"

"Yup. It was some deranged shit. The cult ran several genera-tions deep. The original founder was one of those cuckoo bananas Were supremacist guys who thought that the other species should dedicate their lives to massaging his feet. Weres should control the means of production, that kind of stuff."

"Sounds familiar."

"Totally. Roscoe, the former Alpha of the Southwest, was a bit like that. His wife, Emery, is Koen's aunt. And I'm sure in some East Coast packs they won't let you graduate first grade if you can't spell at least ten Vampyre slurs. The world's full of assholes, and the dung beetles love it. Sadly, the original founder of the cult was just a little too batty for everyone's taste. He was originally from the Southwest, but they politely asked him to leave. Lowe used the word 'exiled.' I'm not sure whether he was being melodramatic or if that's a thing among Weres."

"Why did they kick him out?"

"Ruining the vibes? Unclear. But the dude took his family and friends and made himself comfortable at the border between the Southwest, the Northwest, and the most rural parts of Human territory. Kept themselves busy by writing their scriptures on the inside of cereal boxes. It started as a small settlement, less than twenty Weres. Packs monitored them, even interacted, but nothing significant happened for decades. Until his daughter, or his son's daughter—Lowe tried to draw me a diagram but got stuck—went to a trading meeting with the Northwest and met her mate."

"Constantine?"

"Nope, some guy named Jochem. Originally, the couple were going to live together in Jochem's huddle. But, big surprise, Jochem decided that the cult made some valid points and that the other species should, in fact, show their soft underbelly and let the Weres feast on them. They moved in with the cult. Even brought some friends. And had a few kids.'

"Among them, Constantine."

"You know what? You're clever for a hybrid."

I bite back my laughter until my cheeks bleed. Sometimes I miss Misery so much, it hurts every atom of my being.

"The thing about Constantine, he was also cuckoo bananas, but smarter about it. Early on he figured that if he wanted to take the family cult business to a pro level, he needed more followers. But Weres, even the assholes, were not interested in leaving their cushy packs to sit around a bonfire and discuss their infinite superiority.

ALI HAZELWOOD

So he turned to his Human neighbors. But he needed to offer something of value, and what's more valuable than becoming faster and stronger, living longer, and having a fluffy secondary form?"

"How the hell was he proposing to turn Humans into Weres?"

"Apparently there were bites and mutual blood drinking and a not insignificant amount of sex rituals."

I groan. This is too stupid, even for me. "What about the fact that they are different species? What about *science*?"

"You are so cynical. A little science could never stand between a frat boy and his desire for a monthly howl fest."

"It makes no sense. We both lived among Humans—have you ever met anyone who said they wished they could be a Were?"

"No. But I've also never met anyone with a belly-button fetish, and they exist."

"Do they?"

"Alvinophilia. Look it up. Anyway, fast-forward ten years or so, and Constantine has hundreds of followers. Lots of them are Humans from the rural places neighboring the original settlement, but some are from The City, too. They basically act as servants and free labor, which in turns begets new Were followers. The leadership is fully Were. Constantine's career as a charismatic leader is up and coming. If dudes do as he says, they'll be able to bench-press women at the beach with their pinky fingers. If women do the same . . ." She hesitates. My throat tightens, because I know what she's about to say. "Their children might just be born Weres."

I close my eyes. Wait for the room to stop spinning. This scenario fits my situation better than a bespoke dress. "Like me."

"Well, your mom drinking Were blood had nothing to do with you being a hybrid. But . . . yeah."

"That's why they want me. It's not about who I'm related to.

They think that I used to be Human, and Constantine turned me into a Were."

"Yup. And in case you're wondering, *Why did Lowe and Koen not consider the possibility that I was a child of the cult the second they learned about my existence?* the answer is, they did. They investigated it, but they were sure that every child was accounted for. Anyway, this is where the shittiness of Koen's life starts paralleling our own, because the whole showdown that led to him becoming Alpha—"

"Actually, stop. Don't tell me."

"You don't want to know?"

"No. Yes." I swallow. "I think I should hear this from Koen."

"Aw. Are you guys sleeping together yet?"

"What? No!"

"Well, since it's probably going to happen, would you like a heads-up on the biology?"

"The what?"

"His dick. It—"

"It's *not* going to happen, Misery. It'd be against the law. He took an oath of celibacy."

"I mean, sure." She doesn't *sound* sure. "But you should know that because you're his mate, at the base of—"

"Stop." At the *what* of *what*? "I liked you better when you were a virgin."

"Yeah, well, Lowe didn't. So."

I hang up and massage my eyes till the mental image is scrubbed from my brain, trying to ignore the way my stomach weighs a thousand pounds. Then something occurs to me: this could be my last conversation with Misery. The last time I hear her voice. The last time she hears mine.

I start texting.

Serena: Now that I think about it . . . Our shitty lives? I wouldn't have them any other way.

Misery: Seriously? No other way? You wouldn't, idk, skip over the part where the anti-Vampyre coalition mixed up our rooms and pumped you full of carbon monoxide?

Serena: What I'm trying to say is that I am grateful that our misfortunes brought us together.

Misery: Oh my god. Are you dying?

Shit.

Serena: Is that the only reason for me to tell you nice things?

Misery: It's the only reason for me to listen to them.

I roll my eyes and throw the phone onto the bed. When I walk into the living room, the seconds are still there. I wave at them, listening in as I start the electric kettle.

". . . all of their known hideouts. No sign of recent activity," Saul is saying.

"That we know of," Elle points out. "But our trackers extended their search and still couldn't find any trace. And the cult didn't create problems just for the Northwest—they're despised by everyone in the area. We asked Human neighboring towns if they'd heard anything about them being back, and they were horrified."

"Did you follow the kid's trail from Dr. Silas's home?"

"As much as we could," Brenna says. "He knew what he was doing. Covered his scent in the ocean."

"Any match between his and Serena's DNA?"

"Unrelated. He was a full Were. According to the forensic expert, he spent most of his life in wolf form."

I exhale. Continue puttering around the kitchen.

"Any Northwest markers in his DNA?"

"None."

Koen nods slowly. "The good thing is, there can't be many of them, or we'd have found them by now."

"Maybe we could lure them out," I muse, setting mugs, hot water, and tea bags for everyone on the coffee table.

The room goes so silent, the clicking of the porcelain feels louder than a chain saw.

I don't let it bother me. "They think I'm their miracle Frankenstein baby, and they're willing to go to some lengths to get me. If I were one of them, I'd think that I need *me* to recruit more followers."

I plop down between Koen and the armrest, disregarding the way my thigh brushes against his. Tension swells in the room, heavy with discomfort, but I ignore it and gently press my knee against Koen's thick quad to get him to stop manspreading.

He doesn't budge, so I push harder.

He ignores me.

Until Saul tells me, "We're not sure you were really a cult child, babe. And just to be clear, we would *never* think any less of you because of the circumstances of your—"

"I know." I smile. Reassuring, hopefully. "But the sooner we eliminate the threat, the better for the pack. And since we can't find the cult, using me as bait might be the most . . ."

All the seconds stand at once, like they all received a simultaneous message from an alien mothership. I watch them do those weird, drawn-out nods in Koen's direction, then quickly file out of the cabin. When I glance at Koen, I notice that he's glowering and realize *what* dismissed them.

"Well." I glance at the mugs. "That was a lot of work for nothing."

"You'll survive."

"Not according to multiple physicians."

His expression darkens further.

"Sorry. I was on the phone with Misery. Still in morbid humor mode." It would make sense, now that there are more seats, for one of us to move away. We don't, and Koen's gaze stays on me, the platonic ideal of the concept of a scowl.

"Feel free to stop acting with reckless disregard for your life."

"Aw. Thank you. Anything else I'm allowed to do, *Alpha*?"

His hand comes up to snatch my chin. "You could be fucking good, for once."

"I can try?" I smile. My lower lip pushes against his thumb. "Why didn't you tell me immediately that you suspect that I might be a child of the cult?"

Slowly, keeping his eyes on my mouth, he lets go of me.

"Let me guess: because you didn't want to needlessly upset me in case it didn't turn out to be true." I sprawl against the backrest. "Withholding information to avoid hurting people. Reminds me of something *someone* was recently criticized for doing—"

His palm slides to my neck. Tightens in a threatening curve at my nape.

I laugh, unfazed. "It's okay, Koen. I forgive you."

"Aw. Thank you," he says, parroting me. But his expression is somber. "Remember your interview? Those people outside of the studio?"

"Not really. What—" I gasp. "The man with the *sign*. Yelling something about . . . reborn flesh?"

He nods. "His talking points hit a little too close. I asked Amanda to track him, but it was Human territory, in the middle of a crowd. She couldn't shift and she lost him."

"I see. How many children were there in the cult?"

Koen presses his lips together, clearly worried, and my entire body hurts with how much I care for him. I would give a year of my life, a year I don't even have, to press a kiss against the corner of his lips. Lower, where the stubble is quickly regrowing. I would do illegal, maybe even unethical things, in exchange for the right to bury my nose in the crook of his throat, where the scent of him is densest. "Several. A handful were Weres, and they were taken in by Northwest families. But Humans reproduce more easily, and over two dozen minors survived the cult. We partnered with Human services, kept tabs as much as we could, but we didn't have access to their records."

That's how it went, then. Dozens of orphans, just like me. I wonder if *they* kept their memories. If we used to be friends. Where are they now?

This is too much. I can't process it, not tonight. "I should go to sleep," I say.

"Okay. Which room?"

"Um, mine?"

"Okay. We'll sleep there."

"*We?*"

"We."

My eyebrow lifts. "Uh-oh. Celibacy Threat Alert."

His look withers me, and every garden on the continent. "I'm going to stay in human form and monitor your temperature. We'll catch your fevers early, and they won't get as bad as they did last night."

I open my mouth to say, *I don't want to put you out. I can take care of myself. It's fine.*

But maybe it's not. Maybe I can take care of myself, but I don't mind some help. Maybe he wants to be put out.

Maybe this is equally for him *and* for me.

So what I settle on is "Thank you." I let my head roll back on the cushion. Meet his shoulder. Don't bother hiding the way I'm burying my nose in the soft, worn flannel. He doesn't mind: I can practically taste his satisfaction and relief at not having to fight me on this. It's a sweet, joyful flavor against the roof of my mouth. "You know, your room might be better."

"Why?"

"Comfier bed. Tub." I blink a few times. Leave my eyes closed. "Smells like you."

He grumbles something low that I can't make out. Before I can ask him to repeat himself, I'm already sound asleep.

CHAPTER 23

Well, fuck.

MY FIRST THOUGHT WHEN SOMEBODY SHAKES ME AWAKE IN the middle of the night is that Koen was right.

Which is not something I necessarily love to acknowledge.

"Come on, killer." A large, calloused hand pushes back the damp strands of my hair. The touch is warm and firm, should probably feel like too much, but I don't mind it at all. In fact, when it moves away, I let out a small whimper. "Bath's ready."

I make myself murmur something unintelligible that's half exhaustion, half gratitude. Opening my eyes takes more effort than a graduate degree. I wait for my body to inform me that yes, a lawn mower did just finish joyriding all over us and we do feel like utter shit, as per our regular programming.

Except, we don't.

Yup. Koen really was right. Watch me drown myself in the tub to avoid admitting it.

I sit up slowly, rubbing the sleep out of my eyes. "C'mere," Koen tells me.

His arms close around me and carry me into the bathroom. He's bare-chested, wearing gray sweats and nothing else—ready for skinny dipping. He sets me on the bathroom counter and pulls my leggings down my thighs, somehow managing not to touch me in a single inappropriate spot. He leaves my T-shirt on. Then he picks me up again and slowly lowers me into the tub. My toe brushes against the surface, and—

"No," I say.

It's a soft command, but Koen stops without hesitation.

"It's too cold," I explain calmly. Because I feel *so* calm right now. Why am I usually so full of doubt? I know what I need. I know how to get it. Always have. "I don't want to be cold."

Koen misunderstands. Gently sets me back on the counter. "Let me add some warm water to—"

"No," I repeat, jumping to my feet. I feel weird. Like I'm both speaking and observing myself speak. Awake, but sleeping. The best part is, I'm not just *not* in pain. I'm actually . . .

I feel . . .

I feel fucking amazing. And I *think* I . . .

I step toward Koen, drawn by his heat, the texture of skin, his phenomenal scent. I don't need cold water, because I have *him*. I didn't know anyone could be so perfect, but here we are. I want to touch him, so much so, I'm not sure it's allowed. There has to be a limit to how much we crave. Can't approach infinity, or it'll stretch us too thin.

I move closer and closer. The cotton of my shirt abrades my hard nipples *all wrong*, so I yank it off and toss it as far as I can. It lands in the tub, and I swallow a smile.

Oops.

"Better," I say.

Koen freezes. His eyes, already suspicious, narrow on me. But he doesn't—*Look, Koen*—even glance down—*Come on, Koen*—at my naked body—*I want you to look*. He doesn't ask stupid questions—*What are you doing? Are you okay? What is happening?*—and I'm grateful for it. He just lets me loop my arms around his waist and place an open-mouthed kiss around his rib cage.

His breath hitches. He's *so strong*. And I just . . . I *like* him. His moods. The way he steals my jokes. How full and happy I feel with him. Why have we not done this yet? Sure, *reasons*, but they seem so irrelevant, when there is this needy heat pulsating inside me. He's rock hard, too. He wants me. Half of the time, he doesn't even bother hiding it.

"Serena."

There has never been anyone like him. I could live a thousand more years, and there will never be.

"I need you to tell me what is happening to you."

I hum against the spot between his pecs. Part my lips and lick it, ignoring the soft, raspy curse he lets out. The way his hand combs through the hair at my nape, first pressing my head to him, then pulling it back.

His eyes are nothing but pupil. "Are you warm?"

I think about it. Nod. "In a nice way." A deep inhale. "You smell so *good*."

"What else?" He takes one of my wrists and lifts it to his face. Inhales deeply, as if searching for a lost trail. The brush of his nose against my skin feels better than the best sex I've had in my life. "Headaches? Nausea? Dizziness?"

I chuckle. "I am not, at the moment, experiencing every single prescription drug's side effect." However, my breasts do ache. I writhe against Koen's chest, and I'm not sure it looks dignified, but it feels *sensational*. The friction. The low growl in his throat. "Maybe you and I could . . ."

Okay. Fine. This is about sex. Me, and Koen, and sex. I rub my thighs together, because my lower belly feels like a bowstring, pulled tighter and tighter, warmer and warmer, a pool of liquid heat—

Koen mutters something that sounds like *shit* and spins me around.

My palms meet the counter, on both sides of the sink.

I glance up. See, reflected in what's left of the mirror, my flushed face and glassy eyes. I try to tilt the curve of my ass against his thighs. If I were taller, I could feel his . . .

"You can . . ." *Fuck me.* Even as overwhelmingly aroused, as dripping wet as I am, I can't bring myself to say it. I try again. "We can do whatever you like, I . . ." *Will do whatever you ask me to. For you. Don't you believe it? Try me. Teach me how to deal with all of this.*

But Koen commands "Stay still" and does something very weird.

Swipes the hair away from the back of my neck.

Angles my head down an inch or two.

Bends to run the flat of his tongue against the first few vertebrae of my spine.

And I fucking *die.*

"Oh my *God.*" The sound I let out is indecent. So outrageously shameless, I have to close my eyes and pretend it wasn't mine. It's just—nothing has ever felt as good as being licked by Koen, *there.* Even if the act was clearly not meant to be seductive. In fact, it was more akin to someone tasting a dish to check if they added the right amount of salt.

And there must be something wrong with the flavor profile. Because he mutters a low, deep, soulful, "*Fuck.*"

His tone is like a wrecking ball hitting my belly. It jolts me awake, clears my head some, and . . . What the hell am I *doing*, coming on to Koen like this? Am I out of my *mind*?

I must be. "Is it happening? Am I dying?"

He exhales a soundless laugh that's as clear a no as anything.

I turn around in his arms. Find his cheeks dark with blood. "What, then?"

"You'll be okay," he promises, breathing nearly as fast as me. "It's going to pass. Are you in pain?"

I'm *far* past lying. I look him in the eye and admit, "No, but I'm afraid that if you don't . . . touch me right now, I'm going to start crying. And if that doesn't work, I'm going to beg. And if *that* doesn't work, I'm going to—to break into a million pieces and beg you some more, and I'll do anything if—"

He groans and gathers me. Presses me tight to him for a short, blissful moment. But the heat builds up quickly inside me, and when I start squirming against the hard part of him poking into my stomach, he pulls back and says carefully, "I have to leave, Serena."

"What?"

"You have no understanding of what's going on."

Panic climbs up my throat. "And you do?"

"Yes, killer. I do." He tries to step around me, but the heat in my belly simmers, and . . . I can't let him. "I'm not going to hurt you." His hand is curled around my waist. So close to where I want it. Up a few inches. Down some.

And yet he doesn't move it. I may be about to tear up. "If you don't want me, just be honest about it."

His eyes close. "Serena." He sounds like he's in physical pain.

"Because *I* want to—"

"This has fuck all to do with wanting. You're not in the position to decide—"

"That's *not* for you to say, and—" Whatever clarity broke through earlier, it's rapidly dissipating. Something warm and syrupy builds up inside my abdomen, making me want to crawl out of my skin. Everything's too tight. Too empty. "Whatever this is, it's getting worse. And I dream about you *all the time*, and—" I hold his eyes and take his hand to drag it between my legs, certain that if he feels me there, the mess I've made of myself, the steady, dripping arousal, then he'll get it. But my movements are sloppy and uncoordinated.

What the hell am I doing? Am I out of my mind? I can't *make* Koen touch me. I don't want to make *anyone* touch me.

Except, and I know this with bone-deep certainty, I need *someone* to touch me.

"I get it. You don't have to . . . Is there anyone else who could help me with . . ."

It's a stupid question, and the second I articulate it, I realize that the simple idea of someone else touching me makes me want to tear the flesh off my bones. But going by Koen's deep, guttural, displeased grunt, he doesn't know that.

"You're *not* going to—*fuck it*." He carries me to bed, sits on the edge of the mattress, and pulls me down between his spread legs, facing away from him. *Almost* in his lap. When I try to grind backward, chasing his erection, he stops me with a hold that immobilizes my arms at my sides. It's a little like a straitjacket, made of thick muscles and scent. *Exactly* what I need. *I got you*, it tells me. I no longer have to control myself, because he's doing that for me. I have permission to beg and thrash in his arms.

"That," he growls in my ear, "is *not* the kind of stunt you pull with an Alpha. Not when you're on the brink of a Heat."

"I'm sorry." I'm on the verge of tears. The guilt is like a thousand needles in my chest. "I *wouldn't.* It's just—"

"I know." He kisses the ball of my shoulder, just a brush of his lips. "I'm going to help you. But you need to do as I say. Okay?"

My nod is frenzied. "As long as you touch me. As long as you—"

He nips the spot he just kissed. A hint of teeth. Warning. "Not how it works, killer. You do what I say, no conditions."

Sure. Okay. I'm too desperate to put up a fight. There's nothing inside me—nothing but the need to come. I don't feel embarrassed when he asks, "When you touch yourself, what do you do?"

"I don't—not in months." I had more pressing issues, even though I can't remember what they were. How was anything ever more deserving of my attention than *this*? "I'm sorry, I—"

"Hush. It's okay." He licks a spot on the hollow of my throat, sending a live current down my spine. "I said I'm going to help you, didn't I?"

The help I need involves him bending me over and fucking me into the mattress, so I let out a whiny whimper when he takes my hand, braids our fingers together, and moves them to my lower stomach, where the elastic of my panties sticks to skin.

It feels wrong, that they're the only thing I'm still wearing, especially when Koen seems hell-bent on not touching me anywhere else.

And then my stomach drops. Because I realize that he's not going to touch me *there*, either.

"You're going to use your fingers," he instructs slowly, letting go of my hand. His lips are hot against the arch of my ear. "And you're going to make yourself come."

"What? But I—"

His teeth close around the fleshy part of my neck, just this side of too hard.

I yelp. Squirm against his chest. Moan in frustration. Plead wordlessly.

"Tell me, killer." He nuzzles me. "What makes you think that this is a negotiation?"

"Please, use *your* fingers. Why don't you want to—"

"You need to shut the fuck up about what *you* think *I* want. This is a mess, and you're not in any condition to make any asks. You promised to do what I say." A kiss on my cheek. "Is this who you are? Someone who breaks her promises?"

I shake my head, feverish, panting.

"Good girl. Fingers," he orders. *"Now."*

I shove my hand down my underwear with no grace. "Oh my God." It's just . . . so much. Way too much. "Why am I so wet?"

"It's normal," he says. "You're going to need it."

"F-for what?"

He exhales against my shoulder. "Don't worry about it. Just touch yourself."

I rub myself clumsily, slipping through my folds. I've done this enough times in my life, it should be easy. But it's like there's a balloon swelling inside me, and it won't pop. My hips buck impatiently, and I circle, I rock, I grind, and . . . I nearly burst into tears.

"Slowly," Koen orders roughly. "Can you go slower?"

I can. God, I can. And it's already so much better. His scent is suddenly pleased with me, and I revel in it. Let my head fall back against his shoulder.

"Do you need something inside you? To come?"

I shake my head. Not usually. Right now, though, I *want* it.

"Okay." He inhales deep, like I smell as good to him as he does to me. "You're doing so good, killer."

"Yeah?" I whimper.

"Yeah, baby." His laughter is soft. Wound up. "I'm trying to come up with a list of things I *wouldn't* do just to be allowed to eat your cunt right now, and I can't think of a single item."

"Why don't you, then?" I whine.

"'Cause you've never asked me to before. And no, *now* doesn't count. Open your legs wider. A little more. Yeah." The last word is exhaled. A little choked. Like he's *savoring*. Adding a file to his visual library. "I have no right to it, but fuck, I just want to see enough to imagine what's happening." His tongue runs a broad stroke across a spot on the side of my throat, and a fraction of a second later I'm on the verge of coming.

"W-why does that feel so good?"

"What?"

"When you touch me—there."

"Where?" He briefly lets go of me. Moves my hair over my shoulder again, baring my back. "Here?" This time, he scrapes his teeth against the skin between my shoulder blades, and my head shatters into a thousand pieces.

I arch like a sail, breathless, speechless. Nod frantically as my fingers speed up under the cotton of my soaked panties, and—

"I didn't say you could go faster," he chides with a brief tap of his fingers over the fabric.

I grit my teeth and stop. Resume with slow circles that are somehow too much and not enough. My entire body is *glowing*.

"These are your glands, Serena. Did no one show you?"

"No."

"Might be for the best. I'd have to stop what I'm doing and go kill them." Another graze of his teeth. All my muscles clench, and I'm afraid I'll pass out. "There are five places in your skin where your scent is stronger and your hormones are thickest."

"Five?"

"The inside of your wrists." He brings my left hand to his mouth and nips the area at the base of my palm, making me shudder. "Each side of your throat." He sucks on the right for far longer than would be necessary for a simple demonstration. By the end, I'm trembling so bad, my fingers can barely stay on my clit. "And then there's the back of your neck." Another slow, savoring lick. My eyes roll back in my head.

"'S good," I slur. "This one's . . . good."

The chuff of his laughter makes me even shakier. "This one is special. It's where I would bite you, Serena. High up, where clothes couldn't hide it. And then I'd lick my bite every day to remind you." He sucks on it, and the pleasure is so intense, I have to twist away, overwhelmed. "If you knew the things I think about every time your neck is bare, you'd walk around in a fucking cape."

"I do—I want to know. Tell me."

"That would be unwise, killer. In fact, you shouldn't let me near it at all. Near *you*." One last kiss. He covers my back with the curtain of my hair and taps again at my hand—a silent order to continue touching myself.

I'm instantly on the verge of coming. I think I'll slip over, but something pulls me back.

"What about—*ah*—what about *me*?"

"Hmm?"

"Where would *I* bite *you*, to show that you're mine?"

Koen goes still at the question. And then, after processing it for entirely too long, he lets out a soft, explosive curse against my collarbone. "I hate it," he breathes out.

"What?"

"How *perfect* you are. I spent the last twenty years hoping that if there was a mate for me out there, I'd never come across them. And then I found you, and, Serena . . . there isn't one thing I would change about you. Or one single thing I regret about knowing you."

Suddenly, tears are streaming red-hot down my cheeks. "You haven't answered me," I say, quickening the rhythm of my fingers.

Koen's response is a bittersweet exhale against my cheek. "I think I'd have you bite me right under my jaw. People would glance at it and think that it's obscene. But they'd immediately know who I belong to."

His words hitch me higher, and it's happening. I'm going to come. Koen's hands are on my waist, palms so large, fingers so long, they easily cover me in warmth from hip to hip—and the hard shift of his muscles against my back—his stubble chafing my neck glands in that delicious soreness—and this unbearable tension that pulls me in all directions—

I stay there, teetering. On the edge of a cliff, in constant equilibrium.

I sob. The harder I grind, the more I ache. "I can't— Why can't I come, Koen? Why do I feel so . . ."

"Empty?"

I nod. How does he *know*?

"Okay, it's okay. Put your fingers inside."

"No—not big enough. *Your* fingers."

He groans. "Hush. Do as I say, or I'm going to . . . yes. Good. Like that. I know what you need. Come here." He cranes my neck backward. One of his large hands cups the back of my head, pressing my lips into his skin. "Keep touching yourself and lick the base of my throat."

I do. Gingerly. And—

He exhales a groan.

I freeze.

Because . . . Oh.

Oh.

"Oh my God," I moan against his flesh, but it comes out like a mumbled, shapeless noise. I'm starting to get the whole gland thing, because running my tongue over it is like tasting Koen's scent. The most potent, most perfect narcotic exploding right into my bloodstream.

And I think he likes it, too. He encourages me with low, filthy praises, telling me how beautiful I am, how perfect, what an honor it is for him to be here, with me, how he wouldn't want it any other way, how he would do unspeakable things to have it again. So I suck, and take more, even as I feel his muscles vibrate and the rope of his scent drawing tighter around me.

"*Shit*, you smell so good." He sounds as shaken as I feel. "Fuck the covenant. I want to be so deep in your cunt, you'd be squirming to breathe—"

That's what does it—the picture he paints of him, buried inside me. Of a world in which he and I—*we*—are a possibility. My body clenches, my vision whites out, and the orgasm that follows is so sharp and sudden, I cannot tell the pleasure apart from the pain.

There might not be an after, not following *this*. And honestly, I don't mind. I forget everything—my fingers, my pride, my pounding heart—and all I breathe is him.

Koen.

I'm not aware of being laid down on the bed, in his arms, pressed to him. My nerve endings are unresponsive for a while, but once I'm able, I turn around, luxuriating in the feeling of my bare chest against his, skin to skin, nearly close enough to—

The brain haze clears at once. What just happened hits me like a sucker punch. I'm nauseous. Spinning.

I practically *forced* Koen to—

He's the Alpha of the Northwest, and he shouldn't—

He can't—but I—

"It's okay." He kisses my forehead. I try to push away, but his grip is unbreakable. "Serena. It's fine."

"But I—"

"You didn't."

"Yes. I—"

"No."

"You don't even know what I—"

"I can read your mind, remember?"

He can't. He doesn't. But I feel myself relax against him anyway, too tired to fight. And since we're already so close, since he doesn't seem to mind too much, I hike my leg up his hip, uncaring of the sticky cotton between my thighs. My knee meets the scalding length of his cock. For the first time in my life, I fully comprehend the meaning of the word *throbbing*.

I want to offer him some help with that. But . . . wouldn't it just make things worse? "I'm sorry," I say, and I am. I'm sorry for *every-thing*.

"That's okay." He sighs. Somehow, gathers me even closer. "I've never been less sorry about a thing." Koen kisses me on the forehead. His hold never loosens, and we both fall asleep.

CHAPTER 24

He didn't think she could be more perfect.
Then she offered him her bite.

KOEN'S PHONE RINGS, AND WHEN MY EYES FLUTTER OPEN, HE'S lying back next to me, head on the pillow, the column of his neck golden in the morning light.

Once again, his stubble is on its way to a beard. His features, his hair, the line of his profile—everything about him has become so *dear* to me, I want to bury my face in his chest and scream about it till my vocal cords give out.

That's when his lips part, and he asks, "Are you okay?"

He sounds perfectly awake, but his eyes remain closed. "Yeah." I don't get a chance to ask if he is, too. The arm that isn't wrapped around me grabs the phone, picks up the call, and sets it on speaker.

His eyes are *still* closed. "Sem," he says.

How does he know—

"Sorry about the early call. I may have some news about Serena's condition."

"No shit," Koen mutters.

"Excuse me? I couldn't quite make out—"

"See you at your office. Twenty minutes." He hangs up. Wipes a tired hand down his face and, at last, looks at me.

"What's that about?" I ask.

"You." Gently, he extricates himself. He sits up, displaying an equally unsurprising and annoying amount of control over his core muscles.

"What can Sem have found out in less than twenty-four hours?"

"Fuck all. His partner, however, is a midwife." He rolls his shoulders into a stretch, and I try not to stare at the masterpiece of architecture that is his back. Remind myself that he can hear my heartbeat speed up, and smell . . . everything. "I imagine he talked about your situation with her, and she realized what's going on."

"What do you mean?"

He ignores me and heads for the bathroom. "Get dressed. We're leaving in ten minutes."

"To go where?"

He looks at me from over his shoulder, a small smile curving his lips. "Biology class."

———

KOEN INTERRUPTS SEM ABOUT THIRTY SECONDS INTO HIS CLEARLY rehearsed speech on why he decided to consult with another specialist regarding my situation. "Just call in Layla. We can safely assume that Serena should be transferred to her care."

Two minutes and a greenish, flustered Sem later, Layla comes in and sits behind the desk. Sem never returns. "Koen," she says. "I think it might be best if you and I talked about this for a minute. Alone."

Koen frowns. "Isn't this about Serena?"

She hesitates. Nods.

"Then tell Serena."

"This is . . . delicate."

"It's also about *her* body. I'm not the pack HR rep, but my guess is that she should know before me."

"Alpha, I . . ."

Lines appear between Koen's brows. Layla instantly quiets. "Here's what's going to happen: I'm going to walk out of this office, and you are going to tell Miss Paris whatever she needs to know. Then, if she wants to, she'll inform me of—"

"It's okay," I interrupt. "I'd rather Koen stay, for now."

"Koen," Layla says, and all of a sudden, she sounds less like a pack member and more like a friend. Someone who knew Koen when he was young—who was young *with* him. "You're not going to like me doing it this way."

A merry, careless shrug. "Then I'll have to be a fucking big boy about it, won't I?"

"I feel like I'm left out of an inside joke," I interrupt. "Or like I *am* an inside joke. What am I missing?"

Layla's smile is reassuring. "It's more what your other doctors missed. They were so concerned about the cortisol surges that they rightfully blamed your most extreme symptoms on them, but they missed the broader context."

"Context about . . . ?"

She pauses, clearly sifting through words. Meanwhile, Koen looks as though he's watching a show for the tenth time. Nothing that's about to happen is going to surprise him. He could probably take over the proceedings.

What the hell is going on?

"You see, your estrogen levels are also noticeably past normal thresholds, but because of the existence of CSD, Dr. Henshaw

and Sem assumed that the complex relationship between estra-
diol and—"

"Layla." I soften my interruption with a smile. "It's very lovely
that you don't want me to blame them, and I promise I won't, not
for misreading the blood work of yours truly. But you're saying lots
of things that I don't understand, and the suspense is killing me
faster than the cortisol, so—"

"Estrus," she blurts out. "You're going into Estrus."

"Ah." I nod.

Sit back in my chair, scratching my temple.

Gather all that I know about Estruses—Estri?—which is a
beautiful wasteland of nothing.

"People without degrees would call it going into Heat," Koen
says, and the realization crashes into me like a caravan of armored
trucks.

My behavior last night.

The dreams.

Koen's . . . everything.

"People with degrees, too," Layla adds shyly. "But it can be a
charged word. I wouldn't want to upset you."

"You aren't," I say. *Very* upset. "Is this a thing that happens to
Weres?"

"Yes, it does. Usually in wolf form."

"But I'm . . ." I point at myself. *I'm not in wolf form* seems a redundant statement.

"Breakthrough heats are not unheard of in human form, either.
I've been practicing for about ten years, and I've had several patients like you, triggered by all sorts of things."

"Such as?"

"Stressful events. Medications. The most common cause is

close proximity to a sexually compatible partner." It's remarkable how impersonally she delivers the last few words. One would think she's throwing out hypothetical scenarios, but I can see her hands rubbing under the desk. The fidgety bounce of her foot.

I'm not immune to the rising unease in the room, either. There's a string tied around my neck, and Koen is pulling at it. I want to turn to him more than I want to breathe. But if I did, we'd both be remembering the way I begged him last night, and I'm not sure poor Layla deserves to witness *that* mess.

"If I may ask, Serena, have you been having trouble shifting?" She smiles triumphantly at my nod. "Sorry. I'm not happy that . . . There is a biological premise for this that I could explain—"

"No need," I hasten to say.

"—but none of my other patients were able to shift until their cycle was over."

"Why do the fevers get so bad at night?" Koen asks.

"Simple circadian fluctuations. They're also happening more frequently, because the Estrus is approaching. Given Serena's half-Were state, it's hard to predict with certainty when it'll start, but my guess is . . . soon."

Unfortunately, this is when I cannot put it off any longer. *The* Question. I close my eyes. Mentally laser off the part of my brain that experiences embarrassment. Ask, "What will happen when Estrus starts?"

Maybe I should tell Koen to leave. The thing is, after last night he has the right to know the details of the special dumpster fire in which we're frolicking, and Layla informing the both of us at once seems less painful than having to relay stuff to him later on. Using my own words.

"Well." Layla clears her throat. Longingly gazes at a wall calendar, probably wishing she could turn back time and become a graphic designer. "There's a lot to consider when it comes to—"

"Just tell her," Koen orders. Yesterday, in this very office, he sounded so angry, I briefly wondered if I was going to have to send an apology vase of hydrangeas to the Caine family. Today, I cannot get the slightest read on him.

Layla coughs, just to buy some time. "Some symptoms have already begun. Decrease in appetite. General aches. In the next few days, you'll likely see a spike in nesting behavior."

"Please, tell me I won't be picking up twigs and weaving baskets out of them."

"It has more to do with procuring scents, textures, and objects you find soothing. The goal is for you to build a space that will offer comfort in a time of need."

"What do you mean by . . . What kind of objects?" I'm half terrified that she'll recommend a list of vibrators.

The answer is somehow *worse*.

"There is no hard and fast rule. It can be a particularly soft fabric. A piece of clothing that belongs to someone who makes you feel safe. Some people hoard specific objects and arrange them in soothing ways. Combine different materials."

"Why does this sound like a job that requires a master's degree?"

"Not at all. There is no right or wrong way to nest, and it's a very instinctive process." She scratches her nose. "You may have even already started, in your own way." Layla's eyes pointedly slide to the overly large red flannel I stole from Koen's closet, and I can feel my heartbeat pounding in my cheeks.

"Oh." I think about my room back home—the way I've been stuffing it with blankets of the perfect consistency, pillows filled with the right amount of feather. If Human scientists focused on their work as much as I did on my bed, herpes simplex would be a thing of the past.

God. It's like being told that baby carrots are just regular ones peeled to be smaller: I should have realized what was going on a long time ago, but I didn't, and now I feel stupid. Beside me, Koen betrays no emotion at the idea of contributing to my . . .

Nest.

"There will also be temporary physiological changes. For instance, your scent will become more appealing to potential partners."

"As in, my smell brings all the Weres to the yard?"

"Well, I haven't gotten close enough to you to ascertain whether the enhancement has begun, but—"

"It has," Koen said, settling Layla's waffling.

And that's that. We all marinate in those two little words for a handful of seconds, which happens to be just long enough for me to wistfully imagine being swallowed by a river of magma. "Is this going to . . . Should I be worried?" I glance at Koen, who doesn't get my meaning. "How appealing is my scent going to be to others? Should I get online and order a Taser?"

He blinks. "You already own a knife. But let me reassure you that any Were in this pack who touches you without an express request from you is going to come into a windfall of pain. And then die."

"I'll take that as a no." I smile, disappointed to find that his lips don't curve in response.

Is he angry? He should be. I made him break an oath. And he didn't even . . . But does it matter? Where do we draw the line? Will he feel compelled to do it again in the near future?

"Koen," I say softly. "I think you should leave now."

He doesn't protest. "I'll be outside. Call if you want me back in."

The second the door clicks behind me, Layla asks, "Do you know what covenant the Alpha of the Northwest must abide by?"

I nod.

She seems relieved. When she resumes speaking, most of the awkwardness has melted away, and I realize that the tense atmosphere was due to her awareness that Koen is, by law, not allowed to touch me.

Her newfound directness is refreshing. "The main symptom of Estrus is that you'll want to have sex. A lot. So much so, it might be hard to engage in any other activity. Some people equate the experience to being intoxicated, but that has a negative connotation many healthcare professionals reject. Estrus is its own unique state. You *will* be able to make decisions. The brain fog and arousal noise will just make it hard to think of the consequences and delay gratification. This will last for anywhere from two to five days. You will spend this time alone with a chosen partner, or partners, depending on your preferences."

The idea of allowing anyone but Koen to touch me is ludicrous, but I nod anyway.

"Estrus often accentuates sexual behaviors. For instance, you might find yourself wanting to please your partner more than usual. In turn, a partner tends to become very protective of a Were in heat. They will not take well to threats against them, but they also won't necessarily be able to distinguish a real threat from, say, someone dropping by with a casserole. That's why isolation is usually considered the ideal scenario."

"What if a Were doesn't have a partner? Does anyone just do it . . . alone?"

I'm not surprised by how swiftly Layla shakes her head. "I highly discourage it. Plainly, you won't be able to orgasm without interaction with a partner, which will make the experience miserable."

Keep touching yourself and lick the base of my throat.

Yeah. I can picture that a little too clearly.

"But," she continues, "you'll easily find a partner. I remember reading that sexual activity can be perceived as something shameful and taboo among Humans. Weres have a highly pragmatic attitude toward sex, and I'm sure many would volunteer to help. And I would be remiss if I didn't point out that even though I fully understand how disorienting the situation must be, most Weres who go through a Heat find it a highly pleasurable bonding experience. Not to mention that it's not always easy for us to conceive, so the increase in fertility is often appreciated."

I cover my mouth. "I'm an idiot."

"Why?"

"Pregnancy is the whole biological reason behind this, isn't it?"

"Well, yes. Is that something you're interested in?"

I used to be. Funnily enough, when I thought I was a Human orphan, the idea of having a child was magic: someone who might share my DNA. Someone to take care of. I used to picture it like a do-over of sorts: my child would not be traumatized into forgetting the first six years of its life. My child would suffer zero assassination attempts before its eighteenth birthday—or after. My child would never know true fear or hunger, and its happiness would soak up all the sadness I'd generated and polluted the world with.

Back in college, whenever Misery would catch me playing with the neighbor's kids, pinching their cheeks, calling them cute, she'd roll her eyes so hard, her contacts nearly popped out. *I hear they shit everywhere. And eat all your peanut butter.*

That's true of you, too.

Precisely. Do you really need two of me?

So, yes. I used to be interested. But now . . . "It's unclear whether it's even possible. Because of my genetic makeup."

"I see. Well, in the eventuality that you can, let me make it clear: you will never be asked to put your body through anything you don't want to. And my job is to help you do what's best for you."

I smile at her, genuinely grateful. "In that case, I need one thing from you."

"Of course. What is it?"

"I need you to make sure that I do *not* go into Heat."

CHAPTER 25

*He never thought the world was a particularly fair place.
Still, it's a startlingly vile brand of cruelty on fate's part, to
show him her—what he could have had, if only he'd made
different choices.*

"I N THEORY," LAYLA SAYS CAREFULLY, "WITH A HIGH DOSE OF PRO-
gesterone, we *should* be able to prevent Estrus."

"Perfect. Then—"

"But we don't know how an injection would interact with your
biology." Her eyes fall on the lab results strewn over the desk, and
she starts ticking off her fingers. "Your Estrus started manifesting
much earlier than in any other patient I've heard of, your hormone
levels are still off, and your body doesn't always respond to medi-
cation. When Dr. Henshaw gave you steroid blockers, they were
ineffective, just like antipyretic drugs. You could even get a para-
doxical reaction—"

"We can *try*, though. Right?"

She pauses. "Serena, I will be happy to help you find a suitable
partner—"

"That's not it."

"What is it, then?"

"What if . . ." I close my eyes. "What if my body is set on Koen?" *What if my soul is, too. What if the idea of doing any of this with someone who isn't him makes my stomach turn and my heart shrivel?*

Out of everything I've said, this takes her aback the most. Her eyes widen, and she leans forward over the desk, as if to better reassure me, "I understand that you and Koen have grown close. Heat is a turbulent time, and it's natural to want to spend it with someone you trust. We are not Human, after all, and we communicate through nonverbal signals like touch or scent, and it's normal to want to be with someone who reads you well. But you can still find someone else who qualifies—"

"Maybe it's not about *can*." I swallow. "Maybe it's about *want*." Honestly, I no longer know if there's a difference between the two.

Her lips flatten. "Serena, it's forbidden. To help you through your heat, Koen would be required to step down, which would inevitably lead to a succession war. Even worse, the Assembly might decide to—"

"Secede again. Yes." It's my turn to lean forward. Make sure she understands. "I have no intention of putting Koen, or the Northwest, in that position. And that's why I need you to help me *not* go into Heat."

A flicker passes through her eyes, and I know that she'll do what I'm asking for.

———— ✦ ————

I STEP OUTSIDE SEM'S OFFICE TO FIND KOEN GONE AND BRENNA rolling her eyes. "You know what my favorite pastime is?"

"Um . . . no?"

"Waking up at ass o'clock in the morning because my Alpha

wants me to babysit a halfling who can't take care of herself, and noticing her poorly hidden, crushing disappointment when she sees me. So *delightfully* flattering."

I blush. "I'm sorry. It's lovely to see you, I just didn't expect—"

"Yeah, sure. Yap, yap, yap. Come on." She lifts herself out of one of the plush chairs in the waiting room. "Let's go. Koen wants me to take you home."

I last about four seconds before asking, "Where did he—"

"There was a situation at the border." Her tone is bored.

"Was it the cult?"

"No. Still related to you, though."

"Who was it, then?"

"Don't worry about it."

"Brenna, who?" I hate begging her for little snippets of information. Almost as much as she loves leaving me in limbo for the two minutes we walk to her car.

"Vampyres," she admits once she's behind the wheel. "A lot of them, split in two groups, trying to get to you from the north. Their plan was to have the first team distract our patrols while the second entered the territory to abduct you. Didn't work out."

"Who sent them?"

"See, there is some devious shit going on here. The Vampyres in the first group, the ones we were obviously supposed to catch, were wearing jewelry that would tie them to a councilmember who has historically been pro Were alliances, which . . ."

"Would be incredibly stupid."

"And say what you want about leeches, but they're not. Unless they are, because they think we'd fall for false flags. Food for thought. The second group was harder to identify, so . . ."

"Did they contact Owen?"

"Yup. He was able to recognize a couple of them and believes it's proof that Councilwoman Selamio called the bounty on you. But he needs incontrovertible evidence and possibly a confession, which in turn requires the presence of someone who can be very . . . persuasive. Hence, Koen."

Who's nothing if not persuasive. "Are you planning to return them alive?"

She gives me a pitying glance. "That ship has long sailed for most of them."

"Oh. Right." I clear my throat. "Do you know what the council-woman wanted with me?"

"To study you. Run a whole assay on your lymph nodes. Cut you up in cubes and slap you on microscope slides. That kind of stuff." She grins at me. It transforms the usually dour lines of her face into something so stunning, I have no problem picturing Koen's crush on her when they were younger.

Last night . . . What he and I did. What *he* did to me—he didn't seem clumsy. Or new at it. Or even out of practice. And since Brenna and Koen used to—

"Are you okay?" Brenna asks me.

"Yeah. Just thinking."

"No, I mean . . . You were seeing Sem first thing in the morning. You're not dying or something, are you?"

I blink at her, and all at once I'm not quite sure how to breathe, or speak, or interact with the world surrounding me. It's like I've been locked in a cupboard for months. But its door has been ripped open, and now there's light. There's air. There's a fucking *future*.

I don't have CSD. Which means that I have more than just *months* left. I can make choices. I can go back to the Southwest, see Ana grow up, watch Misery be the worst parent on the planet. I can be a journalist again, or a financial advisor, or dedicate the next ten years to learning how to solve Rubik's Cubes. I can apply for a loan, buy a cabin close to the Pacific Coast, and spend my mornings exploring the shoreline. I can annoy Koen ad infinitum.

The joy of it sings so loudly in my blood, the car is too small to contain it. I have to trap it within my body and let go of it little by little, in slow puffs of air.

"No," I say at last. Because for the first time in months, I can. "As it turns out, I'm not dying."

"'Kay. Good."

"I . . . Brenna, could we stop by the store?"

"Sure. Why?"

"I . . ." A tear slides down my cheek. I cover my smile with the palm of my hand. "I just realized that I'm going to need some sunscreen."

—— ꗃ ——

I SPEND THE DAY ALONE IN THE CABIN, WITH FREQUENT VISITS from the Weres patrolling the surrounding area. A couple of them I know. Several introduce themselves. All of them are naked. I must be adapting well to the Northwest lifestyle, because I barely notice.

They check in, see if I need anything. Ask the same questions, in the same order, with the same wording, which may take away some of the spontaneity but makes them *feel* even more like the proxies of the man who sent them.

I talk on the phone with Ana, then Ana and Misery, then just Misery. It's hard not to share that I'm not yet headed for the mushroom suit. *Can't tell them about the sequel if you didn't let them watch the original.*

I putter around the house. Clean the sheets. I'm not hungry, but

I open the fridge anyway, just to glance affectionately at the still prominently placed unicorn waffles. I play the piano, sure it's silently cringing at how ghostly I pale in comparison to its owner. I try not to think about Koen's hands. I nap, hoping I won't wake up in flames. Or uncontrollably horny.

Heat spotting, Layla called it. *They are surges that happen before Heat itself. Not long lasting, but can be intense. I suspect that your high fevers may have been surges left unattended.*

Koen returns a little before sunset, while I'm going to town on a seven-year-old half-completed crossword I found under his bed. I have a whole speech ready—about what happened last night, about my lifespan's sudden growth spurt, about how I never meant to force him to break his covenant. About how sorry I am that he spent his day dealing with Vampyre commandos who are after me, and the fact that yes, I'm absolutely judging him for letting nearly a decade pass without filling in seven across: *diminishing marginal utility.* But he walks inside, dark circles under his eyes and tousled hair, caught at a rare unguarded time, and all I can squawk out is "I made dinner."

He turns. Stares. Sucks in his cheek. "Did you." He sounds suspicious.

"Yup."

"Saul said you've been asleep for the past four hours."

"I lied. I'm good at it, as you know. Plus, by the fourth person who knocked to ask if I needed anything, I kinda knew the— What happened to your side?" A large stain seeps into the dark gray of his cotton Henley. He glances at it like he'd forgotten about it.

"I'm going to get changed."

The closer I get, the easier it is to smell it—the coppery tinge of fresh Were blood, so different from the iron of mine. "Sure, sure.

'Tis *but a scratch*. You've proven your Alpha unflappability. Your pain threshold is so high, it's wondering if the color blue you see is different from the color blue I see. I am adequately impressed— now take the shirt off."

"And if I'm deathly wounded?" His eyebrow twitches skeptically. "What are you going to do about it, *doctor*?"

I gasp. "Isn't it obvious? I'm going to pretend I know Were anatomy, loudly debate whether you need stitches, decide that you don't, because I have no idea what stitches even are, and clean the general area of the wound with a cotton swab while ignoring the grosser bits. Most importantly, I will *not* pass Go before retrieving my physician assistant diploma. Any objections?"

He hides a smile, but I spot it anyway, even as he reaches over his shoulder, grabs the upper back of the shirt, and pulls it off.

The wound is not a scratch, but neither is it as bad as the pooling blood suggested.

"Alpha," he murmurs from above my head. "We heal quickly."

And yet just last night, he was whole. That very spot beneath his ribs was unbroken and smooth. Except, what do I know? I didn't get to touch him. I touched myself while no one took care of *him*. So unfair, I could scream. "What happened?"

"Vampyre."

"I thought they were all . . ."

"Dead?"

I nod.

"We kept a couple for questioning. One's restraints were a bit loose."

"And then?"

"Then he wasn't alive anymore. No big deal." He disappears into his room, and I shiver, picturing blood the same color as Misery's. I busy myself warming up dinner, setting the table with the few plates he owns, rinsing the—

Koen comes up behind me, hands bracketing my sides. I jolt. The glass slips from my hand, straight into the sink, but doesn't break. His body barely touches mine; it's such an inappropriately intimate, jarringly mundane gesture, my heart cracks.

And then it breaks into a million pieces when his nose nuzzles the crown of my head. His voice is as rough as coffee grounds. "Why does it feel like you're playing house again, killer?"

Because I am. "Playing" *being the key word.* "I'm sorry." My mouth is dry. "I didn't mean to—"

"C'mon. I didn't say stop."

I kill the faucet and turn in his arms. He showered off the blood and put on jeans and a flannel, which hangs open over his bare chest. The look we exchange is worth a million unspoken words but could be condensed to fewer than ten.

It's wrong. Let's do it anyway, though.

I reach up. Fasten the buttons of his shirt. Each one feels like a choice, like whittling the rest of the world away to carve out this night just for us. Excising a moment in time. It's just me and him. And the face he makes a couple of minutes later, when he puts the first bite of dinner in his mouth. "Fuck *me*."

I *beam.* "You are such a better audience than Misery." I don't care if Vampyres don't eat. I'll take her refusal of my cooking personally till the day I die.

"Holy fuck." He continues shoveling pasta with meat sauce in his mouth, and I consider taking a picture of it and scrapbooking it. I've written an award-winning exposé on the largest embezzlement scandals in The City and covered one of the most abstruse monopoly trials ever recorded, but . . .

Okay, I'm still prouder of those. But it's satisfying, watching him inhale something I made. Why do I care about some dude's opinion?

Because he's not some *dude.*

"At the Collateral mansion we weren't allowed to prepare our food, so cooking feels like an insurrectionary action that doesn't require me to put on clothes and go outside."

He says "Please, insurge away" over another mouthful, and I decide to just let myself enjoy this. I ask him if he can cook. He says not well, but I tell him that I don't believe him, not after the piano stunt, and he shakes his head, which I've learned is his way of laughing when he doesn't want to give me the satisfaction of having amused him.

"I can't believe you let me teach you the C major chord. Why are you that good, by the way?"

"My dad taught music."

"And you lied to me, because . . ."

"You didn't ask if I *could* play. You asked if I played. And before this week, I hadn't. Not in years."

"God, I hate you."

"Sure."

He side-eyes me when I make him lift me onto the counter to watch him wash the dishes. "I do have *some* furniture." He points at the two chairs he brought in from the porch.

"I like it better here," I say, tapping the stone countertop.

"Can you Humans just not sit normally?"

"Can you Weres just not mind your business?"

He splashes me with soap suds, and I grin as I cover my face.

After, I make tea. He makes me add several spoonfuls of sugar, and we drink it on the back porch, sitting on the steps, long after the sun has set. From the same mug. His lips touch the same water molecules as mine.

"I can't believe you take your coffee black but sweeten your tea," I say.

"I don't drink black coffee."

"What? Since when?"

"Since I started drinking it, during the High Middle Ages."

"But . . . I've been giving you black coffee."

"And I have been hating it."

I frown. "Are you sure you don't take it black? Like a *real man*?"

His eyebrow lifts. "I wasn't aware of the proven correlation between virility and coffee intake."

"Oh, there isn't one. But you're supposed to be warped by toxic masculinity and not know that. And I'm supposed to be the one who enlightens you."

His stare feels like a kiss. More than any kiss I've experienced ever did. "You're really a nuisance, aren't you?"

I grin so hard, my cheeks hurt. "What do you even do when I'm not here?"

"It's a good question. When you're not around, the entire pack just sits around and thumb-twiddles—"

"Oh, come on." I elbow his biceps. "You know what I mean. What's your corporate mission? What's an Alpha's routine? You wake up and the first thing you do is . . . ?"

"Chase that squirrel we discussed."

"Koen. Don't force me to break into your diary."

He shrugs. Takes another sip, as if thinking about it. "It changes. For the most part, a well-functioning pack is a well-oiled machine. Everyone has their skillset, and everyone has their job. There's lots of delegating, but as the Alpha, the buck stops with you. Which means that when something isn't going great, when there is a decision to be made, that's where I need to be."

I look at him. His strong nose. The set of his eyes. How is it possible that I find him even more handsome than I did the first time I met him? "Do you ever consider . . . you know?"

"I *don't* know, no."

I scoot closer. Conspiratorial. "Do you ever consider going full dictator? I'm talking thirty-foot bronze Koen statue. Koen stamps. Koen as every child's middle name. Senior prom theme: Koen. Mandatory Koen parades with Koen floats *every week*."

"You done?"

I sigh. "Those who have the means never have the vision. Want some?"

I found monster cookies in his cupboard—another Ana souvenir. They're a bit stale but still good. I eat most of one, then talk him into a bite by holding what's left to his face and pouting. His mouth brushes my fingertips, and the memory of it imprints against the pad of my thumb. The scrape of his teeth. An impression of heat.

I pull away. Listen as he lists all the places he wants to show me, here in his territory, and clench my fist to hoard the warmth of his touch. It's getting late, and the ocean breeze has me shivering, but I don't want to go inside. I'm afraid that it'll be over, two doors and a hallway between us, so I lift my closed fists. "Choose one."

"No."

"Pleeeease." He picks the right. "I'm excited to inform you that we'll be solving a crossword puzzle together."

He groans. "What was the other one?"

"You give me a tour of your shop."

"Why do I always pick the less fun one?" He sighs, but we move to the couch and start a new puzzle. His ability to solve it hasn't improved, which delights me.

"This must be so embarrassing for you." I pat his back.

"What shall I do without this valuable life skill?"

I press my toes into the hard muscle of his thigh. Lay my head on his shoulder. Scribble, on twelve down, *Rosicrucianism*. I think about having this, but times twenty. Times one hundred. Times tens of thousands. When two people fall in love, how many nights do they spend together, doing absolutely nothing, before they've had their fill? How many silences and crosswords and mugs of tea do they share? What can Koen and I do, to get as many as—

"Don't," he murmurs into my hair, not even bothering to pretend to read the clues. Yanking me back to our agreement.

A moment out of time.

No before. No after. Just during.

"Don't . . . show you up with my amazing vocabulary and language expertise?"

"Precisely." He inhales deeply from the hollow at the curve of my neck, arms looping around me. He does it again as I pull new words out of the page. *Litigation. Boulevard. Deck. Yorkshire.* He touches me, and yet he doesn't. As close as possible, without breaking the one rule we abide by.

It's nice.

I would give anything for a million more nights of this. Or one.

But I'm getting sleepy.

And he is, too.

And then the fever starts.

CHAPTER 26

Every single time he sets a hand to his cock, he will have this moment in his mind.

I GO TO MY ROOM, AND WE BOTH KNOW WHAT FOR.

Just like we both know what it means when I come back flushed and sweaty, wearing one of his T-shirts and nothing else.

"Didn't work, huh?"

I didn't get a good look at him yesterday. Tonight, the physical proof that he wants this just as much as I do is aggressively *there*, a ridge stretching his jeans in a way that must be painful. Looking away doesn't even occur to me.

"I tried to . . ." It's embarrassing. I'd have thought a piece of information like this one couldn't be waterboarded out of me, but here I am. Giving it out for free. "I tried to lick one of your worn shirts. Around the neck."

I force myself to hold his stare. Wait for him to burst out laughing, mock me, but his eyes are darker than ever.

This is the most unpredictable mix of awkward, devastating, and mind addling. Needing something that I barely know how to

ask for. Standing in front of someone who instinctively understands but isn't allowed to offer it to me. How do we talk about this?

Dear Koen:

Roses are red
   Violets are blue
      I'm about to undergo a period of enhanced sexual receptivity in
which I will require the assistance of a compatible partner
         Could that perhaps be you?

How romantic.

"Tomorrow morning, Layla will give me a progesterone injection. It should make this . . ." I gesture at myself like I'm a magician's
assistant. He takes it as an invitation and studies me from head to
toe, tracks my every fidget, follows the rocking of my heels. "She
hopes it'll make it go away. But she didn't have it at the office, so . . ."

He doesn't bother hiding the depth of his scowl, even if he eventually nods.

"Are you okay with that?" I scratch the back of my neck, which
feels swollen. Tender. "If you have any objections—"

"None that are rational." His smile is slim, self-effacing. His
words sound forced. "I'll support you no matter what. Whether
you take the injection or decide to spend your Heat with someone."

I cock my head. "I thought you said you didn't lie."

"Did I? I must have gotten it wrong. Or maybe things have
changed. Have to admit, killer, that your presence in my life has
been humbling. A fucking revelatory experience. Thought I knew
myself, but . . ." He laughs. Rubs his palm against his mouth. "The

truth is, if you decide to spend your Heat with someone else, they'll have to chain me at the bottom of a well and seal its mouth with concrete."

The gland on my upper back aches, pulsating sweetly with every word he says. Begging for attention. "The idea of anyone else touching me makes me physically ill. So." I attempt a smile. He does, too. We might be in agreement about how painful all of this is. "I can hear your heart."

"Yeah?"

"It's . . . fast." Like a drum. A rhythmic nudge against my skin.

"Must be the tea."

"It was herbal. No caffeine."

"Then maybe it's from earlier today. Busy, y'know."

"I've seen you run, and fight, and it's never been this loud."

"Serena. If you're not going to let me bullshit an answer, just stop asking questions."

I laugh. He doesn't, but the hungry little thing inside me is starting to blur the world, so I go to him anyway. And we must be some kind of perfect, perpetual motion machine—it's that easy, the way my body slides against his as I straddle his lap. His hands lift to hover around my waist, then fall back to his side, fisted.

There is a slight strain on my inner thighs as they open around his hips. His torso is longer than mine, and we're just about eye to eye. Breath to breath. Infinitely close, even if the only place where my skin touches his is our foreheads, leaning together.

"Do you want me to stop?" I murmur.

He says nothing, so I make to move away, but his hand hooks into the soft inner part of my knee.

You know I don't. Stay.

"Okay." I settle deeper into him, trying to get some pressure on my clit. I hold on to the back of the couch, right above his shoulders, and gingerly grind against his erection, feeling the rough pinch of the fabric of his jeans.

Instant pleasure sparks up my spine. The friction is so life-changingly *good*, it rips a breathy whimper out of me. I slowly collapse into him, hiding my flushed face in the crook of his neck, tracing the outline of his gland with my nose.

His response is a silent shudder.

I'm already impatient. Frustrated. Wondering what it would be like, having him inside me. He's hot and heavy. Massive. Would split me open. *Maybe you'd hate it*, I tell myself. *You don't even like guys like him.*

But, no. It doesn't matter that the men I used to have sex with would have chopped off their own middle fingers before acting as though they knew what was best for me, and respected my unwillingness to sleep next to someone who wasn't Misery. There were no orders—just polite requests. But Koen . . . It's so easy to imagine how he'd act. Methodical and self-assured and bulldozer-like. Formidable. Unstoppable. And I'd relish every second of my time with him, like I always do.

"Whatever you're thinking about," he rasps against my ear, "continue."

"Yeah?"

He nods. "You smell *incredible* right now."

"Like . . . how?"

"Like you'd let me keep you here and fuck you for the next six months. Like you *need* me to."

I moan and rotate my hips—an unwise impulse. We both exhale. Our brains glitch, and we have to stop for a few seconds, until that bug is fixed. "You can keep me forever," I mumble into his throat, and his cock *twitches* under me. "Is this okay? I'm making a mess of you, and—"

"Do *more* of it."

I obey, rolling slowly, savoring every little bump. His blood pounds against my ear. I could lick his gland now, but I'm afraid that I'll come, and *this* will end, and I don't want it to. Not yet.

"Last night," he says against my cheekbone, "you fell asleep, and I couldn't stop thinking about your fingers. How they'd been between your legs. How I could have licked them."

I squeeze my eyes shut. Imagine how difficult this must be for him. "What does . . . celibacy. What does it mean?"

He stares up, cheeks flushed dark. "I'll get you a dictionary for your birthday."

"Koen. Where is the line?"

"The line is everywhere, Serena." A hollow laugh. His hand travels up my spine. Cups my nape. Our lips are closer than ever, but never meet. "My entire life is made of fucking lines. And you're blowing past all of them."

It doesn't feel like it. It feels like I'm the one standing still in a storm. "What about this?" More grinding, and my clit catches against something that has my thighs shaking. "What if I'm doing all the work? What if you're just my . . . Mine."

"Stop," he says.

I do. Inhale deeply. "Want me to move away—"

"No," he orders before I'm done talking. "You're so— I just need a fucking second." He squeezes his eyes shut. His head falls back. "I cannot come, Serena."

"Why?"

He takes slow, long breaths. Collects himself.

"Is it because if you don't come, we can pretend that this is not sexual? That it's a favor you're doing for a . . . friend?"

He snorts. Opens his eyes. They are pitch black. "It's been sexual since the second I saw you, and . . . I have *friends*, Serena, and you're not one of them. But yes. It's easier to forgive myself if we make this about you."

I bite my lip, ready to protest how unfair this is, but stop, mortified. I don't want him to have to *forgive* himself. He doesn't owe me anything. "I'm sorry. I—"

He shakes his head. Twists his hand so that it curves around my cheek. "Hush," he croons into my ear. "You're all worked up. And wet. Just a handful of days from your first Heat." His teeth scrape against my jaw. "It's okay. I know how hard this is. I'm going to take care of you, okay?"

I agree with a mindless nod. The need in my blood is rising. I will die without this.

"I'm going to make you come, however many times you need. And then I'm going elsewhere to make myself come."

"I can—"

"No, Serena. You can't. But *I* can. I want you to tell me what you need, and I want the privilege of giving it to you. I want you to use me." A kiss on my collarbone. "If you think there is anything I would like more than seeing my mate through her Heat, you are fucking wrong. If this is all I get, I'm going to make the most of it. Okay?"

I nod again, which gives him a path to my throat. His mouth closes around my gland and it's so sudden, so shocking, I scream. "Koen," I gasp, moving my hips again. The pleasure is white-hot. "Feels so good."

The curve of a smile. "Feels better for me than for you."

"Impossible." My breath tumbles out. "I . . . I tried."

"Hmm?"

"Touching my glands. But it didn't really—not like when you touch me."

"Sweetheart." He nips at it.

I shudder, full-bodied. "It has to be you, Koen. We're like . . . lock and key? It has to be *us*." I rock in his lap, demanding release. Closer and closer, clumsier and clumsier.

"You're my mate, but I'm not yours. There will be other keys for you." A flat-tongued, broad lick. When he bites me again, it feels a little more violent. Like he could easily break my skin, and he wants me to know. "And I'll do my best not to kill them. No promises."

"I don't want them." I sob in pure frustration, pressing harder, all soaked, sticky underwear and hard ridges, marks sucked into tender skin, deep inhales. "I don't want anyone but—"

The first orgasm hits me so hard, I dig my nails into his shoulders. Koen drags it even longer, wrings as much out of it as he possibly can without even touching me, just little slides of his hips where I need them the most. I tremble in his arms and let him take me apart as he tells me how beautiful I am, how good, how lost he is.

It ends too soon. It's not enough.

"Okay?" he asks, and I shake my head.

"I'll never be okay again."

"Yeah." He is hoarse. Desperate but amused. "We're both fucked."

Pleasure inches down my spine. I close my fingers around Koen's palm, which is work-rough and large, and I try to pull it down to my inner thigh. He stops me halfway there. "Why?"

"I can't, Serena. If I touch you there, it's over." His kiss on my cheek is light. "There's this voice in my head, screaming at me that I should hold you down and knot you and shred your gland until it'll scar in the shape of my teeth, and I'm trying very hard to muffle it."

"So, I can touch you. But you can't touch me."

"Correct. Serena—" he warns when I take his other hand, but falls quiet as I splay his fingers open. "What are you doing?"

I grip his wrist and bring his open palm up to my left breast.

"Fuck," he bites out through gritted teeth.

"Technically," I point out through the hitch in my breath, rubbing myself against his rough hand. "You're not touching me. I'm doing all the work, but if it's too much—"

"No." He shakes his head and adjusts his posture, like he needs to see this, how I'm moving. It's undignified. Wild. Frenzied in a way I'll be ashamed of later. But he orders, "Do not fucking stop," and I can *taste* how much he wants me, feel it ricochet against my bones. His desire is so thick, all-encompassing, I don't know how he can stop himself. But when I lean forward and nip at his gland, he simply lets out a deep, rumbly grunt and talks to me like I'm the only person in the universe. "The first time I saw you, I thought that of course the universe would deliver someone with the most perfect pair of tits I'd ever seen and then yank her away from me." I press harder against his palm. He groans. "It's hard to keep my hands off you, killer. And you never wear anything under my shirts—"

"I hate bras."

"I hate them, too. My afterlife will just be me, watching you move around my house in nothing but my clothes. Knowing that you're warm and fed and safe and so damn *soft*."

"Please." I need to come again. Find a spot on the side of his throat, lick it, savor the tremors that shake him every time I cant my hips into his cock. On some strokes, he arches up. Once, I think he's going to come. He does, too, and his intake of breath is so deep, I almost think he'll throw me off him.

But he has better control than that. He urges me softly, patiently. Tells me to take what I want. His voice is hot against my cheek. The skin of his glands feeds me with something explosive. That's why it wasn't enough, my first orgasm. What I need is *him* in my bloodstream. Lock and key.

"Koen?" I slur, almost there. "Do you think this is the last time? Do you think we're n-never going to do this again?"

He doesn't respond. But right as I'm about to come I hear him say, "If it were, I would regret nothing." That's when my mind blacks out, and my body bursts into flames.

After, I wait for the shame to sink into me, but it never does. I revel in the sticky fabric, teeth marks, temple nuzzling. Prickly stubble and faintly green forearm veins as he gets himself under control.

"I can wash your clothes and—"

His hand tightens around my scalp. Something between a mild threat and an invitation to back off. "I'm going to bury my face in them the second you go to bed, killer."

It's heady, how much he wants me. Mixes with what's left of my Heat fever. Coats the inside of my nostrils and the buds on my tongue with delicious, unspoken requests. The idea of denying him is repulsive, plain and simple.

"I want to give you what you need so badly," I say.

His large hand strokes down my hair, soothing me and himself. I burrow into him and feel him shiver in response.

"I know that you took an oath. And I know that this is doomed. But . . . Koen. There is very little that I wouldn't do for you, if you were to ask me."

"Serena." I hear the blurry edge of his smile. A quiet sigh. "I would throw away my pack, my life, and my entire world for you. Which is the exact reason I cannot have you."

CHAPTER 27

His nuisance. That's what she is.

WHEN I WAKE UP THE FOLLOWING MORNING, AMANDA AND Saul are sitting at the kitchen table. Every single ingredient that one might need to make pancakes has been taken out of the cupboards and neatly laid on the counter. A few that one might not, too.

"Out of curiosity, at what point in the process do you think ketchup becomes involved?"

Saul shrugs. "For the stuffing, maybe?"

"Ah, yes. The famed pancake stuffing. That's where the capers go, too?"

He nods so hard, I'm afraid his jaw will detach from the rest of his face.

"And remind me, the vinegar—"

"Listen," Amanda says bluntly. "As much as we love setting our alarms one hour earlier to come visit with Mommy and Daddy, if we knew how to make pancakes, we would not be here."

I cock my head. "Am I Mommy in this scenario?"

"Or Daddy," Saul offers. "You get to pick first, since you provide the pancakes."

"Nice. I'll take it."

Twenty minutes later, when Mommy steps out of his room freshly showered and cleanly shaven, they are in the middle of a bitter argument.

"My editorial position," Amanda is saying, not bothering to finish chewing, "is that it would be like shooting pure, undiluted moon in your veins. A super-soldier. Leviathan, but in space. And on steroids."

"Baby . . . no. There's no atmosphere up there. You'd just be a pincushion for radiation."

"Weres on the moon?" Koen asks, walking up to me in the kitchen. He doesn't look like he slept much.

I hand him a mug of coffee. "Yup."

"Have they been over moonless planets yet?"

"Yes."

"Can't howl 'cause sound doesn't carry?"

"Yes."

"Pluto's five moons?"

"Also yes."

"The asphyxiation?"

"Just now."

"Great. They must be about to wrap up." He reaches for the sugar. I stop him with a hand on his wrist.

"Already in there." It takes a moment for my fingers to let go, and another for him to glance away from the difference in our sizes. My paler, softer skin.

He leans back against the counter next to me, even though there are yards of surfaces for him to use. He could even go sit with his seconds, who were there when he still thought potty jokes were the height of humor and have saved his life countless times. He chooses to be here, though. Looks at me as he takes a sip, while Amanda and Saul's bickering continues.

"A house divided," I say. "Want pancakes?"

He shakes his head. "They've been working on a space Were book for years. The disagreements started early in the planning phase."

"I didn't know they write."

"That's because they don't."

I smile. He does, too, if only with his eyes. The discussion winds down, and Saul and Amanda stare at us, seeing who knows what. "Good morning." Koen cheers in their direction with his mug. "I am overjoyed that you decided to deal with this pressing issue in my home."

Amanda waves a forkful at him. "You can disapprove all you want, Alpha, but the matter is not yet settled."

"Nevertheless, we will proceed with our day. Unless anyone has other important, fully theoretical matters to add to the agenda?"

"Actually." I steeple my hands. "I've been wondering about something for a while. We are Weres, right?"

Encouraging nods.

"But why are we part wolves? Why are there no werebutterflies, or werecrabs? What's so special about *wolves*?"

Three pairs of eyes blink at me. Then Saul winces. "That's just . . . weird, Serena."

"How is it weirder than the moon thing?"

Amanda stands, grimacing like her stomach and her soul are equally upset. "Don't. Just, don't."

"Wait. You guys, tell me how a Were on the moon is any more plausible than . . ."

But they're gone.

I turn to Koen, who's setting his mug down. He shakes his head, an expression that could be mock *or* real disappointment on his face, and follows his seconds outside.

———— ⟩⟨ ————

KOEN NEEDS TO DRIVE BACK TO THE BORDER TO OVERSEE THE EX-tradition of one of the Vampyres to Owen's team but decides to drop me off at Layla's on the way. Saul tails us in his car, listening to dubstep so loudly, Koen mutters something about brain tumors growing in his auditory cortex.

I should introduce Saul to Misery. Maybe meeting someone with the same terrible taste in music is the mirror she needs to re-think some life choices.

"I need a minute with you, before you go in," Koen tells me, parking in front of Sem's office.

I don't like how grave and serious he sounds, stripped of the usual gruff, irascible facade. Then again, we have much to discuss. Preferably, while I'm not squirming in his lap. Last night was a moment out of time, but we're back in it.

"Me too. I wanted to—"

"Not here."

"Oh?" I bite into my thumbnail.

"It's a very small space, Serena, and you are . . . Your scent destroys my focus. It's better if we're not too alone."

He leads me to the green area behind the building, past the playhouse that must have been installed for Sem's youngest patients. The breeze is lovely in my hair. I force myself to enjoy the fresh air, the faint scents of salt and moss, and not to dwell on the fact that the conversation about to happen is a losing game. By my side, Koen is silent. I pick a white bench that's still covered in droplets of dew and point at the spot next to me, but Koen ignores it. Instead he stands, back to the east, the rising sun a halo around his head.

He is so handsome, I have to close my eyes against it.

And I like him so much, I'm going to have to close my heart, too.

But not yet.

"Can I . . . Is it okay if I start?" I ask. "I don't want to . . . It's important to me that I get to say this."

In lieu of a reply, he drops down. Crouches till we're eye to eye. And . . .

I really *am* absolutely gone over this man. Fully, irreparably lost.

"Two nights ago, and maybe even last night . . . I feel like I pressured you. I put you in the position of having to take care of me. Forced you to break a promise you made to your pack. And . . ."

"Serena." He sighs. "You think I didn't want it?"

"The thing is, I grew up with *very* little control of my life, of my choices, of my body, and maybe because of that, I've thought about things like consent and agency a lot. And . . ."

"I grew up sure that one day I would become Alpha, surrounded by people who knew that, too. I also thought about consent and agency. You understand what that meant for me, right? Knowing that the kids I played with felt a pull to do as I ordered? That any girl I wanted to ask out might feel a strong urge to say yes, just to make me happy?" I nod, and he continues. "I get where you're coming from, Serena. But we are Weres. A different species, with different customs. Consent is a value we always uphold, but you're my mate, and you were approaching Heat, which is a Were biological state that has no parallels in Human society. It's more complicated and nuanced than any theoretical scenario you thought through as a Human. So give yourself some grace." The corner of his mouth twitches. "Maybe it'll give me permission to grab some for myself, too."

"You never did anything wrong, though. I wanted you to . . . I *needed* you."

"And I could have walked away at any moment, but I stayed. And . . . come on, killer. There was no need for me to do half of what I did. I had a choice, and I made it."

I want to hang my head. Close my eyes. I want to forget what he said last night, pretend I don't remember, but it feels so cruel. To leave him alone to deal with all this . . . *This.*

The burden should fall on both of us.

"It's not fair. That they won't allow you to—" Fall in love. Have a family. A chance at happiness. A chance with *me.* "It's inhumane."

"Maybe it is." He smiles, a little lopsided, like he has made peace with this. "But we are not Human." He stands, and I can no longer see his expression well. Which, I suspect, is precisely the way he wants it. Because after a pause in which he doesn't take his eyes off me, he says, "My mother was the previous Alpha of the Northwest. And my father was her mate."

My heart is in my throat. This is why he asked to talk. What he meant to tell me. So I fist my hands around the edge of the bench and listen.

"They met young. Teens. They said they knew it immediately, which I was always skeptical about. It was hard to imagine that you could find a person, and they'd instantly become everything. That they'd take up all the space inside you and leave no room for doubt.

Of course, now . . ." He shrugs. Reaches forward to free a strand of hair stuck to my lips. "I've changed my mind. But . . . Well, their bond was mutual. They paired up, were ready for a life together—until the previous Alpha of the Northwest, who'd been a great leader for several decades, lost a challenge to some twenty-year-old piece of shit.

"Highly dominant Weres tend to have other traits, too. Not just strength, but also calm under duress, integrity, empathy. The new Alpha did not, and all of a sudden, the head of the pack was a jackass who couldn't be trusted with slicing a meatloaf, let alone deciding how to maximize resource allocation. Everyone was scared shitless. So, about two weeks into his leadership, my mother took him in the challenge and saved the day. Except, she happened to be pregnant. With me."

I clench my teeth. "Was she allowed to . . . ?"

He shakes his head. "They call it 'the celibacy covenant,' but it's a misnomer. It puts all the focus on the sex, when what's really forbidden to Alphas is to form bonds that might interfere with their ability to serve the pack. An Alpha's decisions should always benefit the Northwest. An Alpha's family could serve as a tool of manipulation. Therefore, an Alpha shouldn't have one."

"But what about an Alpha's siblings? Those bonds can be just as strong. What about parents, or friends? What about platonic relationships, or—"

"Believe me, I know. It's old-fashioned, flawed reasoning, and that's why most packs did away with it a while ago. But the Northwest had no reason to worry about it for decades after most packs began having these discussions. My mother was the moment of reckoning. The huddles didn't stand for it. Became independent. But we didn't close the borders. Socially, we were still one pack, even as each huddle leader made their own decisions. But we wouldn't always share information. And we had different perceptions of what constituted a threat. And that's where things started to go wrong.

"I was born. About five years later, my sister was born, Anki—she lives with her mate in the south." His mouth twitches. "My parents figured that if one of us was going to inherit all those Alpha traits, it would be her. But she took after my dad, who was a musician with no interest in pack leadership. And when it became obvious that I was likely to be the next Alpha, they were relieved. My mother was beloved, and I would take over when she was ready to step down. No need for challenges. The shit Lowe went through with Roscoe? I didn't have to worry about that. Until the cult, at least. Because Constantine was out there, taking advantage of fools, promising them they'd run with the wolves, and . . ." He snorts. "Only Humans would believe this shit. No offense."

"None taken. Well, *some* taken."

He doesn't smile. "Constantine was intelligent. And greedy. And as the cult grew and he kept making promises that he couldn't keep, he decided that what he and his followers needed was an enemy, and maybe a kingdom that was their due but had been wrongfully taken from them. He told his followers that as soon as they took back their birthright, they would become all-powerful, immortal Weres."

I'm starting to feel nauseous. "Was that kingdom the Northwest?"

"And the villain, my mother." He runs a hand through his hair, and the movement angles his face just so, enough for me to see his expression. I was sure he would look angry, and he does. I didn't expect so much sadness. "The details aren't important. But Constantine and his followers exploited the lack of communication between the core and the peripheral huddles. They killed my mother and made sure that the pack knew it was under threat. When the adults in the pack gathered to discuss how to react, Constantine carried out a series of coordinated attacks that wiped out all our leadership and most of our adult members. *Thousands* of people died. And . . . we just had to step up. Amanda, Saul, Jorma, Brenna, me—hundreds of us. We didn't even have a chance to mourn our families. There was a power vacuum, and the cult was trying to use it to take over, and we had to react quickly. Those are some pretty fucked-up memories for a bunch of teens to have to carry. But when I'm about to fall asleep at night, that's not what I think about." He swallows. "You know what is, Serena?"

I wish I didn't. All I want is to have come to the wrong conclusion. "What your mother did."

He nods, and it breaks my heart. "They used my father to lure her out. And even though everyone told her it was a trap, even though her seconds were forming a plan, the idea of my father suffering was so untenable, she refused to wait. And honestly?" He squats down again. Locks eyes with me, so that there is no misunderstanding him. "Now that I'm in the same position, I'm not sure that I wouldn't do the same."

And this is how it all fits together. This is the crux of the issue, and why I can finally make sense of it all.

To Koen, the covenant is not something that's been imposed by the huddle leaders—an arbitrary, unjust restraint. To him, it's a guarantee that history won't repeat itself. And that guarantee has never mattered more than it does now, with the cult threatening the Northwest once again.

And the last thing I want is to ask him to make an impossible choice.

So I reach out. Run my hand through his hair, trying not to sigh at the way he leans into it, like my skin is his North Star. "You know me as a liar, but . . ." Laughter bubbles out of me, sticky. "Can I try honesty? For once?"

He nods, patient, open, in the morning air, like he rarely is. Making it so *easy*.

"I like you more than anyone I've met since Misery. And when I'm with you, I feel . . . a little less like half of two things, and a little more whole. And when you touch me, it feels right. So right that I forget it's wrong. I forget that you're the heart of this pack. I forget that thousands of people rely on you, and that every moment I spend with you, I'm taking something away from them." I manage a labored gulp. My throat is tight and dry. "So this is what's going to happen. I'm going to walk in there and take the drugs Layla gives me. This Heat won't happen. And as soon as the issues with the Vampyre council are officially over and Ana is safe, which will be any day now . . . I'll go back to the Southwest, where I won't be keeping you from the people who need you. And you and I . . . we'll make sure to avoid each other in the next few decades. Won't we?"

Koen doesn't nod, but I smell his assent. His head bends for a long, silent moment. When he looks up, his eyes are emptier than the space between the ocean and the cliffs.

And all he says is "Layla is waiting for you. You should go."

CHAPTER 28

*It's odd, what her absence does to him. She is missing,
but she fills and floods every part of his life.*

I GIVE MYSELF A FEW MINUTES TO CRY IT OUT, THEN HEAD FOR
my appointment.

Saul is leaning against his car, laughing with a young blond
woman I have yet to meet. When she notices me, her eyes double
in size, the *Is that the halfling?* expression that I've grown accustomed to. "Give me a sec, Jess," he says, and jogs up to me.

"Koen left," I tell him. "I'm going to head in and talk to Layla."

"Okey-doke." The corners of his eyes crease with concern. I
don't need a mirror to know that mine are red rimmed, but Saul
saw me disappear behind the building with Koen and has enough
pieces to put together an exhaustive picture. "Do you know how
long it'll take?"

"Not sure."

"Okay. Well, I'll be here, waiting. And hey, maybe later . . ." He
leans forward. Winks at me in a conspiratorial way that has me
bracing for what's to come. I don't know if I can deal with Saul
now—his compassion, his kindness, his terrible music. Where is

Brenna when I want to be bitch-slapped back to my senses by an expert?

"It's okay, Saul, I—"

"Maybe later we can discuss that werecrab thing?"

I frown. "You seemed pretty opposed thirty minutes ago."

"Well, I had to. You know how Amanda and Koen are."

"And how's that?"

"Sticks in the mud. Unimaginative. But the werecrab thing has potential. And I've been thinking of writing a book, so—"

I wave him off, give the woman my least Human smile, and walk into the building.

The waiting room is deserted. I knock at the same office as yesterday. After a few seconds I hear Layla's feeble "Come in."

Weird, I think, wrapping my hand around the doorknob.

So I let go of it. Take a step back. *Why is this weird?* My instincts tell me that something's off. And by now, enough disturbing shit has happened that humoring my instincts feels less like indulgence and more like necessity.

I dig into my pocket, wrapping my fingers around the penguin knife. With my other hand, I unlock my phone and pull up Koen's contact to—

Acute, piercing pain bites into my hand. My phone flies into the air.

"I don't believe so," a voice says from behind me.

I spin on my heels. It's the blond girl—Jess. And she kicked my hand so hard, it might be broken.

I look around. My phone landed beyond the reception desk, so out of reach, it might as well be on the moon with the werecrabs. I hold on to my knife and scream at the top of my lungs, "*Saul!*"

"Saul's taking a nap. Let the boy rest."

ALI HAZELWOOD

I'm willing to—if only because Jess expects nothing from me, which puts me in a good position to slam the right side of my body against her and nick her with my knife.

"You little fucking—" She tries to twist my wrist, but I free myself with a kick, get in another stab, and dart outside. That's when the door to the office opens, and another Were runs out. I realize that Jess is not acting alone, and that I'm fucked.

I throw my self-defense kitchen sink at them, but the most it buys me is a three-foot escape before I'm recaptured. I kick, bite, cry out for help, but I'm quickly muffled with a sweaty palm and dragged inside the office.

Aside from me and Jess, there are three other Weres in the room. The one who helped Jess capture me is around my age. A second, much older man holds something sharp—a scalpel?—to the third's neck.

Layla.

At first, I wonder why she isn't shifting. We'd still be outnumbered, but a wolf would give us a fighting chance. Then I notice her droopy eyelids and limp hand. Her head occasionally lolls around the stem of her neck.

"What did you do to her?" I shout against the younger man's palm. It doesn't come out nearly as intelligible, but he must get the gist.

"Stay calm," he orders. "She's heavily sedated, out of precaution. Now, Eva, you have two choices. I can finish the job." The way the older man waves the scalpel quickly clarifies what that would entail. "Or you can be quiet. Which one shall it be? The first one?"

I furiously shake my head.

"I thought so. Jess, are you okay?"

"I'll live," she mutters. Her blood overpowers every other scent in the room.

"Okay. Eva, I'm going to slowly take my hand off your mouth. Before you do anything stupid, remember that every action has consequences."

I nod, sick to my stomach at the sight of Layla. "What did you give her? Is she—"

"She'll be fine, provided that you stay quiet," the man says from behind me, his breath humid against my ear. "We know this is distressing, but you gave us no other choice."

I swallow a hysterical laugh. "Who the hell are you?"

"The same as you, Eva," Jess says. "We are people who were denied their families. And now we're going home."

"I have no idea what you . . ."

I never get around to the end of the sentence. Because the man presses a cloth with a sweet, chemical scent against my mouth, and that's the last thing I remember.

— ◦◦◦ —

THIS AIN'T MY FIRST RODEO—AND BY RODEO, OF COURSE, I MEAN kidnapping. Still, what I learned in my previous experiences might not come in too handy.

I realize it when I wake up at some unidentified point later in the day, feeling hungover and flattened by an oxcart. My stomach tries to remind me that our usual post-drugs, post-beating routine tends to involve several bouts of vomiting, but I ignore it. My head pounds, but all my limbs are still attached. I'm bruised but not bleeding.

Outside, an incessant rain washes away all other noises.

My muscles shake as I sit up in bed to take in my surroundings. I'm in yet another cabin—two-storied, cozy, sandwiched between a pond and a pine forest. Late morning light filters in from the window,

303

which is notable for its lack of bars. That alone would give me pause, but what really clues me in that this is a clear case of Not Like Other Abductions is the door to my bedroom, which is wide open.

No guard.

I consider climbing down the window. I could run south for the next four to five weeks and stop only when I enter Southwest territory and Misery welcomes me with her infamously cold, stiff embrace. Problem is, it's prisoners who run away. And I might not be one.

So I make my way down the creaky yet sturdy stairs.

"Eva." A slight Were woman glances up from a thick book, welcoming me with a warm smile. She has long straight hair, silver gray all over, but a look at the taut skin of her face tells me she must not even be forty yet. When she stands, her simple, flowy dress drapes down her body in waves of green. *Bet you whatever that she has an herb garden in the back*, a voice says in my head. "Good morning, dear. What would you like to drink?" She glides toward me, all witchy cottage-core vibes. My metabolism must still be working through the drugs, because when she briefly wraps her arms around me, I do *not* violently shove her away. "Anything to eat?"

"Um. No, thanks."

"Are you certain?"

Is this for real? "You already drugged me once. I'm just going to assume that everything you offer me is roofied, if that's okay with you."

The woman sighs, looking remorseful. "You'll have to forgive us. We usually have better manners than this. And please, let me reassure you that you're not our captive. There are vehicles at your disposal if you wish to leave. All we wanted was an opportunity to speak candidly with you. We attempted to bring you here without too much fuss, but the Alpha of the Northwest . . . he is very protective of you. I hope that the unfortunate methods to which we resorted will not influence the tenor of our future acquaintance."

I'm not sure what this lady's grasp of sarcasm is, so I resist the impulse to tell her that it's *No big deal. All water under the bridge.* Instead, I note the frequent use of *we* and glance around. We are alone in the kitchen, but through an open doorway I can see the living room, and three Human women sitting on the velvet couch. They seem to range from their late teens to early fifties. The button shape of their noses and their auburn hair suggest that they're likely related.

They whisper feverishly at each other and watch me with wide, awestruck grins. Clearly, they're guzzling the Kool-Aid. It's all I can do to bite *I'm a hybrid and your murderous prophet dude had shit to do with random genetic changes that lead to interspecies reproductive compatibility* off my tongue. "In that case, I'll be heading home now."

"You are welcome to do so—"

I whirl around.

"—but I thought you might want to visit with me. I am, after all, the only family you have left."

It's so fucking manipulative, I'm disappointed in myself for falling for it. Nevertheless, I halt. Even as the not-rotten part of my brain whispers, *Keep going, Serena. Keep. Fucking. Going.*

When I turn back to the woman, she doesn't hide her smugness. "My mother was Human," I hiss, just to get ahead of *that* specific turd of bullshit.

"Of course Fiona was Human." She plucks a piece of paper from the table and holds it out to me.

Bile climbs bitterly up my throat. "I'm not going to bawl over a shitty stock photo, or some AI generated . . ." But it's a lie that crumples the second my eyes crop to the picture.

It's old. Not quite Kodachrome, but printed out on glossy paper that one doesn't see much anymore, because these days everything lives on phones. The right corners are a little bent, curled into themselves from traveling among hands. Aside from that, it's a very clear photo. Above all, it's . . .

It's me. Or it's not. But it is. The tilt of her head. The dark eyes and darker hair—straight, long, just a hint of wave at the end. The smile, the full lips, the straight line of her nose. There are differences, too. She's on the taller side, her jaw squarer, her complexion olive toned. But I recognize my softness in her, rounded edges that we shared until the last few months wreaked havoc on my body. The necklace at her throat is unnervingly familiar: a silver moon, scratched by a full set of claws.

I glance up at the cottage-core witch. Who has my attention and fucking knows it.

"I have a box full of photos. I was always very partial to Fiona. Out of all the girls . . . I like to think that part of me knew how special she would be. However, if you want to see the rest, I would like for us to sit down." A smile. "Don't worry. You're not making a commitment by hearing me out. I know your friends make us out to be a dangerous terrorist organization. In truth, we are very reasonable, and that's why they've been keeping you away from us. We are *not* attempting to convert you and ask for tithes. This is not Hades. I won't serve you pomegranates."

I don't believe a single word, but my fingers burn to touch the photo. That must be why I find myself sitting at the head of the dining table.

"Irene," the woman says, taking the chair next to mine. "Is my name. I forgot to mention it, since I know yours."

"Actually, you have the wrong one."

"Forgive me. It's out of habit. You prefer Serena?" Her tone is so perfectly sensible, I briefly feel guilty about acting rudely. Then I remember that I've been *abducted* and swear that if I make it out of this alive, I'll go back to therapy and divest myself from my people-pleasing tendencies. "I don't want you to think that we didn't care about you. We would have searched ceaselessly, if we'd known that you survived."

"How exactly are you and I related?"

"Ah, right. Constantine, the leader of the Favored, was my older brother. Which makes me your aunt." Her smile seems genuine. This should be a heartwarming moment, but I shiver anyway. "I know your memories are lost, and even if they weren't, you couldn't possibly recall this. But I held you on the day you were born and adored you from the very start. I will continue to do so, no matter what you decide. Welcome to the family, Eva."

So much for using my real name. "Does this mean that Constantine was my father?"

"Yes, naturally. You were his miracle. His 'little sunlight glint,' that's what he called you."

A sudden chill runs down my spine. I wait for the shock of Irene's revelation to fully sink in, but it never does. Given the cult's interest in me, I was near certain of my connection to them. Constantine being my father . . . well, it was just the worst possible scenario. "Of course it materialized," I mutter.

"Pardon?"

"Nothing. Just excited to hear that the weird jingoistic nutjob everyone hates was my father."

"Is that what they told you about him?" Her head tilts. "What else? That he was insane? Violent? Power hungry? Because I can explain."

I'm sure she can, but I'm not biting. "I'd rather discuss . . .

Fiona." Calling her *my mother* feels wrong. Even if my hands itch to touch the photo. "Why was she with the cul—excuse me, this *totally* legitimate social club?"

Irene chuckles. "Your father would have enjoyed you. This humor of yours, you get it from our side of the family."

"Actually, I get it from the need to proactively cope with a staggering amount of unprocessed trauma. Back to Fiona, please."

"Of course. Your mother was born among us. Her family was very devoted to the Favored. They aspired to become Weres. They would have been so proud of what their granddaughter accomplished."

"You mean, my college degree? That time I ran a half-marathon?" I'm starting to get impatient. My temples throb, and I'm almost certain I'm running a fever. I want the box, I want out of here, I want answers. "Because if what you mean is me being a hybrid, there was very little accomplishing on my part, and a lot of me twiddling my not-yet-existent thumbs as morulation and blastulation happened."

Irene must be getting tired of the family humor, because her lips purse, but she continues, "It's an interesting story. When Fiona became pregnant, she maintained that the baby was Constantine's. At the time . . . there were a lot of women in his life. He was a hardworking man, often in need of rest and comfort. Fiona was one of many who saw to that, and Constantine was a reasonable leader who didn't demand exclusivity. But Fiona was loyal. No one could picture her with another, and no one else would admit to having touched her."

She pulls the box closer, still out of my reach, sifting through photos until she finds a square one. When she shows it to me, I don't lean forward, but rather wait for her to set it in front of me.

The smile on her face tells me that she knows what pissing contest I entered us in but doesn't mind humoring me.

The woman in the picture is the same as before. This time, though, she's not posing. She looks up at a handsome older man who stares into the distance, absorbed by other matters.

"That is Constantine. Your father."

My interest in him is subterranean. He could be wearing a fresh lobster costume, and my eyes would still be drawn to the curve of Fiona's belly, clearly visible under the stretch of her top. She cups it with both hands, a gesture that seems more intentional than a simple *I don't know what to do with my arms.*

And then there's her profile. Several weeks ago, Ana asked Lowe to draw girls-only portrait: Misery, Ana, and me. And, somehow, Sparkles. He chose a three-quarter view for me, and it could have been a tracing of this photograph. Maybe that's why in an odd, inexplicable way, I feel like I am her, and she is me.

I don't owe her anything. Having given birth to me doesn't buy her my love or my gratitude or my compassion, but the problem is—

"How old was she?"

"When she had you? I cannot say for sure. Around twenty."

That is the problem. She was younger than I am now. Pregnant with the baby of a Were cult leader whose restraint was worthy of Caligula's orgies. Lost girl to lost girl, I cannot help wondering whether she felt alone. Overwhelmed. Scared. *Proud*, I'm sure Irene would say, but . . .

Am I just projecting? Because we have the same fucking cheekbones?

Get it together, loser. She didn't love you because she's cupping her bump. Lots of people like babies in theory but not in practice.

"No need to make that face." Irene's tone is gently reproachful.

"She was very happy to become your mother, Eva." More pictures slide into my field of view. Smiling lips pressed to a baby-fat cheek. A tiny infant foot, much smaller than her palm. A candid, breast-feeding. Sitting in a meadow. Smiling up at the camera while a toddler fists the stem of a columbine.

I see the splotch of tears on the mahogany before I even realize I'm crying.

"She was very good with numbers. So are you, I am told. And she loved the ocean. Even though she had little access to it."

I look up, unsure of how to deal with all of these—these *feelings*. Irene, though, seems genuinely sympathetic.

"She also kept a diary where she logged all your milestones. First step, first word, favorite foods. I believe it was destroyed, because I couldn't locate it. We had to be very careful with our records—the downside of being constantly ostracized and persecuted. It was a wise choice, since the Northwest's inability to know the full extent of our ranks is the only reason we were able to rebuild. But I can tell you that she adored you. And you adored her back. You were such a little angel. Very well behaved."

I try to swallow a sob. Fail. This is *ugly*. Shoulder-shaking, tear-slick, full-bodied crying. For a woman I've never even met. What do I care about the tragedy of her life? And why, when Irene covers my hand with hers, do I allow it?

"You may not have any memories of the Favored. But you must recall what it was like, being alone. Away from your people. I can assure you, Fiona didn't let go of you. You were taken from us when the Northwest decided to hunt us down, snuff us out—"

"Why did they do that?" I snatch back my arm. Curl it into my lap. Allow myself one last sniffle before I confront her. "What was the reason?"

"You are too young to remember—"

"But I've been told. Is it a lie that Constantine targeted the Northwest leadership and killed thousands?"

Her mouth curves in a displeased line. "Did they tell you *why*? Did they explain that Constantine won the challenge against their Alpha, but the Northwest refused to allow him to step into the role that was his right?"

I lean forward. "And what about Koen's father, Irene? Did you *not* use him to lure Koen's mother?"

"Koen Alexander is an illegitimate leader." Her dark gaze sharpens. "Your father . . . he may have used the Alpha's mate to draw her to himself. But after, he won fair and square."

"That's *not* how the challenge works."

"And who decides that? Who establishes the rules? The Alpha. The pack. The system was rigged in their favor—but Constantine outwitted them. He should have been the leader of the Northwest, not hunted down like a beast, forced to hide in more and more remote locations, and then killed in cold blood." She closes her eyes. Collects herself. "I struggle to understand why you do not see that Koen is your enemy. But maybe it's your approaching Heat talking."

I recoil. "How do you know about that?"

"Oh, dear. Jess has been good to us. Very helpful indeed. She was one of the Favored, did you know that? They slaughtered her parents and gave her to a Were family. But unlike yours, her memories remained. She gained access to your clinical file and told us that you lost the ability to shift. She delivered the necklace. And, of course, she let us know about your Heat." The line of Irene's mouth softens. "You are very close, I hear."

Fuck this. "I want to go back."

"Ah, yes. That injection. You know, there's no need. We have a handful of Weres who'll be happy to service you. You may choose whoever you prefer among them. And who knows, there might even be a baby from this Heat. Constantine's heir. He has performed bigger miracles than that. After all, we're close to the anniversary of his birth."

"I think I . . ." Just threw up a little in my mouth. "It's a pass for me. I'll be fine."

"No, you won't. Heats in human form are dreadful. I must say, I was surprised to hear that the current Alpha was willing to allow you to avoid yours. But then again . . ." She sighs. "Koen Alexander was always unpredictable. We could never take him by surprise. Before you arrived, that is. We are very grateful to you, for making him a little more like his mother. And his mother, we were able to deal with."

I clench my teeth. "If you're thinking of using me to trap him, he won't come. He's smarter than that. He has spent his entire life aware of how you ruined his family, and—"

"Eva. There is no *smart* when it comes to falling in love. Haven't you learned that?"

"Koen's priority is the pack. He won't jeopardize it."

"We'll see." The tilt of Irene's head gives me goose bumps. "You should ask him when he arrives. He won't be long, dear. But you'll have all the time you need."

"Time for *what*?" I hiss.

"To read your mother's last letter."

CHAPTER 29

He is afraid—not only of what might happen to her, but also of what he might do to the world in retaliation.

A S AWARE AS I AM OF IRENE'S MANEUVERS TO KEEP ME IN THE asscrack of nowhere, I still allow it, and I can't help wondering why. It'd be a good case study. An interesting dive into hybrid behavior. Unfortunately, my temperature is climbing, and I'm starting to feel too shitty to ponder the wonders of the halfling mind.

"You should drink," Nele tells me, holding out a glass. She's the youngest of the women I spotted downstairs. When I returned to my room, Irene instructed her to follow me. I assumed she'd be my designated jailer, but Nele doesn't have the look for it. Could be her homemade cutoffs, or the way her braid reaches nearly past her butt. She seems too sweet and innocent to be part of this mess. "It's not drugged or anything, I promise." She takes a seat across from me and swallows a big, performative gulp to prove it to me.

But I'm not thirsty or hungry. Layla mentioned that the closer I got to my Heat, the harder it would be to keep food down. She didn't say anything about hammering headaches and the burning desire to bite the flesh off my skeleton, but that might just be a side effect of Irene keeping me here by holding Fiona's letter hostage.

"Have you read it?" I ask Nele.

"Um . . . what?"

"The letter."

"Ah." She shakes her head. "I didn't even know Fiona existed until you gave your interview. Hundreds of people died in the Harrowing, and I wasn't even born, so—"

"The what?"

She bites her lips in confusion. I don't think she's had many interactions outside of the cult. "The Harrowing? When the Weres from the Northwest came after the Favored and murdered Constantine."

"Do you know why they did that?" I ask, toneless.

"We were growing in size and power," she recites. "They felt threatened. And Constantine had won a challenge against their Alpha."

This girl is as much a victim of Irene as I am. There is something disturbingly familiar in her mannerisms, something that reminds me of the boy on the cliff. I try to be gentle when I ask, "Why would a pack with tens of thousands of Weres feel threatened by a cult with hundreds of members, no political influence, and no allies?"

She tucks a strand of hair behind her ear. "People don't always act rationally." That, too, comes out a little singsongy. "The unwise is not moved by reality. His behavior is a product of wishes and delusions."

She looks so cogent, I almost wonder if I'm the one who has it all wrong. "Do you really believe that you can be turned into a Were?" I ask her.

"Oh." She blushes. "I wouldn't presume to know if that's what he wants for me. Not everyone will cross that river. Some of us are just here to aid the most favored. Such as yourself."

"Okay. Let me rephrase this. Do you think that a Human can be turned into a Were? Has anyone explained to you that we are different species? Do you study science at all?"

"I . . ." She looks around. Her voice drops to a whisper. "I read a book, once."

I'll take that as a no. "Who gave it to you?"

"It was at one of our hideouts. I . . . We aren't supposed to, but I was bored, and . . ."

"And now you know that it's impossible."

She lowers her eyes. Then lifts them again, to intone, "There are many things that science doesn't yet understand. And there have always been tales, among us Humans. Stories about being bitten during the full moon and becoming Weres. And there's you. You are proof."

"I was born half Human and half Were. I'm a hybrid."

She leans closer, so *sorry* for me, it's impossible to resent her. "If hybrids were a possibility, wouldn't we have thousands by now?"

"That's not how random genetic mutations work." I need Juno. Here and now. To lend me credibility with her doctoral degree and her stern looks.

"It was Constantine," Nele says, with the same gentleness I attempted earlier. The condescension hurts more than the headache. "He proved himself through you."

"Is that why you're here? You're hoping that'll happen to you?"

"I'm here because my grandparents joined Constantine's father, and I grew up among the Favored. But . . . I understand that our beliefs can appear unorthodox." I don't point out that the clinical phrase would be *nuttier than banana bread.* "Every society has its own idiosyncrasies. My parents told me Humans do odd, incomprehensible things all the time. They hoard resources others require to survive. They sometimes murder members of their own groups. They destroy the very place in which they live." Her head tilts. "You were among them. Does that still hold true?"

"Oh, yeah. Big time."

"See? And I've heard that other species are no better. Weres kill their babies for fun, imprison their women, and are violent and cruel to those who are weaker." She must not notice my confused expression, because she continues. "I don't know enough about Vampyres, but I'm sure they have their issues. My point is, the longer you remain with us, the deeper your understanding of our beliefs will be."

Remain. "How many of y—of us are there left?" I feel a tinge of guilt at her delighted smile, but it's too good a chance to find out more.

"About fifty or so."

"Do you all live here?"

"No. This hideout is very close to the northernmost border of the Northwest, and to the Canada pack, too. We almost never use it. But we have better ones. Mostly, we live scattered, hideout to hideout. We meet often, but we cannot live clustered in a compound like we once did."

"Why?"

"Because of the Harrowing. If the Northwest knew, they would come after us. Separate us from our families. Did you know that my grandfather has been in a Human prison for decades? I have never hugged him." Her eyes shimmer with tears. "But we are getting stronger. We'll grow our numbers again. Irene says that you'll bring us visibility."

My throat feels like sandpaper. "Is that her plan? Keep me here like a symbol of the Favored?"

"There is no plan," Nele reassures me, her pretty face guileless.

"Come on, Nele. Did you not hear her downstairs? If nothing else, she's using me to draw Koen here and hurt him."

"Oh, no. You don't know her." Quickly, she comes to kneel beside my chair, taking my hand between hers. My gut churns.

"What does she plan to do to him?"

"Nothing! We're not like that. We just want to live in peace, Eva. We abhor violence."

"You *abhor*—Nele, I was taken against my will. I was assaulted and drugged and—"

"That's different!" Her grip tightens. "We had to bring you here so that you could decide whether you want to be with us."

"I *don't*," I say sharply.

"But you don't have all the information."

"There is nothing that—"

"You can't be sure. You've only heard Koen's side of the story. There are others. And when Irene reveals them, you might change your mind. See that he and his seconds are inhumane."

We are not Human. Funny that if Koen were here, he'd probably agree with her. I shiver and pull my hand away from Nele's to hug my knees. That's exactly what I need—Koen, here. With me.

"I didn't mean to upset you. I just wanted you to know that you are one of us. Will always be." Her smile is apologetic. Young. "Irene sent me up to help you prepare for your Heat."

"Prepare?"

"She said it's coming soon."

My stomach drops. My mind races with horrifying possibilities. "Prepare how?"

"The ceremonial markings." She picks up a small jar full of a thick black liquid. When she holds it closer, I realize that it might be closer to a dark blue. Or green. "Don't worry, the dye will stain lighter."

"Stain . . . what?"

"Your skin. Are you not familiar with the tradition?"

"I've been a Were for about twenty minutes."

"Oh. Well." She glances at the door, clearly considering getting Irene.

"I—I don't care about traditions, I mean." I bite my tongue. To punish myself. "No need for the markings."

"But Were customs are important. And if you don't . . . Irene might be angry." In the slight tremble of her lips, I hear what Nele doesn't say. *At me. And I don't want that.* Irene is a stand-up gal—good to know.

"Eva—"

"It's not my fu—" I stop. Take a deep breath. The abduction/ Heat combo isn't doing my temper any favors. Or maybe I just take after Irene. "Nele, will you please call me Serena?"

"The name the Humans gave you?" Baffled lines appear on her forehead. "You want to honor it?"

"It's not that . . ." *Deep,* I want to say. Except, isn't it?

Serena is the name by which my sister calls me. The name on my diploma. The name Koen whispered in my ear last night. Eva might be what Fiona chose when I was a child, but it belongs to someone who was at the mercy of others, someone who doesn't exist even in her own memories. Serena was a spur-of-the-moment decision by a nurse, but it's my name because I made it so. Everything I built is attached to it.

"Yes. I do." I glance at the jar in her hand. "How do I know it's not poison?"

"It's not at all! Look." She smears a large quantity of the liquid on the inside of her wrist. When she wipes the excess away, the stain is a dark, brilliant green. It reminds me of a forest at night.

It reminds me of Were blood.

"Can I, then? Irene taught me, just for you. I'll do good."

I nod and let her guide me into the bathroom.

———— ⋊ ⋉ ————

FOUR HOURS LATER, THE RAIN HAS YET TO STOP, AND IRENE HANDS me Fiona's letter.

She calls me from downstairs and asks me to join her for tea, addressing me as *dear* once again. I put on the hoodie that Nele laid out for me and stumble out of the room, stopping by the hallway window to press my burning forehead against the glass.

It's bad, this fever. My abdomen is cramping. I desperately need new underwear. My thoughts feel slippery, difficult to chase and impossible to catch. Every once in a while, I snag the tail of one and am dismayed to find that they have little to do with my insane aunt wanting to use me as proof that orgies and drinking Were blood are Good, Actually. It's usually a large, coarse hand closing around my hip. The scrape of stubble against my throat. A soft kiss on the curve of my shoulder. My nest, back at the cabin.

Several new people have appeared, including three male Weres, bringing the total in the house to *too fucking many*. Everyone smells putrid. I need a shower. I need to bury my face into the T-shirt I'm wearing and chase Koen's scent. I need that hormone shot, right now.

"Would you like me to introduce you?" Irene asks when I sit at the table. "You will have to make a choice soon."

The acquisitive glances of the men are hard to miss. They stand by the entrance, fidgety, pupils blown wide. Maybe I didn't overreact by too much when I broke the ceramic soap dispenser in the upstairs bathroom and stuffed the sharpest piece in my pocket. "No. I would like to read the letter, then leave."

She surprises me by handing it over instantly.

"The photos, too," I say.

"You have seen them already."

"And I want to see them again."

"Very well."

"How will I know that the letter is real?"

"You won't. You're going to have to make a decision, but you are an intelligent girl, thanks to your parents. I'm sure you'll figure it out."

The letter is not addressed to me. It's the first thing I notice—the *Dear Irene* in unexpectedly round, neat handwriting. Mine is slanted and messy, hard to make out. *Looks like an ECG line*, Misery always says. *You make people work for every damn letter. No one should have to expend that much effort to know that you want them to buy zucchini.* As if she ever once went grocery shopping.

But this, this is bubbly. Girly.

My *mother's*.

Dear Irene,

I don't know if or when you'll receive this letter. I don't know if you're alive. It's been approximately three weeks since we went our separate ways. Like we agreed, I'll be vague about names and locations, in case the Northwest intercepts our communications. Without going into detail, I dearly hope our time apart has been less eventful for you than for us.

*Originally, it was just C., P., E., and me. A few days later, we
encountered three other Favored on the run and joined forces. A
larger group of adults allows for more night shifts to ensure that
we're not being surrounded, or ambushed. These days, we always
need at least two people to stay awake to sound the alarm. Luckily,
only E., H., and I are still Human. Our senses being what they
are, there is not much we can do. H. sometimes helps me take care
of E., even though she remains wary of men. We have settled in one
of our old safe houses, the most remote we could reach. You may
remember it as the place where our dear friend G. gave birth a few
years ago. It's nice to have that lovely memory as we face this cold
winter.*

*You must be wondering whether C. has had any revelations
about the current situation. Sadly, I don't have good news on that
front. He believes that the Northwest is closing in, and I suspect he
might be right. I feel a great deal of guilt about the skepticism I
expressed when he first informed us of his plan to take over the
Northwest, and I now realize that I shouldn't have questioned the
prophet's word. After long meditation, C. has informed us that
objectors like me are the real reason the takeover did not go as
planned. The least I can do to atone is stay by his side and take
care of him.*

*You probably want to know about your favorite, E. Frankly, I
regret bringing her with us. She is deeply unhappy, and perhaps
even regressing. She eats little, rarely pays attention to us, and at
times she won't speak at all, not even when asked direct questions.
In the first few days on the run, she would ask after her friends, but
has since stopped. She is so withdrawn, the others sometimes make
fun of her. Call her slow. They say that she cannot be trusted to
obey orders, and are worried about her giving our location away,*

and about her behavior in a crisis. Do you recall that battle at Glacier, right before we ran? There was so much blood, and so much death. I tried to shield E. from it, but she hasn't been the same since. All I ever wanted was for her to grow in the presence of her father. C.'s greatness has been a constant throughout my life, and she deserves to be inspired by him, too. But he rarely has time for her these days. I try to carve out moments for just the two of us, slices of the day to play or draw or snuggle together, but is it enough? Would she be better off elsewhere? My love for her is boundless—and much stronger than my pride. Her happiness matters to me, more than being able to say that I am the cause of it.

As you've probably realized by now, this is why I'm writing. You and E. have a special bond, and if you are in a safe place away from conflict, I cannot help wondering whether that's where she should be, too.

There is another possibility. The news has reached us that the new Alpha of the Northwest offered to hear any Favored who will turn themselves in, and will spare the lives of those who were not directly involved in the attacks. C. says that he's an illegitimate Alpha and cannot be trusted. However, I've heard rumors of Humans successfully taking advantage of this stipulation. Would he offer grace to E.? Would it be foolish to expect him to keep his word?

Let me know your thoughts. And whatever you decide, do not let the tone of this letter bring you down. These are hard times, but if we follow C.'s instructions, we will prevail.

Much love,
Fiona

I finish reading, and my timing must be pitch perfect. Because I set the letter on the table just as Irene says, "Ah, he is here. Welcome."

I lift my eyes and Koen is there, blocking the light from filtering through the doorway.

There are more than half a dozen people in the room, but his gaze falls on me instantly, like I'm the center of mass of his universe. The violence of his relief is so strong, I don't think anyone in the room is immune to it. Irene herself recoils, before collecting herself and adding, "We sent our location early this morning. It took you much longer than we expected to get here."

Koen steps inside. He's drenched in rainwater, hands tied in front of his body. His forearms and neck are smeared with blood, green swirled with red. Some of it trickles slowly down his temple, where it mats his thick hair. Just below, a deep cut dissects his right cheekbone. He's wearing a black shirt and black pants, which makes it impossible to tell whether he was injured in any vital spot.

I can't believe he came *alone*. After what he said about his mother, he made the same mistake. He's so outnumbered, even *he* can't make it out of this.

And yet his smirk and "Thank you for having me" fill me with some temporary optimism, even after three more Weres walk inside behind him. It's Jess and her two friends, clearly proud to be delivering the Alpha of the Northwest. They bend their heads to Irene. When she invites Koen to take a seat, the younger man pushes him and sends him staggering forward.

The boy gets to gloat for about three seconds. Then Koen spins around, uses his bound hands to deliver a hook, and trips him with his foot.

Every Were in the room takes an attack stance, ready to inter-
vene, but Koen barely notices. "Tell your boyfriends to get their
hands off me," he orders Irene, not even winded.

"Alpha." She clicks her tongue. "Are you in the position to make
demands?"

Koen's response is a glance toward the boy who's currently in
fetal position on the floor, holding his bleeding jaw.

"Point taken." Irene chuckles, and pulls a chair back for Koen.
She's a spider, willing to bide her time for a juicy reward, and I want
to warn him, but my mouth won't open.

"I see your bitchboys are eager to step up to the plate," he says,
glancing at the male Weres' obvious arousal.

"They are ready to be of service, yes. Would you like some tea,
Alpha?"

"That would be lovely. Chai, two sugars."

"Nele? Do we have . . . No? No chai, unfortunately. Can we offer you anything else?"

Koen sits back. "Lady, fuck you and your tea."

"Oh, there is no need for such hostility," Irene chides. "I have
greatly enjoyed my time with your friend."

"Bully for you. My *mate*, though, doesn't seem to enjoy your
company. She's crying, and smells like she's in distress."

I lift a hand up to my cheek. It's slick with tears.

"You and I have never met, have we?" Irene asks Koen, sizing
him up as she returns to her chair.

"We both know that one of us wouldn't be here if we had."

"That's likely correct. Our families wouldn't have approved of
a friendship between us, would they? Oh, how rude of me—I
haven't even introduced myself. My name is Irene. I believe you
were acquainted with my brother, Constantine." Her smile is po-

lite, even gracious. Too gracious. From my seat, I can see the clench of her right hand in her lap, visceral white-knuckled hatred in her fist. "Ah, I see from your expression that you had no idea."

"We had a list of his siblings, and you weren't on it. If I'd known that any of Constantine's relatives stuck around, we'd have met much earlier."

"Yes. Well, these days I cannot avoid a leadership role, but I used to fly under the radar. I was very young, and the spotlights weren't for me. Then . . . you know what happened." She turns to me. Before I can lurch away, her palm covers mine. "But how can I complain, now that I am reunited with my niece. Family must stick together, mustn't it? It's what her father would have wanted."

Koen walked into this room bound and beaten, but now is the first time I pick up any real tension from him. And all at once, I can no longer ignore the truths that have been drilling at the walls of my skull for the last few hours.

My father killed Koen's mother.

My father killed Koen's father.

My father killed thousands of Weres, including Brenna's, Amanda's, Saul's, and Jorma's families.

My father is the reason Koen was forced to become Alpha at fifteen.

My *father*.

"Koen, I—" *Am not sure what to do. Don't know what to say. Am sorry. Will make amends.* There's no good way to finish this sentence. I stare at him, willing him to meet my eyes.

When he does, the black of his gaze holds absolutely nothing.

Say something. Say something. Please, Koen, say something.

His expression remains closed, jaw set, chest heaving in slow breaths.

A wave of nausea grabs me by the throat. *I'm sorry. I'm so sorry—*

"There is no need to cry, dear." Irene pats my shoulder. "We are just chatting. Let me guess—you feel guilt because of the history between your father and Koen's pack. Maybe you think a debt is owed. But you only know little pieces of the story. That letter you just read . . . Would you like me to tell you what happened after it was sent?"

I nod, ashamed. She's trying to deal me into her game, and I'm allowing it. Because I *need to know.*

"You see, the letter was with a friend, for safekeeping. I didn't read it until months after it was written. But Fiona . . . she died less than twenty-four hours after it was sent." Irene's head tilts. She and Koen regard each other in a way I don't fully comprehend. Two people who have made impossible choices. Two people defined by what has come before them.

And then Irene smiles sweetly, and asks, "Out of curiosity, Alpha. How long have you known that you killed her mother?"

CHAPTER 30

She is meant for him, but they couldn't be more impossible.

I HOLD MY BREATH. STAY PERFECTLY STILL. MY MUSCLES COIL, AS if to keep my body from breaking open, stop my organs and blood from pouring onto the floor.

Then Koen says, "I've been suspecting it for a few days," and I fall apart.

"What?" I sound reedy. Maybe that's why Koen ignores my question. Doesn't look at me. Continues his conversation with Irene, composed, detached, like the topic is only mildly diverting. Broken boilers. The weather. Him, killing my mother.

"And yet you didn't tell her. How self-serving of you."

"I wanted to be certain, before informing her that one or more of her parents were high-profile figures in a cult with a sky-high body count."

Irene sneers. "Now you know for sure." She points at me with a flourish. "Tell her what happened that night. The Favored would like to know, too, wouldn't we, friends? All we had to go by were the rotting corpses."

"Very well." Koen takes a deep breath. Turns to me. Lifts his bound hands onto the table, leaning over his elbows, and locks eyes with me dispassionately.

Then he starts.

"Every raid that was launched against the cult, every search for those who had played a part in attacks against the Northwest, *I* led. And yes, I was the one who killed Constantine. But you knew that." He inches closer. "We found him in a ramshackle cottage up north. He knew that we had him surrounded, and sent his companions ahead to buy time. We worked our way through them. When I reached him, he was in wolf form. I forced him to shift back to human and later brought his corpse back to Northwest territory. I extracted his heart. The rest was left on a cliff for the vultures and other scavengers to feed on. This is the story—no more and no less."

My vision is blurry, whether from tears or the fever, I'm not sure. "I don't care about him. He deserved it. But what about . . ." I can't think over the blood pounding in my ears. I hate it, that I feel grateful toward Irene for asking what I can't bring myself to.

"What about Fiona, her mother? Did you kill her, too?"

At last, a flicker of hesitation. Koen's jaw works. After a moment, he says, "I won't lie to you. It's possible."

Irene scoffs. "Have you killed so many Human women that you can no longer recall them?"

"I don't know. Did you shield Constantine with so many Human women that I lost track?"

"What—what do you mean?" I ask.

He meets my eyes again. Any trace of the anger he showed when discussing Constantine is gone. "When I said that he sent his companions ahead to buy time, Serena, I mean it. If you are certain that your mother was with Constantine that night . . ."

"We are," Irene says.

"Then yes. I killed her." Koen is sorry but not repentant. It's clear in his eyes that he would go back and do it all over again. Then be sad about it all over again

Irene nods, a bitter, satisfied smile curving her lips.

"Was it you?" I ask, trembling. "Or Jorma? Or Amanda? Or—"

"It was me, Serena." His voice is precise. Cutting. "I am the Alpha of the Northwest. Every move, every action, every killing is sanctioned by me. My seconds are an extension of my hand. Whether I tore into your mother's throat myself or not, I'm still her killer. Do you really need me to explain this? Do you understand your people so little? What did I tell you?"

We are not Human.

My insides twist. "What about me? Why didn't you kill *me*?"

"You were not standing between me and Constantine, Serena." For a moment, his expression flickers. Like he's scanning my features. Cataloging them. Comparing them against an image in his head. His tone loses some of its ice. He's remembering something, something that was lost until now. "You were hiding."

"What?"

"In a closet. There was a Human girl with dark hair. She was skeletal and refused to talk." He searches my features. Sandpapers the years off my face.

"W-what happened to her?"

He swallows. "I brought her to the Human social worker."

"Was she . . . me?" I whisper.

Hesitation. "When Lowe first told me about hybrids, we immediately got in touch with Human Child Services to track down children of the cult. We were told that they were all accounted for."

"Then how—"

"A lie. Most likely, someone examined you, realized that you were a hybrid, and alerted Governor Davenport. And after that . . . you appeared in Paris when you were about six. But the girl I turned in to Human Child Services was at least a couple of years younger than that."

"Then, if I'm her . . . where was I during those years?"

His jaw shifts side to side. "I don't know," he says.

My lips tremble. It's hard to shape the words. "How—how can you not remember whether you killed my mother? Whether you met me when I was a child?"

"Serena." He huffs a laugh but seems as shaken as I am. "I killed so many people. I made so many orphans."

It feels like he's killing me, now. Like he's carving my heart out of my chest.

"Did you ever stop to wonder if maybe they were better off among us than with Humans who would never care for them as we could?" Irene asks sharply.

Silence. Did he? He might not remember that, either.

"So you killed both my parents. And then you found me. And then you l-left me alone."

He doesn't flinch away or deflect. Just nods. Admits, "I did, Serena."

I shake my head. Try to wipe at my cheeks, but it doesn't work. There are too many tears coming.

"How do you feel, Eva?" Irene asks, odiously kind.

"I don't know. I . . . I . . ." I cannot look at Koen. Don't want to. "I'm sad. And I'm . . . I'm *so* angry, and you don't even— She was my *mother*, the only person who ever cared about me, and you don't even remember if you fucking *killed her*—"

I stop at the noise of something sliding across the mahogany.

Blink through the tears. Watch it, incongruously pink and cutesy against the paper of my mother's letter.

It's the knife. My knife. The one Koen gave me to protect myself. The one I used against Jess. How did it end up here?

"How angry are you, Serena?" Irene asks. "At this man who murdered your family in cold blood? He took away your childhood and your home and didn't even stick around long enough to make sure that you were taken care of. If he hadn't killed Fiona, the three of us could have been together. There would have been no orphanage. No Vampyres. No Northwest. You could have been happy. But Koen took that away from you. So let me ask you one more time . . . How angry are you?"

"I'm not—" I start, shaking my head—and then stop.

Slowly, I let my eyes settle on Koen. His quiet expression betrays none of the turmoil I'm feeling. How angry am I?

A lot. A *lot*.

"Here." The knife makes its way into my hand, already unfolded. "This man was angry, and he hurt you and your family. Now that you are angry, what will *you* do, Eva?"

This is a dream. A nightmare. I can't be awake as I clutch the plastic handle and walk around Irene's chair, dazed but determined. But I know what I must do.

I know that it's right.

Someone drags Koen's chair to the side to give me better access to him. Four hands keep him still, pinned to the chair, but there's no need. Koen isn't thrashing or wriggling away. There is no pleading, nor an attempt to convince me that I'm overreacting. He sits quietly, looking up at me like I'm a queen. His life and death are but my decision. He wouldn't dream of objecting. If I want to carve his heart out of his chest, he'll crack his rib cage open and lie prone for me.

My hands tremble, but not too much. I can do this. I can.

"You *can* do this," Irene reminds me. "You are owed."

I nod. This is my right. "I'm sorry," I whisper at Koen, letting the tip of the blade graze the soft spot on the side of his neck. I've kissed that spot. Licked it. Buried my face in it.

I adjust my grip. *I'm sorry*, I think.

With a firm swipe, I slice the ropes that tie his wrists together.

CHAPTER 31

The girl was small. He'd have put her around three, but the Humans said she was older than that. At the time he knew little of children and nothing of Humans, and so he believed them.

She clung to him, her little arms skeletal around his neck. Her scent had a strident, chemical note, as though she had been given something that would keep her docile. "It's what they did with the other kids, too," the social worker told him grimly.

The child was asleep in his arms, and as he handed her over, he wondered, Is all of this a mistake? *But when the Human took her, he noticed that his hands had stained the girl's shirt a bright green.*

AFTER A LIFETIME SPENT DISSECTING HIS PARENTS' DECIsions, Koen was bound not to replicate their mistakes. I blame the fever and the drugs for not having realized it earlier, but it all starts making sense when several large wolves jump into the room.

Through the windows.

The *closed* windows.

I count four, then everything turns into pandemonium. Rainfalls of shattered glass. Toppled furniture. Screams and growls and the bone-snapping sounds of the shift. It happens so quickly, when a strong arm loops around my waist, my first reaction is to strike back.

Then I realize who I just hit, and gasp. "Sorry!"

"Fucking sharp elbows," Koen mutters. Jess and another of the guards who brought him in are lying at his feet. The third is outside, being chased by a rust-colored wolf. Jorma.

"Where did Irene go?" he asks the only cult Were who hasn't shifted. "Don't make me repeat myself. Where the fuck did—"

"I don't know! I don't know!"

Koen mutters something about a waste of space and tucks me behind him. "Saul! Here!" A brown wolf quickly defeats his gray opponent, then turns to us. He leaps over Jess's unconscious body and positions himself next to me, snarling at no one in particular. "Do not leave her side."

"What— Koen?" I grip his wrist. "Where are you going?"

"To find Irene."

No, I nearly protest. But why? "If you find Human members, please don't—"

"Serena." His forehead briefly touches me. "We do not hurt Humans if we can help it." Our eyes meet for a split second. I nod. Koen does, too. I feel him take my hand and slip something in it—the pink knife.

A second later, his glossy black fur is in the thick of the fight. He snaps his jaw around the idiot who tries to stop him, then chases Irene's scent. I don't take my eyes off him until I hear a sob behind me.

I race to the living room, finding Nele and her family huddled together in a corner with two Human boys. When I rush to kneel in front of her, they all scream in sheer terror.

"It's just me. Nele, we were together earlier. Alone. I wouldn't hurt you, would I?" I make a show of putting the knife down. Lift my hands. "It's okay. They're not here for you. Saul, can you please look less like you're craving steak? Thanks." It breaks my heart, the way Nele glances up at me, eyes brimming with tears and panic. *Was it like this for me, too? In that closet? Did Fiona push me in there and tell me that it was going to be okay?* "Nele, you and your family will be okay, I swear." Some of the tension leaves her body. "Just stay out of the Weres' way."

"They're going to kill us," her mother says. "They are here to—"

"They only came here to take me back."

"How can you believe that? You heard what he said—they killed your mother."

I clench my teeth. "Am I not your prophet's daughter, too?" Their eyes widen, and I continue, "Trust me." That seems to do it. They look slightly less like they expect to have their livers chomped on.

"What about Irene?" Nele asks, weakly.

"She's gone." *Saving her own ass.*

"Are they going to . . . to hurt her?"

"I don't know." Saul makes a barking noise. "Maybe."

"But she's your only family."

I snort. "You saw that tall guy out there?"

She nods.

"He's more my family than—"

"Serena!" Amanda runs inside the room, naked, covered in blood and other unidentifiable fluids that should never be found *outside* a body.

"Are you okay?" I frantically inspect her limbs.

"Yes." She grins. Saul bumps her hip with his muzzle, looking just as worried. "Come on, you guys. This shit ain't mine. Serena, are *you* okay?"

"Is the fight out there—" The cabin has gone quiet. "Are they . . . ?"

"Yup. And the others went after Irene and another Were who escaped. Serena, we were so fucking worried about you. Shit, you're bleeding. But it's just a graze. Let me make sure you didn't break anything." She gently presses against my jawbone—and instantly pulls back.

"Serena."

"What?"

Her hand touches my forehead. I'm seized by the sudden temptation to break her wrist. "Did they give you something? You're burning up."

"I'm okay."

"You're *not* okay."

"I am. Just, could you . . . not touch me?"

"What?" She examines my face. I *do* feel like I'm boiling.

"My skin. Could you please not—"

"What the fuck?"

Touch me.

"Serena? Serena!"

And that, as they say, is that.

—— ·✦· ——

WHEN I OPEN MY EYES AGAIN, IT'S DARK. THE MIDLEVEL HEADACHE that has been my loyal golden retriever companion is finally gone. In its stead, a dragon-worthy migraine pummels at my temples, clear proof that I'm dead and my corpse was sold to med students for skull-trepanning practice.

And yet.

If I were waking up in any other angle of the observable universe, I'd be rolling off the bed and lurching toward the toilet, ready to vomit my stomach lining. But whoever brought me here had the good foresight to deposit me in the only place where I'm not constantly surrounded by hostile, belly-churning stimuli.

Koen's room.

The scent of him has a morphine-like effect on me. I bury my face in the pillow, take several deep, lung-filling breaths, and use the bathroom. On my way to the living room, I make a pit stop on the bed, inhale a few more times, and walk down the hallway feeling like new.

I expect—no, I *want* to find Koen *alone*. Instead, I count six more people, maxing out every sittable surface: his three closest seconds, Sem and Layla, and Karolina.

I stand in the doorway, and a crystal-clear thought seeps through the atoms that make my being: *How dare they be here?*

It's rapidly followed by: *I'm going to kill them.*

What? No. I'm not. I take a preventative step back. Hold on to the wall and remind myself that I do *not* want any of these people to be dead. In fact, I'm invested in them staying alive. But my instinct tells me that they should *go away, stop invading my space, spreading their scents, their too loud voices, and their bodies in our—*

This must be some new Heat bullshit. I firmly shove it back where it came from and interrupt the ongoing conversations to ask, "Did you find Irene?"

Seven pairs of eyes rocket to me. Six pairs of legs stand and come fuss around me, asking how I'm doing, telling me that I was out for hours, attempting to feel my temperature. My father was directly responsible for the deaths of their friends and family, and yet here they are. Clearly not wishing ill on me. The thought forms a lump in my throat.

I ignore it and focus on Koen, who's unimpressed with me. He sits on a chair someone brought in from the porch, legs spread wide, elbow folded atop the back, and orders the others in his most dispassionate tone, "Get the fuck away from her."

A bunch of *Oh, right. My bad.* Amanda points me at the spot she vacated on the couch. "I forgot about the whole, um, hypersensitivity thing." I take a seat, and they all gawk at me as though I may have forgotten how to perform the complex enterprise of bending my knees. It's offensive, how wonderstruck they are when my butt touches the cushion. Except for Koen, who just exudes a mildly irritated aura.

"You guys, I'm fine."

"Still, I'd like to look you over," Layla says. "I brought my equipment."

Thank God it's injection time. I cannot wait to be rid of these Heat symptoms. "Yes. But first—"

"No, we did not find Irene," Koen interrupts me. "We were able to track her scent for a few miles, but the rain erased her trail. There were eight other Weres in the cabin. Four are dead. Jess is injured and has not regained consciousness yet. Another Were escaped, and we captured the remaining ones, who have been questioned but don't appear to be sharers. We've interviewed everyone who has had prolonged contact with Jess, as well as the family who raised her, and they're all shocked by her ties to the cult. The six Humans are now in Northwest territory and under surveillance, *because*"—he continues, noticing my frown—"Irene left. We're not sure whether they are self-sufficient or, even worse, whether Irene will decide that they know too much and have them killed. We have contacted the Human authorities. In the meantime, they are not our captives, but our guests. They are terrified but unharmed. This is the gist of it, but if you'd like to know more, there is the report"—he glances at Jorma, who appears pleased with himself—"that I was asked to turn in."

"It's not all of them. The cult, I mean. They weren't all in that cabin. They told me that there are—"

"Over fifty of them, yes. We are devoting considerable manpower to tracking the others. Anything else you'd like to know before you allow Layla to make sure that you're not fucking dying?" The last few words are strained. I *really* don't want to make him snap, but.

"Could you—is anyone going to be checking on them? The Humans, I mean."

"Me," Amanda says.

"When you go, could you give Nele a way to contact me?"

"Who?"

"The youngest Human girl. Long auburn hair, freckles? If she needs anything . . ."

Amanda glances at Koen, who nods. "I will," she says.

"Thanks, Amanda, I really appreciate it. Are you okay, by the way? Was anything—"

"Serena," Koen grunts. "I swear to fucking—"

"I'm going, I'm *going*."

"I'm sorry about what happened at the office," Layla tells me as soon as we're in Koen's room.

"Don't worry about it Let's not blame each other for stuff we did at scalpelpoint."

She smiles, but her eyes are shiny. "I was so out of it, I couldn't sound the alarm, and—"

"Believe me, you did everything you could. I would hug you to underscore my point, but the idea of touching anyone who isn't— Well, I'd rather not. Let's do it after the injection."

Layla bites her lower lip. "I don't have good news for you, Serena."

Not being called Eva feels so damn nice, the words don't immediately register. Then they do, and ice pools in my stomach. "What do you mean?"

"You are too close."

"Too close to . . . ?"

"Your Heat."

She's joking, right? "It's not even a full twenty-four hours after we were planning to do the injection."

"I know. In all honesty, I'm starting to wonder whether an injection this morning would have been effective, given how fast you're progressing."

"You haven't even checked me yet. How can you tell?"

"Your scent, for one. Your pupils are permanently dilated. Your resting heartbeat is much quicker than yesterday, your breathing is shallow, and . . . When have you last eaten or drank?"

"I don't know. Probably . . ." This morning? No. Not really. Yesterday? I must have, but—

"Are you thirsty? Hungry? Should I get you something?"

I quickly shake my head. "No, thank you." Shit. *Shit.* "Is it normal?"

"For a Were on the edge of Heat? Absolutely. Once it starts in earnest, you'll have to remember to drink often, or you'll dehydrate soon, and that'll make the post-Heat days a nightmare. We brought over supplies—"

"We?" A wave of horror twists my guts. "Does everyone know?"

She cocks her head. "At this point, no Were of reproductive age would miss it."

I let myself fall back on the mattress. Maybe I could grab a fork from the kitchen, fall upon it, and encounter a swift and merciful death.

"That's not a bad thing, Serena. Your scent is attractive to Weres right now."

Probably better to just make out with a piranha and hope he'll eat me.

"It's a testament to the Alpha's trust in his seconds and his pack members that he's allowing them inside the cabin to be in his ma— in *your* presence, so close to your Heat. And a testament to how much they respect him and you—"

"What if I take the shot anyway?" I sit up. "Why not try, at least?"

"It could make your Heat last longer or be more painful. Worse, it could inflict long-term damage to your reproductive system."

"What if I'm willing to take the risk?"

"Serena." She pins my eyes with hers. *Listen carefully*, they say. *Because I'm in charge.* In her own way, she's as scary as Koen. Scarier. "No self-respecting healthcare professional will give you that shot right now. What I *can* give you, however"—she turns to her bag and pulls out a small packet—"is this."

It's so unsubstantial, as I hold it up to the light, I wonder if she's joking. "What is it?"

"Contraceptive pills."

I blink. "What? I can't even . . ."

"We don't know that for sure. These will prevent pregnancy. If you would like that, take them *after* your Heat is over."

"How will I know—when *is* the Heat over?"

"You'll know, believe me."

I don't want to believe her. *Or* to know. "Why would I need contraceptives? Is there some kind of asexual reproduction . . . I can't get pregnant just by having a Heat, right?"

She stands. Sets a small card on Koen's nightstand. "You have my number. For any question, call me. Anytime."

"Layla, I don't understand."

"If I don't answer, Sem will. But for the most part, it'll be a very intuitive process—"

"Layla."

At last, she stops. She glances in the direction of the door. Then murmurs, "I won't tell a soul. And neither will any of the seconds."

"I . . . Why does it sound like people have been talking about this?"

She swallows. "I know this embarrasses you, but it's not . . . We are not Human, Serena."

We are not Human.

"We don't feel like you do when it comes to our bodies. I know every person in that room. I know Koen. And I really . . . I wouldn't have wanted this for him."

Who else has told me these very same words? Ah, yes. Brenna. Of course. "It's a common feeling," I say flatly.

"I don't mean *you.* It's clear that he's so happy with you—"

"Happy?" Laughter bubbles out of me. "The dude who constantly looks like he's a hairbreadth from slashing every tire in the universe?"

Layla shakes her head. "When I heard that he had found his mate, and that it was unreciprocated, my first thought was that it was a blessing in disguise. I knew from the very start that Koen would put the pack first. It's always been his priority, after all. It would be a terrible choice to make for any Alpha—either renounce his pack for his mate or renounce his mate for his pack. But in your situation, if he chose the pack, you wouldn't suffer from it. You didn't want him, anyway. That made things much easier for him." She swallows. "But this—your Heat, what you are about to experience . . . It changes everything. Koen is now being asked to choose between respecting the covenant or guaranteeing his mate's well-being. And if you need him, he's never going to say no."

"I never asked him. I didn't—"

"Do you really think you need to ask him, Serena?"

I fist the comforter. Clench my jaw shut.

"The thing is . . . *We* need him, too. The Northwest needs Koen precisely because of everything I just told you. And that's why I'm not going to tell a soul." Her lips, I realize, are quivering. "No one will ever know where he'll spend the next few days. He'll be yours for a while, Serena. But after, you must return him. So think of it as a loan." One last, sad smile. "What I always tell my daughter is that all lies come to light. Let's hope that I'm wrong."

A few minutes later, the cabin falls silent. Everyone leaves—except for Koen.

CHAPTER 32

*Indecent. Filthy. Outrageous. Lewd, in the best possible way.
Those are the words he's thinking of.*

SHOWERING FEELS LIKE A THOUSAND FOUNTAIN PENS SCRAP-
ing my body head to toe, but smelling like blood, grime, and
my deranged aunt's homemade tea is worse than the pain, so I grit
my teeth and do it anyway.

Heat, I'm starting to realize, might not be a misnomer. I put on
a sleeveless top and shorts, sweating despite the cool November air.
When I walk into the living room, Koen is facing away from me,
talking on the phone about winning friends and influencing people. Regular Alpha stuff.

I lean against the doorway, eager to observe him, unobserved,
for a moment. The strain in his broad shoulders constricts my
chest. But he must pick up my scent, because he spins around to
face me, and it feels a little like his senses are sloping the room, giving him no choice but to roll toward me, and—

The phone slips out of his hand and thuds against the wooden
floor. Several pieces break off and skitter in every direction, but he
doesn't even glance at them.

"I think you dropped your phone?" I say, pointing at his feet.

He keeps staring at me. Suddenly, I feel immensely aware of my body. The way it pushes against the clothes' fabric. My exposed skin. Koen's dark, shifting eyes roaming it.

In a heartbeat, he crosses the room and cups the side of my head to inspect the base of my neck. That's when I remember. "The stains?" I trace the green ribbon-like twist below my palm. "It's not blood or anything. Just dye."

"Who did it?"

"Nele."

"The Human girl *marked* you?"

"Irene instructed her to. And you know how it is, when you're in the middle of an unlawful detainment and people start asking wacky stuff of you, and you really don't wanna say yes, but you decide to pick your fights and throw them a bone so that maybe later when you refuse to rob a bank they won't take it too personally, and . . . Koen?"

After several seconds and a substantial amount of effort, he manages to tear his eyes away from my neck. His Adam's apple shifts.

"I cannot figure out whether you're offended by these, or . . ."

A step back. He clears his throat. Shoves his fists in the pockets of his pants. "Not offended," he says, hoarsely.

"Glad to know that I'm not a walking insult. What are they?"

"Markings. Around your glands." He licks his lips. "They are used in mating ceremonies."

"Right. Irene had grand dreams for my Heat. I showered, but they didn't come off." I shuffle my feet. His eyes on me are feral. Carnivorous. He's a predator, tracking every movement of a prospective kill. "Koen? You're being a smidge weird about this."

"Right." Another step back—somehow, he drifted closer again. "Did they do the one on your back, too?"

"Yeah, but maybe it washed off." I lift my hair. "You can check—"

"*Don't.*"

I freeze.

He swears under his breath. "The marks are . . ." He jerks a hand through his hair. Opens his mouth about four times before settling on "Beautiful."

"Beautiful." My face tingles with heat. "That's not the word you were thinking."

"No." His jaw tightens.

"I can scrub harder. Or cover them."

"Absolutely fucking *no*." At last, his mouth softens in one of those self-effacing, disarming smiles that I already know I'll bring to my tomb.

Confusing, all of this. I busy myself and crouch down to pick up the phone. The screen is cracked, but the other pieces easily fit back together. "Here. Wanna call them back?"

"It was Lowe. I'll text later. Say that you tackled me."

"Credible. Did you tell him I was missing?"

"And promptly regretted it. The Vampyre called for updates every ten minutes."

"Did you give her your number, or did she just help herself to it?"

"The latter."

Unsurprising. I look down at my toes. Study them for a minute. "Can I ask you not to tell her about *this*?" I make a vaguely neurochemical-imbalance-shaped gesture. "She'd never let me live this down."

Koen crosses his arms, stern. "I doubt someone who's regularly having interspecies sex has a single toe to stand on. Besides, she rarely needs to *ask* to find out shit.'

He's right. I just feel so . . . exposed. Wrung out.

"Why are you so ashamed of this, Serena?" He sounds genuinely confused.

"I don't know." I snort out a laugh. "Maybe it's just easier to worry about what people are thinking than about . . . about the real shit."

"Such as?"

"That my father killed your parents. And you killed mine."

I can't believe it all fits in exactly ten words. Our pasts, woven together. One—no, *four* more reasons we could never work. As though we needed them. They come with a garbled mess of questions that I haven't even begun to wrangle free. Do I resent him? Does he hate me? Am I angry? How much of this is his fault? Should I carry my parents' sins? Can I forgive? Can he? Is there anything to forgive here?

He's just as stumped. Fiddling with these impossible thoughts. Gives me a stuck, resigned look and says, "Couple goals, am I right?"

I laugh. The low, rolling sound that slips out of him could be laughter, too. We regard each other like that, no judgment, no fear of being judged. I could live in this weird limbo for the next century.

"I would do it all over again," he murmurs at last, eyes never letting go of mine. "Even knowing what it did to you. And for that, I'm sorrier than I'll ever be."

We are not Human.

His pain squeezes my chest. "I don't want you to . . . If when you look at me you see Constantine, I don't want you to—"

"Serena." He shakes his head. "When I say that I would do it all over again, I also mean that I would go through what he did all over again. If it brought me to you."

It's a lovely thought: that the mistakes of our parents could have as little impact on our relationship as a butterfly flapping its wings. That *us* is a choice we can make. That we might not be constantly running out of time. *Too* lovely, maybe.

I lift my fists. "Right or left?"

He snorts. "Fuck this losing game."

"Do you really want to renounce one of two prizes, both of inestimable cash value—"

He takes my left fist, gently peels my fingers back, and holds my eyes as he brings my palm to his mouth and—

"Ouch."

"It's what you get." His lips brush against the soft bite he left there. I try not to shiver as he slides lower, to the mark on my inner wrist. His eyes do odd things as he inhales deeply.

"Killer," he murmurs. "You smell . . ."

"Good? Bad? Musty? Like beignet?"

He lets go of my arm. Runs his tongue over his teeth. "Close. You smell *close*."

I *feel* close, too. "You chose left. Therefore, you get a premium—"

"Cut the crap."

"Fine. I'm going to show you something. Come."

He follows me to my bedroom, but when my hand wraps around the doorknob, he grips my wrist to stop me.

"Give me a second," he orders. Trancelike. Foggy.

"I— Why?"

"Your scent is *really* intense here." It takes him a little more than a second, but he does get himself under control. Ushering him inside feels like an epoch-making moment, which might be dumb of me. We're not co-signing a mortgage. I'm not even asking him to be my emergency contact for spinning class. The way I hold my breath doesn't make sense.

And yet here I am. Wringing my hands as some guy looks at the weird, fort-like structure of pillows, blankets, comforters. Everything is plush, knit, soft. Last night I moved the bed into the alcove by the window, and above it I strung the fairy lights Ana must have left months ago. They tinge the place a warm, blurry yellow, much better than the unforgiving ceiling lamp. Also: they make the numerous items of Koen's clothing I've pilfered harder to spot.

"Remember when Layla mentioned nests?" My voice trembles. "I've been working on this for a while. Honestly, I'm just relieved that this new penchant of mine for acquiring shit is just a phase. And . . ." I notice that the placement of the lavender velvet pillow is off. "Sorry, this is a bit . . ." I move closer. Rearrange it over and over until it's just right. Deal with a domino-like cascade of imperfections that need to be fixed right *now*. A minute—or seventeen— later, a moment of clarity smashes into me. I look back at Koen. "Am I being absolutely insane?"

"I . . . believe this might be common," he says. Uncharacteristically diplomatic.

"God. Do you—do you like it?"

He stares at the bed with a blank expression that my single brain cell interprets as disapproval.

"I can redo it. Right now, if you—"

"Don't . . . I'm sure it's pretty. My instincts don't really lean toward the aesthetics and architectural integrity of nesting."

I frown. "What instincts *do* you have?"

"They are much less wholesome." His laugh is a half groan. "Less about making nests, and more about . . . wrecking them."

Because that's the point of a nest. I made it in a fugue-like state, an automaton on a flow experience. But while I was obsessing over every square inch of it, I never stopped to wonder what I'd do once it was ready.

It's obvious now that *I* made this one for *Koen* to—

Yeah.

I should *not* be this blindsided.

"What was in the right?" Koen asks, voice rough-edged. He's behind me. Closer than a moment ago.

"What?"

"If I had chosen the right hand, what would I have gotten?"

"Nothing as exciting as a mound of blankets."

"That's for me to judge."

I turn around. "I would have told you something."

"What?"

"Can't say, or you'll have both prizes."

"Would it be that bad?"

"It wouldn't be realistic. I told you, real life requires choices."

He grunts, annoyed, and leans back against the desk. A thousand warm little pangs gnaw at my body. Comfort and hunger and heartache and love and inevitability, all swirling in my belly.

Maybe tonight is different. Maybe it wouldn't be too bad, to bend the rules of reality. "I would have told you that . . . that you don't have to do what you're about to do." My heart thumps slowly, loudly. Feverish. "If you help me through my Heat, it'll be at great cost to you. If the Assembly ever found out, it would be a disaster.

So I would have told you: thank you, I appreciate the offer, but I cannot ask this of you."

"You don't—"

"Need to ask. Yup, that's what you would have said. And I would have pushed back a little—told you that I'm willing to deal with this on my own, because I wouldn't want you to regret it afterward."

"You can't—"

"But you would have seen through it. So I would have asked you whether you arranged for someone to cover your absence in the next few days. And you'd have said . . . Amanda?"

He nods, displeased in that endearing way of his.

"And that's when I would have told you how . . ." I take a deep, shaky breath. "I would have told you how vulnerable I've been feeling in the past year. Stripped of my life. My identity. My agency. My health. And now, of the most personal thing of all. A few hours from now, I'll be out of my mind. I will be a creature made of *need*, beyond thought. And you will take care of me exemplarily, like always. You will . . . You will kiss me, and touch me, and fuck me, because it's what I require, and those will be the memories I carry for the rest of my life: you, satisfying my needs. And I would have tried to make you understand that I . . . I want *more*. I would like some *real* memories of us. Not because we've been cornered into it by biology and circumstances, but because being together is what we both want. So, while I'm still in control, I would have asked you to . . . to kiss me, and . . ."

Koen doesn't come to me. He leans forward and pulls me into him with a tug at my wrist. I offer no resistance and stumble into his arms. "Yeah?"

I nod. He hunches forward. Cups my head and uses his thumb

to tilt my jaw upward, lips brushing against mine. Then he makes me wait.

And wait.

We stay there, on the brink of everything. I feel him everywhere. His scent. The steady warmth of his skin. His fingers, traveling to curve around my rib cage. "Let me make something very clear, Serena. I'm never going to regret any of this, okay?"

Our mouths are touching. I feel as though we're made of the same stuff. Me and him, set apart from the remaining matter of the universe. "I think . . . this is going to hurt, Koen."

"After, yeah. But not yet."

"Not yet."

Our first kiss is about as romantic as our first meeting, the first night we spent together, or my first visit to the ocean with him. It's a pattern for us: unmemorable (at best) or questionable (at worst) firsts. This once, though, it might be my fault. The impatience. The lack of harmony. I should have thought this through better, but it ends up being a scrape of teeth against the corner of his mouth, the delicious drag of his stubble, a lot of sharing air and breathing in between us. My upper lip slides against his lower, because that's as high as I can reach. He doesn't kiss me back, but there is a faint groan in his chest, just loud enough for me to hear.

"Serena," he sighs, and makes it better. Flips us so that I'm sitting on the desk, him between my legs, and then it's the rough swipe of his tongue against my lips, loud breaths, the heat of our open mouths. Fingers pulling at my scalp, new angles, tongues stroking. He tastes like a distilled version of his scent. I laugh against the seam of his mouth, giddy, and he grunts, "What?"

"Just—" He doesn't let me finish. Deepens the kiss. Slides a hand under my top and the pleasure startles me. I grip his forearms. When he sucks the gland on my neck I exhale roughly, and say, "Just, for someone who hasn't made out with anyone in over twenty years, you're not as bad as you— *Oof.*"

He tosses me on the nest. Air whooshes out of my lungs. I'm belly-down, spread-legged. Laughing without oxygen. "It was a compli—"

My shorts and underwear are *forcefully* pulled down. The mattress dips between my legs.

"I was joking!"

"So am I," he says, dead serious, pressing an open-mouthed kiss at the base of my spine.

I quiver. Take in a big gulp of air, but my throat won't comply.

"I saw these the first day we met. Been thinking about them." He lifts the hem of my top and just stares. I squirm as he presses his thumbs to each side of my spine. "Dimples. *Very* cute. Wholesome, really. Ready to be defiled." He leans in, and his tongue traces the cleft of the right one. "C'mon, Serena."

"W-what?"

"I thought you were joking. Joke some more."

I would write him a whole comedy special, if his hands weren't squeezing my ass, making my brain ring like some kind of . . .

"Phone." I drag myself up on my elbows.

He hums like he heard me but keeps staring down. His fingers tighten on me, acquisitive, like he can't help *taking*. I turn and find him heavy lidded, his breath shallow. His biceps are tense, prepared, anticipating. His fingers stroke between the globes of my ass.

"Koen," I gasp, "it's your—"

"Fuck my phone," he says, distracted, bending to lick the other dimple, and—

"It could be Nele, or they could have found Irene, or—"

He groans against my right asscheek. Then bites into it like it's a piece of fruit.

"Koen!"

"Sorry," he says. Before doing it again.

"Koen!"

"I said sorry." He presses a kiss against the small of my back. I roll around just as he leaves the room, catching his small smile.

The caller is Lowe, wondering whether Koen's toaster oven exploded and took him out. "All good. Serena tackled me," I hear him say. And, after a pause, "Told you, she beat me up. Slapped the phone out of my hand. What is there to understand?" I bury my laughter into a pillow. And there, in a nest that smells like Koen, listening to talk of pack jurisdictions and Human authorities, I fall into a calm, deep sleep.

CHAPTER 33

This is it, then. What he was born for.

I WAKE UP WHEN IT'S STILL DARK, FEELING LIKE AN ABOMINATION. My skin itches, too tight for my body. I arch against the mattress and press a palm to my abdomen: something hot and angry is pulsating inside me, and if I let it rip me apart, maybe it'll stop clawing at my insides. I'm sticky. Covered in sweat, strands of hair glued to my throat. My inner thighs are so wet, I refuse to think about it.

This cannot be normal, even for a Heat. It must be my ever fucked-up biology. Layla—I need to call her. Maybe she has something for the pain.

Are you really going to do that in the middle of the night? Wake up a woman with a small child who may very well be teething, just because you have a boo-boo? Are you that self-centered?

A whole-body cramp splits me in two, and— *Yes, I fucking am.*

Layla's number is on the desk across the hallway. I can get there. I can hike the Rocky Mountains. I can swim to outer space. I may even be able to do all that *and* keep quiet enough to let Koen sleep.

He's wrapped around me, chest to my back, and I gently slither under the arm he draped around my hips. I pause when his grip tightens on me, but it's a reflex, and a moment later I'm free.

Sitting up sucks the air out of me. My head swims, so I take a well-deserved break and beg my racing heart to slow down, giving myself a little pep talk. *You are able to breathe, Serena. Have been for years. If your life had a performance review, it would* not *be marked as an area of improvement.*

Then I hear, "Serena."

Shit. Woke Koen up.

"Just going to the bathroom," I lie. It comes out slurred, a chain-reaction crash of vowels and soft consonants, so I add, "Go back to sleep," making an effort to enunciate better.

"Are you okay?"

His voice rolls over my skin. Makes the thing pulsating inside me purr sweetly. For a second, it almost *feels* nice. "Yup. Don't worry." It's a bad idea, trying to answer him *and* to stand at the same time. I'm in no condition for simultaneous activities: all it gets me is jelly knees and more pounding in my head. I remember, once upon a time, being able to walk and chew gum. Ah, past glories.

"Serena." Rustling behind me. The mattress dips as weight is redistributed. Koen, always one to show me up, gets into a sitting position with ease. His hand closes around my upper arm to pull me back into him, and his touch, the sheer *ecstasy* of it, it hurts. My entire body clenches. "What . . ."

He goes unnaturally still. So quiet, I wonder whether he's feeling poorly, too. I turn to scan his face in the semidarkness, and after a long pause I hear him say, *"Fuck."*

"I'm sorry," I blurt out. "I didn't mean to—"

Make a mess of the bed.

Make a mess of you.

Get this grossly sick.

Lose my mind.

"I'm going—I'll shower and call Layla and figure this out and—"

"Serena, come here." He scoops me back into him, shushing me with his lips against my temple.

I'm on the verge of tears, and I'm not sure why. "Maybe you could help me to the bathroom—"

"Hush, killer. I got you."

He holds me. I'm tacky and gross and don't want to lean on him, but every inch of contact is pure heaven. "Koen?"

"Relax."

"I'm really not feeling well."

"I know." His nose nuzzles behind my ear. My heart could explode with joy. "You'll be okay. I'll make you okay."

"I need to call Layla—"

"Sweetheart."

"It's just that I need—"

"You need to do what *I* tell you." His tone is gentle and firm all at once, commanding in the exact way I need. It quells my anxiety. Loosens my restlessness. Koen's scent is so pleased, my body blooms in his arms. "See, killer? We can fix this." He licks across the gland on my neck, and I slump against him. It's bliss. "You don't need to call Layla. And you definitely don't need to stay away. You know what you need?"

I shake my head. His cool lips press against my heated, blotchy cheek.

"You need to be fucked, Serena."

Oh. It makes so much sense, I can finally compute the last few minutes. Of course. I'm about to go into Heat. Everything I need is here, in this bed. How did I not realize this sooner? "I . . . I forgot?"

"I don't think Heats are when people are at their most lucid." His laughter rumbles softly against my throat.

"So I just need to . . . ?"

"Be fucked, yes. I'll be taking care of that. Okay?"

"Please." I nod, desperate, all brainstem. This is all I want. I'm hollow, and he's going to fill me to the brim. The prospect scorches me blank. My vision whites out.

I'm also . . . The idea of water sloshing over my body makes me want to gouge my eyes out, but: "Can I . . . shower?"

Koen inhales deeply. Rolls us over until he's hovering above me, murmuring something about how "fucking unbelievable" I smell. Nips at my jaw, teeth just a little too tight, just this side of dangerous. He *could* hurt me, but he would never.

"Wait. Before we . . . I'm going to shower."

Koen props himself up on his palms to stare down at me, mystified. "What?"

You're annoying your mate, a pick-me voice whispers in my ear. *In your nest, no less. What is wrong with you?* I shrug it away, and say again, "You'd like it better if I washed up."

A silent snort. "I very much would not."

I have no idea how to explain what's happening to me and keep my dignity. "It's just, I'm sweaty and kind of disgusting, and also . . . You could say that I'm eager, but it doesn't really convey the depth of my . . ." I shut my eyes tight, mortified. Feel a single, shameful tear slip out of one corner.

"Serena, do you *want* to shower?" He sounds befuddled. "Or are you asking because you think I find your body disgusting?"

"The . . . latter."

Koen exhales. Indignant, maybe. "Open your eyes," he orders.

I can't. Don't want to. But realize that's not an option when he shoves my top up, licks one of my nipples, then bites into it hard enough for my back to wind high.

"Serena, open your damn eyes."

I do. For a long moment we regard each other. Then he explains, tone level, "The reason you are so wet is that your body has been preparing for what is about to happen. Believe me, you will need all the slick you can spare."

Slick. "I feel like I smell . . ."

"Fuckable. You smell *ready*. You smell transcendent and filthy and delicious. You smell like you're *this* close to losing your mind, like you might hurt me if I don't take care of you, and you know what that does to me, knowing that my mate needs me? You understand what this is for, right? What Heats are for?"

I nod but squirm underneath him. I might be lying.

"You always smell like you were made specifically for me. To fuck. To be around. To worship. But right now, you smell like you'd give me anything I asked for. If that's the scent you're planning to wash off . . . don't do it on my account." He bends to suck on my neck gland, then lets go with a lurid, popping sound.

I shudder. Watch him take off his shirt. Gaze never leaving mine, he spreads my legs open with his knees. When he stares down at me like *that*, I feel like I could . . .

He inhales deeply and closes his eyes. Like he needs a minute. "Fuck."

I watch him stroke himself through the fabric of his sweatpants. I've been around Koen a lot in the past week, and I'm not so unobservant to have missed his erections, but the ridge of his cock always gives me pause. He is . . . large. Perfect. Already leaking through his clothes.

I want to touch him. I want to do *everything* with him. Anything he asks for, he can have.

"Is this what worries you?" he asks. "That you're too wet?"

I nod. Cannot bring myself to say anything.

"You really have no idea, do you?"

A moment later, his face is in my cunt. His eyes drift shut as he laps, sucks, presses kisses against it. I can't tell whether he's doing this for me or for himself, but I arch in a surge of pleasure and tremble, gasp, beg for more. He pulls at my clit, strokes every fold with his tongue, and bites my inner thigh. The noises he makes are fearsome. Animal. They should make me flinch, but . . .

"Please," I keen. Fist my hands in his hair. Grind his face against my mouth. But my ass is in his hands and he controls my every movement. *"Please."*

"Wanted to wash this off, huh?" he growls against me.

"I— Yes."

"Good. Just helping you out, killer."

I nod, breathless, and fist the sheets as he eats me—wolflike, with teeth, feral, the rough flat of his tongue scraping against me over and over, teasing the fluttering rim of my hole until I'm puffy and pink and taut, a violin string begging to be snapped. I chase the end of it, press my heels into the meat of his shoulders, feel the pressure balloon inside me, building up and up and . . . "Why can't I—" I writhe, desperate, frustrated. He is ruining me. I feel the slide of his thumb through my slit, the broad first joint slowly pressing into my entrance.

"Tight," he mutters. But he pushes it deeper, then hooks it just a little, and the pleasure crests so high, I know I'm there. I should be there.

Why can't I? "Koen," I whimper.

"I know. I know." He drinks more of me. I'm trembling, right on a cliff. "You can't come from this, killer. Not when you are so close to Heat."

"Then why are you— Please, I need you to—"

One last bite, strong enough to quiet me down. A warning. *Be obedient.* "You just want to be fucked, don't you?"

Yes. Please.

"We'll see about that." His tone is ominous, but I exhale in relief as he pushes down his pants. He lowers himself on top of me, and his scent is *breathtaking*. But when I look down at the space between us, I see him nudging my opening with the blunt head of his cock, and . . .

My breath hitches.

"This is why," he says, stroking himself.

He's faintly terrifying. He pushes against me, but instead of slipping inside, he goes nowhere. I cant my hips to help, but nothing happens. A mewling sound rolls out of me. "Is it—" Normal? Am I fucking this up?

"It's not you," he reassures, leaning on his side, along my body. "Never been easy." He braces himself on his forearm. "I hoped it would help, that you're almost in Heat, but . . ." His hand spreads against my belly and slides down. He sinks a single finger inside me, and it's *so much bigger* than one of mine. When his progress stops, he gently works me open. Licks my gland, a broad swipe on my neck, and maybe half an inch gives. A single step on the staircase to Machu Picchu.

"It hurts," I sigh.

"Does it?" He kisses my cheek. "Are you too full? Or too empty?"

"I want more." I try to take it, too, thrusting my pelvis upward. Koen stops me so easily, it's embarrassing.

"Hey," he says, soothing. "I want to fuck you really, really bad. You know that, right?"

I nod.

"Good. I can't rush this, killer, because if you become sore or hurt or God fucking forbid, torn, you're not going to get a couple of days to recover. Once your Heat starts in earnest, you're going to want me inside you, whether it's painful or not. So I'm going to move slowly. And I need you to do what I say. Okay?"

Another, more subdued nod. A "My good girl" brushed against my jaw helps his finger sink deep enough that he can slowly, relentlessly work another one inside, tucked next to the first. I clench around him hard enough to make him grunt. The stretch burns so nicely, I cannot help but squirm. My fingernails dig into his arm, his wrist, searching for purchase, a counterpoint. My hips won't stay still, my entire body twitches, I still need *more*, but I'm being good. I'm doing what he says.

"Yeah, you are." His laugh is rough and shaky. Another loving, soft kiss, this time on the corner of my mouth. "You were *born* for this. A little more, huh?" Reality fuzzes over. Sweat drips from his body onto mine. I shake head to toe, contracting around fingers that are too thick and not thick enough. I'm on the edge, and the finish line keeps moving farther and farther, and—

"Can't come like this, either, sweetheart? It's okay, almost there. Take them a little deeper, and we can try again." A few low encouragements—*yes, good, look at you, just a little more*—and then he's on top of me again, biting my lower lip as he eases inside. This time, the first couple of inches slip right in.

"Yes," I say, drawing up the knee he's not pinning to the mattress. "Yes, yes, *yes*."

He winces and smiles at the same time, and there is something youthful about it, something that looks fresh on Koen's face. "See, we're getting there." Teeth close around my earlobe. "You just need to be patient. Don't you?"

Yes.

"I thought so." He wraps his hand around my throat, thumb and index finger on either side of my jaw. He doesn't press, but it's a warning, a reminder of who's in charge. I wonder what's wrong with me, that I experience so much gratitude for it, tears stream down my face.

We are not Human.

We really aren't. *I* am not. I've never felt it so much as right now, with Koen licking the tears off my temple. "Quiet," he whispers against my ear. "Don't make me come too soon. Let me get you used to it."

I still my lower body, obedient. Or not. When I tip my head to the side and scrape my teeth around the gland on his throat—

"Fucking hell." His control vanishes. Our eyes meet. His hold on my neck moves upward, fingers splayed open, pressing on my chin. Index and middle dip in my mouth, slide over my tongue, the grip tight enough to stop me from moving my head again. Then his cock drives deeper inside me, sustained, unrelenting, long and fat and far too much. I beg for more of it around his fingers, even as every sinking inch has me pushing my palms against his shoulders to shove him away. My heels twist against the sheets. I try to make room that doesn't exist.

"Breathe," he tells me. "Just breathe, Serena."

I'm trying, I can't bring myself to say. I want everything. Nothing.

No—everything. I babble things that make no sense, clawing into the muscles of his upper arms, holding on to the large expanse of his upper back until the sweat makes my palms slip. All throughout, Koen does exactly what I need. We're past words and gestures. Past the ability to lie. We're Weres, and we communicate through scents.

He understands what I want: to be broken in. "It's okay, Serena. Almost all in. Easy." A little more. A little more. There's no room, but he'll make it. One tweak of my nipple, one kiss to my gland, one flick on my clit at a time.

"I think I like this," he says, strained. Hazy eyed.

"You t-think?" The words muffle against his fingers. My internal muscles are overextended. "T-that's flattering."

His laughter is a choked huff. "I meant—having you this way. Exposed. Pinned." His hand slips to cup my head. He kisses my lips, gentle. "In a matter of days, you're going to leave, and I'll spend the rest of my life as your fucking servant. Whatever you ask me for, you'll have. But here you are. Defenseless. Mine for a short time."

He almost pulls out. Pushes in again. My moan meets the air rushing out of him. He repeats the same motion, wild eyed, lips curving in a dumbfounded, incredulous smile. I feel him rearranging my cunt, my soul, my entire damn life, and lose control of my body. My head falls back. My thighs tremble. His thrusts are slow. Shallow. Redefining.

"'S good," I say, meaning that it's the best thing I've ever felt in my life, bar none.

"It's good," he agrees, looking like he means the exact same thing.

Another stroke. Another one, slow, like he wants to make each last as long as possible. He luxuriates. Indulges in every second of friction. "Serena," he breathes out against my cheekbone. "I think this might be it, for me."

His arms slide under my back before I can ask him what he means. Gather me up in a viselike embrace. The drag of our skins. Wet noises. A terrible, all-consuming heat. His eyes, never leaving mine. It all whirls together and winds down to the place where Koen is fucking me.

"I'm going to come," I gasp, and convulse around him before I'm even done announcing it, pawing desperately at his shoulder. He stays still while I do, waits it out crammed inside, pressing against all those spots.

When I'm done, he kisses my cheek, tells me how beautiful I am, and orders, ruthless, "Again."

I want to laugh at him, but he makes me come in less than a minute with slow rolls of his hips and watches every second of me falling apart.

"Serena," he says, except there's no sound other than the whimpers in my throat. "Again."

"I can't," I tell him, but I'm so wrong, and his pace is measured, a patient, unforgiving rhythm, and this time my release is so intense, I forget to breathe.

"Absurd," he says, and I know he's going to ask me for more. It occurs to me how terrifying it must be, for an Alpha whose existence is predicated upon control, the unraveling that comes with pleasure like this. I wonder if he knows. I wonder if anyone has seen him this vulnerable in the past two decades.

I reach up to cradle his face in my hands. Kiss his hot lips. Say, "Koen. Next time, I'd like for you to come, too."

He can't say no to me. The steady, controlled movements become frantic, pounding, the thick of his cock filling me over and over, words of adoration and filth murmured in my ear. Another orgasm crashes into me. His cock gets even bigger and fuller, and—

My breath catches in my throat. "What— Koen?"

He kisses me, deep. Lovely. He's not really moving anymore, just grinding inside me, trying to find a perfect spot, and the feeling of fullness becomes unbearable. I feel a tinge of alarm. *Stop*, I should say. *Stop. It's not normal. It's too much*. But it's not. And Koen knows it.

"Take it." He shoves deeper. "Be good and take my knot."

"I—I don't—"

"You *do*. You were made for it. How could I ever think of fucking anyone else, when you take it so well?"

His cock starts jerking, and he holds me tighter, groaning against my gland something about his "perfect mate" and her "perfect, tight cunt" that almost sounds like poetry, and his orgasm lasts for . . . for minutes, I think. "That's it," he grits out. "That's where my come goes."

It's perfect. I comb a hand through his hair and wrap my arms around him, feeling his heavy breaths reverberate through me, the sounds of his pleasure. Being filled up, witnessing him let go, it's all so good, another orgasm crashes into me, so violent that everything goes blurry around the edges.

I stay there, spasming, holding tight, for a long time.

So long, I startle when he says, "I'm crushing you." He rolls me on top of him, my breasts flattened against his ribs, and he's still inside, still as hard as when we started. In fact . . .

I squirm. Shimmy my hips. Tug at whatever is happening down there, whatever is making it so that we can't quite separate yet. It's like he's lodged inside me. *Locked*.

I test the connection, finding that it holds strong. The rational part of me says that I should be panicking, but my hindbrain is in charge at the moment, and it's profoundly okay with what's going on.

Instincts, Layla said. And one of them is to squeeze my internal muscles to make sure that there is no give.

"Fuck," Koen swears, and he's coming again, a short burst that has him driving his hips up into me, and he mumbles into me that "there's no need," that he's "already fucking gone" over me, that I'm "so good," it's going to "destroy" him. So I do it again, just to watch the way the pleasure transforms his face, the tendons of his strong neck in relief as he arches back, his muscles tensing and releasing.

And once more, because he's *losing his mind*, and I love it.

I could continue. Instead, I ask, "Koen?"

He's too out of breath to reply, but he presses a kiss of acknowledgment against the crown of my hair.

"Please, don't take this as a complaint."

His hand was tracing my spine, but stops. "Did I hurt you?"

"Nothing like that. But I think I'm going to need a Were anatomy lesson before we . . . Actually, I think I'm gonna need it right now."

His chin dips. He studies me to figure out whether I'm joking.

"Well," he says at last. "Fuck."

CHAPTER 34

One stolen moment. And another. And another.

CANNOT *BELIEVE* LAYLA DIDN'T MENTION IT!"

"She probably assumed you knew." Koen smiles a little and keeps drumming his fingers on the curve of my hip. "*I* certainly did."

"This is mind-blowing. Does Lowe have one?"

He scowls. "I have not personally witnessed it, but—"

"I didn't mean . . . I'm not interested in my best friend's husband's penis. Or, I am, if she wants to, you know, talk about it because of issues they're having. Say he was struggling with erectile dysfunction and Misery wanted to confide in me, I wouldn't be like, *I don't care, shut up*, but I also wouldn't solicit nudes of Lowe—"

"Serena."

I clear my throat. "I think Misery may have tried to warn me."

"About knots."

"I thought she was on her usual bullshit, so I ignored her."

"Understandable."

"There's a Human urban legend that Weres have inflatable dicks, but it's widely believed to be made up. Like the rumor that Vampyres pulverize in the sun? But lo and behold, we found a single conspiracy theory grounded in reality. Of course it's the one about genitalia."

Koen doesn't reply, so I lift myself up on my forearm and look at him. The *knot*—here I am, using new vocabulary in full sentences—has deflated, but I'm still half on top of him, clearheaded once again. He plays with my hair, marks every inch of my skin, squeezes the fat and muscles of my body, moving from curve to bone like he couldn't stop even if he wanted. I wonder if he's storing every little touch for later. If he's even aware of what he's doing, staring at me with a faint half smile that is just . . .

Lovesick.

It's like a boulder in my stomach, the transience of this. Of us. We're momentary. Impermanent. Doomed.

He deserves better. "So," I say lightly, a little forced. "You do like sex, after all."

"Did I say that I didn't?"

"No. Just . . ." I chew on my lower lip. "Amanda said you never looked like you missed it."

"Because I didn't."

I swallow. "Do you think . . . After this is done, do you think it'll be harder for you to go back to not having it?"

"Serena," he says, deliberate, level. "None of this is about sex."

"Then what—"

"You. This, all of it, is purely about *you*."

I sit up, desperate to find the right thing to say. The sheet slides down to my hips, and Koen doesn't pretend to look anywhere but at my breasts. "Still *spectacular*?" I joke, fighting the impulse to cover myself. It's a little uncomfortable, being on display, even after what we just did.

"I hope you never find out the things I've done while thinking about them."

I flush. "I was so self-conscious about my body. For the longest time."

"Why?"

I draw up my knees. Cover myself. "Just the side effect of being the short, busty sidekick to a tall, elegant, cypress-like princess creature." My cheeks are hot. "It's nice, I guess. That you're not disappointed in the way I look."

"Disappointed?"

"Yeah. I mean, it could have shaken out in a different . . . Why are you staring at me like I just told you that angels' wings are made of porridge?"

He exhales, speechless. "You know what? You wouldn't get it."

"How so?"

"Leave it alone."

"But I want to know."

"Just . . ." He bites the inside of his cheek, looking for the right words. "You are my mate. I would have wanted you no matter what. I *will* want you no matter what. But you are also . . ." He licks his lips. "If someone had given me a piece of paper and asked me to list everything I liked, everything I dreamed of, everything that I was sure would make me happy, you would have been the final product of it."

My heart thuds in my chest. *Good line*, I want to tell him, just to dull the way it stabs through my ribs. *No need to waste it on me, I'm already a sure thing.*

But it's so obviously *not* a line. He's trying to explain something to me, something that he knows in his belly, and I . . .

I guess I'm listening.

"There could never be disappointment, because there were never any comparisons, or expectations, or hopes, or standards to meet. There's only . . ." He casts a glance around the room, searching. Then his eyes settle on me. "There is only you, Serena."

It's unacceptable, his adoring expression. I hide my burning face in my knees and scramble for something, anything to say, but my mind is blank and—

"Hey." He pulls me closer into his arms again. "It's a Heat. It's normal, feeling unsteady. I've got you, okay?" I nod, and he twines his fingers with mine. Lifts my arm and inhales the skin in the crook of my elbow, where my scent pools. "I could live here," he murmurs. "In this crease." A kiss, soft lipped.

"I thought my elbows were too 'fucking sharp' for your distinguished taste."

He smiles. Nips at me. "It's going to build up again. Soon. You'll feel more and more out of control."

"More out of control than earlier?"

"Yes."

"How do you even know?"

"I'm the Alpha of this pack. I know everything."

I squint. "What's the square root of pi?"

"Zero point nine."

"Okay, I should have asked you a question *I* know the answer to. I'm just surprised, since you've never had the exigency of spending a Heat with—"

"I educated myself when you started smelling like *you'd* have the exigency." He lifts me into the curve of his body. Spoons me. "Just fucking believe me for once."

"Hmm."

"Rest while you can," he orders.

Why not? This is nice. Perfect, even. I fall asleep nestled under his chin. Still thinking that—worse than earlier? Probably an exaggeration. I'll be fine.

—◦◦◦—

IT'S NOT. (AN EXAGGERATION.) BUT I AM. (FINE.)

Better than.

It hits me halfway through the first day, in the late afternoon light, a fleeting spell of clarity as I stare at Koen's wide shoulders glistening above. He rocks inside me slowly, a languid, wet rhythm. I just came. A couple of times. He hasn't yet. He tries to make it last as long as possible, every single time, and this is the best I can recall feeling in years. My world, when narrowed to just Koen and our nest, is light and kind and full of revelries.

I lean back. Study his slack mouth. His eyes, closed, squeeze tighter with every thrust. Like he has to brace himself. Build a dam every time, to keep his orgasm from spilling out. Pleasure is written all over his features.

I smooth his damp hair back with my palm and say, "Koen."

His eyelids flutter open. He nuzzles into my hand like a big, half-tamed beast. Presses a biting kiss into the flesh right under my thumb, an invitation to continue. It makes my insides spasm.

"Thank you," I tell him. "For this."

"I told you not to—"

I arch to shut him up with a kiss, and with a soft curse he slides one arm between my back and the mattress to pull me up.

"You're welcome. Lucky for you, I'm so fucking"—a harder stroke—"*selfless.*"

I inhale sharply, already quivering along his cock. My orgasm builds quickly, violently, a warm rush that has my thighs locking around his hips. "No, I . . . Thank you. For making this so—"

Before I can tell him how disorientingly *good* this feels, his knot is growing, thick, inescapable, and he's too busy hiking one of my legs back toward my chest to hear what I have to say.

This is how things should be, I think. *Always.*

———— ❧ ————

AFTER WEEKS OF TRUANCY, MY APPETITE RETURNS AT THE WORST possible time.

I decide to give it the cold shoulder and focus on what's rapidly becoming my favorite thing in the world: thrashing around and begging Koen to do something, anything, *everything* to me. Unfortunately, he really did educate himself about Heats. Not only did he memorize some doctor's office pamphlet, but he's also extremely literal about it.

We can start again after you have a strawberry, he tells me.

One more sip of juice. Like that. Be good. Give me one more.

Open up. No, not later—*now.*

You have to drink. A kiss against the flushed skin of my throat. *Girls in Heat only get what they ask for if they finish their water.*

"You know you're not going to get a surprise visit from the Heat inspector, right?" I ask between shallow gulps of electrolytes. "There are no thumbs-up stickers for doing exactly what the textbook—"

He grasps my chin and taps the pad of his thumb against my lips, pushing against them until I have no choice but to open. "Since it's obvious that your mouth is not nearly busy enough, you're having another glass before we continue."

The nutrition is a boon. For the first time in months, I'm not exhausted or dizzy or confused. I don't have a headache. In fact, I feel surprisingly healthy, even as I rub myself against Koen to get him to pay attention to me. The rational, cortical part of my brain knows he hasn't so much as cast a glance elsewhere since the day we met. But as my Heat progresses, his scent becomes compulsive, and my wants snap into unprecedented focus.

Koen is perfect. Koen is strong. Koen is maddening and beautiful and *mine*, and I want what I am due. At my best, I am enamored with every inch of his body, with every word he rasps against my ear. At my worst, I am a savage, impatient, rude creature that tolerates no competition. Possessive. Impossible to reason with.

"Spoiled," he mumbles against my lips, but there's a touch of a smile at the corners of his eyes, in the webs of wrinkles irradiating from them. "Nuisance."

So he seats me on his cock and splits me open, and as I strive to relearn how to breathe with him inside, he feeds me slices of fruit, whispering, *Sweetheart. This is really fucking good*. He rubs his thumb against my clit, and I clamp hard around him. My mind empties. I don't think about the day I arrived here, unicorn waffles and too few chairs, and I bury my face in his throat as I try to finish chewing so that he can go deeper, so that we can *move*.

"Such a damn *nuisance*," he repeats when my thighs squeeze around his waist, punching a grunt out of his chest.

I gasp for air, and he shouts out his pleasure when I suck his gland as hard as I can.

———— ❊ ————

BY THE END OF THE FIRST DAY, WE'RE BOTH A LITTLE OUT OF OUR minds. The hormone bomb went off inside *my* body, but Koen wasn't spared.

"Okay?" he asks, before starting to rock inside me the second his previous knot goes down. "I just can't—"

I nod. Lift my arms above my head, trying not to squirm as he kisses, licks, sucks, nibbles, *worships* my breasts.

"Fucking spectacular," he says again. I cannot help my smile.

By now, he slides in like a dream, and I cognitively reframe the concept of having sex: not an act with a beginning and an end, but a continuous exchange of pleasure and hushed words. I know, rationally, that Koen and I are separate beings. It just doesn't feel like it.

I come a lot. So does Koen. My ex-boyfriends are pale gray memories with no hope of bursting through the pink haze surrounding me. I do know, however, that sex has never been like this for me, and I cannot help but wonder, What's the hinge? What makes the difference, really? The biology of the Heat? Or the fact that it's with Koen?

I'll never know. That's the stipulation: afterward, we'll go our separate ways.

I stroke my fingers through his hair. Pull him in for a kiss. Our eyes meet, and his face lights up with a grin.

"Hey," he says.

"Hey." I force myself to smile back and forget about after.

———— ❊ ————

THINGS GET REAL ON THE SECOND DAY. I THOUGHT THEY WERE before, but . . . I should just accept that I know nothing and go with the flow. Yeah. That's what I'll do.

We don't sleep through the night, but I do doze off at dawn, while Koen's knot is inside me and he's still twitching with pleasure. The last thing I remember is him coming and whispering in my ear, "Unbelievable, how fucking unreal you feel, soft and wet and warm and every good thing in the world, baby."

I open my eyes to orange sunlight streaming through the window. Birds chirp in the tall trees surrounding the cabin, and Koen hugs me tight, my back pressed to his chest, both hands closed around my breasts.

He's already moving inside me, shallow, staccato strokes that feel nothing like usual. I tilt the curve of my ass back to meet him, and his sharp inhale tells me that he wasn't quite awake yet.

"Shit." He buries his face in my hair. "Sorry." My scent must broadcast how little I mind, because he doesn't stop. His long fingers splay on my abdomen. Curl against my hip. He moves me against him in little circles, like I'm a doll, like my body is the most precious object he'll ever own. He develops a quiet rhythm, chants things that have me questioning whether he's still partially asleep. "This is it. How I want to wake up for the rest of my life."

I must be asleep, too. I tell him, "Yes, yes, please." Wonder: *What if he just took me? What if I lived here, in this nest, hidden, stolen, stowed away? What if my entire life were just to be here, to make him happy? What then?*

It sends him into a frenzy. He pounds inside me, his cock deeper than ever, bottoming out. I feel him in the back of my throat. With a snapping motion he splays my thighs open and rams me into the mattress. The heel of his palm presses between my shoulder blades, flattens me, and it's *sublime*.

"Good. C'mon, killer, you can do it. Take it like— Good."

Heat licks down my spine. Thrums in my belly. I try to grind against him as he swipes away the hair from my nape to find the green swirl on my upper back. Muffled obscenities vibrate through my body. Praises, slurred. His tongue against the thin, fragile skin of my gland.

He hasn't touched me there yet, not since my Heat started.

One of his arms wraps under my rib cage to lift me up, fingers bruising me as his grip tightens. A hint of claws grazing against my flank, like he's starting to lose control of the shift, the borders between man and animal becoming blurrier.

It's the best thing I've ever known.

"Please," I beg, not sure for what. But he knows. A low groan. He stuffs me so full, I wail at how good it hurts. Hot breath puffs against my hair, and he once again presses hot, open-mouthed kisses over my gland. I come instantly. His teeth scrape, then touch, then brace. He's ready to pierce my skin. To sink them inside me.

It's like the world stops spinning. Every cell of my body coalesces on my upper back, where my gland lives. Ready for Koen's scar. Welcoming it.

I feel his knot starting to swell, and all at once I know what I'm asking for.

"Do it," I say. "Please."

He groans.

"*Please.*"

"God *fucking* damn."

Koen rips himself away. He pulls out and turns me around, landing me on my back. His hand hooks under my knee, spreads me open, and he knots me like that. I come again. So hard, I think I see the edge of the universe.

"Don't let me do that again," he orders, catching his breath.

I peer up at him, trying to gauge his tone. I've never seen him so serious. "What?"

"You don't want me anywhere near the back of your neck right now."

"Why?"

"You smell beyond belief. And . . ." He covers his eyes with his palm. "I don't know my limits. I might not be able to stop myself and might just bite you."

It's *exactly* what I want him to do.

I don't say it, but he hears it anyway.

"No." He gathers me closer. "It'll just make things worse when you leave."

Any response that comes to mind involves me shouting at him that I know what *I* need. I know what *he* needs, too, and it involves his wolf teeth as deep inside me as physics will allow. But I just came, and I'm too clearheaded to push his boundaries so shamelessly.

So I let him kiss me. I let him tell me how much he loves every single part of me, even as he doesn't mention the whole. I let him touch the place where we're joined together, where his come and my slick overflow and dribble out, like we're the only thing that matters in the history of the universe. I let him make me come again, and I massage his knot till he's coming, too.

I let him do everything he wants, and pretend that we have more than a short time left together.

———— ✦ ————

I WAKE UP IN THE EARLY AFTERNOON AND WATCH HIM SLEEP. MY heart flutters and my stomach bubbles at how beautiful he has grown to be to *me*, specifically. Everything that his face *means*. The sides of him no else can see. Cheekbones that dust with dark olive when I loop my arms around his neck. The long, straight nose he scrunches as he calls me a nuisance. The scars that split his face when he cannot help a smile, and the shallow dimples hidden under the stubble he can't be bothered to shave.

I could spend the next hundred years cataloging new things about him, and never be done. He could be the project of my lifetime.

Just like I'm his.

The Heat mounts, but I let Koen get some rest and I go to the kitchen to grab a new bottle of water, trying not to dwell on how wrong it feels, being out of my nest.

That's where he finds me two minutes later, and he immediately crowds me against the fridge. The stainless-steel presses against the backs of my thighs, and I shiver.

"Are you wearing fucking *clothes*?"

"It's just your sweater. I can—"

"You're not supposed to leave."

He's not joking. He's genuinely upset that I . . . walked twenty feet and put on a hoodie? Hormones, man.

"I'm sorry," I say, appeasing. He can't help this any more than I can. "I didn't mean to worry you. Let's go back to bed."

But we don't. He silently flips me around and bends me over the table, uncaring of the papers scattered all over or the bottle rolling into the living room. He maneuvers me until one of my knees is on the edge, and once I'm spread open, he pushes inside me so roughly, I come halfway through the first thrust. He knots me quickly, in a few unceremonious, glorious strokes. For him it seems to be more about locking me closer than about coming, but my thighs shake with my orgasm and the effort to stay upright.

"Poor killer." He hugs me and kisses my cheek. "She didn't do as she was told, and now look."

It doesn't feel like punishment, not when his knot grinds inside me. That little bit of friction, coupled with his hand strumming my clit, makes me come so many times, I don't even remember making it back to the bed.

ON THE MORNING OF THE THIRD DAY, THE URGENCY SUBSIDES. Somewhat.

"Is it over?" I ask Koen.

He scoffs. Twenty minutes later, when I climb on top of him, desperate for relief, I understand why.

But it *is* getting better. Less intense. With longer spells of normalcy. The *fuck or die* is waning in favor of . . . "Fuck or cry, maybe?" I tell him, and he laughs.

The end of this is in sight, and I do *not* want to look at it.

I feel good enough to take a shower, but Koen tries to talk me out of it, protesting that I won't smell like him anymore.

"We are in your house. You are right here. There's no way I'll smell like anyone else."

He grumbles for a while, even as he joins me and helps me clean up, looking morose the entire time.

Cute. He's so *cute*.

For the first time in weeks, the water doesn't sucker punch my skin into submission.

"What came before Neanderthals?" I ask him afterward.

He shrugs. Pouts.

"Whatever they were, you're the one *before* them."

He tosses me an apple, and his *shut up and eat* look is wry enough, I think I'm forgiven. But I'm deluding myself, because afterward, once the fever rises again, he makes me pay for it with his mouth on my cunt.

"I didn't mean to—"

"You didn't mean to wash away my come like it's a bad thing?" He sucks on my clit so hard, I almost pass out.

"I'm sorry. I'm *sorry*. Koen, please, you said—" I sob. It's too much. Too good. Is this what happens when people slowly descend into madness and despair? Is *this* the feeling? "You said that I can't come from this."

"You can't." He leaves a bite on the tender strip where my thigh and my abdomen meet. I yelp, even though the pain is better than the constant, unbreakable tension.

"Then why are you doing it?"

"Because unlike you, *I* can."

He can. And he does. A minute later I watch him, wide-eyed, as he comes just from eating me out. He growls his orgasm into my flesh, twitching with pleasure, kissing me throughout, and even though I'm left trembling and unsatisfied, even though I'm still in my twenties, I know that it's the most erotic thing I'll ever experience.

When he moves up, he's still hard, tacky once again, and I cannot look away. My hands shake. I'm rapidly approaching the point where I'll beg him, but this is my first chance to truly look at his knot. Since it's usually inside me.

"Can I—"

He sits back in the nest. Pulls me into him, wedging me under his chin. "What?"

"Can I touch it?"

"My cock?"

"No, your . . ."

He laughs. "Out of all the things to ask permission for, touching my knot is not one you need to worry about."

"Is it sensitive?"

"I'm not sure. The knot and I are still making each other's acquaintance."

I peek up at him. "Does celibacy include . . ."

He snorts. "No. Though the Assembly would love to monitor the frequency of me jerking off."

"Then . . . why?"

"It only happens when we're with our mates." His pecs rise, then fall as he catches his breath. "Or after we find them, anyway."

"Oh." My chest tightens.

"It'll go down soon. Never lasts as long when I'm not inside you. Or maybe it won't. It gets really happy when you're around."

I sit up on my knees. Observe him, fascinated by how free he is with his body. Even after three days naked, I still feel a little bit shy when I catch him staring.

But he said I could. Or, he said I didn't even need to ask for permission. So I reach out and gingerly run a finger down his cock. The soft heat of him is a small shock, and I realize that I haven't done this yet. Touched him. Enjoyed him.

I trail down to the base, where his knot is still distended and dark with blood. Koen shudders, eyes fluttering closed. His hand white-knuckles the comforter.

"Does it hurt?"

The question amuses him. "No."

It's an impulsive decision, leaning closer. And maybe the twenty years of forced celibacy did leave a trace. Maybe teenage Koen didn't do it *all* and left some things off the table. I can point my finger at the exact moment his quiet, curious expression morphs into wide-eyed understanding: not until my mouth is just a hairbreadth away from his cock.

Caught by surprise, at last.

"Serena—" he starts, then stops with a choked groan.

I swirl my tongue around him. Suck a bit. He tastes like a drug. Pulsates in my mouth. Sends me into a stupor.

"Fuck," he swears.

I don't attempt anything fancy, but Koen seems dazzled enough. Speechless. His neck falls back, brow drawn tight and beaded with sweat. The head of his cock catches against my throat, and he runs a hand through my hair.

"I'm going to— You need to— No." His cheeks are dark with blood.

I hum in agreement, but his scent is like a leash, tugging me closer, begging me for more. He needs me, *now*. It's heady, having him at my mercy. Knowing that his pleasure depends on me. I smile, truly happy, and lick his knot *once*.

It's so rewarding, how he immediately starts coming. The out-of-control guttural sounds he makes. He grips my scalp so tight it hurts, and then he's pulling me into his lap.

"You are so fucking—"

His cock doesn't flag. He drives inside me, hard, elbows hooked under my armpits, crossed on my back. The knot won't allow him to go as deep as we want, but he certainly tries.

I snake my arms around his neck, hold him tight, and refuse to let go.

———✧—✧———

THE HEAT BREAKS ON THE FOURTH DAY.

The morning sunlight sneaks inside the room, dappling every surface. I stretch, pop my eyes open, and realize that a pyramid-sized boulder just rolled off my shoulders.

I haven't felt this good in months, even though I'm approximately thirty hours behind on rest and badly need another shower. My stomach is a cavernous pit clamoring for nourishment. I'm sore between my legs, but the usual suspects are gone: no headache, no pulled muscles, no overall fatigue.

It's paradigm shifting. The symptoms of my Heat rose so slowly, they became my new normal. I forgot what it's like, *not* feeling like a box of stale saltines left open in a cupboard in 1947. It's nothing extravagant—I doubt I could spring out of bed and run a half marathon, or even a 5K, without needing immediate resuscitation. But I'm decent. After being on the brink of croaking, it's kind of a big deal.

I lift my arm up, right into a sunbeam. Stare at my hand and, without stressing too much, think about the *other* me. The crunchy sounds that rise from the bed of the forest. The cold rush of the first dive into a stream. The inescapable tug of the moon.

Yes, my body says. New cells knit together as old ones break apart. My nails grow three times their size. My ulna and radius reshape, and the flesh around them merrily follows suit. *At last.*

I exhale giddy, delighted laughter, turning my midshift limb back and forth, savoring the beauty of—

"I still haven't seen your wolf form."

Koen's scratchy morning voice rolls into my skin. He's still holding me, his arm heavy across my belly. I doubt he plans to let go.

"Don't even know the color of your pelt," he adds, musing.

I force my arm back into human form and turn on my flank, facing him. He is—perfect. Mine, mine, *mine.*

Not mine at all.

My exultance at once again being able to shift turns into dread. "Koen." My throat seizes up. "It's over."

He doesn't tell me that he knows. Doesn't agree that it sucks. He just stares at me with a small, content smile at the edges of his eyes. Like I've given him everything he could ever want, and he's not planning to ask for more. Like he's too happy about what we had to be sad about what we'll soon lose.

Since I cannot bear it, I do what I know best: I lie. To myself. To him. Without even speaking.

He makes it easy for me. Goes along with it as I roll us around. Helps me keep my balance as I kneel atop his hips.

I ignore the strain in my inner thighs and stroke myself against his fully hard cock. My palms trace his chest. Shoulders. The V of his torso. Rib cage. I want to touch him everywhere, and I do. Until his hips buck upward of their own volition.

"Serena," he murmurs.

It's an apology, I think. His hands find my ass, my waist, my hip bones, but they don't grip or cage. Instead he takes deep, calming breaths and peers up at me, waiting for guidance. It's up to me. I'm painting a picture, and he doesn't want to mess with my vision.

Whether it's the position or the end of my Heat, taking him inside me is difficult again. Koen does nothing to help and stares, swallowing encouraging noises, fascinated by the way I have to stop and restart in increments. He's too thick. Then there's a sudden, wet give within me, and he's not. His nostrils flare, and his fingers twitch in the sheets. It's not until I have him right at the hilt, our hips flush, that I get rewarded with a pass of his thumb on my clit.

The stretch fills me to the edge and beyond, but this time neither of us cares about comfort. The urgency is still there, simmering between us, in a different form. The goal is no longer having an orgasm. We want to ... I'm not sure. Make a memory, perhaps. So we go slowly. We make it last, hips angling, slow rise and slow fall, empty, then full. Our eyes keep wandering down, to the place where he's stuffed inside me.

Sweaty, tacky skin.

Desperate grasping.

Pleading, drugging kisses.

In a way, it's our first time. In *all* ways, it's the last.

"Koen," I exhale. I want to explain to him that he's rebuilding me from the inside out, molding me into a more solid, resilient shape. But I can't. Not when he looks up with a stupefied expression, like the existence of me, of what we're doing, is something he hadn't taken into consideration. Like I make the world a different place.

"Koen," I repeat, coming, clutching wetly around his length.

Still twitching with pleasure, I lean over. We kiss, long, leisurely, incriminating. Messy and deep.

"Koen," I say again.

He remains silent. No words—just the rasp of his breathing, his parted lips, and everything left unsaid trapped behind them. But it's good, the quiet. It gives me a chance to say the one thing I've been holding back. To lean over and whisper in his ear, "I love you. And I'm never going to stop, no matter what."

I come again, and he comes, too, knot swelling, the pleasure sharper than a knife, slicing right through us. Irreparable damage that doesn't hurt enough. Koen's grip notches against me, leaving marks the size of his fingers in my flesh. He is a sting of wordless noises and unseeing eyes, wide with something I cannot comprehend.

He never says that he loves me, but it's written all over my skin.

CHAPTER 35

His duties, the one to his pack and the one to his mate, should be tearing him in two. And yet he has never felt more intact than he does right now.

THE FIRST THING AMANDA TELLS ME IN THE LATE AFTERNOON, when I emerge from Koen's empty cabin, is a firm "Don't."

"Hello to you, too." I bend down to pet Twinkles, laughing at the enthusiastic wag of his tail. "Don't . . . ?"

"Dwell on the intrusive thought that everyone knows the nasty shit you and Koen have been doing to each other for the past few days."

I stop dead. "I wasn't going to." Until now.

"Good. Keep it that way. Koen's inner circle is very happy that Mommy and Daddy got it on."

I have so many questions about that, I decide to ask none. I take a resigned seat on the porch, enjoying the way Twinkles curls up against me, the breeze caressing my skin.

I want *more* of this. I want to explore the cliffs and the shores as a wolf. I want to go for a run. My cells itch for it.

"Are you . . ." Amanda eyes me, circumspect. "All intact? I know Heats can be, um, tempestuous situations. He didn't . . . ?"

"Mommy did not hurt Daddy. Or vice versa," I say dryly. "What about you? How was it, being substitute Alpha?"

She groans. "Not much happened. The worst of it was a dispute between a twelve-year-old who kept kicking his soccer ball in his neighbors' yard, and the elderly curmudgeon who decided to burn it. The parents intervened, then the entire village, and it got blown *way* out of proportion."

"Exciting. Who did you side with?"

"That's the thing of being Alpha—you don't *side*. You mediate. You fix. You have the authority to make people stop doing stupid shit, but it takes a while to cement that. Koen? He snaps his fingers, calls everyone a cumbucket, and everything runs smoothly. Me? Pack members push back. They whine. They need to be cajoled, and I'm not cut out for it. Jorma can take over, if he wants."

"Fascinating." At the very least, this explains Koen's utter bewilderment when things dare to not go his way. "Anything else? Are Nele and the Humans okay?"

"They are. Nele said she'd love to talk soon."

"Cool. Maybe I could—" A sharp thwack interrupts me. I tense. Track Twinkles with my eyes as he runs behind the cabin to investigate.

"Oh, it's just Koen. He went for a run and now he's chopping wood."

My heart flickers. "Thought he was gone." I rise to my feet, flushing at how unceremoniously I'm ditching Amanda. "Is it okay if I . . . go say hi to him?" Her smirk is so knowing, I stop feeling bad for her.

Koen's right there, by the shop, and it all mushes together for me—the strain on his thick muscles as he swings the ax; the scent of pines; the sheen of sweat on his shirtless chest, trickling into the waistband of his jeans. He's breathing hard but doesn't stop to take a break.

I observe him for a while, wondering whether it's normal, feeling—feeling *so much* about a single person. Surely, it's unfair. Surely, a love this deep should be reserved for the universe as a whole. But what if, to me, he's the linchpin? What if he's the stitch that keeps it all together?

Is this what finding a mate feels like? Is it possible that—

"Everything okay?" he asks without looking my way.

My heart trips all over itself. "Yeah." Deep breath. Good. "So, you *do* chop wood."

He turns, mouth twitching. "Occasionally. This is for the Humans." He shifts his grip on the ax, lodges it in the splitting block in a single smooth movement, and stands there, arms at his sides.

What would he do if I went to hug him? I picture his hand, coming up to cradle my head. His heartbeat under my cheek. The enveloping quality of being in his presence. It's all so *vivid*.

But I can't. There were conditions. We signed off on them.

The breeze breathes through the trees. A too-long silence ticks by. I briefly avert my eyes, and he does the same. There's a tic in his jaw, and I'm wringing my hands.

"If—" I start, just as he says, "You—"

We stop. His lips curl into a smile. Mine don't. This territory, it's uncharted.

"You first," he says.

"Right. Thanks." I don't know why my throat feels like it's seizing up. "The business with the Vampyres . . . is it over?"

"Owen cleaned up the council," he says evenly. "There no longer is a bounty on you and Ana."

"Good. Yeah, I . . . Good. In that case . . ." Why am I having to remind myself that this is precisely what I wanted? "I no longer have my phone, because of the . . . Can I borrow yours? I need to get in touch with Nele and . . . and Misery. We need to figure out . . . well." My turn to smile. Koen's mouth tightens. "Everything."

He nods, like *yes, of course*, he's going to hand me his phone. But says, "C'mere, killer."

I hang back, unsure.

"Serena. Come."

This time I go. Stop a foot away from him. Pretend his scent doesn't feel like home, like a blanket, like he's holding me already, and that my heart doesn't drop into my stomach as he says, "I'm going to step down."

I ask, "From what?" But I already know, so I don't give him time to answer. "Why?" Regrettably, I already know *that*, too. That only leaves me with "You can't."

"See, that's the thing about being Alpha. I can do whatever the fuck I want."

"Are you— Please tell me you are joking."

"While I'm widely known for my prankster personality and comedic timing, no. I'm not joking. Not about this."

"You . . . We talked about this." I sound shrill. "The pack is too important to you. And you are necessary to the pack."

"Things have changed."

"Things—*nothing* has changed. You love the Northwest more than anything."

"Not more than anything, Serena."

His words are like a rock in my gut, sinking further by the second. I'm surprised I'm still upright. "You can't," I whisper. "You don't have a successor picked out."

"I'll wait until the situation with Irene is resolved," he says, like he has a *plan*. "Then one of my seconds will take over."

"Who?"

"Amanda is the most—"

"Amanda doesn't want to be Alpha. And she's not established like you—people would challenge her."

"She can win any challenge."

"All of them? Are you sure? Because it would only take one loss, and she'd be dead. And even if she does win, what about Saul? They're off now, but who knows when they'll be on again?"

His lips flatten. "Whoever takes over, it wouldn't have to be permanent. And we will stick around. I can act as an advisor for a while."

"We?" I sound frantic. "We're not— Don't say 'we.'"

"It doesn't have to be Amanda. There are several dominant Weres in the pack. Most are young, but they could take over in a couple of years, and I would trust them to—"

"Koen, no. You actually *like* being Alpha. You *live* to order people around."

He holds back a smile. "Guess from now on, you're going to have to be people."

"No. You'll step down, and then what? Run away with me? Be my deadbeat boyfriend? We're gonna live in the woods, argue over what to have for dinner, and—" I close my eyes and press the back of my hand to my lips. I'm in physical pain. Because . . .

"Sounds that good, huh?" he asks knowingly.

And yes. Yes, it fucking does. But.

We need him, Layla said. Amanda. Brenna. Dozens, countless people. Even Irene.

My eyes lock with his, willing him to understand. "You are the heart of this pack, Koen."

He nods. Even as he says, "And you are mine, Serena."

This is unthinkable. "If you leave for me, and anything happens to the Northwest . . . I'm going to hate myself for the rest of my life. Your life. *Our* life."

That besotted half smile, again. "That was a 'we.'"

"It wasn't." I steady myself. "Just a few days ago you listed several reasons why you had to choose the pack over me. What changed?"

He roams the inside of his mouth with his tongue. Waits out the end of a particularly strong gust of breeze. "You told me that you loved me, Serena," he says simply. His eyes are earnest, liquid. So profoundly *good*. "And while I'm willing to resign myself to an existence without the person I love, I refuse to condemn you to it."

I square my shoulders. *Don't cry. Don't you fucking dare cry.* "It was very good sex, and I—I made it up, Koen. In the heat of the moment."

His eyes are compassionate "I read your letter."

"My . . . ?"

"The one on your desk. With my name on it. It changes everything, Serena."

The letter I wrote for him to read after I died. I shut my eyes tight, trying to block the memories of what's in it.

I feel close to you. So much so, sometimes I wonder if fate really does exist.

   When you're around, the universe feels more bearable.

   This mate business—does it feel like I have you in my palm? Like we're tethered to each other? Like I changed you at the nuclear level? Asking for a friend.

No. None of this matters. I know Koen: if he were to step down, over time he would grow to hate himself. And *me*. "Do you have clear memories," I ask calmly, "of my Heat?"

His eyebrow lifts. "They'll be what I last see before I die."

"Good. Then you will remember that I asked you to bite me. Several times."

His throat works.

"And you didn't. I begged you, and you didn't."

"Ask me now, and I'll do it. I'll do it *right here*—"

"Why didn't you *then*?"

There is a tic in his jaw. "Because you weren't in the position to make the choice."

"You're right. I wasn't. Would you say that I am in the position now?" His shoulders tense. He knows where I'm going with this. "I'm lucid. Clearheaded. I'm making a choice, which is to let you know that if you step down, it will be for nothing. I will not stay with you." My chin trembles. I power through. "So don't bother—"

"Serena."

"—doing that, because it's not going to—"

"*Serena*."

He steps toward me, and I swallow back my tears. His hand travels to my cheek but drops to his side before making contact. As though he's no longer sure he has the right to touch me.

I did this, I think, nauseous. *I did this to him.*

"I don't know," he says, soft, barely audible. He stops. Restarts. A lock of hair falls on his forehead, dark against tanned skin. "I don't think I can go on without you. Above all, I don't think I can go on knowing that you need me, and I'm not by your side."

"I'll be fine," I lie.

"I wish . . ." His mouth has to work to shape more words. "I wish I could believe you, but—"

"Hey!" Amanda's voice pierces through the narrow space between us. I shift my attention to her, even as Koen's eyes stay on me.

"What's going on?" he asks.

"The Human girl, Nele? She just asked to meet in person with Serena. But I think it might be better if you came, too, Alpha."

He finally turns away from me. "Why?"

"She mentioned something about Irene. And her . . . plans."

———— ✢ ————

ON THE PLUSH, CLOUDLIKE COUCH, I WRAP MY ARM AROUND Nele's shoulders and let her lean into me, squeezing her tighter whenever her heartbeat grows more erratic. Koen sits across from us, an obvious attempt at giving her space. When it doesn't ease her anxiety, he says, "None of what has happened, or will happen, is your fault. No matter what you say, we're *not* going to hurt you." It's his reassuring tone, the one that works wonders on Weres, but I'm not sure Nele buys it.

"What about . . . What about my grandfather?" she asks feebly.

"You said he was in prison," I point out, curling her hair behind her ear.

"Yes. But Irene s-said that you would f-find him and k-kill him, and that . . ."

"Nele, I have no authority in Human territory." Koen's voice is firm but kind.

"She said that it doesn't matter. That you would . . ."

"I'm sure she did. Here's why it makes no sense: Who do you think turned your grandfather over to the Human authorities twenty years ago?"

"I don't . . . You?"

"Correct. We did not kill Humans unless they were active participants in the attacks on the Northwest, or standing between us and Constantine. More importantly, we discovered soon enough that there were no birth records for Humans who were born within the cult. You understand what that means?" Nele is silent, so he continues, "We could have done whatever we pleased with them. If we had wanted to kill them, they'd be *long* dead."

Nele's eyes widen, and she starts shaking uncontrollably. I shoot my best *thank you for that tactful explanation* glare at Koen, whose response is an unironic *You're welcome* nod.

"What Koen's trying to say is that he believes that your family has been punished enough, and holds no resentment toward them." Koen appears to have minor quibbles with my translation but wisely keeps them to himself. "Is everything okay?" I clutch her hand tighter.

Is this what Fiona felt like among the Favored? Constantly scared? If someone had been kind to her early enough, would she still have made the leap from victim to accomplice? By the time I was born, was she already both? Did I tip her over?

"In the last few months . . . Since we found out about you in the interview, really, we've been . . . It's been different." She casts a quick, skittish glance at Koen. It shimmers with unshed tears. "Things became more . . . And then they sent Job to get you."

"Job?"

"The boy by Silas's house," Koen explains.

"Oh." My heart squeezes. "Were you two . . . ?"

"He was my friend. And they told him that if he couldn't bring you back, he shouldn't bother returning at all." For the first time, the hurt in her voice is tinged with anger. "So he didn't."

"I'm sorry, Nele."

She nods. Casts a lost glance around the room, taking in the impersonal but welcoming decor. "It's not like they said it would be. Here, with the Weres. I thought you'd hurt us and treat us like we're unworthy, but we've been able to come and go as we please. It's not dangerous for Humans. The Weres are . . . You have been kind."

It's so depressing, Amanda told us in the car. *Every time I bring them clothes and food and books and tell them that they don't need to ask for permission to walk around nature, they look at me like I must be drinking mercury. Can you believe it?*

A cult lying to its members to control them, Koen mumbled, driving with his elbow hanging out of the window. *Unheard of.*

Honestly, fuck Irene and Constantine and the Favored. Fuck them all. "The Northwest is kind," I say, "but what they are doing is the bare minimum. You deserve respect, and more. You should have had it your whole life."

I can see the cogs in her head turning as she tries to grasp the concept of basic decency. "I know . . . I know we're Humans. But would it be possible . . . Could we maybe stay here for a while? I think that if we did, the others would see it, too, that maybe there can be a life for us, even outside of the Favored."

"You can stay for as long as you like," Koen replies before I can turn to him.

"Thank you." Her smile wobbles. "Maybe you and I could be friends, E—Serena. I enjoyed the afternoon we spent together."

"I did, too," I say, instead of *We could be friends if I stayed, but I won't. I can't. You'll be fine, though. And so will Koen. And so will I.*

Good liar, and all that.

"Maybe I could help you," she adds, tentative. "I could show you where some of our hideouts are. We could go together—"

"No," Koen and I say in unison, forcefully. We share a glance, and he continues. "How old are you?"

"Sixteen."

"Son of a bitch." He briefly hangs his head. Massages the bridge of his nose. "You're way too young to be caught in this. We don't know if they are guarding their hideouts, or whether they will treat you as a threat. You've been through enough. Your involvement in this bullshit ends now."

Nele blushes, looking scandalized.

Koen cocks his head. "Did you really just offer to escort me into a life-or-death situation, only to balk at the word 'bullshit'?"

The flush deepens. "The thing is, after what happened last week, there are . . . a little less than fifty Favored left. About half of them are Weres. And . . . my older sister, she's currently with them."

My stomach sinks.

Koen sighs. "Could you write me a list of the members?"

"I already have. It's in my room." She averts her eyes. "What will you do to them?"

"Provided that the Weres don't resist, we'll capture them alive and put them through a tribunal. Humans are not our concern."

"Will you . . ."

His face softens. "We'll do our best not to harm anyone. Humans are easy to subdue. However, if my pack is in danger, we *will* defend ourselves."

Nele exhales slowly. The silence stretches until she says, "I just want it to be over, you know? A normal life, for me and my family." She lets go of my hand and wraps her arms around herself. "I don't know where Irene is right now. But the prophet's birthday is in two days, and it's our most important day of worship. Irene might call

it off this year, but she never has. In fact, I think that she might . . ."
At once, she smells intensely guilty.

"None of this is your fault," Koen reminds her.

She nods. "Ever since Serena's interview, there has been a lot of anger toward the Northwest. More than usual. Many Favored saw that as proof that they'd been right all along, and people have been thinking about the Harrowing." She swallows. "In the past few months, they've been accumulating weapons. Firearms. Some bigger ones, too. And . . ."

"And?"

"And . . . they've been teaching us how to use them."

CHAPTER 36

She would make for the perfect Alpha's mate.

I CAN'T BE THE ONLY ONE EXPERIENCING A STRONG SENSE OF déjà vu," Saul says, but no one laughs.

I wouldn't describe the Northwest seconds as the jolliest of bunches, but they usually tease each other, dish out jabs, and exchange inside jokes that go way over my head. Tonight, however, the atmosphere in Koen's cabin is very gothic manor, mid-nineteenth century. The huddle leaders are on their way. Most of the pack leadership is in attendance, and all agree with Koen's decision to go after the cult before Irene can strike.

"It's the same strategy Constantine used," he says.

"Target the Alpha and the closest seconds," Amanda recites. "When the pack is trying to regroup, they work their way down."

"They don't have the insiders they had back then," Mai points out. "Or the manpower."

"The attack might not be as widespread," Amanda agrees, "but if something happens to Koen?"

"That wouldn't be ideal. There's always a slew of cumballs with no leadership experience who decide to try the challenge at the worst possible time." Koen leans against the counter and stares into the middle distance. "It's not enough, getting Irene. We need to make sure that no Were related to the cult remains free. Otherwise, two years from now some fuckwaffle who happens to be Constantine's third cousin will be back with some shitty claim and rile up all the other fuckwaffles."

"What are the chances that the Human girl is lying about the weapons?" Jorma asks.

"None," Koen says. "She adores Serena and wants to see her safe."

"Easiest solution," Elle says, "would be to lure as many of them as possible somewhere where we can easily neutralize them. Maybe we could feed them false information that we're gathering for a leadership meeting."

"We don't know the extent of their weapons," Koen points out. "Last time we underestimated them, and you know what happened." *We* meaning his parents. *What happened* meaning mine.

"And would Irene be that easy to fool?" Colin asks.

Slowly, Koen shakes his head. "She's deluded but not stupid. She believed that Serena would side with her over the Northwest, and that was shortsighted of her. She won't make the same mistake twice."

"Could we use Jess to plant false information?"

Pavel shakes his head. "She's not being cooperative."

"We could still use her as bait."

"Irene doesn't give a single fuck about her," Amanda says.

"She cares about me, though." It's the first time I speak in the meeting. Everyone turns to me, and it's like a floodlight right in my face. "I'm her niece. Constantine's daughter." It's not news to anyone, but some seconds lower their eyes, like the reminder is hard to swallow. I don't blame them one bit. "I'd be bait worth her while. I could set up a meeting with her, tell her that I changed my mind about the Favored."

"She won't buy it," Amanda says. "You clearly made your choice."

"She might even know that we're using you to lure her there, and turn it against us," Mai adds.

And they're right. However. "What if *they* were to use *me* as bait?" The question gets me lots of confused stares. A couple of skeptical *I think the halfling is slow* glances are exchanged. "Irene wants Koen gone," I explain. "She knows that Koen will come for me if I'm taken, because he already has. She knows that he'll bring several of his seconds with him, too. It's the ideal scenario for her."

Silence. Amanda squints. "I'm not sure I follow?"

"If Irene had me at her disposal right now, she would use me to lure the Northwest leadership to a place where she could easily dispose of you. So let her do that. Let her think that she's ambushing us, while *we* are ambushing *her*. Like you said, her manpower is limited. She's going to have to use all her resources on the ambush—"

"And have none left to pay attention to us." Saul nods slowly. "This isn't a bad idea."

"It isn't," Elle concedes. "Except for the small detail that Serena is *not* with Irene."

"That might be easy to fix," Amanda says, sounding on board. "Nele told us where the hideouts are. We could parade Serena near one, someone would snatch her to please Mother Irene, and then—"

"Enough."

The entire room falls quiet. Every second's gaze slips down to their toes, like they're children being collectively reprimanded for not flushing the toilet.

I guess this is the effect it has—the Alpha's voice. Except, Amanda's eyes bounce back up. It doesn't surprise me—I've always felt that there was something sturdier about her relationship with Koen, something that comes from her being his closest friend. Maybe that's why she's the one with the guts to push against him. "Koen, this is not some dumb *final girl running upstairs* plan. Serena knows that Irene is unlikely to harm her. She's too important to the cult."

"Can you guarantee it?"

Amanda looks away, but mutters, "I can't guarantee anything. I can't guarantee that Irene's weapons secretly aren't embalmed gerbils. But I can make an educated guess."

"No, you can't. Not in my pack." Koen's voice is harsh, and a hollow, terrible silence follows, in which everyone, including Amanda, performs one of those weird eye genuflections.

I rise to my feet, cross the room, and walk up to him. "It wasn't Amanda's idea. It was mine. So if you have something against—"

"You fucking know I do, killer."

We're the only two in the kitchen area, which gives an illusion of privacy. But that's just it—an illusion. Everyone can listen in. Everyone *is*. "Do you have a better plan?"

He glares. My heart flutters with fondness, and a bit of sorrow for what I'm about to do to him.

"Clearly, you don't. This is the best way to keep the pack safe."

"I'm *not* letting you—"

"That's the thing, Koen. You don't have to *let* me. I can do whatever I want. I could walk across the Human border right now, and you couldn't stop me."

His jaw tenses. "I am the Alpha of this pack."

"You are. And everyone else in this room is going to follow your orders. But I won't."

Suddenly, he seems larger. Angrier. He towers over me in a new, unfamiliar way, and hisses through clenched teeth, "You are under my command. If I say that I want you here, you'll fucking stay here. Your plan would put you in danger and out of my protection, and that's unacceptable."

"Koen." I smile.

He leans forward. I should be scared. I'm just *not*.

"I love you," I say simply.

His eyes close. "You are *mine*. My mate. My—"

"More importantly, you love *me*. And that's why you have no authority over me." I reach up to caress his face with the back of my hand. Let my arm fall limp at my side, suddenly cold.

When I turn around, I meet Amanda's eyes, and we nod at each other.

———— ⋈ ————

THE PLAN FALLS INTO PLACE LIKE A WELL-CHOREOGRAPHED DANCE.

The following day, Amanda and I are escorted to the territory of the easternmost huddle. Anneke, its leader, meets us under the tall trees on the riverside and welcomes me with a curious tilt of her head. "I hope you know what you got yourself into," she tells me. When Koen and Saul get out of the front seats, she bows her head. "Alpha. I'll take her from here."

"Yeah. Give us a minute."

Anneke and Amanda take a step back, and Saul feels my upper arm for the GPS tracker embedded in my flesh. "Still doesn't hurt?"

I shake my head.

"Good. It's a little bit reddened, but that's for the best, since it'll make it easier to notice for Irene. If it hurts—"

"Shut it, Saul," Koen grumbles. "She's an adult Were and doesn't need you fussing over her."

Saul's eyebrow perks up. "Excuse me, *Alpha*. I must have misheard when you threatened to chain her to the radiator to prevent her from stubbing her toe."

"She is my mate," Koen snarls. "*I* get to treat her like she's made of mother-of-pearl. *You* do not."

Saul hugs me, wishes me good luck, and disappears from Koen's sight at record speed. Then it's just us. Across the sky, a bird of prey calls in a loud, descending pitch.

"I should have," Koen mutters. In the sunlight, his eyes look darker than usual.

"What?"

"Chained you to my fucking radiator. I still could. I will."

I laugh. "No, you won't. But I'll be all right. They don't know I can shift again. If things get dangerous, I can always run."

He clenches his teeth. "If anything happens to you, I'm going to—"

"Kill me, yes. I know the drill by now." I would love to hug him, but Anneke is right behind me, and she's part of the Assembly. I don't want to make things harder for him. "I think it's gonna work, Koen. We'll get rid of this threat, and we'll . . . move on." I smile. More or less. "Consider it my parting gift to the Northwest."

"You already gave the Northwest enough."

I swallow thickly. "I like to think that I simply didn't take away one of its most attractive features." It's not funny. Neither of us is laughing. The pangs in my chest feel more like stab wounds.

"Sure." He exhales. "I have to go, Serena. Before I chain you somewhere for real."

I nod, willing away the full, prickling feeling at the back of my throat. Watch Koen spin around and put some distance between us.

But he stops.

Takes a deep, shoulder-heaving breath.

Turns again and marches back to me, taking my face in his palms and pressing our lips together.

It's a simple, bruising, marking kiss. My fingers grip his wrists, and he smells like we never left his cabin. We're still in our nest, measuring each other's breathing. Marveling at how quickly we fall into rhythm.

"Whatever you need, you have to come to me. It's a fucking order." His voice is strained. "I don't care where you are. I don't care what it is. I want you to promise me that for anything you—"

"I promise, Koen."

He nods. Fills his lungs with air. Shakes his head. "Fucking nuisance," he mutters, and then he's walking, driving away.

Amanda and I enter Anneke's car.

—⋊⋉—

MY GRANDFATHER'S HOUSE HAS BEEN EMPTY FOR NEARLY FIVE DE-cades. The outside, however, looks surprisingly intact, and no one seems to have initiated a stone-throwing contest toward the living room windows.

"Could I claim this property?" I ask, standing on the balcony. "Does it belong to me?"

"Technically, everything on pack territory belongs to the pack itself," Anneke's assistant tells me, a little pedantic. *We should introduce her to Jorma*, Amanda whispered to me earlier, after she offered us a croissant and pronounced it like we were fine dining in Toulouse.

"Is anyone taking care of this place?"

"Yes. People will stay here occasionally, mostly when they are
between residences. They would be welcome to move in, but . . ."

"They know it's the house where Constantine's father was born
and don't want to commit?"

She nods.

"Fair enough. There's probably lots of black mold in those
walls." It would certainly explain the family history.

"It's also very close to the border," she points out. "Over there,
that line of trees? That's Human territory. Very well patrolled, and
we haven't had issues in a long time. But . . ."

"Interesting." I pretend to be learning something new. "Thank
you for showing me."

"No problem. I have to say, I was surprised when Anneke said
you'd want to visit your grandfather's home, but . . . I guess it makes
sense."

I smile. Ten minutes later, I lie in the grass with Amanda, staring up at the cloudy sky. My fingers play with my mother's necklace. *Put it on*, Saul suggested before I left. *It'll make the lie that you're
all about reconnecting with your ancestors even more believable.*

"This place gives me the creeps," Amanda says, but my mind is
on something else.

Someone else.

"Did I ruin it for him?"

She glances at me. "What? Who?"

"Did I irreparably undermine Koen's authority?" When I publicly stood up to him, his seconds' faces covered the not-small
gamut from shocked to scandalized.

Amanda laughs. "Oh my God, no. Believe me, we're all very clear on our respective roles in Koen's life. No one would dream to assume that because *you* get away with bitching at the Alpha, so would *they*."

"I don't want to make things complicated for him, now that I'm leaving."

She is silent for a long beat. When I turn to face her, I find her staring. "Thank you, Serena," she tells me. Serious, and uncharacteristically heartfelt.

"For what?"

"For not taking him from us."

"Oh." I rub a hand down my jeans. "How do you know that he . . . ?"

"I didn't. Or maybe I did, but not because he told me. I knew from the start that it would come to this. From the moment he returned from the Southwest and told me that he'd found you." She chuckles, shaking her head. "He was so mad, Serena, for actually *liking* you so much. And I took Saul aside and said, this is how we lose Koen. He doesn't know it yet. And if I told him, he'd ask me to fuck off and call me a . . . a prickhound, or something. But I knew it." Her expression sobers. "I would have forgiven him if he'd left the Northwest. But I don't think he'd have forgiven himself. So thank you."

That's when her phone rings, as planned, and Amanda walks inside the house to take the call, leaving me alone.

As planned.

——— ·✦· ———

THIS TIME AROUND THERE ARE NO DRUGS INVOLVED, AND WHEN I find myself bound and gagged in front of Irene, I'm feeling grateful.

Honestly? I set the bar too low. I need to start asking more of my abductors.

And then there is a hideout about eight miles from there, Nele told me yesterday, pointing at a map. *It's inconvenient, because it's so close to pack territory, the risk of being caught during patrols is high. But Irene never gave it up.*

Because of its proximity to her father's home?

She nodded. *There were rumors that the previous huddle leader wanted to tear the house down, and Irene decided to keep an eye on it to make sure it was still standing. We don't really have a burial place for Constantine, so it's like a memorial. It inspires us.*

I looked at Koen. *It would make sense for me to take a trip there, since I just found out about my family. Someone like Irene, who's spent her entire life upholding Constantine's legacy, wouldn't find it weird.*

I took Koen's gritted teeth as assent, and here I am. Blinking at Irene as she kneels in front of me. Trying to avoid her touch as she cups my face with her thin, soft hands, and tells me, "You made a mistake, choosing the Northwest over your people. I know you are young and untrained, but you should have known better."

I thrash around a little, mostly for show, but this is cathartic. I've never had a family to disappoint before, and it's a bit of a power trip. Lots of fun. I don't understand what Misery has been going on about.

"I'm not giving up on you, not if I can help it. You are Constantine's only direct descendant, and my only blood relative."

One of the Favored, a male Were, approaches to whisper something into her ear. Irene nods, looking pleased, and he leaves. I wonder where we are. We drove about five hours south.

"The thing is, Eva." She lowers her voice. Her smile is wistful and threatening. "I might simply not be able to help it. If you refuse your birthright and don't allow me to elevate you to the symbol you should be . . . I'm going to have to turn you into a martyr."

She glances at my arm, where the tracker is implanted.

I pretend not to notice the gleam in her eyes.

———— ><•>< ————

MY EYES WIDEN WHEN I SEE THE WEAPONS THEY HAVE AMASSED, and it's not another example of award-winning acting. I was prepared for the firearms, but not for the explosives.

This has clearly been a while in the making. When night comes, I pretend to fall asleep, and gather snippets from conversations floating around. They were almost ready to strike, and my presence is just an opportunity to expedite the proceedings.

We don't have a long time, but . . .

. . . that tracker? They can see her location, are probably on their way . . .

. . . ideal situation, but we need to hurry . . .

. . . might not come. He left her alone close to the border, after all, not the act of someone who cares.

. . . nonsense. He had his closest second guarding her. The woman. She screwed up.

. . . is very attached to the girl . . .

Poor Koen is probably grinding his teeth to stubs. I wonder if he's called Amanda a testicle yet, just for siding with me about the plan. I wonder if this is shaving a couple of years off his life. I wonder if it'll be better for him, once I'm back in the Southwest. *Out of sight, out of mind* will never be our thing, but maybe not knowing whether I'm in danger will save the lining of his esophagus?

I should talk to Jorma. Make sure that someone is there to take care of him, even if I can't.

"Eva," a voice calls, and my eyes pop open. It's a Human man, holding something sharp. "I'm sorry. This won't hurt."

I'm out before I can wonder what he's referring to.

———— ❧ ————

MY NEXT MOMENT OF AWARENESS IS IN THE MIDDLE OF THE NIGHT. I'm groggy and confused, in the same safe house where I fell asleep. Except, it's no longer bustling with activity.

It's just me and two Human guards.

My upper arm, where the tracker was, hurts like an open wound. Dried blood clings to my biceps, pools in the inside of my elbow.

And that's when I realize that I may have underestimated Irene.

CHAPTER 37

*She's a small wolf. Cream and white colored, with the same
dark brown eyes as her human form, and pale yellow ears
that are large for her body and more pointed than most. Her
thick tail and delicate muzzle have a few light markings that
make her utterly unique. So pretty, he thinks that if she were
the last thing he saw, he wouldn't mind. Not at all.*

THEY TOOK MY TRACKER AND LEFT ME BEHIND, WHICH IS NOT
how I thought it would go. Irene must know that the Northwest is going to notice that it's no longer attached to my body, which
could mean a handful of things. At best, she's aware that something
might be off and decided to be cautious. At worst, she knows exactly what our plan is and opted for using a less valuable bait, outfit
it with my tracker, and let it be a casualty of the fight that will
break out.

It, because I don't want to believe that Irene would sacrifice one
of the Favored.

The moment I'm fully awake, I yell into my gag. Writhe. Make
a scene. One guard, a man with gray hair and a long beard, watches
me for a few minutes. Then he sighs, comes closer, and frees my
mouth. "What is it?"

Where the fuck did they go? would be my conversation starter of
choice, but I settle for "I have to go to the bathroom." It's not even
a lie.

He and the younger guard share a look. "Just . . . go."

"Where?"

They seem confused.

"You want me to just piss myself?"

"I mean . . . yeah."

I consider pulling a *Do you know who my father is?* but decide to go a little subtler. "Irene would let me keep my dignity." Classy, if I say so myself.

"Would she?" Beard seems doubtful. He glances at the gun next to his right hand, then at the younger man, who's clearly *not* in charge. Unlike Beard, he looks properly intimidated by the idea of being on Irene's shit list. "Maybe. But I've watched enough TV to predict how the *take me to the bathroom, untie me for just a second* she-bang always ends."

"Have you?"

He nods, proud of his clairvoyance.

I sigh. "Okay, listen—don't untie me. Don't even take me outside. How about you just lower my pants and underwear so I don't have to sit in my own urine for the foreseeable future? Your buddy can hold me at gunpoint so I don't try anything. Not that I could, since my arms *and* my feet are tied up."

Beard thinks it through, finds no objections, and the rest is easy enough. Not very smart of them, to assume that I'd need someone else to untie me. Then again, they have no idea I can shift.

I feel the rush of power, of *rightness*, as my fingers sharpen into claws. In Were form, my wrists are slim enough that I can easily angle them to tear into the rope. Beard comes closer to help me with my bathroom emergency, and overpowering him is a matter of a couple of blows. As I suspected, his young buddy is far too intimidated by the situation to shoot the gun and kill Constantine's prodigal kid. Once Beard is groaning on the floor, he tosses the weapon and runs away.

I savor the delicious pain in my bones as I shift into my wolf form. It's been a long time, too long. Every single one of my cells welcomes me as I settle into them.

Whatever's left of my Human mind feels a bit guilty about tackling the boy and leaving him out of commission, remembering what Koen said about the cult and its habit to shield Weres with Humans. A bit, but not enough to stop me.

The forest is my home. She beckons me. Urges me forward. Embraces me like I'm worthy of her, always will be. I set off after the cult, tracking their scent, following every trace of their passage. Humans, in particular, are easy to stalk. Tire marks. Shoe prints. The occasional littering. *They didn't bother concealing their trail*, the forest whispers. *I'll tell you everything you need to know. I will lead you to them.*

I lope for ten minutes. Or hours. I can't tell time in this form, only sequences. Events. Cause and effect. My hindbrain is larger, and everything is instinct, clear cut. Either good or bad. Want or *fuck, no.* Friend or foe. There is no compromise, because I'm the undiluted essence of myself. I am insignificant. I am hunger and love and joy. I am the pack, and the pack is me.

Then I spot flames.

Hear screams and shots.

Smell smoke.

My wolf brain doesn't *understand*. All it sees is chaos and hurt, adrenaline and anger. I gallop toward the battleground, leaving behind the thickest part of the forest. There is a fire, one that started in the clearing and is rapidly spreading to the trees. I can barely breathe. The heat is so intense, my fur feels singed.

Leave, my instincts scream at me. *Leave.*

But I spot Pavel. His neck is almost entirely in the powerful jaws of another wolf, a fawn-colored one I don't recognize. When Pavel unsuccessfully tries to free himself, I race toward him and sink my fangs into the vulnerable side of the other wolf's belly.

No one has taught me how to fight in this form, but I know anyway. I *know*.

The fawn wolf manages to throw me off. By Were standards I'm not a fearsome creature, but I puff myself up, trying to appear larger. I growl. I raise my tail. When he crouches, ready to charge, I do the same—and then howl in triumph as Pavel takes him by surprise and pins him to the ground.

Around me, Humans scream, firing their weapons. A glance tells me that the cult is overwhelmed and rapidly losing ground. That's when I spot Koen and learn what real fear is.

He's still in human form. I growl—*What the hell is he waiting for?*—but he cannot hear me. Unlike everyone else, he's running toward the source of the fire. I dart after him, ready to hook my teeth in his neck and pull him away. Then I realize what his goal is.

A girl. A Human girl that I can barely make out through the flames—except for her auburn hair. She's on the ground, unconscious, and he's trying to rescue her.

Nele's sister.

Waves of heat lick at me, and I watch Koen disappear through the blaze. I let out a soft whine, running around the perimeter of the fire, turning away to cough. I snarl. I bark. I wait for him to reappear for several seconds. Or years.

Then, like the idiot that I am, I follow him in.

Stupid, a voice yells at me. But it adds, *Help! Him!*

It's impossible to breathe. Jaw open wide, tongue lolling, I track his steps and leap in relief when I see him exiting the fire from another direction, carrying the girl's unconscious body. I chase after him, trying to keep the smoke out of my lungs. Koen runs past the flames, lays the girl down on the grass, and puts his ear by her mouth, looking for a sign of life.

I'm trotting to him, and that's when I see Irene.

She's naked and barefoot. Doesn't notice me, because Koen and the girl are right between us. Unfortunately, I'm almost sure Koen doesn't notice *her*, either. He's focused on giving CPR to Nele's sister, and he never turns around, not even as Irene lifts something that looks a lot like a rifle.

My fur bristles along my spine. In an instant, my fear explodes into pure, roaring rage.

Not on my fucking watch, Auntie.

I clack my teeth, meaning to warn Koen. The problem is, he turns toward *me* and instantly recognizes me, despite never having seen my wolf form. I feel his relief and joy and *everything else* like a shock wave, reverberating through me.

Behind him, though, Irene is taking aim.

My next move is primal instinct, something beyond reason and thought. I watch her adjust the mouth of the barrel, and sprint toward her as fast as I can. I leap above Koen and the girl, careening toward the rifle, ready to rip into Irene's throat.

Someone yells my name.

The wind blows the fire toward us.

A sharp, loud *crack* reverberates throughout the forest.

That's the last thing I remember.

CHAPTER 38

"You pathetic asshole." The Vampyre voice jostles him awake. He's asleep beside Serena's bed—has been for . . . He doesn't care. "It's kinda gross, how madly in love with her you are. But please, continue. Pitiful, twitterpated men are very entertaining."

I THINK IT WAS ALL A DREAM.

Not just the fight and the fire and the abduction. Not just Koen, me being a Were, and my time at *The Herald*. I think I'm still in college, wondering who the hell is getting kickbacks for putting a chemistry requirement in a finance degree. I think I'm at the Collateral house, wondering whether the new landscaper's resting asshole face means that he's secretly an anti-Vampyre activist.

The last six or seven years were all a nightmare. Nothing else could explain that the first thing I hear when I regain consciousness is Misery's cackle. "Oh, boy. He's gonna be *so* pissed."

"Who?" I wheeze out. My palate feels coated in kelp. When a straw is thrust into my mouth, I latch on to it and take about twelve gulps.

"Who what?" Misery asks.

I am, obviously, in a hospital bed. She is, obviously, in the chair next to it. Judging by how my bedside table is covered in electronic devices, an empty blood bag, and even the last installment of the

Were mystery series we both swore we'd stop hate-reading, she's been here for a while. "Who's gonna be pissed?"

"Koen. You've been out for four days, and he literally just agreed to leave this morning."

"Where did he go?"

"Something something *pack*. I think he's getting yelled at by . . . Is it possible that Amanda mentioned an Assembly?"

Yup. "Am I . . . Is this the Southwest?"

"What? No. Look out the window. It rains here. There are trees and shit. We're in the Den." She leans back in the chair, kicks off her shoes, and stretches her long legs at the foot of my bed. Her pretty, fay-like face curves into a happy smile. "Anyway. I'm sure you're very confused. And have questions. I'll be happy to fill you in," she offers, magnanimously.

When is Koen coming back? seems like a shitty thing to ask my best friend, who's clearly been watching over my sickbed. So I go with "Did she shoot me?"

"Irene? Yup, but only in the arm. Leg? I don't know. You were in wolf form."

"Where is she?"

"Um, so. Koen was, um, mad."

"Ah."

"You have been de-aunted, I fear."

"How tragic," I say, not giving a single fuck. "The girl?"

"The redhead? The one they put your tracker in? She's fully re-covered. I met her sister, by the way. She has a crush on both you *and* Koen. It's kinda cute, honestly."

"She's sixteen."

"I think it's a platonic crush. But also, when you were sixteen, you wanted to pork Mr. Lumiere in the mudroom."

MATE

"Did I?" I groan. Yeah, I did. "What about everyone else? Anything I should know?"

"Let's see . . . The cult members are either in custody or with Irene. Which, I am sure, will delight them. The fire was put out. No one from the Northwest died, though there were minor injuries. Can I just say—I've had a lot of time to consider recent revelations, and I'm not *at all* surprised that you come from a long line of cult leaders. You've talked me into so much weird shit through the years, and I always wondered why I kept falling for it."

"I'm glad we figured it out." I sit up. It's a pleasantly easy and painless process. "Not that I'm unhappy about it, but why are you here?"

She pouts. "Because my sister was on the brink of death?"

"Was I, though?"

"Well, critical condition. Interestingly, not because of the bullet. You hit your head hard when you slammed into Irene. Basically, you are responsible for the worst of your own injuries. Way to show agency." She holds up her hand. With a sigh, I high-five her. "Lowe flew in with me. He left yesterday, when they cleared you. Today I had to drink fridge blood, and it's like going from gourmet peanut butter to diarrhea."

"Such vivid imagery—"

The door opens. "Misery! Look at this frog that I . . ." A gasp. "Serena is *awake*?" A second later, the frog is leaping away, and a soft, bony weight lands on me with all the grace of a flying squirrel. I return Ana's boa constrictor hug, trying not to burst into tears at how much she's grown in the last few months. "Hey, baby."

"Your hair is so long," she says. "Can I braid it?"

"Sure."

"Misery and I got matching tattoos!" The back of Ana's right hand is suddenly in front of my eyes.

"Is that a . . . narwhal?"

Misery nods proudly and lifts her arm to show me hers.

"Also, did you know that next week is Misha's birthday and my present for her is a bouncy castle? Also, Sparkles says hi." I glance at Misery, who slowly shakes her head. *He doesn't*, she mouths at me. *He cannot talk.*

Ana chatters in my lap for a few more minutes—Lowe is gone on pack business but he'll come back soon, Uncle Koen bought her unicorn waffles, what's my favorite cheese, there's a kid at her school she totally does *not* have a crush on but *will* marry as soon as she's of age, I'm still her favorite because we're the only two "hybrids" in the world, but Nele is her new best friend.

"Nele?"

"They've been getting on," Misery tells me. "You and Ana might have to split custody. Hey, pest, why don't you go tell Nele where you are before she worries?"

Ana blinks at her. "Are you trying to get rid of me so you can have a grown-up conversation with Serena?"

"See? I told Lowe that you're too smart to fall for this crap." Misery rolls her eyes.

"What are you two going to talk about?"

"I'm going to rip Serena a new one."

"What does that mean?"

"You know how right now she only has one butthole? I'm going to—"

"*Ana*," I interrupt, "why don't you go find, um . . . another frog? To keep this one company?"

Ana leaves in a peal of giggles, and I shake my head. "Wow. She learned to pronounce your name."

"It's tragic," she says mournfully. "Every day I do my best to delay her cognitive development and keep her a child forever, and that's how she repays me."

"My condolences."

"Anyhoodles, how do you feel?"

Honestly, not bad. There is no smoke. Not much hurts. Everyone I love seems to have survived the week. "If I say fine, will you be yelling at me?"

"I'll yell at you either way."

I frown. "Why? You would have done the same. You *did* do the same—you married some dude you didn't know to come look for me in enemy territory. How is that less irresponsible than a calculated bait plan to—"

"You think *that's* why I'm mad at you?" She lowers her legs and leans forward, showing me her fangs. Which means that she is *very* angry. "Miss Girl, I don't give a shit about that."

"Then what—"

"Why do I have to find out from Lowe what a Heat is?"

I freeze. Did she just say . . . ?

"Yup, I know. And I will be reminding you that I know every day for the rest of your natural life. Which, as it turns out, you thought was going to *end soon*? Not that I would have known if *other people* hadn't told me."

Shit. Shit, shit. This is *bad*. "It turned out to be nothing. And the Heat, I would have told you the second I came back to live in the Southwest. And—"

"I don't believe you."

"Well, you should, because—"

"No, Serena, *I'm* talking. Remember when you didn't tell me you were a Were? And we agreed that you should have? Clearly you learned nothing. You acted selfishly again. And you know what? I'm sick of this. I'm sick of you shouldering everything like you're the fucking guy with the stone."

"Sisyphus?"

"No—the other guy."

"King Arthur?"

"No, the asshole who carries the planet."

"Atlas!"

"Yes!" Her victorious smile mirrors mine. Then she remembers herself, and her expression becomes disheartened. "Serena, I can't keep wondering what you're not telling me. I can't keep finding out that you're facing enormous problems alone."

"Misery, it's not . . ." I have no right to cry. So I try very hard not to. "I just don't want you to have to worry—"

"I worry anyway. I worry *more*, because I don't know whether you'll reach out to me when you're in need. Listen, you've seen me stuff my bra with math homework. I've seen you with your eyebrows shaved. There's no dignity left between us. We've been with each other at our worst—"

"And now you are at your *best*," I blurt out. "And I don't want to drag you back down with me."

It's what I feel. Really. Genuinely. I didn't fully know it until the words slipped out, and now I'm looking at Misery, my beautiful, beloved sister, and the hurt in her eyes makes me want to step off a cliff.

"Is that what you think?" she whispers. "That I'm too . . . too *functioning* for you? That I wouldn't want to be with you because . . ."

"It's just . . . ," I start. But anything I can think of saying feels so profoundly myopic. "You have many people who love you now. You're not alone anymore. And I want you to be able to enjoy it without having to worry about your loser hybrid unemployed maybe-terminal friend who now has weird mating cycles and is a liability for everyone because of the undiagnosed narcissism in her family tree." I wipe my cheek with the back of my hand. And Misery is silent for so long, I wonder if this is it.

She's had enough.

But then she says, "I'm not. At my best. And I . . . I feel alone and insecure and lost all the time. I wonder whether people's lives are worse because of me *all the time*. Having a Vampyre mate doesn't buy Lowe any favors. And Ana? I have this fucking *child* who looks at me like I'm a role model. Serena, she's so fucking small, basically held together with spit and duct tape, and one of these days she's going to join a biker gang or ask me how children are made—"

"You're probably good for a while."

"—and I'm ruining her, because I forget that I'm not supposed to swear around her. And some classmates at school have been making fun of her for not being able to shift—"

"What?" I pull back the sheets and jump to my feet. "Those *cunts*!"

"I *know*!" She shoots up, too. "Can you believe that Juno won't let me go suck their fucking pets dry in front of their fucking useless eyes?"

"I can, actually. The pets did nothing wrong. But we could shank the classmates themselves—"

"Juno forbade that, too! *No violence against minors*," she sing-songs, in the worst imitation of Juno I've had the pleasure to witness. I'm still pondering avenues for revenge, but Misery continues.

"It sucks. I constantly feel like I'm not equipped for this. And the reason it hurts so much is that . . . I *want* to be. I adore her. But would she be better off if I went away? And Lowe, his life would be so much easier with a Were mate. I should leave him, right? But I love him so much. Almost as much as he loves me."

I laugh, and some gross snot comes out.

"But, Serena, the thing about Ana and Lowe and Juno and every other person I'll meet for the rest of my life is . . . they're not *you*. They don't get it. They're never going to get it." I think—I *know* that if she could cry, she would. *I* certainly am. "Just like Koen or Amanda are never going to get it. They'll get other things. They'll get other moments—they'll get their own exclusives. But they won't get *this*."

What a shameless abuse of the verb "to get." And yet. "I can't believe I know exactly what you mean."

"It's because you—"

"Get it. Yes."

Two normal friends would exchange a hug. We just sit back in our respective places and stare at each other, fondly amused by our very own idiocy. "Ribbit," the frog says, and we both nod in agreement.

"You haven't even told me that you're in love with Koen," she whines.

"How do you—"

"Come on, Serena."

I shrug. "He can't be with me, anyway."

"Yeah. It's just . . ."

"What?"

"I don't know. Koen's not the kind of guy who lets himself be limited by stuff like people saying no."

"And yet."

"Yeah. What else have you been hiding? Don't bother saying 'nothing,' because—"

"I might want to stay here," I blurt out.

"Oh." Misery looks around, like she doesn't quite know what to say. Honestly, it's endearing as fuck. "In the . . . hospital?"

"No, I . . . I love this place. The Northwest. I don't know if it's because part of me remembers being here when I was a kid, but it feels like home. And I think I might want to live here, even if I can't be with Koen. This is such a large territory, and I could be out of his way, and . . . Would you hate me?"

"What? No. We'll still see each other all the time. I mean, look at Lowe and Koen. They are just as codependent as we are."

"Are they?"

"Oh, come on. Koen is Lowe's . . . If I said father figure, would that make things weird?"

"*So* weird."

"Okay, then let's say, the older brother Lowe always needed. He basically saved his life when he took him in, and I think Koen is proud of Lowe. I once overheard him say that 'raising the kid' was the best thing he'd ever done. If they can make it work, so can we. I don't care if we're close geographically. I just want to feel like I know what's going on with your life."

I nod gratefully. "Since we're being honest: Deep down, aren't you glad you had to skip through the whole death false alarm thing?"

"Yes, but that's beside the point. *And* you deprived me of the pleasure of making fun of you for having a three-day compulsory fuckfest." She sighs. "Serena?"

"Mmm?"

"Should we cut each other's toenails and talk about the knot thing?"

I think about how little I want to do it. How overdue we are. "Are there clippers in the bathroom?"

She stands and goes to look for some.

CHAPTER 39

"I know it might seem like a difficult decision, but it's for the best, Koen," Xabier tells him. The rest of the Assembly nods with varying degrees of enthusiasm.

He feels as though the ground beneath his feet is no longer solid.

I DON'T KNOW," AMANDA TELLS ME WHEN I ASK HER IF KOEN WILL be forced to step down.

"It's not that simple," Saul adds, sticking closer to her than he has in the last few weeks. They entered Koen's cabin holding hands, or maybe it was an optical illusion. "They can't demand that he steps down. They don't have that kind of power. They're not, like, our real fathers."

Amanda stabs him with her eyes. "What they *could* say is that they are unwilling to stick with the Northwest."

"Was it Anneke who told them? Is it because he kissed me in front of her?"

"It's not just that," Jorma explains, looking up from a ream of paperwork that's thicker than my wrist. "Anneke, Xabier, and Conan were there when you were hurt. It left little doubt that Koen is emotionally compromised. This is less of a controlling body sanctioning a misbehaved child, and more of a conversation between adults regarding the future of the pack. Most likely, they'll give him an ultimatum and ask that you leave the core."

"I'm sorry. I—"

"Serena. Honey." Saul gives me a square look. "You *literally* took a bullet for the Alpha of this pack. I'm going to need you to never apologize again. And yes, I'll have another slice of that coffee cake."

I feel obscenely guilty. I think about it for the rest of the day, through the steady stream of visitors whose names I barely remember, and hardly sleep overnight. "That's ideal," Misery says, exchanging a mutually distrustful look with Twinkles. Ana decided that if he wants, he should be allowed indoors, and who was I to tell her no? Hopefully, Koen won't mind that he's fully moved into his room. "Since I'm here. We can spend our time making fun of Were Alphas and the sticks up their asses together."

Koen doesn't return until the following afternoon, when Ana is at the local airport with Amanda, waiting for Lowe to land. Misery is asleep in Koen's closet, and I almost step on her when I go to steal another one of his hoodies. Clearly, it wasn't just the Heat that made me partial to them.

Then, as I make toast to satisfy my newfound, ravenous appetite, a brilliant idea occurs to me.

The closet would be a *spectacular* hiding place. I can picture myself calmly talking this through with Koen. *I could live under your bed. Have you heard of the concept of "dirty little secret"? Let's be real, it's not as though I love hanging out with people lately.*

I press the toaster's lever. Which won't stay down.

I could hide in there with Twinkles. We could share some tasty bones. Push.

Read. Sleep. Find some remote finance job and pull my weight. Push.

I can't be used against you if no one knows that I exist. So really, this is the best solution for all of us.

Push, push, push, push—

Two things happen in rapid succession. First, the spring mechanism in the toaster gives out. Then the door opens. When I whirl around, Koen is at the entrance. His eyes linger on my face for a moment, then flick to my fingers.

Which are still grasping the lever.

Which has fallen off.

"It's not what it looks like," I blurt out, feeling caught red-handed, even more than when Misery saw me draw hearts around Mr. Lumiere's name.

Koen nods, closing the door behind him. He looks . . .

I want to throw myself at him. I want to bite his neck and squeeze him and inhale his scent so deep, it'll never leave my lungs. Instead I take in his long-suffering expression and try not to flinch.

"I think your toaster is broken," I inform him.

"You don't say."

"No, I mean—it was broken *before*."

"Was it?" His gaze travels to a spot on the counter. I follow it, and . . .

Okay. Fine. The damn toaster wasn't plugged in, and I have learned nothing. Cool. "You, um, might need a new one," I say, with all the dignity I can muster. Which is appallingly little. "Because I'm a generous person, I will pay for it."

"Will you."

"Yeah. I'll even go buy it at the store." I hold out my hand. Why am I close to tears? "Give me the keys to your car."

"You want to break that, too?"

I wince but stubbornly don't retract my arm. Koen never gives over his car keys, but he does reach for my hand and pull me into him.

He has held me many times, but never like this—so close, it almost hurts, like he's trying to swallow me inside his body. "There's always something with you, huh," he mumbles, for the fifth or millionth time. And for the fifth or millionth time, I melt into him and forget that there's a whole shitty world out there.

"I'm sorry," I say. It comes out muffled against his flannel.

"About what?"

"I don't know. Everything?"

"Hmm." The sound reverberates through me. "The thing is, I don't think any of what happened is for you to feel sorry for. Aside from the toaster." He picks me up, one arm under my knees, and carries me outside to sit us on a chair on his porch. My head fits perfectly under his chin, my legs drape across his thighs, and this is a terrible idea. *Anyone* could see us.

But I'll be gone in what, twenty-four hours? If it's all going to shit anyway, let it go to shit while I'm in his lap.

"Can I tell you something?" I force myself to say before I lose the courage. "And it's not . . . I'm not asking for anything. I just want you to know, because . . . I just think that maybe you'd enjoy knowing?"

His chin bumps against the crown of my head. A nod.

"I was wrong. When I said that you weren't my mate, even if I was yours. And I know what you're thinking: 'No, you idiot, you just fell in love with me like any regular person would, that's what happens when two people who like each other spend time together,' but this is . . . more. I liked you from the very start, in a way that had never happened to me, and all these feelings . . . I don't think I have the words to explain, but I . . ."

His chest bounces under my ear. I pull back to find that he's laughing silently.

"What?"

"Nothing." He tucks a strand of hair behind my ear. "I'm just glad you figured it out."

"You mean, you knew?"

"Not for sure. But there were signs."

"Oh." I blink. "Really?"

"Serena, our first meeting sent you into Heat."

I flush. "Well, we don't know that. It could have been a coincidence." He looks doubtful. "Seriously. Maybe Alex the IT guy sent me into Heat."

"Yeah. Except, you couldn't bear to be touched by anyone but me." A smile plays at the corners of his eyes. "People without mates are much less discerning when they're in that situation, believe me."

"Oh." I stare into the distance, then back at him. "So . . . you *are* my mate?"

"We might never know, since your biology is different from a full Were's. I don't care very much, because . . ."

"Because?"

"Because you're perfect."

I lower my eyes, feeling too full of . . . of *everything* to hold Koen's gaze. "Well. I guess it doesn't matter much. I didn't tell you, because . . . I wasn't trying to give you a reason to step down."

"Good. Because I'm not stepping down."

I swallow past the lump in my throat. It's fine. Better than fine, it's *exactly* what I wanted. Koen, staying with the Northwest. The right thing to do. "Good," I echo. I need to change the topic, before I beg him to do something he really shouldn't. "Were the huddle leaders fuckwaffles about . . . stuff?"

"No more than usual. They said that I'm emotionally compromised over you. Which is true." His thumb traces my lower lip. "Has been true for a while, really."

"Maybe. So you have—so you have feelings. Big deal." I might be indignant on his behalf, which is ridiculous. Koen doesn't need me to protect him or advocate for him, and yet here I am. "It changes nothing. Every single decision you have ever made has taken into consideration the good of the pack."

"Yeah. They would agree with that."

"Good. Because it's bullshit. You can—you can be in love with someone and still be a fantastic Alpha. The thing is, I love you, and mate or not, I wouldn't love you half as much if you weren't the kind of person who deserves it. And one of the reasons you deserve it is that you *care*." My stupid eyes are leaking. And Koen . . .

Koen is failing, abysmally, to bite back a smile. "Everybody agrees with you, killer. Including the Assembly."

"Good. They fucking *better*."

"That's why they rescinded the covenant."

I don't get it. Not at first. "What?"

"They know what happened. They know how you stood up to me. They know that I let you be our bait. They know that you saved my life. They said exactly what you said." His hand runs through my hair. His eyes follow its path. "That your presence doesn't influence my ability to do my job. But I think they're wrong."

"Wrong?"

He nods. "I think it does affect me. I think you make me a better leader." His smile widens. "You make my world better, for sure. And mate or not, I wouldn't love you half as much if you weren't the kind of person who deserves it."

My own words, thrown back at me, and it's like my entire life reorients. The breeze, the trees, the grass, the moss, the seals, the waves—they stop, immobile, for a fraction of a moment. Then they resume blowing, rustling, swishing, whispering, splashing, lapping, but in a slightly, enormously different way.

"Does it mean that . . . ?"

He nods.

"We can . . . ?"

"If you want to."

"If I—" My laugh is thick. Watery. "If *I* want to? Do *you* want to?"

He laughs, too. "Let me think about it."

I lean forward and bite him on the jaw, hard. I feel his smile grow between my teeth. "So we can just . . . stay here? In this cabin? And I'll find some job? And you'll do your Alpha stuff? And we'll . . . we'll go for runs together? And be boring?"

"That sounds like a dream, actually."

"And I'll cook? And we'll see Misery and Lowe? And you'll build me more chairs and let me decorate the cabin?"

"Whatever you want, sweetheart."

"And we'll have Twinkles as our wolf dog who sometimes sleeps on our bed?"

"Is that why I nearly walked into a water bowl earlier?"

I nod. Burrow into him.

He sighs. Tightens his hold on me. "Such a fucking nuisance."

I wonder why it took me until this very moment to realize that it's been his way of saying *I love you* all along.

EPILOGUE

HE MANAGES TO HOLD IT TOGETHER FOR A LITTLE OVER SIX weeks.

As feats go, this one is so Herculean, so strenuous, so immensely exacting, Koen is certain that it'll make up for every single shitty thing he's done during his wretched, questionable life. He is able to control his instincts and deny himself the one thing he wants with an all-consuming, ferocious, overwhelming passion. That, if nothing else, will guarantee him a place in his particular brand of Were heaven.

Which, he's come to realize, requires only one single thing: Serena.

"ARE YOU BORED YET?" SHE ASKS HIM A MONTH OR SO AFTER MOV-ing in for good. It's an absurd question. And yet, in a rational, detached sort of way, Koen understands what she's getting at.

They had a rocky start. The near murders and the kidnappings and that other bullshit. The medical scares. The fact that he had to push her away over and over even as keeping his distance tore him apart. Bottom line, their first few months were very eventful. Compared to all that, the last few weeks have been strikingly low stakes.

They wake up in the morning. He leaves for his job. She does hers—remote, for Karolina, something about money or stocks that reminds Koen every day how much smarter than him she is and fills him with glowing, besotted pride. He returns home. The end.

Taken at face value, it does seem boring. But there's so much hidden in the crevices of their daily rhythm, Koen can't imagine ever finding his time spent with her anything less than thrilling. Not that he'd be caught dead admitting it to anyone, but he's just fucking . . . enamored, that's the word. The way she needs to be coaxed out of bed with tea and kisses in the morning. Her unabashed joy at discovering every corner of their territory. The fact that every mundane little action feels new and shimmery and magic when she's around.

And yeah, it's ordinary stuff. Boring, he supposes. She sits in his shop doing her crosswords while he builds her more goddamned chairs. She makes him buy her a TV and forces him to watch stupid Human movies she grew up with, and it's just not plausible, that the twins came back from camp having switched places and the parents did *not* immediately figure it out from their scents. She chatters and mumbles to herself and tells him things, all sorts of things, funny and serious, big and small, and the more she talks, the more he wants to do nothing but listen to her. She asks him to play the piano for her, so he finds some Bach sheet music. She wants to go on runs, and that's when he takes her to his favorite places, deep in the belly of the forest. She cooks, and that's—he's so fucking lucky. Especially because when she doesn't feel like it, when he hunts small game for her and drops it by her feet, tail wagging and tongue lolling out expectantly, she also acts happy and satisfied and pleased with him. Alpha instinct doesn't normally concern itself with external approval, but Serena . . . she feels like another part of him.

His heart, in another body.

"Are *you* bored?" he asks her, instead of replying. They're on the porch, and she's brushing the wolf dog with some de-shedding tool she bought online. He now sports a collar, equipped with a heart-shaped charm that sparklingly proclaims: *Twinkles*. Koen keeps expecting to see betrayal in the beast's eyes, but he seems genuinely happy to have been domesticated and bedazzled.

Koen can relate.

"No," Serena tells him. "No. I'm not. This is everything I've ever . . . It's just, you're an Alpha. Maybe you like adventure?"

To him, it feels like an adventure. This. *Them.* Waking up every morning wondering if he'll survive the intensity of his feelings for her. Seems unlikely, and yet. He always makes it to the night. "I'm good," he simply says.

"Okay. As long as you don't mind." Another swipe of the brush. "The whole boring, married routine." Her teeth bite fussily into her lower lip. She is so enchantingly beautiful, sometimes Koen loses track of time and space. Sometimes he finds himself wanting to snarl at other people for looking at her. He's going to have to work on that. "As long as you don't change your mind," she adds.

Koen doesn't immediately follow, too taken by the soft curve of her neck as she folds her hair behind the delicate shell of an ear. He considers asking *Change my mind on what?* When it finally occurs to him what she's talking about, he takes the brush from her hand and pulls her into his lap.

To kiss her in the least *bored* way he's capable of.

———— ◦◦◦ ————

HE HAS WANTED IT FROM THE MOMENT HE FIRST SAW HER IN Lowe's living room, on her knees to receive Ana's hug, her hair pinned up and her expression sad. That is to say: he has wanted it for a long time, but now he aches for it. He itches.

He might even *need* it.

"She might not know that it's a thing," Saul says after Koen almost snaps his spine in two during play-fight.

"She does know," Koen mumbles.

"How can you be so—"

"I told her."

"Did you tell her *what* a mating bite is?" Amanda asks, as obnoxiously shrewd as always. "Or did you tell her that *you* specifically want to bite her to finally seal the mating ritual, and that restraining yourself is driving you banana pants?"

Koen glares. "She was fucking Human until three hours ago. The decent thing to do is let her get used to being a Were before I mangle her with my meat-mincing jaws and leave a scar, for my own personal pleasure."

"The former, huh?" Amanda smirks knowingly. "Did you explain to her the immense peace of mind the bite would give you?"

"How would that *not* be pressuring her?"

"The thing is," Saul points out, "I understand wanting to give her space, but until you bite her you'll be sullen and ill-tempered and crusty. I bet Serena's not enjoying it very much, either."

"Oh, come on, Saul. Be for fucking real," Amanda scoffs. "Koen's crusty with us, not with *her*."

That's correct. Because when he's with Serena, he's in a great fucking mood. When he's with her, she's *his*. And it doesn't matter that he hasn't bitten her yet, because her soft throat is just inches away, because she smells like she needs nothing else but him, because she has the unspeakable ability to turn him into a creature of patience and bliss and repose.

The problem . . . well, the problems mostly occur when she's *not* around. Six weeks after all that shit with the Favored went down, for instance. When he's in Human territory for a three-day work trip. The purpose is, ostensibly, to help the Humans figure out what to do with the bunch of not-yet-deprogrammed cult members the Northwest just turned in to the authorities. Koen is a hairbreadth away from asking Lowe and Maddie why the fuck he had to come all the way here only to get roped into business that no longer has anything to do with his goddamn pack.

Until his patience runs out, and he growls, "Why the fuck did I have to come all the way here only to get roped into business that no longer has anything to do with my goddamn pack? I don't give a shit about Humans. Give them therapy, or send them to rot at the bottom of a ditch, or put them on an all-inclusive cruise ship—just don't involve me."

Maddie's eyebrow arches. "I would have thought you'd want to see with your own eyes the people who tried to invade your territory brought to justice."

Lowe snorts, and Koen shoots him a *Don't you fucking dare* glare.

Lowe, unfortunately, dares. "He's *mated* now."

"I've heard." Maddie smiles. "I hope you and Serena are very happy."

"At the moment I'm pretty fucking unhappy." Because he's here, and Serena is *elsewhere*. The months he spent away from her *before* were abominable, but Koen foolishly believed they'd taught him how to bear her absence. He's starting to realize that might not be the case. He counts the hours and the minutes. He smells shadows of her scent in places she's never set foot. He's not a restless man. Why the hell can he not stop bouncing his leg, then?

It doesn't help, that he doesn't hear from her more often while he's gone. He refuses to become the kind of person who sends little heart emoji texts every ten minutes, but by God, can't *Serena* shoulder the burden of being the needy one? Can't *she* blow up his fucking phone?

"How does Koen's recent mating relate to his lack of interest in Were-Human relations?" Maddie asks Lowe, as if Koen weren't in the same room.

"Indirectly. He misses Serena. Can't be bothered with stuff that's not her for long."

"Has this been a long trip for him, then?"

"Nope. Two days."

"Two and three-quarters," Koen mutters.

Maddie ignores him. "Is that why he checks his phone every two minutes?"

"Yes," Lowe says, just as Koen grunts morosely, "I have a *Tetris* addiction."

"It's complicated," Lowe continues. "Being away from one's mate. On many levels. And the fresher the mating, the more unpleasant the distance." He looks like he knows from personal experience.

"Does it get better with time?" Maddie asks.

Lowe winces. "Not as far as I know. *Although . . .*"

"Don't you fucking dare say it," Koen growls.

Once again, Lowe dares. "There are things he could do that would make it more bearable."

"And he isn't doing them because . . . ?"

"Your guess is as good as mi—"

Koen chucks his phone at Lowe and is proud of how squarely he hits his mouth.

So—yeah. Fine. He'll need to bite Serena. Then there'll be a tangible sign of the mating, this whole business will be complete, and the instinctual, feral part of him will be soothed. He'll feel less like his world could explode for lack of her, less like absconding with her and tucking her in the trunk of a tree and keeping her as his precious, beautiful secret. He *will* bite her—the alternative is inconceivable—but first he'll give her time. Space. A chance to settle.

Just be fucking patient, he snarls at himself. *You're not the center of the fucking world.* She *is*.

But it feels like torture when he returns to her after three days (and three hours and twenty minutes) away. Serena's with Twinkles, waiting for Koen on the cabin's porch, but sprints toward him before he even slows down the car. He's terrified he'll run her over, so he parks right in the middle of the driveway, gets out of the vehicle, and lets her softening body slam against his when she throws herself into his arms.

She stretches up for a kiss, two, a million, but she's too little and maybe too eager and clearly hasn't planned this out, so he has to pick her up and slide his hands down to squeeze her thighs as she wraps her legs around him.

"Can you," she says between kisses, "never"—kiss—"leave again?" Kiss. "Like, ever?" Kiss.

The only response he can manage is a groan. He breathes her in, nose buried into the gland at the base of her neck. Yeah, of course he'll never leave again. He'll do her one better: they'll stay in his cabin forever. Brick up all entrances. Sounds like a pretty fucking good deal.

He'd love to be a gentleman for once—carry her inside, give her the snacks he brought back from Human territory for her, ask how her week at work went, tell her that he missed her and—God, the banality of it sounds outrageously enticing. Problem is, it doesn't go like that. Koen can rarely stay on task when it comes to Serena, which is his fault, his weakness, yeah, sure, but it doesn't help that her scent is phenomenal, or that she no longer smells as intensely *his* as when he left. Not to mention, he apparently *does* require sex in quantities and frequencies that are . . . humbling. And he won't be able to let go of her until he's certain that she's unharmed and whole, because that's the bottom line: he doesn't really trust the world to treat her right if he's not around. She's simply too beautiful.

Koen wishes he could help himself, but that's not the case. She's pliable in his arms, and the couch is enticingly horizontal, and at least he manages to kick the door shut behind him before laying her down and pulling at her shirt so hard that—"Fuck"—the neckline tears. He should be sorry, but now he has full access to her tits, and maybe the universe is a good, just place after all.

"I think," he pants against her ear, ragged, "you should just start coming on these trips with me." His hands are trembling. He wants her too much.

"I missed you," she says instead of yes, licking the gland under his jaw, and he doesn't bother telling her that he missed her back, because it feels so fucking redundant when he's trying to inhale her.

"Serena," he mouths against her temple. It really is terrible mate behavior, fucking his partner before even saying hello, but she's squirming underneath him, and the friction is unfuckingbelievable, and he can't control himself. Maybe she can't, either, and *that* is when it happens.

The most life-changing event he'll ever experience.

It almost feels like a miscalculation on her part. Because one moment she's kissing and sucking his gland, and the next her teeth sink into the skin of his neck.

The pleasure is as stupefying as it is annihilating. He doesn't come in his pants, but it's a close thing. The only reason he's able to stop himself is that the world grinds to a halt. For several seconds, it doesn't spin. Koen and Serena stay like that, still, tethered by her bite, for long moments. And then . . .

Then she pulls away. She licks her lips, and he discovers that they are dark.

With his goddamn *blood*.

This time he *does* come a little bit.

For a few seconds, Serena's eyes are full wolf. Then they transition back to human, still that beautiful, rich brown he fell for, and she's with him once again, present, aware, and—

She blinks. "Holy shit. Did I . . . ?"

Yeah.

"Oh my God. I bit you?"

She did. She fucking did. Koen is inordinately proud of her. How deep her little teeth got. The sharp blades of her canines. It even hurt a little. Okay, not really, but he *felt* her seize the inside of his soul.

She *owns* him. It's *official*.

"I'm so sorry. I—I didn't mean to. I was just—I've been think-ing about you and I . . . I've been having these dreams and—I got carried away. Your neck was *right there* and . . . Oh my God. Are you okay?" She seems highly alarmed. "Is it going to stick? Leave a scar?"

Nothing has ever given Koen more joy than being able to tell her, "Oh, yeah."

"Are you sure?"

He doesn't have much experience with it, but . . . it damn *better*. He hopes it'll be twisted. In relief. Beautiful in its own ugly way. He hopes it'll be a mess of thick, ropy lines that no one can pretend not to see. He's hers. He always was, but now she has claimed him, and he's going to rub it in everyone's fucking face until they plead with him to stop, and even then he will not. Instead, he'll beg her for another one. On the wrist, maybe, so that he can look at it every second of every day. On *both* wrists. Why not? How many mating scars is too many? Frankly, whoever said that less is more was—

"I'm *so* sorry. I probably should have asked if—"

A deep sound snaps out of his throat. *No.* There was no need for that. The thought is so ridiculous, he decides to focus on something else.

Like taking off her pants.

"Koen? Are you okay with me having done that?"

He's dazed. Overwhelmed in the best possible away. He truly is not sure how to communicate to her that he's never been harder, happier, and more certain of the existence of a benevolent God than he is right now. "Yeah," he grunts.

"Okay. Good. I . . . Good." There is some blood trickling down the column of his throat, because she *butchered* his gland. He feels her arch up to lick it, and—

Perfection. His mate is perfect. He'll massacre whoever tries to take her from him, of course.

She smiles at him, and he smiles back as she asks, "Would it be okay if . . . ?"

He stops what he's doing—trying to get inside her—and looks up. Waits for her request, whatever it may be, even though he already knows that his answer is going to be yes. It's not like he's ever going to deny her anything. He has tried and always, always failed. "Yeah?"

"If you . . ." She's flushing a little. Her pretty pink cheeks—such a weird fucking color, and yet so enchanting.

"What?"

"Um, do you maybe want to bite me, too?"

That's when Koen passes out for a minute. At least, he thinks so. His vision blacks out, and sound recedes. He's suspended in nothing. Then, when he comes to, she's still soft underneath him, and clearly in the middle of a little speech.

". . . did it to you, so it would be only, you know, fair. And you said, a few weeks ago, that you wanted to bite me, too . . ." The cheeks—now that he's regained his eyesight, he can tell that they're even *pinker*. He thinks that he might come again just from looking at them.

And then the true meaning of her words sinks in.

"You asked me to bite you," he rasps out.

She nods quickly.

"The mating bite."

More nodding.

"Mine."

Nod.

"On you."

"You never really brought it up again. I was wondering if it was something I did, or—"

"I was fucking—" A deep growly, unspeakable sound rises from deep in his chest. Koen had not known he was capable of that. "I was giving you space."

She frowns. "What?"

"I was being a patient, considerate, respectful, non-intrusive, accommodating mate. I was trying to—"

"Koen, you are the most intrusive mate *ever*. You never stop staring at me when we're in the same room, you wake me up to have sex in the middle of the night, you keep tearing my clothes, and you want to be with me every second you're not gone on pack business. You're not really the space-giving kind of partner, and—"

"I'm *trying*. I could be way fucking worse."

"—*and* I'm not complaining, because I wouldn't have you any other way."

He swallows. Works his jaw. "You've been through some shit. And I'm trying hard to seem more . . . evolved than I actually am."

She stares up at him with so much pity, he knows how miserably he has failed.

"I assumed," he continues. "that you didn't want me to shred your skin and make you bleed and scar you purely for my own sexual thrill, and—"

"Koen. My love." Her hand comes up to cup his face. She's clearly holding in laughter. "Could you please shred my skin and make me bleed and leave a scar purely for your own sexual thri—"

The force with which he flips Serena onto her belly is not *evolved*, nor is the way he tugs at the thick hair at the nape of her neck. The thing is, it's in the way. So is her underwear, which means that he has to tear it off, and—okay, maybe Serena has a point.

Koen enters her quickly, maybe too deep and too soon, no time for adjusting, but she can take everything he dishes out. He hears her gasp and regains a smidge of control, trying for slow, unhurried thrusts, somewhat managing. His knot is already pulsating, starting to inflate, pressing against the tight walls of her cunt. She's warm inside, glowing with heat.

He would die for her, and he would kill for her. More importantly, he will live for her. She'll be the purpose driving every second of his every day.

"I'm going to do it," he says, licking up her spine, a promise. She's already nodding, arching back into him, and when he opens his mouth, the skin of her gland is soft under his tongue, under the scrape of his teeth. "I'm going to mark you," he tells her, because that's what this is about, and he wants to make it clear.

She doesn't reply. But he feels her come, clenching around his growing knot. When he can't wait any longer, his teeth cut into her supple flesh. The iron tang of her blood is strong and sweet.

It tastes, Koen thinks, like forever should.

ACKNOWLEDGMENTS

To start, I would like to acknowledge James Cameron: thank you, my good sir, for picking up *Battle Angel Alita* and changing the course of history.

Second (but really first), thanks to every one of you who read *Bride*. It was a departure from my previous books, and a bit of a gamble. As I was writing it, I knew that I wanted to give Serena a much-deserved happy ending, and it's your support that made *Mate* possible. Once again, thank you for embracing the knot.

Many thanks, as usual, to: Thao Le, my agent; Sarah Blumenstock, my editor, and Liz Sellers, her assistant (and Cindy Hwang, her editor-mother); Kristin Cipolla, Tara O'Connor, Bridget O'Toole, and Kim-Salina I, for marketing and publicity; Jennifer Myers, my production editor; Christine Legon, my managing editor; Janice Lee, my copyeditor; my proofreader; Megha Jain, my cold reader; Daniel Brount, my interior designer; lilithsaur, for the best cover illustration; and Vikki Chu, for the cover design.

Also, my undying thanks to Claire, for being my cult consultant. To Jen, for making me write the bitey epilogue. To Alison, Becca, Christina, Danelle, Lauren, Leslie, Paola, Stephanie, and Susan, for immediately clocking the boobs situation at the Meet Cute dinner. To my family, and to all the people who I am lucky to call friends.

But above all: thank you, Dr. James Francis Cameron. The world is a better place because of you.

ALI HAZELWOOD is the #1 *New York Times* bestselling author of *Bride* and *The Love Hypothesis*, as well as a writer of peer-reviewed articles about brain science, in which no one makes out and the ever after is not always happy. Originally from Italy, she lived in Germany and Japan before moving to the US to pursue a PhD in neuroscience. When Ali is not at work, she can be found crocheting, eating cake pops, or watching sci-fi movies with her three feline overlords (and her slightly-less-feline husband).

VISIT ALI HAZELWOOD ONLINE

AliHazelwood.com

🄾 AliHazelwood

♪ AliHazelwood

LEARN MORE ABOUT THIS BOOK AND OTHER TITLES FROM *NEW YORK TIMES* BESTSELLING AUTHOR

ALI HAZELWOOD